To: Julie and Jeff,

Hope you enjoy.

Best wishes
&

God Bless,

Jim Damiano

2020
A SEASON TO DIE
A parable of love and war

A NOVEL BY

Jim Damiano

JIM DAMIANO

Austin, Texas

2020 – A Season to Die
By Jim Damiano

Copyright 2005 V. R. Damiano, Jr.
2020 – A Season to Die

F&F Publishing
1st World Library
7600 Burnet Road, Suite 510
Austin, TX 78757
512-339-4000
www.1stworldlibrary.com

First Edition

Senior Editor
Barbara Foley

Editing
Louanne Jones
Katherine Bishop
Brad Fregger
Susan Ondrasek

Layout
Brad Fregger

Cover Production
Ashley Underwood

Library of Congress Control Number: 2005904810
ISBN: 0-9765821-2-0

    All rights reserved. No part of this book may be reproduced or utilized in any form or by any means, electronic, or mechanical, including photocopying, or recording, or by an information storage and retrieval system, without permission in writing from the Author.
    This is a work of fiction. Names, characters, places, and incidents are either the product of the author's imagination or are used fictitiously, and any resemblance to actual persons, living or dead, businesses, government agencies, events, or locations, is entirely coincidental.

A NATION DIVIDED

Where eagles once ruled, only ravens scavenge,
Barren land wasted by political greed.
Plunder, not worth the taking!
A nation laid to waste,
While brother fights brother,
Once again, once again.
A nation divided cannot long stand,
Or so it must go,
But purpose united in mortal combat,
Only sheds blood with little conscience,
Reason halted and war the only voice heard.
Nothing of peace can be recalled,
Or times that could have been.
Or times no longer available to enjoy,
As the evil of war corrupts,
And soldiers divided in their quest,
Though knowing the end,
No matter might or right will divide,
With just the best aim of a weapon,
Well intended and deliberate,
Will in earnest begin a story,
Of what can be or what could become,
Future in this land of the free,
And home of the brave.
Life in these free and individual states
Rushes blindly forward to an involuntary moment,
A challenge in history to be,
Foundation for which building and treachery has begun,
Portends only what could be,
For the enemies that surround us so,
The strongest, most determined this writer envisions
Could someday be the internal foe.
History teaches to learn from our past,
To refuse this easy lesson
Only serves to invite the tragedy of this saga.

Jim Damiano

DEDICATION

I dedicate this novel to the one person who has been my inspiration, my cheerleader, my best friend, and my chief critic, my beautiful wife and life's companion, Betty J. Rockwell Damiano.

I am forever grateful to my grandchildren, Justin, Taylor, Savannah, and Brooklyn for their inspiration; may they never witness the tale this fiction has wrought!

To my children, Cheryl, James, Rebecca, and their spouses, Shane, Candace, and Christopher, thanks for your support and help in the editing and many suggestions along the way.

And last, to my parents, now both with God, who always encouraged me to be honest to myself and to my dreams. Their love of reading was passed on to me at an early age. They always pushed me firmly, but gently, to allow my creativity to blossom. They will never see this novel. Yet, somehow I feel they have read it already.

I love and thank you all.

Jim Damiano

ACKNOWLEDGMENTS

Time is really the only true asset we ever have while on this earth. Therefore, it is with great pleasure that I acknowledge the following people who have helped me make *2020 – A Season to Die* a reality and not just a dream.

Captain Tony Arbisi, USMC, retired, for his military advice and encouragement, and Ray Strickland, Vietnam War era veteran, for his honest commentary;

My daughters, Cheryl Humphrey and Rebecca Gebhardt, for their tireless copyediting efforts and extreme diligence when the novel was but a fresh idea, filled with more mistakes than I care to remember;

Klaus and Anita Gebhardt, for their encouragement and help, and the use of their business office;

John Sissala, my brother-in-law and friend of forty years, who read the seventh of my twenty-plus revisions, while on vacation.

Kathy Zaharek, my sister-in-law, but really my little sister, who encouraged me to write a story about a bad dream;

Kimberly Evans, whose photography skills made my old mug look acceptable;

Carol Witt for her artistic and creative ability capturing the perfect scene for the novel's back cover;

Brad Fregger and his team at 1st World Library, who had faith in my story and took my book and ran with it with a gusto that went far beyond expectations.

And last, Betty, my life partner of forty-plus years, who knows each page of this story as well, if not better, than I. Her sometimes-stabbing critique and loving kindness kept me balanced and focused.

I thank you all from the bottom of my heart.

Northcutt Family of Prosper, Texas

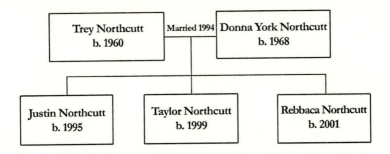

Rinaldi Family of Utica, New York

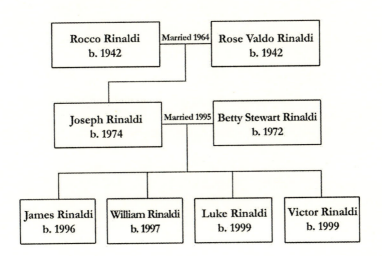

OPEN LETTER TO THE EDITOR

Dateline Utica, New York, April 19, 2009

Please consider the following:

> *Dear Editor:*
> *The streets of our fair city are filled with rioting. Local citizenry is divided, not by religion or cultural differences, but by a new idealism called "Freedom." Soldiers representing the government have shot citizens dead in our streets, citizens whose only crime was their disorderly conduct. A free black citizen has been among the first killed, not because of his race, only his views.*
>
> *Today's government surely will tax us to death, punishing those who produce by taxation without true representation, while freebooters and government lackeys find reward for benign activity.*
>
> *Government, at its will, has the right of search and seizure, breaking into homes of law-abiding citizens, without cause, except what it determines as well-founded suspicions. Government troops are billeted in homes of unlucky citizens who foolishly believe freedom of speech a God-given right. Owner and tenant alike must find lodging while their homes are pillaged. Rumors once thought unreal are now common. Government agents will search, confiscate, and apprehend militia arsenals considered a threat to the very peace they defend. I, my dear editor, fear for our once blissful city on this robust spring morning of April 10, 1775.*
>
> *–Signed Anonymous*

Couldn't this ironic editorial, printed in Boston, Massachusetts, except for billeting, have been written today? We do not billet soldiers today. Our extensive taxes allow troops and various agents of government to travel and live the good life at the expense of the hard-working taxpayers.

Our media has often been chided for its liberal bias. This humble writer believes that the media gets far too much credit for this high accolade. To suggest that our media is biased only raises it to a higher level of professionalism, something it lost long ago. Today it feeds and prospers on reports bent on sensationalism and open attempts to spin, even manufacture, the news, all aimed at corporate profits, not conveying the real happenings of daily events.

Like many, I cried a father's tears in seeing events unwind on TV when tragedy hit our television screens on September 11, 2001. I, like every freedom-loving American, was numbed by the event. For a brief moment we were a caring and united country. Patriots all, we became furious and resolute to the bitter, daily reminder of terrorism's presence.

Someday we may regret the truth, when our nation tallies the cause underlying why this happened. I do not feel we will truly be able to indict the militia, the terrorists (both internal and external), the crazed individual, or whoever shall attack the domestic tranquility of our nation. No, not until we first look inward and indict ourselves for our fear of being politically correct, which has become more important than the constitutional rights for which our famous and brave forefathers bled.

We must return to our God, no matter what our belief. The value of religion is in knowing that no God, no matter what name He is called, no matter how He is worshipped, would condone the bombing of the government building in Oklahoma, or the World Trade Center on 9-11, or the terrorist acts that have followed us to this very day. Terrorists try to use God to justify cowardly acts. God in His omnipotence cannot be pleased.

I am one man exercising my right to speak. I love this country. It has been the greatest and best experiment in known history for freedom, democracy, and the republican form of representative government that this world has ever known.

But our government has become too big and too large a part of our daily lives. And worse, it has become a government that is more focused on the mundane than the critical issues facing our nation. Nations that forget their founding principles eventually forget their citizens. It's become a government that slowly forgot its original intent: that ours is a government formed of the people, by the people, and for the people. Its politicians are only servants of the people, not the new royalty of special interest groups, compromised media, and elitist politicians. Didn't we rebel against royalty and its ilk once already?

Let us pray we reach our 250th anniversary as a unified nation. The only real threat we have is not from terrorist nations; it is not from outside rogue

Third World dictatorships, nor is it from the remaining Red threat of communism. Our greatest fear should be from the putrid decay within our very own borders. History teaches us that every great civilization's demise started from within.

Perhaps today I will be criticized and even treated with disdain for my beliefs. I'm thankful for the right to free speech and for the opportunity to express these ideals. I am an old man and have been privileged to see our nation at the height of its greatness. I have fought for and served my country, and have always freely paid my taxes, no matter how unjust they seemed. I want the peace and the freedom that our founding fathers willed us as their posterity. In practicality, our nation needs to rethink itself. I sincerely hope this epistle helps to jar the reader to action to preserve our Union, not just for our children, but for all the freedom-loving people in the world at large, before it is too late.

There is so much that is so wonderful about our nation. Clearly the good has mostly outweighed the bad. Now it is in our hands to adjust the indifference and correct what's gone wrong, if we choose.

A nation that allows dissent and free speech is good. A nation that creates and sponsors a spirit of resentment for any segment of its populace is doomed to stir the ire of its majority and eventually fail.

The Great Experiment of 1776 works today only if we, its citizens, work to keep it alive in spirit, action, gratitude, and love.

Signed,
Rocco V. Rinaldi

One of the great liberal documents of the world is the Declaration of Independence. One of the great conservative documents of the world is the Constitution of the United States. We need both documents to build a country. One to get it started—Liberal; and the other to help maintain the structure over the years—Conservative.

—John Rohn

Prologue

April 19, 2019—Utica, New York

Rock Rinaldi unfolded his morning paper with grave reluctance. He already knew what the headlines would be. The riots were the only focus of the news media. His main concern right now was the whereabouts of his grandson Luke's 10th Mountain Division. Street fighting was its specialty, and it was reported that Regular Army units were being sent to Texas when the Texas National Guard refused to intercede. It was logical to Rock that President Collins might call in this elite outfit. Scanning several pages, he found nothing to ease his fear. In frustration, he tossed the paper on the table, startling his wife, who was about to take a sip of coffee.

"Darn paper. You never get the news you need."

"Rock, why the fuss? This mess will all go away in time. The country's leaders are too smart to let this go on." Rose was the eternal optimist in the Rinaldi family. Happily married since 1964, she was Rock's best friend and alter ego.

"Honey, I sure hope you're right. This is a great country, but it has contracted an illness that has gotten us off balance. I hope that my predictions of worse times are just my own worries. I can't help but feel that this time it has lingered too long to cure. Our president has stirred up a hornet's nest in Texas with the way he's handling this. It was pure stupidity when he blatantly ordered the shooting of any citizens without regard.

Of all places, why did Collins pick Texas to make an example right now? This may backfire and turn into something worse."

"Well, Rocco, your letter to the editor seems to be coming true."

"Rose, I pray that you're wrong."

Rose saw a sadness in Rock's eyes that only she could understand. Grim eyes—a harbinger of things to come, Worse, a reminder of Vietnam, another hostile time when everything seemed out of control.

January 3, 2020—Prosper, Texas

Today was the first time that the Texas rebels attacked the Federal Army with the weight of their combined militias. Organizing the army had been a painful experience, filled with confusion and blunders. But that all ended when men like Raif Sinsome took the reins and fast-forwarded the cause to a higher level of achievement. Guerilla warfare had taken its toll upon the Federal invaders. Yet it was not enough to tip the balance. Only a well-organized army with an adequate plan for victory would do this. The Texas governor, Barbara Collins-Smythe, ironically the younger sister of the President of the United States, was the catalyst for such a plan.

Lieutenant Taylor Northcutt looked at his men, who were all hugging the ground awaiting orders to move forward. The early morning light was breaking through the misty fog that was concealing their ambush.

Somewhere in the dark, Taylor's brother, Colonel Justin Northcutt, was preparing to give the order for his regiment to lock and load. Word had reached him that his Rangers, stationed at the end of the defensive perimeter, must seal the fate of the enemy.

Sinsome's courier message lay hard in his hand. It stated, in Raif's quickly scribbled handwriting:

> *Justin, let their troop convoy pass your position without taking action until the last vehicle passes. Advise by radio, using the SOS code only, when it does. Then, and I repeat only then, you must fire upon the enemy once you hear any action commencing north of your position. Your primary responsibility is to prevent their retreat.*
> *Good luck, Raif*

Justin reread the order, took a deep breath, and sent word to his company commanders. His 800 men, almost all natives of Prosper and Celina, were primed and ready. Desire for revenge motivated them. He knew, though, that his men would need more than hatred to defeat the well-organized enemy.

The last vehicle passed. Assurance came from Justin's scouts that no more were in sight. The weather would prevent the Federals' massive air advantage from giving them support, especially in a close battle. Moments seemed like eternities to Justin as he awaited the reassuring sound of conflict. It came with a thunderous report.

Justin shouted, "Move forward!"

As one, his Rangers executed a wide sweep northward. Eight-hundred men, in three-column formation, each man ten paces apart, advanced at a trot with old Preston Road as their center, just a mere mile south of Prosper, Texas. They reached the enemy, flanking them at their rear. The battle commenced immediately. Any Federal trying to retreat was cut down mercilessly. But the enemy would not give in lightly. It wheeled to the west and worked its way into the city. Battle plans and any thought of order retreated with them as the Rebels diligently followed. Each army gave its all. The battle turned ugly as hand-to-hand, building-to-building combat took its toll. Reaching the city, the Federals took fire from resolute citizens, many of whom died heroically for their efforts.

The battle raged for hours. Justin's regiment fought the hardest of any, for most of his men came from this very city, and it was in their homes the enemy had chosen to take refuge. In the end, this would be the first major victory for the Rebels. Up until now, there had been many smaller skirmishes and minor battles. Today, 30,000 Rebels defeated a Federal column of more than 20,000. Most of the Federals managed to escape northward when the foreboding skies cleared. Their air force made certain of this, as it played havoc with the victorious Rebels, tainting their first victory. It would be one of the few times the Rebel forces would outnumber their adversary, but it was a beginning.

Retreating northward, Federal Sergeant Luke Rinaldi counted the men in his platoon who had escaped the enemy's ambush. It wasn't good. More than half were missing and presumed dead. He had been lucky. When the attack started, his position was far forward of the action. His men had fought desperately to survive, giving as much as they received. It didn't matter. *This war is so unnecessary*, he thought, wondering if he would ever see his family again. He marched double quick, pushing to survive. Somehow, it mattered, but he wasn't sure why.

April 19, 2020—Battle of Utica, Utica, New York

Rebel Sergeant James Rinaldi loaded his M-16 rifle and gathered his men before him. He looked at his younger brother Billy, always the card. He smiled; Billy winked.

What's he up to now? James wondered. *He's always so damn reckless, yet so predictable and dependable.* James worried about Billy's safety. He had promised his father he'd look after him. However, that was easier said than done, especially during an unpredictable war.

Tim Rockwell stood to his left. Tim, his boyhood friend and constant sounding board, was pensive as James talked to his squad.

"Men, we are about to attack the enemy. This is the first time we feel able to wage a full battle. All I can say is do your best. Many of us are from this city, so it is personal. Be careful. Remember, a dead Rebel only helps the Federal cause, not ours. Good luck."

James was correct. Never before had the New York Rebels tried to go beyond harassment of the enemy. Guerilla fighting was the norm, not committing to fully pitched battles. Now Rebel leaders thought the time right. It was up to the First New York Volunteers to make it all happen. It was a risky gesture. Failure was not an option.

James's platoon was a small part of a massive movement attempting to effect a change in the order of a once peaceful life, in a country gone crazy. He gave the order to advance. Slowly his men walked down Deerfield Hill into the enemy fire. The Adirondack Mountains would no longer protect them. Now only the cover of darkness gave comfort. They reached Genesee Street, its normal familiarity erased by war's fury. Fighting from building to building, the battle raged into the day and then merged into the night, finding its way into the next day's early light.

Slowly the Rebels gained ground and momentum as the Federals, routed, retreated into the southern reaches of the city's hilly area.

A small personal battle raged at an old house on Conkling Avenue, long abandoned. Today it contained several Federal snipers and a machine gun. It was James's platoon's misfortune to run into their devastating fire. James signaled to his men to sweep wide of the building to try to flank it. Two men were immediately cut down for their efforts and two more wounded. It didn't look good.

James looked at the lieutenant, hoping he'd signal his men to leave. *We can bypass this motherless place, damn it. Why now, when we are so close?* Knowing it was foolish wishing, he ordered his men to take the building. The first to respond was Billy. Moving forward with the speed of an Olympic runner, Billy reached a wounded comrade and carried him to safety. Miraculously he was not hit. He returned for the other wounded comrade, a woman. He reached her and returned her to safety, but it was too late. She soon died from her wounds.

James shouted, "Billy, stay put! I need you to go to our right."

But Billy didn't hear him above the roar of battle. Instead, he moved forward, grenades in his two hands, fury in his eyes. Somehow the enemy's bullets failed to find him. He took advantage of their surprise, hurling his grenades and then unleashing another two—all hit their target. Billy had been an ace pitcher for Proctor High School and the enemy now felt confirmation of his accuracy. He reached the safety of an old maple tree and pulled his rifle from its sling around his back. He settled in for the continuing siege of the building, alone, several yards from his platoon, or at least what remained of it. Taking a deep breath to clear his mind, Billy realized what he had just done. He didn't know why he had taken the chance. He only knew that he had done what he had to do and that somehow it felt right.

April 21, 2020—Rome, New York

Spring rains cascaded down the empty street, falling into the sewer on their journey to the Mohawk River. Vic Rinaldi sat in silent contemplation across the street from Fort Stanwix National Park, the site where Betsy

Ross's Stars and Stripes flag was first flown in battle in another war for independence. The early morning light, hidden by bilious clouds, cast an eerie feel to the moment.

"Hey Vic, how the hell long do ya expect us to sit around this dump? Don't cha think it's time we mosey on?" Randy Parker wiped the rain from his stolen hat as he guardedly floated his request. Vic, known for his edgy temper, had to be handled carefully.

"We move when I say so." Vic stood, his five-feet-ten muscular frame moving menacingly toward Parker.

"Vic, don't get on Randy. It's a fair question. Shit, we've been here two days and we're pushing our luck." Vernon Walters, the educated bad boy of the wild bunch, was not intimidated by Vic. He stood six feet tall and had the muscle to have his way if he intended, but Vic's proven leadership needed leeway. This was one of those moments where a little room for maneuvering was required, if only to be prudent.

"Look, guys." Vic signaled them to come closer. Five rain-soaked marauders picked their way to his side, none willing to exert individualism. Vic, their chosen leader, had kept them alive. None dared defy him, at least not to his face. Vic continued, eyeballing each man with a penetrating glare. "I agree we need to move on, but where? The Rebs are in control of this sector. Unlike the Feds, they still are disorganized, leaving us a lot of room to do as we please." Vic's large, brown eyes glared into the rain. A snarl formed upon his lips. "Where do you propose to go? Damn, the pickings are good here. This city's all but empty, and no one's going to bother us for at least a few more days. Then we'll strike north and see what we can run into there."

Parker, feeling suddenly brave, spoke. "Vic, we're pushin' our luck. The Rebs hunt us down like dogs, the same as the Feds. I'm for pullin' out now." He shouted above the din of the thunder. "This friggin' rain looks like it's stayin', and we need more shelter than our damned Humvee."

Vic's ignoring Parker only served to rile him more. "Damn it, Vic, don't turn your f-ing back to me."

Without warning, Vic quickly turned, his right fist balled tight in fury, and struck Parker, breaking his nose and knocking him down. Parker's blood, mixing with the rain, found its way to the gutter.

Vic, right fist still curled, purposefully faced his men, his left hand placed menacingly on his Luger, while grinding his booted foot into Parker's exposed stomach. With deliberate intensity, he slowly spit out each word. "We move only," he hesitated for effect, "and I mean only, when I damn well say so, and only when I get the lay of the land. I'll decide when that is, and no sooner. So don't push me."

His index finger moved to the Luger's trigger as he took his foot off Parker. Parker did not dare move. The others waited, not certain what to expect. Vic's tendency toward violence often went unchecked.

Vic sneered. "First we get diesel. We're not going anywhere without it. Next we'll need supplies, or do you all suppose we'll get by on our looks? We move out when we figure where the troops aren't. And last, we need more ammo. In case you haven't noticed, we're about out."

No one said a thing. Collectively they knew Vic was right. Life as a marauder was hard enough. Acting stupidly was the surest way to an early end, though few expected a long life. Vic, seeing the squabble was over, returned to the Humvee, his right hand lovingly fingering his pistol, just in case.

Parker, trying to stanch his bleeding, was left to himself. The others sensed that helping him might prove dangerous to their own health.

Vic looked with guarded indifference at the scene before him. Never in his wildest dreams could he have imagined himself here, in such a low position. Being a marauder was easier than he thought, and Vic always took the easy way out. He felt a sudden pang of disgust with his life. By most odds, one would never believe a Rinaldi boy would stoop to such low levels. His family, mostly well-respected businessmen and educators, produced better progeny than he. Their family tree was not a place where a criminal mind would be expected to dwell. But this was 2020, and nothing was what it should be.

Jim Damiano

A nation that allows dissent and free speech is good. A nation that creates and sponsors a spirit of resentment for any segment of its populace is doomed to stir the ire of its majority and eventually fail.

—Rocco Rinaldi, from his letter to the editor dated April 19, 2009

PART ONE

Overview

The United States had been in a war of insurrection for a year, and most of the country's infrastructure had been destroyed or badly compromised, causing great pain to its citizens.

The Federal Army, in its zest to maintain order, had gone overboard in Texas, committing one atrocity after another. The president's initial plan to stop the rebellion at all costs had been indifferent in its violence. As a result, many loyal citizens were driven to join the Rebel cause.

The U.S. techno-military, created to fight terrorists and enemies outside the country's borders, consisted of fewer than 800,000 personnel, with more than sixty percent of them stationed outside the borders in places like South Korea, Japan, Iraq, and Iran. It was woefully unprepared and untrained for an internal conflict.

The war did not have any easily defined boundaries as in the first Civil War of the 1860s—then, northern states fought southern states mostly below the Mason-Dixon Line. By 2020, the rebellion had advanced from a guerilla action to full, conventional warfare. Its deadly path spread terror across a frightened nation.

Jim Damiano

We hold these Truths to be self-evident, that all men are created equal, that they are endowed by their Creator with certain unalienable Rights; that among these are Life, Liberty, and the Pursuit of Happiness—That to secure these Rights, Governments are instituted among Men, deriving their just Powers from the Consent of the Governed, that whenever any Form of Government becomes destructive of these Ends, it is the Right of the People to alter or abolish it, and to institute new Government laying its Foundation on such Principles, and organizing its Powers in such Form, as to them shall seem most likely to effect their Safety and Happiness.

—Declaration of Independence of the United Colonies, July 1776

CHAPTER ONE

April 19, 2020, 0100—Southwest Sector, U.S. 2nd Army Corps

Sergeant Luke Rinaldi lay in his forward foxhole facing the Rebel front line. The constant pound of raindrops on his battered helmet went unnoticed as he rested in the muddy puddle that was now his home. Every second was a test of survival, with every minute an eternity of fear.

He briefly recalled a peaceful time from his boyhood, now so far away. It helped him to escape for a moment from the hell his life had become. He laughed sarcastically, remembering how crowded he once felt in the little room that he shared with Vic, his stubborn twin brother. But that was back home in Utica, New York, and a million miles ago. He and Vic were identical twins, but all similarities stopped there—they were different in every other way. Luke remembered with fondness how messy his twin's side of their bedroom was; Luke, however, loved order. The army usually allowed him this comfort, yet this hellish hole was far from order. The deep, rainy night did little to lessen his anguish. *This Satan's foxhole will have to do for now*, he sighed, while trying desperately to get comfortable.

Looking to his right, the heap of humanity that was once his best friend lay like so much garbage. Only the shattered shell of his body remained, twisted in its last agony, shot by a sniper's unerring aim. "This damn war," he mumbled. Then he pleaded as if talking to the rain, "Why, God, why?"

But Luke still cared. That was his problem, and it bothered him— he cared too much. He looked frantically to find something positive in this unholy environment, searching for anything that would ease his dismay. Instantly he knew that it was a fool's errand, and worse his foxhole seemed like the last scene of a bad play, and he couldn't wait for its end so that he could go home.

Well, he thought, looking at the body resting in two inches of water, *at least Bobby's death was quick*. His earthly remains would have to lie in a puddle of gore and muddy rainwater until it was safe to move for burial, or worse, left unceremoniously to rot if a quick retreat became necessary. And they had been retreating a lot lately. *Yet in this war, sudden death's a mercy not to be overlooked. Bobby Rockwell's war is over, and damn it, mine's not.* Luke shivered, but not from the rain; he was used to the depravity of his life now. His fear was more subtle. He was going mad.

If only I could just walk off into the sunset. He chuckled hysterically. Aloud, to no one in particular, he said, "Like I'll ever see a sunset again with this stinking rain. I hate goddamned Texas!" His eerie shout echoed in the dark.

The zip of a sniper's round whizzed past, about two to three inches from his shoulder, another cruel reminder of where he was. It burrowed into the mud with a quick thud. The mark of its presence disappeared quickly as water crept continuously into his semi-safe haven, soon obliterating it from memory like it never happened.

Luke had turned twenty-one a few days earlier and wondered if he'd ever reach twenty-two. A year is forever in combat. He tried to concentrate on the sniper as he carefully scanned the area immediately to his front, searching for the cowardly bastard. The gloomy light made his search all but impossible. He was constantly distracted by visions of home; he wondered why he was here in the first place. *How did I ever get to the Texas-Oklahoma border?* This was neither something he could comprehend nor anything he really wished to consider in this dull-witted moment. *But here I am.* He shuddered.

"How stupid!" Luke shouted again, as he slapped the rain from his face. No one could hear him above the roar of the natural and artificial thunder. The night and the humidity of the spring's summer-like heat were appalling. The incessant rain drummed a staccato rhythm on his helmet, making his situation all the more unbearable.

Shit, here I am like a bull's-eye target at Basic, waiting for an unexpected, unwelcome bullet from a fellow ex-citizen. The thought unnerved him. He patiently searched for the chance to reciprocate. He saw the sniper and snapped off a shot, and appeared to hit him. "Hot damn!" he shouted into the night. "I got you, you bastard." It felt good for a moment, but his effort was rewarded with an increased barrage of enemy fire. Suddenly, as if for the first time, everything seemed out of place. *Here I am hundreds of miles from Utica, sitting in two inches of water, wishing for a cold Saranac beer and a slice of mom's homemade pizza.* He laughed outwardly at his crazy craving.

The United States in 2020 was far removed from the United States of Luke's innocent childhood. His past life seemed so carefree and so long ago. "When was that, yesterday?" he pondered aloud. *Shit, even with the world crumbling it's unlikely a kid will notice, unless of course he's thrust like a guinea pig into the middle of a war. God, am I going mad?'*

With a sickening impact, he realized how numbed he had become to his surroundings. And then everything was abruptly silent in his sector. The snipers seemed to have relaxed their relentless terror. Silence could be good or bad. It didn't make much sense to dwell on it. *Enjoy the moment.*

The quiet lulled him, enabling him to think. Thinking, however, was not always smart in the middle of combat, especially when one was a platoon leader needing to be ready to respond at any given moment. *Hell, I was raised protected by the love of my family. The outside world was once a place of no real concern to me. Then I matured, and look at me now.*

"Well, here I am," he growled to no one in particular, and then the real world broke into his reverie.

"Hello. Did you say somethin', Sergeant?"

"No, and who the hell are you?" Luke asked in a high whisper. "Get your ass down here quick before it gets shot off!"

A tall, skinny kid stumbled into Luke's foxhole. Luke snapped, "What's your name and where the hell did you come from?"

"Tony Martin, Sergeant. My unit arrived late last evenin'. I guess we're your reinforcements."

"How many men came with you, Private?"

"Not many. About a company, I'd guess."

"Damn! That will get the brigade to about ten percent of the strength we had when we retreated about two days ago. We need at least two full battalions to get us to something like full strength." Luke rattled through his company's predicament as if unaware of Martin. "What's your training, Private? Any action yet?"

"Sergeant, Sir, I was a civy nine weeks ago, but I'm more'n ready to do what I hafta do."

"Soldier, didn't they teach you anything at Basic? You don't call a goddamned sergeant 'sir.' Get it? And don't say it again unless you want your sorry ass kicked from here to the enemy."

"Sorry, Sergeant, it won't happen again."

"It better not." Luke didn't want to come down so hard on the boy, yet he was regular army, and it was the only way he knew to give the kid a chance to survive. "How old are you, Private?" Luke brushed rain from his eyes.

Why am I asking this? Up until now, he had made it a point not to get to know replacements. It made their inevitable death easier to bear if you knew them only as a "dog tag," another expendable.

"Sergeant, seventeen, but don't worry. I can shoot. I was a marksman in Basic. Hey, Sarge, what the hell's this war about? One day I'm in high school, and the next I'm taken out of class and sent to training camp, issued a uniform with patches sewn over some bullet holes, eighty pounds of equipment, and told about the glory of defending the Union. Now, I'm in your mud hole a thousand miles from Cleveland, rainwater up to my ass."

Luke would normally just laugh and ignore the question. It was usually best that way. Something, though, dragged him out of his training and dulled his sense of survival. In this weakened moment, he felt a need to explain to this rookie why he might die in the next few moments. *Listen to me*, Luke marveled. *I'm thinking this kid's a young man as if I was old. I suppose a year of combat makes me qualify as an old man. Damn war!*

"Look, Private, I won't pretend I know all there is to this freaking conflict. In fact, truth is, I don't know shit. But as long as the lines are quiet and we're safe in this hole, I see no reason not to give you what I know and what I've seen. Maybe it'll keep you alive. First, you can start by staying low and hugging the mud."

"Thanks, Sergeant." Martin carefully pushed his body as far as possible into the gummy, uncomfortable muck.

"You see, Private, I don't know if anyone really understands why it started. From what I hear, one of the things that set off the fireworks happened about twelve months ago when the Great State of Texas chose to break from our Union. Rumors were that Texas had about forty million small arms weapons all by its Lone Star self. Seems the Texans said that our Constitution gave them the right to bear arms through one of the amendments. Damned if I remember which one. But our good president felt otherwise, and so did his congress. So he got several new laws passed regulating the ownership of firearms, with the requirement that all citizens must turn in all their weapons except for one, if it was used only for hunting and properly registered with the federal government. This kind of pissed them Texans off a bit, and that, in a nutshell, is why we're in this hell hole." Luke shifted his legs to reduce the intense numbing in his body.

"Yeah, I heard about that. I was in school at the time. Most people in Cleveland seemed to think it was a good idea, even if the president skirted around the right to keep arms. None of us thought it mattered much. Hell, you could buy about any gun you wanted in Cleveland anyway, law or not, if ya had a mind to."

"Well, Private, what Cleveland accepted as OK didn't set well in Texas, and the local and state governments refused to enforce the law. The federal government figured it had the right to enforce the president's edict. So when the locals refused to comply, after several opportunities, the president said 'screw it' and ordered in the FBI and the ATF gang. When the federal agents entered the state like bulls in a china shop, intent on confiscating as many weapons as they could, they never figured on the resistance they received. The Texas ringleader is a mid-sized black man named Raif Sinsome. He's one of the Rebel generals across the way trying to kill us as we speak. I also heard tell the bastard's a West Point grad."

"Yeah, Sarge, I heard he's one hell of a fighter."

Luke ignored his comment and continued, feeling good about the chance to unwind. "My dad is, or at least was, a professor of American history. When we were kids, he'd talk to us about the Constitution. It was his passion. He sure loves America, yet somehow he always felt that we were heading toward this conflict. Pa often said that the first U.S. citizens were given the right to bear arms but not just for protection against Indians and foreign invasions as some would like us to believe. You see, in our nation's beginning, militias were often the only defense citizens had. Back then there wasn't much of a standing army. But citizens also wanted protection and defense from a corrupt government, like the one they kicked out with our first revolution. I'm told Texans believe that a government that can't protect its own citizens isn't worth its salt. Terrorist bombings in Dallas about five years ago plus the undefended, open borders supported their worry. As far as I can tell, the Texans also believe that's what they're fighting—a corrupt government." Luke checked the protective covering he had placed on his rifle.

"That's bullshit, Sarge, they just can't decide they're not going to follow our laws! That wouldn't be right."

"That's why we're here, Private. It's up to us to show the Texans and anyone else that they're part of the United States and duty bound to support and defend our nation and our laws."

"Sarge, surely there's more to this war than what you've said."

"Private, you're probably on target, but I'm only a GI grunt like you, so I can only know so much. What I do know is in the last few years there's a lot about our country that was not quite working. And, for whatever reason, one day Texas exploded, and our unit was one of the first sent when the Texas National Guard plus supporting militias took over all the military bases along with their armament and military hardware.

"Private, am I boring the hell out of you yet? It sure is better than thinking of nothing but sleep." Luke tried unsuccessfully to suppress a yawn.

"No, Sarge, this is interesting. Tell me more."

"Well, Private, let me tell you this, and you hear it good. Regardless of what or who got this damn war of rebellion started, it doesn't matter a rat's behind. All that matters is the here and the now and the guy to your left and to your right. When it all comes down to it, the only loyalty we have is to the men in our platoon. It's them that will help keep you alive—that and following orders. Look out for those men with you, and they will look out for you. Whatever the damn cause that started this mess, it just doesn't matter. What matters is that we're here, and if you want to survive this shit, you won't waste your time thinking too much about anything except living through each goddamned minute."

Suddenly a sniper bullet whizzed by, inches from Martin's helmet, sinking itself into the soft mud on the opposite side of the trench.

"Damn it! Private, hug the ground like it's your first love! Those frigging Texans can shoot," Luke snapped. "They aren't much to look at in their odd assortment of uniforms, but their snipers are brutally good at what they do."

Luke felt a deep respect for his enemy, a respect learned from well-earned battle hatred. The enemy seemed to be able to use weapons in ways that his troops, even with formal training, could not surpass. Fighting to defend their homes from the invading Federals gave the Rebels a controlled fury.

"Kid, since it's stayed pretty quiet, I'm going to try to rest a bit. Stay low unless told otherwise. I need some shut-eye bad."

But sleep would not come. Luke's mind rambled. *Strange, I can no longer doze off unless it's loud.* The quiet was unnerving.

Why am I here? He pondered. Relentless in his self-torment, he tried to summon his mind to the reality of the moment, but his thoughts involuntarily raced back to when he first joined the Army's 10th Mountain Division. The drumbeat of long-ago summers came relentlessly back to haunt him; the constant memories underscored the folly of his present situation and reminded him of his youth.

Three short years ago, desperate for work, Luke was among the many that actually joined the all-volunteer army. Most of his fellow recruits were now either dead or deserters. Luke was so unlike his brothers. He didn't really hate books, only the discipline of study, and he foolishly traded it for the discipline of the army. It all seemed right at the time. Now he saw it as the greatest cop-out of his life. That hurt his ego. *I'm here because I am a fool.*

He remembered laughing sarcastically at his brothers when they encouraged him to reconsider joining the army. They tried to get him to go to a Freedom Rally, but he refused. He had no interest in bullshit political talk. Who would have thought that meetings like those would lead to rebellion? Nor had he ever imagined that his brothers would join the radicals, and now they could actually oppose him on the field of battle. Even his twin brother was involved in the opposition, but not in a manner he was proud to hear about. His last letter from home, months ago, had hinted that Vic was thought to be a renegade. *Why in the hell would he do that? And why would my brothers go against the very United States that we were all taught to love by our parents? It all makes no sense.*

Luke opened his tired eyes, glaring into the early morning light. He peered at Private Martin sitting pensively with his M-16 clutched to his chest as rain cascaded off his helmet. Luke could see the fear in his eyes and smell his youthful ignorance. How could Martin's horror be any different from anyone else's? Cold, damp fear was uncomfortable enough. Add sitting in this mud with the stench of new death in one's nostrils and that terrible taste of bile one gets while awaiting fate moment by moment. God, how he remembered his first taste of action. The inner panic was beyond comprehension. Now he stoically faced death, uncaring. Martin would have to learn to do the same. *There is no substitute for experience.*

When things quieted down, Luke resolved to ask Martin about his life. This was again in direct contradiction to common sense. *Avoid feeling at all cost.* The thought hammered at him. It was a simple rule. To make it from each difficult day to the next, you had to avoid getting close to the new guys. They were usually the ones killed more quickly, battle experience being an expensive commodity learned only by the lucky survivors of the school of hard knocks. *Here I am, living proof that life is cheap and expendable, a lowly sergeant of a platoon that has only seven effective men, including this raw kid.* Yesterday, the company roster showed thirty-four men, a paltry few of the original 250 that left Basic. The last statistics from HQ said that the company had over a 200 percent turnover. *So why get to know anyone? Why waste the energy?*

Even worse, you never knew when you might be called on one of those countless firing squad details. This duty did little to encourage morale. At least twenty men from Luke's company had been shot as deserters. The current U.S. Army was based as much on fear of its own command as on fear of the Rebels. The citizens felt it, too. And none of this was helped by what seemed to be the unnerving vicissitudes of a self-centered president. The nation, in its past, always seemed to have the right man to lead it out of a fix. Washington, Lincoln, Wilson, and Roosevelt were a few names that came to Luke's mind. President Rex Collins was not a Lincoln, but his sister, ironically the Rebel Texas president, seemed to have the grit to do the job. ... Luke caught himself, embarrassed at even thinking this was a good thing.

Many recruits, like Luke, joined the army because of lack of work and just for something to do. The country had been in another recession-turned-depression, one of a series of many in the past two decades that had crippled the economy. The restless fever of the citizenry created a new street rabble. The military offered one of the very few jobs available if you wanted work. No one had thought a war was possible—much less a rebellion for independence. The lingering War on Terrorism was considered a joke by most.

Luke made corporal after one year. His promotion came about the time President Collins had issued his famous order for the military to assist, "at its fullest capacity, the local and state police organizations in their fight against extremists, militias, and weapons stockpiles." Collins had ordered swift, harsh punishment to any who resisted the seizure of weapons. Collins kept his word.

The president was undeterred, even when many innocents were included in the widespread sweep. This was when desertions started and the silent militias, slipping under the radar of the weakened CIA and FBI, had made their presence known. And it had all started in Dallas, a few short miles from here, like a forest fire raging uncontrolled.

Martin interrupted Luke's thoughts. "Sarge, how much time before something starts?"

"Damned if I know, Private. It'll come soon enough."

"Sarge, I've been thinking …"

"Bad habit out here, kid. Leave the thinking to the generals." Luke grinned. He liked Martin.

"From what you said, it sounds like we're undermanned. How bad off are we, or is it some military secret?"

"It's hardly a secret when you are in the middle of it." Martin's question reminded Luke of all the carnage. And he knew it would only get worse. "We're under strength by about eighty percent."

"Well, I hope our boys made them pay the piper."

"Private, we gave as good as we took, but you've got to give them credit. Their damn militia, those out of control Texans, and the deserters from our side have given us one helluva fight. And lately it's been backwards for us."

"Sarge, don't we control the air? Why aren't we bombing the living shit out of them?"

Luke grunted, "We did. But we got frustrated pretty quick with the restrictions on collateral damage. When we rolled those back, our pilots went overboard, which ended up being one great recruitment tool for the Rebs."

"Don't we have more damn planes …?"

"Not anymore. The deserters not only stole some of our good aircraft, the bastards raided the plane bone yards in Arizona, grabbing stuff dating back to the '50s. Our brass scoffed at first, but they ain't scoffin' now. The Rebs got the junkers up. They ain't pretty, but they still fly, and they still kill real good. Easier to manage, too, given the crappy situation with fuel."

"What about the mercenaries? Are there any in our outfit?"

"None that I know of. Rumor says the Rebs welcome anybody who will fight for the cause. Most of 'em are from England and Western Europe, or so I've heard. I'd guess its fewer than we think. I know this unit never killed or captured one."

Luke spat to the side, into the mud. "What bothers me the most is the pillaging that goes on, especially in our outfit. Hear this and hear it good, Private. I won't tolerate any crap like that in my platoon. When this is all over, my men's consciences will be clear, even if I have to kill them myself to make sure." Martin nearly cracked a smile, but it died when he saw that Luke's face showed no humor whatsoever.

"Yes, Sarge, I understand."

"Good, now let me get some rest."

April 19, 2020, 0500—Texas/Oklahoma Border, Rebel Forward Line

The staccato rap of machine gun fire penetrated the pre-dawn mist along with the lingering stench of death. Colonel Justin Northcutt focused his night-vision binoculars, scanning across the deadly field of no-man's land, wondering if the Federal forces opposing his sector would attempt an assault. The battle had not been going well for either side. Casualties were extreme. Something would have to be done—and soon—to break the impasse.

A vivid memory of glazed, staring eyes looking up at him brought him up short. She must have been a beautiful child, about ten years old, he guessed. She lay strangled and broken in her last agony after craven Federal soldiers had brutally raped her. They left the city of Sherman in flames, retreating to safety and their present position at the Texas border. The memory of this little girl's needless death drove him onward. This war had become personal.

Justin, a native Texan, was the newly appointed commander of the 2nd Ranger Regiment, 1st Brigade, 36th Ranger Division. Although only twenty-four, the war had made him an old man. This new war for freedom and independence had started over a dozen months and countless deaths ago. *Was it only yesterday that I was a boy growing up in Prosper, Texas?* Prosper was only a few battles and scant miles from this tattered field.

He crawled in earnest, mud seeping through his uniform, to his command post. Once there, he stood and stretched to ease the damp pain from his six-feet-five frame. Oh, how he longed for the creature comfort of a nice warm shower and a soft bed to lay his weary bones on—wishful thinking. Taking off his helmet, he brushed back sweaty, dark brown hair.

Justin had been up for forty-eight endless hours. His Aggie ROTC training didn't prepare him for the continuous Federal attacks upon his position. His unit had the enormous responsibility of defending the extreme right flank of the Texas line. It was becoming more difficult to cover the area. His once-proud unit of 800 strong Texan souls was reduced to a mere 300. Justin sighed wistfully. S*o many good men gone*. His thoughts melted into the hazy mist from his eyes.

A massive explosion, not very distant, interrupted his brief reverie. He seldom took notice anymore of the war's manmade thunder and the destruction it signaled. He had become conditioned to it. Before he could determine the Federal shell's direction, the shadow of his brother Taylor filled the entry to his rough headquarters.

Lieutenant Taylor Northcutt was clearly Justin's opposite. Standing shy of six feet, his blond hair and casual good looks and spirit emphasized what a twenty-year-old living in any other time could have enjoyed. He was the deliberate baby brother, without the adventurous spirit that marked Justin's personality. His actions were carefully contemplated, whereas Justin usually acted first, depending on his instinct, and calculated later.

Taylor took off his helmet, clunking it on the improvised table, glad to be in the stale and musty bunker away, if only temporarily, from the fury outside. His long, unkempt, matted hair did not match his personality; constant battle had given him little time for grooming.

Of the two, Taylor was always the straight-A student. He also had been the class clown, or in Justin's words, the "Class Smart-Ass." He somehow managed to get away with it, while Justin, who had his moments, usually got caught. But today, looking at his brother, Justin saw a very intelligent, tough smart-ass and, more importantly, a leader of men who could be depended upon in a crisis. Men like Taylor helped give the Rebel cause its limited success.

It was no surprise to Justin that Taylor failed to salute. Military protocol was not Taylor's strong suit. He was not, nor ever would be, considered regular army. His spirit, almost Peter Pan-like, caused him to purposely do things to irritate his somber brother, but only in private, and only when he saw a need to lighten Justin's load. He started to talk as Justin motioned him to take a seat on a crate near his makeshift desk. He sat gingerly on the rickety structure, afraid to place his full weight.

"Justin, I have orders from command. I thought I'd bring them myself as, well, as …" He hesitated and then spit it out. "You know, as we may not make it to see each other again. I don't know why, but I wanted to see your ugly face, you know, in case." Taylor couldn't fully express the obvious concern of both men, and though he tried to make light of his concern, fatigue had cost him his edge.

Taylor stood, handing Justin the sealed orders. Justin quickly ripped open the folded paper and slowly read. His face gave away his concern. Taylor watched, patiently waiting. Justin turned and read its contents aloud.

Colonel J. Northcutt, Commander, 2nd Ranger Regiment. First Brigade, 36th Division
19 April 2020

You are commanded to commence a coordinated attack at 0800 today upon the sector immediate to your position, against Federal forces believed to be preparing for an assault. Your only advantage is surprise; artillery cover will commence at 0755. You must move quickly. Your regiment must hit their lines as the barrage lifts. All regiments of Second Brigade will join you, along with the 5th, 6th, and 7th regiments of the First Brigade. Your orders are simple but FIRM. We must not fail as reinforcements to the Federals are expected shortly. Therefore, instruct your men that Texas must be defended at all costs. For God and Texas, we must prevail.

M. Gen. Raif Sinsome, Commander, 36th Division, Army of the Republic of Texas

Justin stood, as did Taylor. Justin grasped his brother's hand and then did something he hadn't done in years. He put his long arms around his brother and hugged him. "Thanks, Tay. You take care, ya hear, and don't take unnecessary chances. That, Lieutenant, is an order."

"Don't worry, Justin, I'll watch my backside, but it's you that I'm worried about. You be careful too. We've got too many women we haven't met yet."

"Let's hope women will soon be our biggest and only concern." Justin felt a rare smile forming as his brother smartly returned his salute, an uncommon courtesy that spoke volumes.

April 19, 2020, 0630—Headquarters, 2nd Ranger Regiment

Justin spent the next hour with his officers, readying for the attack. Reserve units from other regiments slowly and efficiently started to reposition in case the attack failed or they were needed to fill any gaps created by the enemy. Justin thought, *If only the rain would continue for a few more hours. It would hinder the enemy's air power.*

Luckily, the air force they might face today was not the same powerhouse of a year ago. Many Federal pilots had deserted the service to join the Rebels. Unlike the early stages of the war, both sides now enjoyed sufficient aircraft to make life miserable for ground troops. However, almost all the modern technology had been lost in the shuffle of the Rebellion. The great advantage of pinpoint, laser-guided air power was minimized or rendered ineffective.

Justin looked fondly upon the Lone Star patch emblazoned on the uniforms of his Rangers forming for the assault. The flag insignia patch sewn on the right shoulder of each shirtsleeve had the red, white, and blue of the Republic of Texas. The left shirtsleeve had the historical T-patch of the 36th Ranger Infantry Division. Its green capital T, emblazoned in a field of blue, set in an inverted arrowhead had seen many of the nation's wars. His secret wish was that someday the flag of the United States would once again fly. He wondered what terrible cost in human life it would take to make it happen.

Perhaps the revived flag would represent a true republic—one with states' rights as important as federal rights, and more notably, one that stood united under the principles of freedom for all. *Are we fighting only to replace one bad set of politicians with another? ... Stop these incessant thoughts. You'll drive yourself nuts!*

Calmed somewhat, he thought, *Our job is to fight for our freedom and the protection of our families, even when the invading enemy are our own countrymen.* Texans had seen what the Federal Army did to communities they had conquered, even those that had only minimal rebel leanings. This was a new America, and the rules of engagement included the torture or murder of innocent civilians, no matter their age or sex. Federal atrocities gave the Rebels something important to defend against. Even when there seemed little hope, the tinder for revenge kindled the fires of war. Texans understood they were defending their homeland, and that knowledge gave them mythical courage and the strength to carry on the fight for independence.

April 19, 2020, 0755—Rebel Advance Line

Artillery started as planned. Justin commanded his Rangers to start the attack. In an instant, the incredible Rebel Cry penetrated the morning rain. All along their line, Federal forces heard its fearful resonance even above the awesome din of artillery.

Justin thought, *Could this be how the famous Rebel Yell of the last Civil War sounded?* He could never know but guessed that it was. Its eerie cry struck fear into the Federal lines unlike anything else. The horrific sound meant no mercy for anyone caught in the web of its onslaught. With chills running up and down his spine and adrenalin pulsing throughout his body, he rushed forward with his men. Glancing quickly to his right, he saw his brother, head low, advancing with his depleted platoon. Their eyes met briefly—no words were needed.

April 19, 2020, 0800—Federal Forward Line

The five-minute Rebel barrage seemed an eternity to Luke as he hugged the dirt, almost smothering in the putrid, bloody water at its bottom. No sooner did it stop than he heard that terrible, now familiar, eerie howl as the Texans attacked the Federal line in force.

The barrage seemed to let up, allowing Luke to survey the area.

Luke pushed at Martin's back. "Martin, get ready. You're about to get to see first hand what we've been talkin' about. Martin!"

Luke turned the kid's body. There was a mass of blood and grizzle where his face used to be. Luke's worst fears about getting to know this kid from Cleveland were now realized. He shook off his dread, like the veteran he was, and prepared himself mentally for what was about to happen next.

Machine-gun fire, combined with mortar shells, rained down on Luke's muddy world. He shouted above the din, "Keep down; they're throwing everything they have at us!" He could not look over his foxhole to see the oncoming enemy. If he did, he'd die. He tried to look through all the smoke and dimly saw a few men who appeared uninjured, though many suffered crippling or deadly wounds. Several Federal troopers fired back as often as they dared. Mostly, they just lifted their weapons over the muddy ramparts and without seeing, pulled their triggers on automatic.

Good God, Luke thought, *the only answer is surrender*. Luke's instincts took over; common sense took command of his inner thoughts. However, he did not have the courage or desire to just give up. The constant zip of bullets, shrapnel, body parts, and dirt surrounded him. The sulfuric smell of battle covered everything. The horrific danger gave his mouth a terrible, dry taste.

They were coming forward. He heard their continued unearthly yell. It sounded as if the Rebels were on top of him. Mud splashed while the constant sound of rain and natural thunder competed with the man-made echoes from the returning Federal artillery rounds, exploding shells, and small-arms fire. The smell of death was a constant.

Luke was encouraged by the slight change in the sounds of the battle's direction. It appeared to his practiced ears that it might represent a Federal counterattack. On this day, the Federal Air Force consisted of one plane. Luke looked up from the safety of his foxhole to see it screech low over their position. The jet's afterburners seemed to explode in defiance at the Rebel advance as it strafed and bombed any and all visible targets.

Luke shouted, his adrenalin peaking, "We still have air, damn it, and we'll keep this ground." He savored the fact that he was still alive. Calmly he looked at his rifle, as if transfixed. Then, instinctively defending his position, he slammed one magazine after another into his piece until he was out. Luke's intuition told him that he was on his own. He saw no living men from his squad—only parts of men and tragically crumpled bodies. He yelled for anyone to respond. But even if some were alive, no one could possibly hear his calls above the roar.

To continue firing his M-16, he had to leave the safety of his position to rummage through the pockets and ammo belts of dead companions. The urge to survive erased his fear, though the taste of bile continued to burn his throat. The ammunition he found on Martin's twisted body was quickly slammed into the hot pit of his rifle's chamber. After he unloaded that magazine, he was again out of ammo. He decided to stay put. Reason returned—searching for more ammo meant instant death.

A sudden, disarming quiet was followed by a massive impact that smothered the area outside his foxhole. Luke screamed, but no noise came from him as his body was thrown unceremoniously into the air. He landed on the rain-softened ground, his impact partially cushioned by a Rebel body. He lost consciousness as he slumped into an uncontrollable heap, his battle over.

The wet soil turned a deep red, as if drowning him. The eyes of the dead Rebel that had lessened his fall stared blankly, almost as if focusing on Luke's crumpled body. It seemed as if the dead Texan was pleading, "Why?"

The torrential rains continued as the battle raged on, trying, but failing, to cleanse the gory field, as if God wanted to erase what His creation, man, had so foolishly wrought.

Jim Damiano

It is not the critic who counts; nor the man who points out how the strong man stumbles. ... The credit belongs to the man who is actually in the arena, whose face is marred by dust and sweat and blood ... who at the worst if he fails, at least fails while daring greatly, so that his place shall never be with those cold and timid souls who know neither victory nor defeat.

—President Theodore Roosevelt

CHAPTER TWO

April 21, 2020—Rebel Army, Northeast Sector, Utica, New York

Sergeant James Rinaldi breathed a sigh of weary relief as he dropped the spade. He collapsed to his knees in silent prayer for his brother William, killed yesterday in the aftermath of the battle to take the city of Utica. It was an unkind death—as if there were any good deaths in this struggle. But the death of a brother is always harsh to grasp.

It had been a bit of chance, a brief moment of glory and adrenalin as they captured a house that held a few stubborn Federal defenders and one desperate enemy trooper who would not surrender. Tears streaked James's face, liberally soaking his bearded chin. *At least I was able to kill the man who slaughtered Billy.* Retribution was seldom possible in war, which is simply an organized effort to kill in a commonly archaic and impersonal way.

The recent Battle of Utica was the first major engagement in the northeastern theater of the war where Federal and Rebel armies clashed openly. Guerrilla warfare had been more the norm until this recent battle.

Tim Rockwell stood in silence, respecting the moment. He had come with James to bury his boyhood friend. "Billy deserved more," he said quietly. "Hell, he saved my life at least twice in this damn battle alone." He looked at the mound of fresh dirt outlining the final resting place of Corporal William Rinaldi. Tim felt the lift of an encouraging calm coming from deep within his soul. "Jimmy, at least Billy is at peace and with family.

Heaven knows most of our troops are buried where they fall, and then only if it's convenient."

Tim placed his hand on James's shoulder. He felt his friend's deep anguish. "Why don't we talk about Billy for a while? Maybe it'll help." Tim beckoned his friend to sit on a nearby boulder.

"It's so damn impersonal putting him in the ground like this, Tim, with no one but us to say a few words over him. He was such a good kid. Hell, we knew this could happen to any one of us. I just didn't believe it ever would." James fought back tears.

"One thing's for certain—nothing about this war is predictable." Tim fidgeted with his hands, looking for the right thing to say. "Look at us, for instance. We each have brothers fighting with the Feds. My brother Bobby is God knows where, along with your brother Luke, most likely with guns aimed at some Rebel right this minute. I hope, deep in my heart, that they're both OK and, well … if something happens to them that they'll be properly buried, like Billy, here."

"I don't know, Tim. Somehow sitting on this peaceful knoll, overlooking the ruins of our hometown, I can't help thinking that making peace seems so right, so important. I know it's a pipe dream, but it'd sure be nice to see an end to this war, and the sooner the better."

"Can't disagree with that, James. And don't you know, it sure has been one miserable year. Look at all the graves in this cemetery; all of 'em standing here like sentinels of death. Yeah, each stone marker represents a human life and a personal history. And each one is nicely tucked away, orderly and silent, lost forever to the avalanche of time. It makes me wonder what life really is about. We live, we die, and somewhere in between those realities, we survive. Life is difficult enough, and then you throw a damn war into the maze."

Tim gazed intently at the view of the once scenic and now charred city below him, now blotted with war's wreckage. "You know, Jimmy boy," he said, using his friend's childhood nickname, "this place and that city have a lot of meaning for us. I look at Utica and wonder if it deserves this fate."

"Tim, I love Utica as much as anyone, but let's be honest; this city has been doomed for years. According to Grandpa Rock, its decay started in the late 1950s. We just put it out of its misery with this battle. Maybe, by some freaking God-sent miracle, it'll come back like the legendary phoenix. Look, Tim!" James's excitement at seeing a landmark startled his friend. "The Gold Dome Bank still stands!" James cheerfully pointed his finger several blocks beyond, toward Genesee Street. The sun gleamed majestically off the bank's undamaged golden roof.

"You're right; I can see it still standing proudly. That bank has served the city of Utica for over three centuries. I wonder if my tiny little bank account is still open."

"Good luck there, buddy. The bank's dependable, but you won't see your money as long as this war keeps all the banks closed." James laughed, feeling relief for the first time in days. Suddenly he stopped; guilt overcame him as he looked upon Billy's grave.

Tim, sensing the abrupt change in James, spoke. "A lot of our boys died retaking this place; far too many." Tim looked painfully at the mound of fresh dirt covering his friend. "Utica will survive. It always does. Heck, maybe when the war's over, it'll get a rebirth, perhaps even return to the glory of its heyday." He brushed a fly away from his face.

"You're right, Tim. Time will surely tell. Most of our friends and relatives left Utica for greener pastures years ago. Thankfully, Dad chose to stay. He loves the history of this place and especially his job at Utica College. But all his well-meaning instruction only helped to encourage ambitious students to seek a better life elsewhere."

"I can sure picture Rock standing here, saying, 'Gaze upon this valley boys.'" Tim smiled as he continued his pantomime. "'Isn't it beautiful? Over there, you can see the foothills of the Adirondack Mountains and behind us the beginning of the Catskills. Look how the Mohawk River winds, the same path it has for centuries, majestically through the city. From this hill, it looks like a perfect picture postcard.'"

"Yeah, right on, Tim! I can almost hear him, too." James became animated, enjoying the moment, seeing the beauty of the day for the first time. "You know, this cemetery's a nice place to spend eternity. It's been here for almost two centuries. Almost all my immediate family rests here, going back over 120 years." The Rinaldi plot was surrounded by magnificent ceremonial stones that stood prominent in the shadows of several towering blue spruce trees.

James tried valiantly to fight back tears. In a strained voice in between fighting sobs he whispered painfully, "Mom, I should've been here for you. I'm so sorry." He looked into Tim's eyes, seeing tears flowing, as his friend put his arm around his shoulder.

James paused and then said, "Yeah, Tim, here lies a long procession of my people, right up to these two fresh graves. It's sad there are only two wooden planks to mark their final resting places. Someday I'll get stone markers."

"Don't worry, Jimmy. If you can't and I survive, I'll be sure to do it for you."

"Thanks, Tim. You're a real friend."

"Hell, I know that. You're welcome."

"When Mom died a month ago, it hurt badly that I couldn't come. It still hurts." James looked at the fresh dirt still outlining his mother's grave. James walked carefully around each grave. Kneeling, he smoothed the disturbed earth.

"Jimmy, the freaking city was occupied by Feds. You can't keep blaming yourself."

"Grandpa did say it was sudden and merciful. Mom was a wonderful lady." James sighed, wiping away a tear. "Poor Dad, he must be taking it hard; first Mom, and soon he'll hear about Billy. I wonder where Grandpa Rock is." James's mind rambled, scattershot, as the stressful fatigue of battle, tempered with constant death, melted his usual solid resolve.

"My guess is he's safe somewhere in hiding. Heck, no one around knows these parts better than Rock. With all the hiking he does and his survival experience in the Vietnam War, he's OK. You can bet on it!"

"Thanks, Tim," James gently touched his friend's shoulder. "You know, when I was a kid, I'd come up here a lot. I always felt close to these souls, most of whom I've never known. I'd plant flowers, visit Grandma Rose's grave, and sometimes I'd talk to her. It would somehow solve what was troubling me. This place has always been my sanctuary. I suppose it still is.

"At least for now this hill remains distant from the war. The last time I was here was about a year and a half ago. I came with Grandpa Rock. It was in the fall. The leaves were almost gone. We came for the comfort of the visit and to just talk. Rock somehow knew I was troubled. He has a way about him that sees through things. He always talked to me like an equal, even when I was a kid. I wish I could talk to him now. Talking to him was always an event for me. Remember the last thing Rock said to us before we joined the volunteers?"

"Yep, I'd sure agree. The old Green Beret turned grocer never missed an opportunity to get across his point, especially when flavoring it with his special Rinaldi School of Reasoning routine. Yeah, Jimmy, I remember like it was yesterday. He said something like this." Tim mimicked Rock's stern voice and began to talk with his hands, a familiar trait to James. " 'Until our country gets back to the basic principles upon which it was founded, we'll never have peace. You boys do the best you can to bring that about. Go with God and my prayers, and damn it, be careful. I love you all. Jimmy, Billy, and even you, too, Tim. Remember that your brothers are out there somewhere on the other side. Try to avoid them if you can. The thought of my grandsons and their best friends warring on each other hurts like hell.' "

"Good imitation, Tim. Rock sure is everyone's grandpa, and he loves it. Remember him and Dad going on about what led up to war? Rock, ever the amateur historian, to Dad's dismay, held his own and was seldom swayed. You know, Rock was a major influence on Dad's decision to become a Doctor of History. When they got together to discuss events and how history was repeating itself, it sure led to some serious conversation. Rock always held his ground with Dad."

"Sure, Jimmy, I recall. Wasn't it about two years ago? We were sitting in your kitchen listening to them go on and on. I think it was the first time that I really understood what this mess was about."

"I remember that day. You're right. Wasn't it about this time of year? Grandpa had been talking about growing up in the '40s, harping about high prices and reminiscing about penny candy and nickel sodas."

"Yeah, Jimmy, it was the time he said he was born in 1941 and his only memory of World War II was the sadness it brought to his mother when she thought of her brother, killed in France, and how they never found his body."

"What I recall most is when he mentioned he lived on Webster Avenue across the street from the old cemetery and how he often watched the returning caskets of soldiers killed in the war being buried. Remember, Tim? He said he'd asked his ma why the soldier was blowing a horn and others were shooting guns over the grave. He said Great Grandma told them they were sad for the poor soldier who had died during the war and that the government was giving him the respect he deserved because his earthly home was here in Utica. And most important, she had said, it wasn't right for him to be buried so far away on foreign soil and that it was good the government brought the soldier home for the comfort of his family." He hesitated, taking a deep breath. "I remember going out of my way to drive to that cemetery on Memorial Day to look at Old Glory and think on the day's real meaning."

"Rock always said there were too many flags on too many graves on Memorial Day. He'd recall with pride how people remembered and cared with big parades to honor the fallen, followed by family picnics. I remember he stressed how all the stores were closed in respect, not the way it was when we were teenagers. He was saddened at how it was slowly being lost, this respectful memory for those patriots who gave their all, so we could be free."

"Yeah, he often said that the real cost of freedom lies under those flags." Tim noted a quiet smile forming upon James's face.

"Tim, chatting about Grandpa makes me think of when he reminisced about how good it was for men to fight for their country for a just cause. He once explained to me what had happened as he saw it and lived it. His war wasn't the same as the war his father had served in. Great Grandpa served with the 36th Division in Italy in World War II. Rock was wondering that day about how good it must have been for his dad's generation to have the United States unified as one nation, fighting for the freedom of the world—something tangible. Rock's bitter about his war in Vietnam. He'd say he made it through one year of hell, only to return to an ungrateful nation whose only concern was for its own comfort. And worse, no one seemed to give a damn for soldiers who were dying in the jungles." James stood, dusting the dirt from his knees, pensive.

"Then he'd go on and say," James now imitated his grandfather, "'We fought the Communists for freedom as much as in any other war, but we were spit upon when we returned. No one gave us a parade to welcome us home.' That was about all we ever heard about 'Nam. Rock never elaborated. Now we've seen a giant piece of his hell first hand and know what he must have felt."

The past year for James was full of vivid and horrible memories, most of which he wanted to forget. He gazed at the graves of what was now two of those memories and gulped a sob aside.

Tim stood, dusting his tattered uniform, stretching to remove the kinks from his body. "Do you think we need to be getting back?" Tim's eyes were alert to movement in the valley. "I can see a lot of activity below."

"Tim, you go ahead. I'd like to take some time to be alone with my feelings. The lieutenant gave us the day, so I plan to take him up on it."

"OK with me, Jimmy boy. I'll walk and leave the truck for you so you won't be AWOL. There's only four hours left to our leave."

"No, thanks for thinking of me, though. I want to walk. It's only three miles; nothing compared to what we're used to. Thanks for coming; I couldn't have done this without you." James firmly grasped Tim's hand.

"Given the opportunity, I wouldn't be anywhere else. Watch your backside, Jimmy—there's still Fed stragglers about that would like nothing more than to put a Rebel sergeant's stripes on their gun notch."

James watched Tim leave. A sudden faraway feeling engulfed him. *Damn, I need to think and make sense of all of this chaos. This past year has been one continuous blur, filled with hit-and-run guerilla fighting. The Feds made our lives miserable with their damn laser-guided aircraft—at least this kind of warfare made most of the special weaponry useless.*

Shouting to no one but the unfeeling dead, James let out a mournful howl, "Leave me be, you damn war. Please, Lord ... let me return to what once was." He fell to his knees—stillness absorbing the frightening quiet, pondering his helpless state.

The howl helped ease his pain. Letting out his anger always helped. From his vantage point, James could see for miles across the Valley of the Mohawk. He saw harried movement about two miles away through his field glasses. James's unit—Company C, 7th Regiment, 4th Brigade, 121st Division of the First Corps of New York Freedom Fighters—was somewhere down there. *I guess we'll move out soon*, he thought.

The 121st Division continued to grow in talent, from hard-knocks experience, desertions from the Federals, and from citizens who saw it as a chance to get back at the roving bands of marauders. Organization, which they had only managed to achieve lately, was the only way to ensure success and survival. James recalled how disorganized the movement had been when it started twelve months earlier. They were lucky then. The Feds did not take advantage of the Rebel incompetence. They had their own problems, created by their poor management and the cruelty of President Collins's policies. The Rebels learned quickly that freedom and independence were expensive and that experience and unity were the only way to keep from losing.

James, a true student of military history, thought the Rebel strategy was brilliant in its simplicity. The Northern Rebel units were fighting ever northward to merge with similar units from other sectors and eventually amass a great army from the north that would meet up with the Texans and their southern allies. Strong military leadership was now the norm, as the Rebel Army matured from its rabble beginnings to its present formidable force. Each success gave momentum to their great offensive. Defensive and guerilla warfare would remain part of the overall strategy, as would hundreds of minor skirmishes, but Rebel leadership understood that hit-and-run was no longer the best way to bring the conflict to a quick conclusion. The country, and especially the Rebel movement, couldn't afford a long struggle.

Presently, 50,000 Rebel troops were in the valley awaiting orders. James felt certain his unit would move out. He hoped silently that it would stay for a little longer in Utica. He was ready for a little less combat.

It was good to be alone. It hurt too much to reflect, but James couldn't stop the flood of thoughts. Another brother, Luke, whom he loved and missed, was somewhere in the Fed Army. He looked at the wooden grave marker, and tears flowed. Not all the death he had witnessed had hardened him enough to accept the death of a brother. He said one last prayer for Billy. He continued to blame himself.

If only I had been with Billy instead of flushing out that other building. Billy was always so brave and reckless, ready to take action before anyone else realized its necessity, and it cost him his life. It was so much like him to act the hero and to die a hero. But unless we prevail, his gallant acts die with him. As Dad said, "The winners usually write the history."

James remembered his brother's last deed. Billy had single-handedly carried two wounded comrades, struck down by machine gun fire, while under heavy fire from that same gun. Having brought the wounded soldiers to safety, he then crawled back and took out the gun with grenades, only to be killed by an unseen sniper hidden in a home they thought was cleared. If James survived this war, and if the Rebel cause prevailed, the world would know about his brother's last heroic deed; perhaps it might get Billy a posthumous medal. *But a medal will never bring him back.*

This might be a grand history lesson in some future classroom. James could almost hear his father's lecture, or even his own—the thought of teaching appealed to him as well. He cleared his throat and began speaking aloud as if in rehearsal.

"Dad would most likely say something about the commitment and pride of the Texans and how it helped unify the Rebel movement. Most likely, he'd reach back into Texas history to the mindset of the early Texans, and he'd tell about their original war for independence from the Mexicans, and the Alamo and the sacrifice it stood for. Then he would talk about the Civil War and how it influenced the South for over 150 years."

James had heard that the Texans chose to wear tan and green dress, avoiding the camouflage dress of the last century. They even had a new flag. It was a lone star to the right, with the American flag's fifty stars and thirteen stripes in the left-hand portion. It reminded the world that they weren't fighting to change the country, but to get it back.

James continued quoting his dad's imagined lecture out loud, clearly picturing his father addressing his class. " 'The Texas Lone Star always represented independence, states' rights, and some ideals that were sadly forgotten. That's why our late flag had fifty stars, to represent the union of single states, but Texas was the only state to emphasize its independence within the union. The ideals that this war was about included honor, integrity, loyalty, fidelity, justice, and love of a nation indivisible and under God. A new United States where one could choose to not worship any God if they so desired, for this new nation continued to separate church and state. But it would not forget God, either, by restricting the rights of citizens to worship and speak freely about religion and God, as some suggested we should do in the recent past.'"

James's mind continued to play out his father's lecture, knowing now that if he lived, it would also be his. College had been cut short by the war. He vowed then and there to return, at least for his master's degree, if he made it through. He mused. *The Texans were the rallying point for the rebellion. There was neither North nor South like the previous Civil War; there would be no definitive dividing points. Almost all the states were involved after one year's combat. This Federal government had no catchy rallying point as emotional as slavery. There was equal representation of all minorities on both sides. Since the North had won the Civil War, it had written the country's history, so states' rights, a primary and very real issue for the South, was buried in the sands of time—until now.*

James thought deeply on this and mulled over in his mind what he had been telling potential recruits to give them reason to take up arms, especially when confronted with the rebellion's historical similarity to the Civil War. He had told them it was more like revisiting the Revolutionary War for Independence. But many recruits knew little of that or any war, since educational institutions in the United States had de-emphasized the teaching of the nation's history. Programs focused more on social issues and student self-esteem. When James's father gave his dosage of realistic, down-to-earth, unflavored, and not politically correct American history, he was often criticized.

With the April sun to warm him, James continued his ideal lecture. "This war was a fight about many things: unfair taxation, too much government, career politicians, a faltering immigration policy, and numerous issues beyond the scope of imagination. The Federal government did not have the slavery issue to dissuade any civilized nation that might want to recognize the Rebels. So now every state had a North, a South, an East, and a West. Every state's population was hopelessly split on all the issues.

"When the draft was reenacted, most went unwillingly. There were riots, similar to and as deadly as those seen in the racial riots of the last century. This resulted in the perceived need to impose a strong military presence in every major city, spreading thin an extravagant military and infuriating the populace. The military now was needed to defend against problems within, though its primary responsibility was to defend us from problems outside our borders. The military strategy to use technology and a much smaller army to fight outside enemies enabled the Rebels to get a real foothold after a desperate year of hit-and-run battles.

"President Rex Collins said he would never give in to Rebel demands. Collins, a corrupt, self-centered man, had fought his way to the top, often climbing remorselessly over the bodies of those who once helped him. He was a man of low scruples who would do anything, including desecration of the Constitution, to get his way. He was the consummate politician gone wrong. The irony of the conflict was that Collins's younger sister Barbara, lovingly known as Babs to the Rebels, was elected the President of the Texas Republic by an overwhelming margin.

"It's a long story, that of the Collins family. The Collins's saga goes back almost two centuries, with each Collins child probably taught the value of a vote before he learned to crawl." James chuckled, pleased with his ironic twist of words.

He became momentarily stymied as he wondered how his father would cover Collins's corrupt administration. Dismissing the thought, he continued, "Collins had declared a constitutional crisis before the actual outbreak of civil war, to avoid a national election and certain defeat for his party. The required end of his eight-year term in office, only two months off, was delayed until the crisis was ended."

James thought, *Dad would probably say Collins, a byproduct of his time, lived for political payoff and corruption. He clawed his way to the top with greed and lobbyism, using the broken political system to his advantage and to the dismay of his adversaries.*

"Collins was the consummate, over-confident politician. He was aided by mistrust and encouraged by personal gain, slashing an immoral path to the top. As a young state senator in Texas, he learned the art of politics as he slowly and patiently carved his empire. His five terms as a

U.S. congressman furthered his ability to stealthily acquire power and fool his constituents, who thought him a god.

"His rise to the presidency gave immediate cause for concern about lost constitutional rights. The long-standing War on Terrorism had eroded many of these privileges as time, fear, and necessity allowed the government to make changes relatively unopposed by the people.

"Collins's uncanny ability to maintain a united front slowly degenerated as definitive points of disagreement became apparent." Ironically, until just a few days previously, the western states had not been involved beyond sending recruits to both sides: those drafted by the Feds, and those who volunteered to the Rebel cause.

James continued his father's lecture after he caught up with his thoughts. "What initially was a giant nationwide riot turned into the third revolution and a fight for independence. What Collins and his cronies could not grasp was that the United States could never return again to what it once was without a fight. There was just too much hate, hurt, and damage done to overcome and forgive the abuse of his tenure and the moral decay of his predecessors.

"In contrast, his sister, the Texas governor when the war started, had somehow been conceived with values from a tribe that appeared to have none. This won her the respect of the Texans, and more so, of the fighting force. She unfailingly did what was morally right in the eyes of her people. She was not only considered a leader but also a grandmotherly figure. She acted with fixation and purpose to be part of the reconstruction of a nation founded on the principles of the original Founding Fathers." James realized now that he was unable to continue with the lecture, since the outcome remained an unknown.

He took a deep breath. He had pondered too long. He looked at the pale blue sky as it filtered through the clouds racing above him and became aware that he had better be getting back. Sunshine was sometimes a rarity in upstate New York, and James had enjoyed basking in its warmth. He gathered his backpack, canteen, and rifle and took one last mournful glance at the graves of his family, unsure if he'd ever return. Recharged, he calmly walked down Oneida Street toward his encampment in old Proctor Park.

x x x x x

Walking east past his girl's home below on St. Agnes Avenue, he was swamped with fond memories of Jenny. Where was she now? He sure missed her. The last time they talked was over nine months ago. He reveled in blissful contemplation of her beautiful blue eyes, windows to her loving, angelic nature. He felt a sudden emptiness and a need for the comfort and warmth of her company.

He turned, walked north on St. Jane Avenue, and was passing his home when a sudden movement in the bushes in front of an abandoned house awakened him from his daydreaming. James instinctively opened the safety on his M-16 and warily scanned the bushes, shouting in an agitated voice, "Come out, you bastard, or I'll shoot to kill!" He triggered a warning shot into the air as he dived for the ground behind the safety of a huge maple tree.

"Don't shoot, don't shoot!" a feeble voice cried out, as a tattered, bleeding enemy soldier crawled from behind the slight refuge of the lilac bushes standing in front of James's home.

James approached with the wary cunning of a veteran, his M-16 never leaving his target less than twenty feet away. The enemy soldier appeared to be unarmed. Caution was wise in any case. Nothing was ever as it seemed in combat.

"Lay flat and still. Surrender now or you're a dead man."

"I surrender, man. Please, help, I'm begging you. I'm hurt bad."

James approached, looking for anything that would necessitate killing this man, hoping not to find anything. The empathy James had for anything weak or injured, whether man or beast, caused him to slip back to an earlier time before he had been forced to kill on sight. All of a sudden, caring felt right to James.

"What's your name and rank, soldier?"

"Corporal Washington, 2nd Regiment of the 20th Mountain Division, U.S. Army, Sergeant."

"Where are you hit?" James asked, while he rummaged in his backpack for his first aid kit. Taking off his helmet, he brushed back jet-black hair from his eyes as he surveyed the wounded man.

"My leg and my arm both hurt like fire."

"Do you think you can walk?" The last thing James wanted to do was carry this big hulking Federal soldier, who probably weighed at least 200 pounds, to the nearest aid station about a mile or more distant. James assessed the situation to surmise if his solid, almost six-foot frame could carry the man.

"Sorry, Reb, I can't go another step. I think I've bled too much and have no energy left, 'cept to talk," he stammered.

"Well, Washington, if you promise to behave, I'll do what I can for you, though it would be easier to just shoot you. But I won't as long as you cooperate. Lie still while I bind your wounds with what supplies I have." James used his last dose of morphine and bound Washington's wounds after he washed them as best he could with water from his canteen. He looked directly into the big, friendly eyes of his prisoner. He was no doubt a good man caught up in the same confusing mess of war.

Still wary, he slung his rifle over his shoulder to his front for protection from the wounded soldier and then lifted the semi-conscious enemy to his shoulders, balancing his weight. He started the long trek to his base, hoping to see friendly forces early so he could release his charge. James's strong, young back tired as he took each difficult and deliberate step.

"Hey, Reb, why are you doing this? I'd a probably kept going if I'd been you."

Struggling but not about to give up, James answered. "From what you just said, you'd never be me, so shut up, you heavy SOB. You can thank my mom for this act of kindness. She taught me to care for my fellow man, no matter what the circumstance."

"Well, when you see your mom, you can thank her for me, Sarge."

"Corporal, you need to shut up and rest as best you can. You're not out of the woods yet. You've lost a lot of blood."

"Who do I owe my thanks to, Sarge? It's nice to know that there's still some kindness left in this crazy world."

"Just call me James, and you're welcome. Where are you from? Your accent sounds like you are from nearby."

"Caught me, Sarge. I hail from Albany, was drafted ..." Washington paused, his voice showing painful fatigue. "... about two years ago, and wish I was back playing college ball again and not playing war. I was once a first baseman for RPI."

"Well, ballplayer, I was at Syracuse. And I recall we whipped you boys good quite a few times." James's reflections raced back to college, a simpler time, now so far away.

"Sarge, you can kiss my sweet black ass, but I don't recall your Orangemen ever beating my team."

"Soldier, you rest and we'll talk later." The statement was unnecessary. Washington had passed out; his weight seemed heavier on James's shoulder.

This damn war, James thought, as he slowly trudged back to his battle-scarred company. To his chagrin, the aid station had been moved. Once he found its new location, he turned his captive over to a nearby field hospital's MP. Weary, he walked to his bivouac. The 121st Division's insignia, a blazing orange cross in a field of white, flew defiantly on its standard. A similar patch adorned his uniform's left shoulder. The prominent orange cross had seen its share of war in other times, long ago.

James's sad thoughts formed a broken wall around his fractured world. *How quickly death arrives, especially when you least expect its sting.* He wondered in his silent grief, *Did Billy know he was going to die? Does anyone?*

Yeah, life still has value even in this wilderness of death, in my beautiful Valley of the Mohawk. He took one last look at the hills to his north and saw a lone hawk soaring with the updraft, free from the carnage below.

Jim Damiano

Once it was written, beneath the sky,
Life seems its best in days gone by,
Now time in the land of our birth,
Seems gone forever from the earth,
Thrown to the uncaring winds of war.
— Jim Damiano

CHAPTER THREE

May 19, 2020—Prosper, Republic of Texas

The city was deathly quiet this hazy morning. A hush surrounded it like a warm blanket covering a newborn baby. Most of its citizens, at least those brave enough to live this far north, were sleeping. Northern Texas, a battlefield for the past year, and in particular the city of Prosper, wore their scars of war with pride. Recent freedom from the Federal Army's repulsive occupation, along with vivid memories of the ravages it engaged, incited even the average law-abiding citizen to hatred surpassing imagination. War's aftermath filled the air while fear of another Federal invasion fostered a real need for constant alert. Poorly armed local militia, made up mostly of older men and boys, protected the city. The badly bruised Texas National Army and its many militia units were on the offensive only a few miles north, leaving the city vulnerable to any intensive action from a determined enemy. Luckily for Prosper, the enemy was retreating, a victim of Texan wrath and its own miscalculations.

After a bloody major engagement near the Texas/Oklahoma border, the Rebel line was a few miles north of the Red River. War's chaos briefly abated while both sides regrouped.

Justin had been ordered to Austin to meet with Central Command. He took his brother Taylor as his newly appointed adjutant. It was an opportunity to take advantage of Taylor's organizational skills, and more important, to spend some valuable time together. General

Sinsome personally chose Justin to represent the 36th Division at the strategy session. His confidence in his young protégé to represent the 36th Division's severe needs was warranted. The dispatches Justin carried from command bore evidence of this, though Justin was not privy to their contents.

Justin had been surprised by his promotion. In addition to receiving a Silver Star for bravery for his action near Denison, he was promoted to brigadier general and given command of the 36th Division's 1st Ranger Brigade. War's high-speed pace had overtaken Justin's restless expectations.

"Justin, what the devil's on your mind? You haven't said a darn thing for almost an hour," Taylor said as he turned to look at his brother, momentarily taking his eyes off the road.

"Sorry, Tay, I'm just thinking about Austin. Everything's moving too fast. How in the hell did I get this additional responsibility? God knows I didn't look for nor want it. And to be honest, it scares the crap out of me. Hey," Justin shouted, "watch out for that hole in the road!" Taylor swerved to miss the giant pothole, another souvenir of war.

The near miss didn't deter Taylor, "As I see it, brother, command somehow thinks you're the best man for the job, or in my humble opinion, one of only a few in our ranks who can best serve the needs of the brigade. You know I'm always breaking your chops, but hear me, General; they picked you because you know how to lead. Men respect and follow you. It's an important ingredient for a commander, Sir. And Justin, I say 'General' out of respect. I'm damn proud of you."

"Taylor, I know where you're coming from, and I appreciate it," Justin replied, hands clasped tightly, his manner tense. "Unfortunately, a lot of those poor souls who trusted me are dead. I don't know if I can keep sending so many to their deaths. It's so goddamned hard to sleep anymore. Worse yet, I sometimes think our army must be freaking desperate to appoint the likes of me to be a damn general."

"As I see it, you have no choice. To be honest, Justy old boy, you care. That's why more Rangers live than die under your command, even when the odds are stacked against them. I see that as real important.

Regardless of the army's plight, you, my brother, are stuck with that general's star."

Taylor checked the gas gauge. It was low but that didn't seem to faze him. "Damn, we've always been outnumbered, and we have always survived. Maybe it's the mystique of our old division's history or just plain luck. Nevertheless, a lot of it is your superior leadership that's got you this far. So why don't you just go with the moment and let it be."

"Yeah Tay, thanks again for the encouraging words. This brass star seems a bit heavy right at the moment, and I'm not sure it fits."

"You're welcome, you big pain-in-the-ass, General, Sir." Taylor winked and continued. "Do you think we'll be sent back to the Mexican Border after we return to HQ? From what we heard back in Austin, it appears that the marauders and the Mexicans have breached the border and things are gettin' hot again. If rumors are true that the Mexican Nationals have joined the Feds, well … shit is sure to hit the fan. And the Ranger division will be needed to clean it up once again."

Justin looked at his often goofy but more perceptive brother, wishing he could be as calculating and deliberate.

Taylor absorbs anything he studies, whatever the subject, and he's a good man to have on my team and will make a good adjutant. There is no way he'll stay a lieutenant.

"Justin, are you still daydreaming?"

"Sorry, I was off in another world. I heard you," he lied. I was wondering what my new command is up to. If I had a say in this, we'd be sent to the border due to our previous experience down there. They could fill the gap left by our brigade with Oklahoma volunteers or Texas militia units."

Taylor took his eye off the road again. "By last count, our division is 20,000 strong. If we're sent to the border, I really hope they find a way to get us more help. If the Mexicans try something big, our division may not be able to handle it. It won't be like before, a few banditos here and there. Heck, we never faced a large concentration or an organized invasion."

Justin's once happy-go-lucky spirit returned momentarily as he chuckled, poking his brother's arm. Then his solemn side returned quickly. "Taylor, we're Rangers, and like the Rangers in the past, our

20,000 should be equal to any 100,000 Mexicans. If there's one thing we have, it is *esprit de corps*."

Then Taylor laughed openly at his brother's bravado. "Well, General, Sir," he said sarcastically, "at least I don't have to supply my own horse, gun, knife, bullets, and food like our predecessors did." Feeling contrite, Taylor added, 'Sorry, Bro, I couldn't help myself."

"Yeah, well, most of the time we don't, and we do know how to ride horses, too," Justin shot back. "My backside, though, would prefer the comfort of a Humvee." Justin thought briefly of happier times when he, Taylor, and their younger sister, Becky, rode horses on their grandfather's ranch near Sherman, Texas.

"Don't you think this here Ranger badge we wear on our lapel must have secret powers, or at least it gives anyone who wears it the need to live up to its stellar reputation?" Taylor fidgeted with his shirt, pointing to his badge as if for the first time.

"You know, when we did border patrol last summer, I couldn't wait to be moved to the front. I thought it might be less demanding. Boy, oh boy, was I wrong. Nine months of non-stop fightin' can get pretty ugly."

"Oh, I suppose you're referring to those nostalgic days on end with no rest, crossing the border to go after anyone daring to do anything nasty, as being easy days of song and joy." Taylor's sarcasm made Justin smile.

"I agree, Taylor. Mostly, though, I remember those damn Mexican marauders gave us no mercy. We'd track down the sons-of-bitches and likewise give them no quarter, just like Rangers of old. When we received orders to assassinate any marauder caught, it bothered me at first; then the atrocities worsened, and it became easy to act as judge and jury. I've seen more than enough of the raiders' dirty work. Killing them wasn't punishment enough." He snickered, "However, we Texans are still civilized to a point."

The lines on Justin's face reflected the many horrors and gruesome deaths his young eyes had seen. He had ordered troops under his command, as often as necessary, to kill their adversaries without mercy. Near the Texas border he had slain many thought to be the enemy, but one never really knew if they were enemies or just unlucky souls. Experience had often proved that it was too costly to take a chance to find out.

The rules they followed were simple: If you entered Texas and a Ranger caught you or found you in his sights, and you weren't wearing a Ranger uniform or carried evidence you had a right to be in Texas, you were shot dead. It was that cut and dried. Renegades seemed to be everywhere, on or near the border, filtering slowly northward. The Texans' unforgiving, almost Biblical, method of justice sent a clear signal, and eventually the problem dwindled as the craven bastards took to easier prey, going elsewhere.

The desperate few who dared to challenge the Rangers learned quickly the full wrath of their vengeance. Skeletons dotted the rough landscape, adding to the eternal Texas dust. The Rangers' efficient annihilation of their enemies often caused Justin's conscience pangs of guilt. *I feel like a butcher, not the civilized Christian boy left behind somewhere in Prosper.* This thought hit him with a sudden shock as the brothers' Humvee passed their family church. Justin exclaimed, "There it stands, glorious in the aftermath of battle, a celestial sign, representing peace on earth ... or, at least, it once did."

"Justin, we have two days at home. Do you suppose we can try to forget the war for a few minutes?"

"Seems like a plan to me, Tay, but damn it, if we run into anything resembling military, try to remember that I'm your general and forget the personal stuff for once."

"Spoil sport." Taylor feigned hurt. "OK, you got it, General. Hey, here's Main Street. Let's see if there's anything left to our house. Maybe we can get a bath and even locate Becky's whereabouts."

"No, Becky's somewhere with her hospital unit, probably close to the front. But I agree it'd be good to see Sis."

They passed the old post office, now converted to the command post for local militia. "Will we need to report our presence to the local militia commander?" Taylor asked.

"Probably be nice to, out of courtesy, I suppose. Let's do it after we see if there's anything left of our home."

Prosper, like so many cities surrounding Dallas, had been part of the boom of the past several decades, growing to a city of more than

50,000. They drove slowly through the empty streets. The city's quiet gave off an eerie feeling.

"It seems more like a disaster area than the home we left a year ago." Justin said.

Taylor drove the Humvee slowly to the front of their home on Fifth Street. The roar of the vehicle's ancient engine competed with their voices.

"I doubt this junker will last until Oklahoma, Justin, ah, I mean General. Think you can pull your rank to improve our ride?"

"Look, Lieutenant Smart-Ass, we'll see if the locals can repair it. Otherwise, we'll need to commandeer another. We're about out of diesel anyway; and I know the spare cans are empty."

"Yeah," Taylor quipped, "and once we turn over these dispatches to Regular Army in Celina, we can come back to Prosper and get some R&R and maybe rustle up a long shower or perhaps even two."

Taylor began scratching himself in such an exaggerated manner that Justin slapped his brother's hand to get him to stop, but Taylor kept scratching himself anyway.

Trying to ignore his own itch with difficulty, Justin continued. "Tay, at least Texas still has some oil. Maybe fuel won't be a problem." Taylor just snickered and playfully punched Justin's right arm.

From staff reports, Justin had garnered that oil supplies were all but gone. Every existing well was now pumping overtime. Fortunately, Texas still had an abundance of untapped oil. Its liquid gold hadn't been pumped much in past years because of the government's policy to purchase cheap oil from the Middle East and other oil-producing nations. Additionally, developing alternate fuels, which had never been a priority for the oil-drinking old United States, now served to aid its internal enemy. Both policies had become a blessing for the Rebel forces.

"Taylor, I hear currently Rebel strategy is to secure Oklahoma's oil. The threat is that Federals will blow the wells. They didn't in Texas, even when they had retreated, so maybe Oklahoma oil is safe. Truth is, the Feds need the oil as much or more than us. Destruction of the wells would serve to underline we're winning."

Taylor answered, "Me, I think it's the War on Terrorism and the weakened Federal Navy that has made every drop of oil precious. You know there's no problem-free oil source remaining for either side to replenish rapidly dwindling supplies."

"Kinda sucks, doesn't it?" Justin said.

The first thing the Northcutt brothers noticed in Prosper were the signs of the battle fought a few weeks earlier. The ravages didn't deter their excitement. It was still their home, though sometimes they had to use imagination, for where homes once stood prominent, only rubble remained.

As they left for their brief run to Celina they drove past their old high school, damaged but still standing. The football and baseball fields held many fond memories. Taylor slowed the Humvee to a crawl, looking wistfully at the high school he had attended before beginning at the University of Texas. He had left his college studies a year ago to join Justin in the 36th. He missed college life, its books and learning, and he especially missed the social scene.

"Justin, there were sure some good times here; it seems so long ago. I can still see you scoring that last-minute touchdown in your senior year, beating the Celina Bobcats."

"Yeah, it sure brings back fond memories. I can recall you pitching a few great games for the school pride there as well, not to mention the baskets you made. And you sure enjoyed the soccer season, too. You loved to beat the hell out of Celina every chance you could."

"Justin, I think I miss girls the most; sports come in a long second place, though you're right on about Celina. If we beat Celina and then lost every other game, the season was always considered a success."

"You're right on, Tay. When we get back, let's come here and throw the old football for awhile."

"Sounds like a plan to me, General, Sir." Taylor made a mockery of a salute as he drove, his eyes off the road more than on.

"Well, Lieutenant, you meatball, just don't forget you're with a general when we get to Celina," Justin chuckled, as his brother edged into his comical routine. *I hope Taylor never changes.*

Celina, once a thriving community of about 70,000, was more heavily damaged than Prosper. Justin pushed aside thoughts of the furious battle as they drove through the old historical square to the local Regular Army command post. His regiment had suffered over 100 casualties here, including his best friend. He looked intently at his brother. "Lieutenant, let's get this over with so we can get on with our leave."

"Yes, Sir," Taylor barked out with a bit too much enthusiasm.

Justin scanned the square. Recalling more pleasant days, he wondered, *How many times have I ridden my pickup to this very spot to visit friends or just to walk around and pass time? Celina may have been a major rival, but they had had some pretty girls.*

"Time can sure change things."

"What did you say, General?" Taylor, so pleased with himself for remembering military protocol, almost missed Justin's answer.

"No, nothing, never mind, Lieutenant. I was just remembering." Justin wanted only to dispense with this duty to turn over the dispatches and return to Prosper to learn whatever they could about their family.

"These damn dispatches," Justin muttered. "Why the heck did I volunteer to drop them off? They could have just as easily been carried by someone else."

Taylor turned to look at Justin. "Yeah, I wondered why. Your reason, I recall, was we were passing this way, so why waste a messenger."

"Taylor, kick me the next time I get a silly notion. This one is costing us some R&R."

"You got it, General. But will I be court-martialed if someone sees me?"

When the Northcutt brothers pulled up in front of the command post in the old Humvee, two sentries immediately approached with guns at the ready. "What's your business, Sir?" the tall one asked. His eye caught the new shiny star on Justin's shoulder.

"Private, we have business with command at your brigade HQ. Set up a guard for this vehicle, and make sure it's here when we return," Taylor said with authority.

Taylor was more than aware that vehicles were scarce and open prey for anyone willing to steal them. He had been known to commandeer a vehicle now and then, if necessary, for his brother. The private noted the

Ranger insignia and quickly decided to do as commanded. He did not want to get on their bad side. They were, after all, the shock troops of the army and known for their disregard of other units of lesser valor. He would guard the vehicle.

The brothers ambled with an air of confidence and a well-earned arrogance up the steps of the old city hall, now serving as military command of the 4th Brigade of the 2nd Division of the Army of Texas.

When they passed through the door, two sentries sharply saluted. A young lieutenant, who looked vaguely familiar to Taylor, sat behind the counter while a weathered sergeant manned his post, sitting at the well-worn counter's edge.

Sergeant Rodgers, old Regular U.S. Army, snappily saluted the unknown officers—it appeared almost with an air of contempt. It immediately roused Taylor's inner anger and the raging temper he rarely showed, unless provoked.

"Yes, Sirs, what can I do for you? I'm busy, so let it out."

Taylor, the recently confirmed professional adjutant, snapped back with argumentative insistence. His return contained the roar of a young lion, edged with lieutenant's bars to back his brag. "Sergeant, Lieutenant Taylor Northcutt, with orders for the commanding officer of this post. I suggest that you comply with haste or I shall forget that we're on the same side."

The sergeant noticed the safety was off on the young lieutenant's M-16 and that his finger was grasping the trigger. He also noted the fire in Taylor's eyes and realized he couldn't scare this young officer with his bullying. The Rebel Army had some loose discipline, but the Sergeant immediately figured correctly that this young officer would not take his shit.

Justin hid his true feelings, enjoying his brother's action. Though Taylor was far from Regular Army, he was not a man to fool with. Now a side of Taylor that he usually kept hidden—the one that was best to avoid—was on full display. Justin was relieved that Taylor spared him from losing his own monumental temper.

The lieutenant remained seated behind the counter saying nothing; his knowing smile said volumes. The lieutenant turned in his chair, starting to call into the office directly behind his desk; but without getting up, Sergeant Rodgers beat him to it. "Captain, there's two Ranger officers from the 36th with orders to see you, Sir." His words did not hide his contempt, and neither Northcutt missed his arrogance.

Captain Robert Long didn't need the announcement, since he couldn't help overhearing their exchange. The captain, angry, hesitated briefly before he answered. *If this upstart's general weren't with him, I'd have some fun disciplining that smart-mouthed, arrogant, Ranger hotshot.*

"Send them in, Sergeant."

Abruptly, Taylor responded, "Sergeant, don't bother to get up, we can find our way." The brothers entered the shabby office. Its unkempt décor raised Justin's ire. *Organization was one thing he respected. A war is no excuse for mass confusion.*

"Lieutenant Northcutt, 1st Brigade adjutant, 36th Division with dispatches needing delivery to northern front HQ's Command."

Long stood at attention. "General, Lieutenant," Long said as he looked into the eyes of each officer, "I'm Captain Long at your service. How am I expected to deliver this dispatch? We have no vehicles available."

Justin took this opportunity to assert his authority. Leaning forcefully over Long's desk, his enraged eyes met the startled captain's. "Captain, I suggest," he spoke with restrained emphasis, "you find a vehicle, even if you must build one. We've been on the road, without rest, for two days. I order you to find a way with extreme haste. Your obvious ability to make excuses rather than perform your duty is not acceptable or appreciated. Am I clear, Captain?" Justin was so close to the captain's face that spittle sprayed into his startled eyes.

"Sir, I'll see to it myself."

"Good, Captain. We'll just wait here in your office until you've made arrangements before we take our leave. And Captain, I have two days I intend to spend at my home in Prosper. I expect you'll move with haste, or I may be forced to invent a way to get your ass to the front and out of this luxury you call duty."

Justin had had about all he could take. He was tired, dirty, and needed rest. The captain's freshly cleaned uniform set off a side of him that he liked to avoid.

"General, Lieutenant, please be seated and make yourselves comfortable while I make the arrangements." Long left the office and talked to the quiet lieutenant they had seen earlier.

"Lieutenant Jackson. ..." The conversation faded to where the Northcutts could not hear it.

"Taylor, now I know why the lieutenant looks familiar. Isn't that the Jackson that Becky once dated in high school?"

"You know, I thought he looked familiar. The last I saw him was when Becky graduated two years ago," Taylor said. "He attended Prosper High. I recall he was a year ahead of her. I guess I couldn't place him with that ragged beard."

"Maybe Jackson will have an update on Becky or news about our family," Justin said.

"Justin, wasn't Jackson with the 36th, in the 4th Regiment?"

"I think you're right. Wonder why he's here?"

Before they could conjecture more about Jackson's circumstances, Long returned to his drab office. "General, I hope momentarily to see what options we have. I've sent my lieutenant to see what he can muster."

"Since we have a moment, Captain, why don't you fill us in on any recent news you have from the front. We've been out of touch for over forty-eight hours."

"General, you may not have heard that your division's major general was promoted just yesterday to command the Texas Army. You probably passed him on his way to Austin." Justin was not surprised at Raif Sinsome's promotion. In fact, he felt the Republic's Army would be in capable hands with him in charge.

"By any chance did you hear who now commands the 36th?"

"I heard it's Major General Phillips, Sir."

Justin smiled at the news. "He's a good man and a damn good leader. The 36th is well served with his promotion. General Raif Sinsome will make us proud, Captain. I'd guess your boys will have to continue rapidly moving your HQ to catch up with his front, once he gets moving."

"Well, Sir, it looks like he may have hit a few snags in Oklahoma. The Feds are dug in and will not give up the Okie oil without a hot contest. I also heard through the grapevine that some of our allied states are west of Oklahoma City waiting to join our main army once it breaks through from the south. It's rumored the Feds not only see the significance of defending the oil, but they're capitalizing on that terrorist bombing of so many years ago. It's become a rallying cry for the Feds, like we had anything to do with that misfit McVeigh," Long said and slammed his fist on his cluttered desk, causing some papers to fall to the floor.

"The quicker we take Oklahoma City the better. It's just a matter of time before forces from other freed states converge with us," Justin said.

Taylor sat listening to his superior officers, wishing to leave this place and go back to Prosper to start his leave.

"Supplies, that's the real problem we face," Justin spoke as if to no one. "If we do not get a constant flow established, we'll have to slow our drive or we'll be in trouble. The last time I talked with Raif, he touched on this problem."

"I agree, General. Living off the land can only go so far. It's one thing to ask Texans to give up what they have, when we're invaded. Texas' survival depended upon it for success. It's another when you ask a city or state we just conquered, in particular where allegiance may be questionable."

The conversation was interrupted by Lieutenant Jackson, who limped into the office and saluted. An ill-fitting artificial leg caused his hobble. "Captain, I have secured a vehicle and an escort, but Sir, I must advise the vehicle is not very acceptable."

"How's that, Lieutenant?" Long's voice did not hide his irritation.

"It's on its last leg, Sir. All serviceable vehicles have been taken by the main army for use at the front and for supplies. I doubt it'll make the fifty or more miles it must go to reach the front."

Justin interrupted. "Captain, take our Humvee; it's not much, but it got us here from Austin. All it needs is fuel. We'll take the old heap and return it in two days and take back the Humvee, which I fully expect to be returned."

Long forced a smile. "Thank you, General."

"All for the cause, Captain, all for the cause."

"General Northcutt, we got off on the wrong foot, Sir, and I would like to apologize."

"Apology accepted, but not necessary. We both started off on the wrong side."

"Would you gentlemen join me in a cup of coffee?"

"Thanks for the kind offer, Captain, but we must run. However, I would like a quick word with your Lieutenant Jackson. He's from our hometown—a friend of the family."

"Certainly, Sir, I'll call him. Use my office." Long motioned to the space and left.

Jackson reentered the office, wondering what was needed so soon. His hobble, due to the constant pain from chafing caused by movement on his new prosthesis, was even more pronounced. "Yes, General, may I be of service? The Captain advises you wish to speak with me."

"Yes, Jackson, that's correct. You can cut the formality for the moment, though. It's good to see you; it's been a long time. I'm sorry to see you've been injured."

"Thank you, Sir, I lost my leg to a mortar fragment about six months ago at the border near Del Rio. It could've been worse. I'm happy to be alive."

"I remember that skirmish. Our regiment was in Laredo at the time. I'm really sorry about the loss of your leg. ... How's your family?"

"They got out of Prosper just in time, but I haven't heard from them in months. I think they went to the Hill Country with several families. I believe your parents were in that caravan."

"Ed, do you know what happened to them?"

"Sorry, Justin, I don't. I only know Becky's serving with a forward field hospital. I think it might be the 77th, somewhere near the Oklahoma border. I hear things are quiet up there, at least for the moment. We haven't had an air attack in days. I guess the Feds are saving their fuel, just like us. We see an occasional helicopter gunship come in, but without support, they usually end up suicide missions. Our defenses are now well honed."

"Thanks, Ed. It was good seeing you. Take care."

"You too, Sir. Say hello to Becky when you see her. Now, please allow me to introduce you to your transportation."

Taylor and Justin followed Jackson to an old beat-up Jeep Cherokee that had seen better days. "Will this thing make it to Prosper?" Taylor asked.

"I hope so, but no guarantees," Jackson replied; his facial expression gave away his doubt.

Taylor sighed, "I never thought I'd miss that Humvee. May I suggest we get started, General? It may literally be a long push."

They puttered along on their return trip to Prosper, anxious to finally start their R&R; yet their conversation returned to the Celina headquarters. "Justin, did you notice that freaking sergeant I snapped at was also missing a leg?"

"Yeah, I suspect that 'behind the lines' in the regular army currently translates to only the aged or the invalid, while more able-bodied men are at the front lines. We can't afford to continue to lose men at the rate we're losing them. It's good that some can still serve, yet it must be particularly difficult for an athlete like Jackson."

"Then how do you account for the likes of Captain Long? He looked like he was still in one piece."

"I don't know, Tay. Maybe he got assigned duty with the invalids because they do need at least some able-bodied personnel."

The short trip from Celina was touch-and-go. It had been over a year. Justin knew Becky was close by. She had volunteered as a nurse's aid, but Jackson hadn't been able to shed light on his parent's whereabouts. Justin couldn't allow himself to think of them as dead. He felt that his dad would move the earth itself to contact his sons even with the unreliable, occasional mail service.

The old jeep died within one block of their home. "Looks like the ride ends here," Justin said, reaching into the vehicle's back seat and grabbing his knapsack, automatic rifle, bayonet, spare pistol, and bandoleer. A Colt .45 and an old Bowie knife, a throwback to the first Ranger outfits on the frontier, were already on his belt. All this armament represented a heavy but necessary load for survival. Taylor grabbed his kit, which was similar, but he had six hand grenades strapped to his belt and the helmet he seldom wore. With their meager possessions, the brothers walked down Fifth Street to their ransacked home.

Few men or women actually leave their imprint on history, yet those who do must often face the wrath of those who never will, to retain their grandeur.
—Jim Damiano

CHAPTER FOUR

May 10, 2020—Denton, Republic of Texas

Restless, Becky Northcutt lay on her cot in her small, humidity-drenched tent. She gazed at the canvas ceiling and watched flies flit in crazy circles. Despite her grimy appearance from the stress and fatigue, her natural beauty still shone through. She had just returned from one of many endless rounds where she'd been caring for wounded Texan and Federal soldiers. Her mind wandered endlessly, trying to forget, if only for a moment, the long line of broken men, mostly boys. *Will it ever stop? Could I ever completely wash the blood from these hands or erase the memory of the stench of war?* These and many other unpleasant thoughts kept her much-needed rest a distant possibility.

One badly wounded P.O.W. kept haunting her. It wasn't a feeling of dread but of consternation that pecked at her conscience. The soldier, in his delirium, kept calling out names. She'd repeatedly asked him who these people were, trying to reach him despite the fever. His beautiful blue eyes, so like her brothers', stared blankly at her, protecting his inner thoughts as if they were a military secret or perhaps an embarrassment. He was now beyond danger, though in his sleep he suffered what appeared to be terrible nightmares and doubt. He regained consciousness from time to time but remained confused.

His dog tag introduced him as Luke Rinaldi, blood type O, Catholic. He wasn't much older than she. Yet, like so many of his peers, he had aged in tiny bits and pieces. One moment he called, "Jimmy," another frantic moment it was "Billy," then "Vic." In his delirium, he'd shout, "Please don't! Please don't! Stay in New York! Don't come here!" Strange, she thought, he never called for his mother like the severely injured were apt to do.

Becky had seen more in her nineteen years than a teenager should have. Yet she didn't begin to care or to understand why this particular dark, good-looking Federal sergeant intrigued her. He was delirious when first brought to triage. The medics said he'd been blown forward out of his foxhole. Both legs were broken, his left arm was cut badly, and shrapnel had cut up both legs and part of his back. He stayed in a coma for days; it was a wonder he survived. The head triage nurse had suggested he be comfortably medicated and left to die. However, the lead surgeon, a captain and empathetic thoracic surgeon in civilian life, refused to allow anyone within his power, no matter their politics, to die a needless death.

Rinaldi's surgery went well. His strong physical health aided the prognosis for an expected, but long and gradual, recovery. But his mental state was another matter. His delirium caused continued concern. And unfortunately, his malady was an all too common scene.

Becky tossed and turned in her cot, trying to get comfortable. She couldn't get him out of her mind. *What have young Rinaldi's eyes seen? What miseries has he witnessed and lived through? Is his recovery a blessing or a demon meant to haunt him for the rest of his life? What happy memories does this mysterious soldier possess? Does he have any?*

Becky could not grasp her interest in this particular enemy soldier. For, she reasoned, wasn't he on the other side of this turmoil trying to kill Texans, maybe even trying to kill her brothers? She knew from reports that Justin and Taylor's division fought in the battle that wounded this man. Now fleeting thoughts raced to another direction of uncontrollable concern over her brothers' safety. The last time she had heard from either had been weeks earlier, when their overconfident unit of Rangers passed through Prosper on its way to the Oklahoma border. She'd heard that the Rangers were in the thick of battle. She smiled thinking of her two handsome brothers, but concern quickly replaced happy thoughts as her mind raced back to her Federal sergeant.

The stretcher-bearer who found Rinaldi said the soldier had his M-16 still clutched in his hands. In fact, they had to pry it from his vice-like grip. It appeared he'd been blown some forty feet from his position, yet he still clung to his rifle. *War does crazy things*, Becky thought. She shook her head in wonder, hoping she would not ever have this experience.

Pleasant memories tried nudging their way again into Becky's troubled mind. A carefree child, she enjoyed her life and status as the youngest of the Northcutt children. She idolized her older brothers, in between tormenting their equilibrium. In quiet abandon, she laughed, remembering their overprotective watch over her innocence. She longed for another glimpse of Taylor's clown-like antics.

Her fidgety mind shifted to concern for her parents, whom she hadn't seen in months. *Where might they be?* Deep down she feared the worst, shuddering violently on her cot at the possibility. This war was a killer scythe. Right now Texans bore the brunt—over a third of Rebel casualties—and the civilian population was a greater part of the carnage. However, the rest of the country was quickly catching up.

Becky spoke out loud, "Damn!" She quickly glanced at her beat-up Timex, realizing, too late, that she had wasted her four-hour respite with her ramblings and must now return to her nursing duties. Looking again at her watch, she wondered why time, even in war, was so darn important. At least a watch gave one a feeling of presence and bearing. It trumpeted with certain uncaring abruptness that it was time to go back and face the real world and to nurse the wounded. She was sometimes bitter when deliberating on her charges' recoveries. Many would eventually go home as invalids. The lucky—as if it were good fortune—would return to the front lines to again face war's hell. As for Federal Sergeant Rinaldi, his eventual recovery would mean a prisoner-of-war camp, probably near Huntsville.

Prisoner of war! Somehow the thought that Rinaldi would be sent there gave Becky a severe chill. A soldier once told her there were over 4,000 war prisoners spread across Texas, overcrowding the nearby prisons. The inhumanity of this move was soon evident when regular inmates made life difficult, if not final, for the enemy soldiers placed in their population.

Laws quickly changed to accommodate need. It was decreed by government proclamation that anyone on death row, or thought to deserve such a dishonor, was to be executed to make room for war prisoners. Inmates were sent to other prison centers, adding to the already overcrowded situation. More dangerous felons were crippled to prevent escape, lessening the need to police them. Minor felons were given the opportunity to join the army; others considered dangerous to society or thought to have the psychological makeup of a marauder were executed. It was difficult for a nineteen-year-old girl to comprehend. She was not alone in her dismay.

But there was no longer room for an extreme, bleeding-heart liberal doctrine where criminals were given an opportunity to commit additional crimes. Prisoners' rights, as far as convicts were concerned, had been tossed into the garbage heap of necessity. Now if you stole a car, just like in days of old when a horse was stolen, you were shot dead, unless there was time to hang the perpetrator. There was no point in coddling felons any longer, not with a desperate war blazing away. Such was law, and such was the high price set for those who would break it. Insurance for a peaceful future once the war was over took more import than a thief's comfort.

"Why am I thinking this stuff?" she shouted at her image in the cracked mirror, as she attempted to comb her unmanageable blonde hair. But the mental pictures kept pounding at her—things most young women would or should never care about. Yet here she was perplexed by her moment of weakness and fatigue, and with thoughts caused by her infatuation with an enemy soldier. "Stop it," she yelled again at her reflection. But her mind continued to ramble with thoughts difficult to put aside.

Becky then recalled with happiness a song her grandfather had sung. It was from an old 1960 John Wayne movie about the Alamo, about a time to live and a time to die. She didn't know its title, only that she'd heard him sing it. She tried to remember all the lyrics as she sang in her soft, beautiful voice while stepping out of her tent. *Grandpa said the words were also in the Bible. I should know this, but I don't.*

> "A time to be reapin',
> A time to be sowin',
> The green leaves of summer,
> Are calling me home.
> It was good to be young then.
> To be close to the earth,
> Now the green leaves of summer,
> Are callin' me home."

With a tin pail in hand, she washed the grime from her face and hands, putting some respectability back into her life for the difficult duty she had to face. Wounded continued coming with rapid regularity. When she had checked she was told that the fighting continued to be fierce about twenty miles north near the city of Durant, Oklahoma. Earlier in the week it had been reported that Oklahoma City was expected to fall soon. Becky felt certain its cost would be too high in human destruction. So far, casualties at the huge field hospital lingered at around 5,000, most cut down at the border where her mysterious Federal prisoner had fallen.

She put on her last clean military-issue tan blouse and her best face, flipped open the personnel tent flap and walked forward, determined to meet her next shift moment by moment. As she walked, she resolved not to think. "Thinking is a dangerous thing to do," she said aloud. *Whatever challenge or shocking, unforeseen moment awaits me will be dealt with positively*, she said to herself—trying to find encouragement.

Her medical station was in Tent B, one of several dozen large circus-size tents set up on the Denton High School football field and campus. Here, patients who would live occupied all seveny-five beds. Becky felt lucky. At least this was not the death tent. She smiled at the MP guard at the entrance.

"How are you today, Nurse Northcutt?"

"Very fine, Private Wilcox. And you?"

"Much better since your lovely presence appeared."

Becky had known the much older Pete Wilcox since childhood and was always happy to see him. He had been a patient of another hospital unit just a few weeks earlier and was now reassigned to duty more suitable for his injuries and lingering disability. He was missing a left hand, but he often said, "My *right* trigger finger is still good."

She walked to her station, checked the record sheet, and relieved Nurse Edwards.

"Anything I need to know, Ginny?"

"No, not really. The last four hours were enjoyably quiet."

"How about the lone Federal patient in bed nine? Has he come out of his amnesia?"

"Oh, you mean Sergeant Rinaldi. Yes, there seems to be some slight improvement; he now realizes he's a prisoner. He put up quite a ruckus once he found out he was in a Rebel medical tent. He kept yelling for his men, sort of like in a roll call. In particular, he kept telling a Private Long to keep his head down or something like that. It must be a dreadful thing for these boys to face such terror."

"What else did he do? I want to know every detail."

"Well, let me see." Ginny's experience as a nurse spanned several years, so she instinctively knew Becky's interest went beyond simple responsibility. She had seen her share of nurses falling for good-looking vulnerable men.

"He screamed on and off that he didn't belong here, to let him go, and that we should've left him to die with his men. I told him that some would agree with his wish, but as long as he was in my tent, if he knew what was good for him, he'd get better, even if I had to beat it out of him."

"You didn't!"

"Perhaps the thought of our notorious prison camps frightens him," Ginny frowned.

"But he's hardly back to conscious life. Awakening from whatever hell he faced must be a frightful, if not confusing, experience. Oh, this war has ruined so many lives, hasn't it, Ginny?"

Ginny shook her head in agreement. "Look, Becky, it's none of my business, but don't get too close to any patient, especially an enemy soldier. It's not healthy for you, and not for him either."

"I know where you're coming from, and you're right, Ginny, but he sort of reminds me of my brother Taylor. The only difference is his dark hair, but his deep blue eyes, body type, and damn determined look, even in a coma, make me think of Taylor. It's like I know him. There is so much more to this soldier than his dog tag."

"Except your Taylor is a lieutenant in the Rangers, as I've heard you say, and a bit of a rake."

"Oh yes, he's all that, as is my oldest brother Justin, who is a colonel in the same unit. It's tough to see them in positions of authority; both are such cut-ups. All I can envision is their total penchant for life, not rampant destruction and death. It's hard to imagine them as soldiers, let alone officers. Oh Ginny, I fear they might end up here, or worse, in some unknown grave."

Ginny put her arms on Becky's shoulder and looked directly into her eyes with a warm, motherly smile. "Who knows, with the fighting so close by, maybe they'll get a chance to visit. It looks to me like it'd be good therapy for you to see them."

"I sure hope so; it's been a while."

"Listen, Honey, I'm tired and hungry, so I'll see you in four hours." Ginny hugged Becky and turned to leave.

Becky, feeling both comforted and alone, resumed her duties. She checked all her charges and dispensed medicine and care, working swiftly and efficiently, logging everything in her precise handwriting. Ever diligent, she attacked the day's work as one would any other job, except this day's work included thirty broken bodies with thirty different stories.

x x x x x

Becky completed her initial rounds and then walked purposely to Rinaldi's cot. This was the fifth day since he'd been slipping in and out of the coma, and she had yet to speak directly to him. She hoped his memory returned, regardless of how traumatic it might be. However, her constant need to know more about him still confused her.

Her heart beat rapidly with sudden fear and resentment of this unknown young man. Up until now, everything she fitfully imagined had resided somewhere in the recesses of her mind. She didn't know what to expect. Today was different though; Rinaldi's eyes gaped intently with the awakening of his damaged spirit. Becky was unnerved, as it appeared he was looking right through her to her most private thoughts. His broken smile was a likeable smirk, although perhaps more the result of the influence of the heavy painkillers. *Was it,* she wondered, *a smile that hid his inner fear? Ginny said that in an earlier awakening, he had realized his predicament.*

With a rapid jolt, the smirk left him when Becky's angelic presence entered his field of vision. He'd always heard that Texas women were beautiful, but the first Texan woman he'd ever seen was Nurse Ginny, and she couldn't have been pretty even to her mother.

He tried to smile, which was difficult because it hurt. His words sounded harsh yet pleading. "Who are you? I didn't know the Rebs had angels working for 'em." He hesitated, then, just a touch more softly, "Whoever you are, you're the best thing these eyes have seen since I don't know when." This was the first rational speech, though slurred, she had heard from him, and it intimidated her.

Becky's initial thought was to slap his sorry face. Stopping short in mid-swing, knowing she could never hit an injured man, she defiantly snapped back, "You damned Federal, I'm here to take care of your sorry carcass. I won't take your smart talk no matter how hurt you are."

"Sorry, miss." Again, he tried to smile. "I meant no harm. It's just like, you know, it's like I know you from somewhere. Your voice seems so familiar to me. You make me feel safe."

Becky thought perhaps he did recognize her voice. During his coma she had talked to him often, using as soothing a voice as she could muster, often volunteering to work overtime, adding to the strain of her overworked days. She treated him as she hoped her brothers would be treated if they were in the same circumstance. She shuddered knowing deep down, though, that she'd never think of him as a brother.

"Sergeant, you've been in and out of a coma for several days. You've had temporary amnesia from the trauma of your wounds, and today's the first time you appear to know who you are."

"I guess all that was explained to me by that nice, ancient nurse. I think her name is Virginia. You know, her Texas twang just about drove me nuts, although I can stomach yours. It's a heck of a way to wake up; you know, being greeted by Nurse Virginia saying, 'Welcome back to planet Earth, Private.' I guess I must have gotten demoted when I was captured."

Becky tried to hide her smile but couldn't. She knew instantly he was telling the truth. Ginny was ever the professional and would never give her nickname to a patient, in particular a Federal. She probably called him a private to see if he remembered his true rank. Ginny always preached to her nurses, in particular the younger ones, to keep things impersonal. It was better that way.

"Your harsh Northern dialect's not so enjoyable either, Sergeant."

Luke feebly held his hand to his chest in mock protest, pretending an arrow penetrated his heart. "Let's start over again, nurse. My name's Sergeant Luke Rinaldi, late, and not so sad at the departing, of the Federal Army. Please call me Luke." He held his hand out to hers in greeting. "Can you tell me what's happened to me since I first paid my untimely visit to your fine hospital tent?"

"Sergeant, I'm Nurse Rebecca Northcutt, and what's happened shouldn't concern you right now." Becky, flustered, raised her voice, "You need to rest and let your sedation work. You're a medical prisoner of war." *Soon you'll probably be carted off to prison with the rest of your kind to rot for all eternity, or at least until the end of the war.* She sighed. *For all I give a hoot.* Her parents' strong Christian upbringing stopped her from saying the profanity she had on her tongue. She felt a strong sting of embarrassment.

Becky, with sudden guilt, wondered, *Why was I so curt to him? Here he's finally awake and talking to me and maybe even ready to tell his life story, and I'm acting like a fool.*

"You don't like us Federals much, do you, Nurse Becky?" His mannerism was so much like her brother Taylor that it took her back for a moment.

"Sergeant, I said my name was Nurse Rebecca Northcutt."

He sputtered, speaking slowly, "You don't like me much do you, Nurse Rebecca Northcutt?"

Becky could picture Taylor acting in the same way, always a cut-up, always ready to strike a path for the quick way to one's heart.

"No, it's not personal, Sergeant. As a matter of fact, I don't like what your army stands for. I have two brothers in the Texas Army. They were down protecting the border and fighting marauders for awhile, but I suspect you might have run into them recently at the Battle of the Red River."

"So that's what history will call that border fight I just attended." Smiling, he continued, "No, Nurse Northcutt, I'm afraid I didn't make their acquaintance, at least not while I was awake. All I saw of the last attack was smoke and fire. My memory will forever recall the ear-piercing Rebel yell and that last blinding moment of fear and silence." Luke's pained expression melted Becky's resolve.

"You know, Becky," he paused as he noticed her slight smile, "I've got three brothers myself. Two are fighting with the Rebs in New York. My twin brother, his name's Vic, has somehow stayed neutral; he's off hiding somewhere. He's the smart one of the litter. If only I could have followed Vic's lead."

"You have Rebel brothers?" she asked.

"It's a long story. Maybe someday when we get to liking each other we can talk about it."

Becky was surprised to hear about this soldier's divided family. It was too close to home. She became bitter and snapped back.

"You asked me why I don't like anything Federal. It's simple. Most of my friends are either dead, hiding, or carrying arms for the cause. I don't know where much of anything is anymore except this place and this time. I couldn't care less what you want or need to know. My job is simply to help you recover so that we can send you off to a prison camp. So, Sergeant, enjoy the food before it gets scarce."

She continued to ramble on and could not stop her verbal attack. "The prisoners get no better than our soldiers. Now that you're awake, you'll find our supplies are slim, even though the government gives the best to the hospitals. It's hoped it'll give those men capable of recovery a chance to return back to the lines a bit faster. As for prisoners, well ..." she hesitated, "we're a bit more humane than your people have been."

"I didn't know they had declared war yet." Luke's energy was on the wane and it showed in his voice. "Last I heard it was an insurrection and that we were trying to put it down. But I'm really sorry for the pain this so-called war has given you, Nurse Becky." His voice trailed as he fought the medications' effects. However, he noticed how she ignored his personal use of her name.

"You go on and call it what you want. We call it a war," chided Becky. "I don't expect you to understand our side, nor do I want you to. So as far as I'm concerned, lie still and recover, so we can get rid of you. We need the bed!"

"Aw, come on, Nurse Northcutt," Luke chided. "I didn't mean any harm. I haven't talked to a woman in over a year, and certainly not one as beautiful as you. To you, I'm the enemy, but we do have some things in common, don't you know?"

"What things could we possibly have in common?" Becky had fire in her eyes, her hands balled tightly in a fist.

"Aside from our common language, that is except for a few flaws you Texans have, we both have two brothers fighting for the Rebs. And frankly, I am not so sure anymore if they haven't taken the right course." Becky couldn't hold back her sudden smile; Rinaldi's charm was as contagious as she had feared.

"Tell me, what are your brothers' names, Sergeant?"

"My oldest brother is Jimmy. The next in line is Billy, and then there's my twin, Vic. I really miss them. My biggest fear was of the day when we might face each other in battle. I prayed often it wouldn't come to that. Now that I'm a prisoner, I'd guess my worrying is over. You see, up to now, my unit's been down here, not in New York where they are. Quite honestly, I'm relieved that I won't have to face that day."

"Sergeant, I'm not familiar with the New York Volunteers, but we do hear that the northern Rebels are in the thick of it. I'm only familiar with what's going on down here. Sure, most Texans are fighting for our Republic as well as independence and freedom from you invaders. But, there are still a few Texans who have slipped over to the Feds for their beliefs and loyalties. Some of them are, or were, friends. You know, this isn't the first time brother fought brother in this country. It's the third I'm told. In any case, I don't think anyone can ever get used to it."

"I only remember one other," Luke fibbed. "The Civil War, which I suppose could be likened to this mess in some way."

Becky laughed. "You don't know your American history very well, do you?"

"I should," Luke replied, "but I never paid much attention to my grandfather or my dad. If anyone knows history, they do. Hell, my father's a history professor, with a doctorate, no less."

"Even we ignorant Texans know that this is the third time Americans have had a civil war. Let's see, the first was the American Revolution, where brother often fought brother. Next came the Civil War, or as ex-Confederate States like to say, the Second War for Independence. You could almost say that Texas has had four civil wars. Our first war was for independence from Mexico, and some families were split on that one, too."

Luke was becoming very tired, and he feared Becky would pick up on it. His conversation with this fabulous young woman seemed to be the elixir he needed. He would continue talking with her, even at the expense of his health, even if it meant he must pick an argument with her. He didn't care. He hadn't told the truth about his knowledge of his country's history. He had grown up absorbing American history, as if through osmosis. He wanted to see her fired up. It brought out a beauty in her that attracted him—stirring up feelings thought forgotten.

"I guess you're right, Nurse Becky," Luke slipped her nickname in to see if it got a rise out of her. It didn't. "I should know. I come from a little city in upstate New York, a place almost forgotten, called Utica. All around it are monuments to heroes who fought battles around the area, most of them from the Revolution. There the Rebels mostly fought Indians and Tories, or what my dad called loyalists to Britain's King George. The Tories wore green uniforms, or so Grandpa always said, but unlike your Rebel green and tan, their green was on the side of the king's government. I guess you know what side your people are on." Now his smile was contagious.

"Yeah, so you do remember." Becky grinned openly for the first time. Luke did not miss it, enjoying the moment. She also noted he had called her by her nickname, but she chose to dismiss it for now. "I'll come back and check on you later. You look pretty tired, and you do need your rest."

"Sorry we got off to such a bad start."

"Yes, but we are on opposite sides, aren't we?" Becky asked. "And what of it? It looks like our rambling got your blood up and running, and heaven knows you need to have some circulation to flow through that thick Federal skull of yours. You know it's the first I've seen some color in your arrogant face since they brought you in. You looked as white as snow."

"What does which side we are on matter? We're both people in a place we'd rather not be. Now don't get me wrong, Nurse Becky. I do want to be in your presence. Tell me, what do you know about snow?"

"Luke, I know it comes here about once every five or six years, and sometimes it lasts longer than a day." Luke was thrilled. She used his name for the first time. It sounded so sweet coming from her melodic voice.

"Becky, snow in my hometown is as natural as breathing. We get from 100 to 130 inches every year. I could go for some of that cool snow right now. This tent is damn hot. What is it, still only May? Yeah, it's May." Luke answered his own question, his voice trailing off. "It's already May, and I'm lucky to be alive. My foxhole had three casualties in it. Two of my best friends are gone and a new young recruit. He was just a boy. I'm lucky not to have made it unanimous."

There was now more than physical pain in Luke's voice. He continued to talk, but the medicine began to take effect, slurring his voice. "All I did the last several months was fight for my comrades in arms. Now they're all dead. I'm so damn confused. I never believed in this struggle. I only joined for the pay and to get away from a boring town. Damn, why did they all die? Why did that kid have to die? He didn't deserve that."

The painkillers seemed to be working like a truth serum. Tears rushed down Luke's troubled face. Becky, seeing his tears, looked away, not wanting to embarrass him. Her heart went out to him, and silently she cried, too.

"Nurse Rebecca Northcutt ..." Luke sighed. "It was very nice meeting and talking to you. One last question, if I may?" He struggled for the correct words. "It was you I heard in my dreams, wasn't it?"

"Yes, it was me."

"I thought so; I'd never forget your beautiful voice, even if I was only dreaming. Thank you for caring."

"I was only doing my job."

"Were you? I wish the times were different and that we could get to know each other better." Luke closed his eyes; his body finally gave in to the medicine.

"Rest, Sergeant," she soothed. "I'll be back to look in on you later. I've a few other boys that need my attention." But he didn't hear her. He was fast asleep.

Becky left Luke to care for a Texan soldier in the next cot. She turned back to look at Luke and felt a growing warmth—a feeling she wished would go away, but somehow she knew it wouldn't. *I must find a way to keep him from the horrors of Huntsville.* She decided to use all of her little sister charm on her rugged Ranger brothers and seek their help. *I must,* she affirmed silently. *Luke is not a true Federal. I must help him realize that he can switch or go neutral.*

Luke's face was serene, something Becky had not seen before. He had fallen into a deep, morphine-induced, welcome slumber. It was the first peace he had experienced in several months, and his body reacted blissfully to its blessing.

A cool breeze, like a breath of spring,
Doesn't always invite robins to sing,
Only the Hawk can circle its prey,
On wisps of air, this new dawn's day,
While restless nature serves to blind,
Nobler men to reciprocate in kind.
　　　　　　　　　—Jim Damiano

CHAPTER FIVE

May 05, 2020—Adirondack Mountains, near Tupper Lake, New York

The old grandfather clock ticked away slowly. Tick, tick, tick … the monotonous sound was soothing to the troubled, resting man. Rock listened to the timepiece in the silent seclusion of the old summer retreat in the paradise of the ancient mountains, in a place he sometimes called home. He had left Utica two days after he buried his daughter-in-law next to the grave of his beloved wife Rose.

Betty had been a wonderful lady who Rock thought of as his own daughter. It troubled him deeply that her sons and husband were not with her at her end. She bravely fought her last few days; an illness that medicine available in peacetime would have cured. Yet, no matter how hard he tried to get medical help, he was told there was none. Rock's eyes misted with tears at the thought of her last painful days. Betty's death was pointless and unnecessary; she was as much a casualty of the rebellion as any soldier struck by a bullet.

His only son Joseph must be told, but how? Joseph left weeks ago and hadn't been heard from since he joined the Rebels. Rock feared the worst: that his son had not survived. He remembered how hard he tried to convince him to stay and wait out the hostilities. After all, Joe was forty-five and should leave the fighting to his sons, but when James and William left with the 1st New York, Joe soon followed.

Silence became Rock's enemy. It allowed too many memories, peeling away his peace into his loneliness, haunting his innermost soul, giving him longings and a nagging hunger for better times. The ticking clock struck a chord in him that life, his life, was slowly marching toward its inevitable end, with each measure marking time.

Rock felt fortunate finding this fully provisioned home, hidden away in the hills he loved. An honest man, he was ill at ease taking refuge and repast from unknown hosts. If possible, he would do something to improve the place to repay the unintentional kindness of its nameless owners.

He considered this place a sanctuary, even though the electricity was off and the generator out of fuel; it wasn't safe to use it even if he desired, for its noise might draw attention, and Rock's quest for survival needed to stay hidden. The fireplace gave little comfort; its smoke could invite danger. So he used it sparingly and only at night.

Luxuries of the 21st century were scarce. Harsh seclusion gave Rock too much time to invite thoughts of his happy childhood with family surrounding him with love. It was a good time, when family was the number-one importance in the United States. Would those happy times ever return? He prayed but doubted they would.

A gloomy mood crept over Rock, giving reflection to his isolation. The smell of the cold, stale room awakened his senses to new depths of understanding. It was time to pick up his spirits. It was necessary for his survival and sanity. Outside waited a beautiful spring day—melodious sounds of birds chirping their collective songs, inviting, welcoming daybreak to the mountain.

He wondered, *Would the Rebels, if they prevailed, only succeed to represent another failed chapter in the history for the country?* In the years since his birth he had seen the nation go from high elation after winning a world war to its present state of devastation. The war's destruction hadn't equaled that suffered by Europe and Asia after that terrible war, but it was quickly catching up.

A typical brisk Adirondack morning beckoned. He put on his jacket and, as a precaution, picked up his rifle, an old 30/30, six-round lever-action Winchester. Rock checked its safety and walked out into the new day.

From the porch he took in a panoramic view of the rolling hills and picturesque lake close by. He guessed the cabin had been built in the 1950s. *God,* he thought, *that would make this place about seventy years old.* That seemed old to him, even though he was seventy-five. The home had been built with the environment in mind, several years before anyone cared to worry about such things. The stone probably came from nearby quarries. The builder had placed it in this secluded spot commanding a great view of everything below. A large hedgerow of tall pines acted as a windbreak from the strong Canadian winds. Rock wondered if the present owners had planted these majestic trees. It was difficult to imagine that a vengeful war was only a few miles from this peace. Rock absorbed the grandeur, fearing it was a dream.

No sooner had he felt good about everything than the terrible feeling of remorse set in to plague Rock's serenity. His idle depression was set off by his battle-sorrowed, over-active mind. He purposely force-fed good thoughts, and they pleasantly turned to his grandsons, the pride of his life and probably the only family he had left.

Luke, a GI, was somewhere in the Midwest fighting in the Federal Army, while his brothers, James and William, were somewhere near Utica fighting for the Rebels in the recent battle that had prompted his swift departure. And then there was Victor, his difficult yet loveable twin grandson. He had left home over two years ago. Victor and Luke were like bookends, identical in every way but disposition. They were the Dr. Jekyll and Mr. Hyde of the Rinaldi family.

No matter where they were or what they were doing, Rock would forever love his grandsons, even the wayward Vic. When he last saw Vic, it was on his nineteenth birthday. He and Vic had a terrible argument. By that time, James and Billy were off somewhere in the Rebel army. Vic had left home when he was seventeen, and no one expected to see him that day. But here he was visiting his grandparents, though not really intending to visit, only there to play on sympathy and ask for money. He said he was leaving to get away from everything. He vented that he didn't fit in and wanted to be his own person. Rock remembered saying, perhaps a bit curtly, that what he needed was to go back to school and also to relearn some respect for others and, more importantly, respect for himself. Vic had been upset with Rock, but the youthful reverence and love he still held for his grandfather caused him to remain quiet. Then Rock, though he knew he would regret it later, pulled out all the money he had in his wallet and handed it over to Vic, saying, "Take it. At least you'll eat."

As soon as Vic had left, Rock wondered if he'd eat or use the money to buy drugs or other illicit comforts so readily available. Vic was not blessed as the most intellectual of his grandchildren. He never cared to listen to Rock's ramblings about history or much else. Everything seemed to bore him. His mind always looked for the easy and quick way around every path in his life. He'd rather spend an hour conniving on how to get something for nothing than working for an honest wage and buy it with a good conscience. How Vic went wrong was known only to God—it was difficult to believe he came from the same blood. Still, Rock wished he had a chance to reach out and hug Vic, to hold him and reassure him that he was loved. *If only I had succeeded in settling him down.* He resigned himself to the fact that he couldn't change anything, even if given the opportunity.

Rock had no illusions. He figured Vic was not with either opposing army. Most likely, he was a marauder. That would be the easy way out, and he knew his grandson. If only he could see Vic again, maybe he could knock some sense into his stubbornness this time around.

Rock peered down the long driveway, looking at the highway below. He shuddered with a sudden sick feeling in his stomach as he saw an odd-looking vehicle approach at a slow deliberate crawl. Whoever its occupants were, it was apparent they were neither Rebels nor Federals; civilians rarely had access to fuel except that which burned naturally. Electric vehicles could not run without the current to recharge them, and only those with weapons authorized by war's necessity had the power to confiscate what little fuel was available. The rule of the day was simple: the strong ruled, the weak accepted. Rock wasn't weak.

With instinct born from his combat experience, combined with that of an avid hunter, he ran for the security of the hedge north of the cabin. He found a good hiding place with a clear view of the highway and drive below. It would be about a 300-foot climb for the intruders to reach his hideaway. Rock glanced sadly at his temporary little home, which was no longer a safe haven, not with this new threat approaching to destroy his quiet. He could've done worse than stay here, but once these people saw the house they most likely would come to pillage and find refuge.

Rock didn't have long to wait. The roar of the ancient military vehicle announced its presence as it climbed the drive. The road, as he'd feared, did little to hide the cabin. He could now see them clearly; they were definitely thieves. He took the safety off his rifle, though he would not be the one to start anything; they clearly outnumbered him, and their firepower outclassed his old 30/30. He only had six rounds in his chamber and two idle rounds in his jacket pocket.

The driver saw the home and turned into the gravel drive to investigate. Rock rechecked his rifle. He would not do anything foolish to reveal his hiding place. *Damn*, he mused, *all my gear is in the house. They'll figure someone's here*. His sweater, ammunition, medical supplies, knapsack, and knife were on the table. Somehow, he had to get his belongings out. It would mean the difference between surviving or not. He'd wait to see what happened, but patience was never one of Rock's virtues. The raiders opened their doors, and six men spilled out of the old Humvee.

They were a boisterous band, laughing and trying to out-swear each other in bravado, which often, in Rock's experience, revealed true cowards. It was difficult to hear all they were saying, but by the hand signals and body language expressed, it appeared their loud kidding had turned to insults. The group seemed hovering on the edge against one man who looked very familiar. They jeered and chided him, one pulling out a pistol, screaming at the object of his derision.

It was clear to Rock a confrontation was in the making when one of the opposing five shouted, "Look, prick, we've had enough of your shit. Either you start doing it our way or you're a dead man, right here and right now." The familiar-looking, unkempt man never wavered as he threw his main adversary his middle finger in an arrogant manner that revealed his identity. It was his grandson Victor. Of all the coincidences—not a hundred yards from his hiding place was the younger twin he had thought about just moments earlier.

Vic snarled at the ringleader of his opposition and yelled, "Look here, you rotten SOB, I'm the leader of this group. None of you would've gotten by without me, so what I say, you do! Understand? If any of you don't like it, screw off and leave! But don't take anything with you except your life."

Rock sensed Vic had more than one opponent in this altercation and feared his grandson would be killed in a few seconds. His intuition didn't often lead him astray, and Rock always went with his gut feelings. The marauder who had drawn the pistol made a threatening motion that Vic didn't miss; his reaction was swift and deadly as his youthful reflexes sighted and fired his pistol in one motion with unerring accuracy. As his first challenger fell, his head destroyed, another marauder took quick aim with obvious intent to kill. With natural instinct a man has for his family, Rock, who was already aiming at potential targets, let off a round, hitting the man squarely in the back. The Winchester's loud report totally confused the whole melee; the marauders dove for cover, alarmed by the sudden awareness that they weren't alone. It was the first man Rock had killed since returning from Nam in 1968. It wasn't a good feeling; bile filled Rock's mouth with a foul taste of death.

What had seemed an abandoned house suddenly appeared to have at least one defender. The bandits realized too late how foolish it had been not to reconnoiter first. Greed is often a deterrent to common sense among thieves.

Vic, reclaiming his role as leader, shouted, "You in the bushes, whoever you are, there's four of us and we're well-armed. I suggest you give up. We're going to kill you anyway, so save the pain of delay for yourself."

At that last outburst, Rock's anger heightened and his adrenaline reached a dangerous level. "Look, you mangy weasels, and you, Victor, you little bastard, I'm your grandfather. I don't want to kill you, but I will," he stammered with apparent, controlled anger. "I just saved your worthless goddamned life, but for the death of me, I don't know why."

"Grandpa, Grandpa Rock, is that really you? How in the hell did you get here?" Vic yelled to his shaggy crew, "Hold your fire, it's my grandpa."

"We don't give a flip who the hell he is," said one of the three. "The old fart just killed Jake."

"Yeah, and Jake was about to plug me. Don't say another word or this pistol is going to give you another hole to eat with." Vic meant it and his men knew it.

"Come on down, Grandpa, we won't do anything to you."

Rock was tempted, but instinct told him it was safer to stay put. He didn't trust the rabble before him. He had more respect for his old enemy, the Viet Cong, right now than these mangy fools. At least the Cong were efficient little bastards. "Look, Grandson, if you want to talk to me, you come up here and do it slowly. Tell your buddies to stay right where they are. The last we talked was two years ago, and I don't know you anymore, and what's more, during these times I won't trust anyone, especially now that I see my grandson acting the role of a damn cut-throat and a no-good thief. I'm disappointed, I'll have you know. You little shit!" Rock took a deep breath to calm himself.

"Stay put, you lug heads, and I'll see what he wants. Blood is thicker than water. He won't hurt us, and I won't have you hurting him."

With violent death now as common as breathing, no one seemed to notice the two lying sprawled in the New York dirt, their souls on the way to visit Satan. They did take note of Rock's rifle; they just could not see where he was. Vic walked with care, almost in a backward stance, facing his men and their potential wrath, strolling in careful silence towards the direction of Rock's voice. Vic was leery as he half suspected and feared that Rock might have some of his old cronies with him who might be less inclined to spare his life.

He reached the tree line, and his grandfather whispered to him. "Over here, Vic."

Vic looked at his grandfather. He was just as he remembered him: clean-shaven, no matter what, and so damned self-assured, you'd never know he was almost eighty. And here he was holding off three of his men, not to mention himself. Then Vic recalled the knowledge, somewhere tucked away in his brain, that Rock had been a reluctant warrior once before. *This situation is not a new experience for him.* Rock, an expert in survival, had learned decades ago what Americans now, thrust by the necessity of living day-to-day in chaos, were quickly learning.

Rock looked with business-like precision at his grandson. It was as if he were checking stock on a shelf in his grocery store. He looked like hell—long, greasy unwashed hair, and a ragged beard that matched his more ragged clothes. Everything he carried was no doubt stolen or taken by force from someone weaker. He did have on a good pair of boots, and in his right hand he held an old, familiar Luger—the pistol Rock's father had taken home as a souvenir from his tour of duty in Europe during World War II.

Rock's dad had served two years in the Italian campaign as an interpreter with the Army. Rock remembered the arrow patch with its green capital T emblazoned over a blue inverted arrow, representing the proud 36th Texas Division. His presumably safe role as interpreter didn't prevent him from earning a Purple Heart for wounds received in southern Italy. Rock's dad had given the pistol to him, and he in turn gave it to his son, Joseph. He wondered silently how Vic came to possess the gun. He didn't want to know.

Vic took the automatic rifle's strap from his shoulder. The two men acknowledged each other with a nod; although their personal philosophies separated them, a genuine love still existed.

"Sit down, young man; I'd like to talk to you. Yell down to your friends and tell them all's OK, but tell 'em to stay put where I can see them."

Vic complied, turning all his attention toward Rock, who started to talk again. "Vic, I don't trust your friends, and I'm sorry to say I'm uncertain about you. It appears you haven't been leading a stellar life since I last saw you, not that you were then. Don't you know they're shooting marauders on site, no questions or trials? What in God's name are you thinking?"

Ignoring Rock's question, Vic got to the point. "Well, Grandpa, I suppose it's intended somehow for us to meet here, though it does appear we're in a bit of a fix over it."

"Vic, maybe there's hope yet that you'll straighten out. I believe in you, Grandson."

"Look, I didn't come up here to be lectured. I left that world behind a long time ago."

"Did you really, Vic? Certainly with your upbringing, you know what you're doing's wrong. Wrong, goddamn it!"

"Look, Grandpa, once again, I don't want a lecture. I came here out of respect for you and to save your ass from some really mean bastards down there."

"I can take care of myself, so don't worry about me."

"I don't know how you got here or in this mess, but again, I came here out of respect, so don't push me." Vic's face showed the strain he was trying to hide.

"Oh, now you're the big man, you going to shoot your grandfather? Yeah, that'll look good on your resume when you approach the Pearly Gates. I can just hear it now. Well, Saint Pete, I belong in Heaven because I was a good thief and well, uh ... I did kind of kill my grandfather once."

"Give me a break, Grandpa. You know damn well that I won't do that!" Vic's face showed genuine pain.

"But you have killed, haven't you, Vic?"

"Oh, I've killed a few, but none who didn't need it."

"I suppose like that fellow down there next to the one I sent to hell. One of your gang, I assume, vermin that he was."

"It was him or me, and I didn't want it to be me."

"God, what's happening to this country? I never thought, not in my wildest and worst dreams, I'd be talking to one of my grandchildren like this, worried about what he's become and, worse, fearing that he may take my life."

Vic's injured look stared a hole into his grandfather. He felt sudden embarrassment at what he had become. "Look, Grandpa, I would never harm you, you've got to believe me. My companions, well, they're another story."

"Where the heck are those bums? They're gone."

Vic looked down to where they last were seen and quickly feared the emptiness it represented. The Humvee was still in the drive, clearly giving away their intent to do harm.

"Blood-thirsty bastards, they probably want to kill us both and keep this nice site here for a couple of days' rest, and God knows we need it. We've been on the run for over thirty hours."

"Well, if it's rest they want, they came to the right place. I'll give them a permanent rest, if they try to come for me. I'm not about to put up with their crap. Are you with me or against me? I need to know right now, Vic." Rock pointed the rifle at his grandson's chest, his intent very clear.

"I'm with you, damn it! Why would you even ask?"

"You've changed, Vic, and we haven't had much of a chance to really talk things out. I don't really know you right now." Every second counted, and Rock, trusting his instincts, accepted Vic's temporary alliance.

Vic said sullenly, "I'm with you; I just wish you didn't have to ask." Rock could feel his sincerity.

"We better start thinking. I know this area, and I suspect they don't. They seem tired, and we have the upper ground. There's only one way they can get around us, and it will take them time to find it. Our best bet is to just sit tight and wait till they make their move or we hear something, anything. As soon as we do, we can't hesitate."

Rock took full command. Vic didn't argue as Rock whispered, "You run to that boulder over there about twenty yards to the left. See it?" Vic nodded.

"It's well hidden, and there's a small ditch-like incline right behind it. You can slip down in it very nicely. No one should see you, and if they do, it'll be too late for them to react. I'm going over to my left. See it?" Vic nodded. "You can see behind my position, and I can see behind yours, and at this angle of placement, we can catch 'em from either direction."

Rock's quick military thinking impressed Vic. He was suddenly very thankful the old man was on his side. He knew these men. They would stop at nothing less than killing him and the old man.

It seemed like hours, but only about five minutes passed before they heard the distinct sound of a branch cracking about 100 yards off in the deep brush. The marauders, street smart but none true hunters, were careless in this new environment. It would take them awhile to find their way to Rock's hiding place.

Rock looked at his grandson crouching in steady readiness across from him. Vic looked tense and strained. In the two years since he last saw him, he had aged beyond his twenty-one years. Rock noticed his grandson's jaw set and ready to take a life as easily as snuffing out a candle. Rock, still a bit sick to his stomach after taking out his target, took deep breaths to calm his mind. Reason continually reminded him he had little choice. It had been the marauder's life or his grandson's. Reason did little to lessen his repulsion.

Rock had been a hunter since he was seven, yet even after each successful kill, he always felt sadness for the animal. *It's funny*, he thought, *what goes through your mind before action.* He shuddered at the memory of his war, once so safely tucked away, for sanity's sake, in the far recesses of his mind, now back to haunt him. Now was not the time for a diversion into his past. *Why am I thinking of the first rabbit I killed as a kid?*

He adjusted his crouched position to prevent numbness. His mind went back to that darn rabbit. He recalled looking at the poor creature, wondering why he'd killed it. His dad, sensing his concern, had explained that hunting was an acceptable habit of humanity going back to the cavemen, and that as long as you consumed what you killed, it justified the sport. "Heck," his dad had said. "Every time you bite into a hamburger you shouldn't create regret for the cow providing the meal. We'd go nuts from the worry and never eat meat, becoming blooming vegetarians. Do you want to be a vegetable-eater, Rocky?" It was humorous to think of that poor rabbit as he waited, now the hunted, anxious for the coming altercation. But when the adrenaline goes up, all men react differently. It helped him to focus on the peril ahead.

In a matter of seconds, his life or that of his grandson could be over. Like anyone who ever faced a similar situation, he had his fears. But he was an old man who had lived a good and wonderful life and one who was satisfied with his lot. Rock felt comfort in knowing that his last act on earth might be to die defending both his and his grandson's life. If it were to be, he would not die in vain.

Only breathing and the wind's movement interrupted the deafening silence of their solitude. Rustling leaves stood as a keen reminder that life still pulsed through their numbed bodies. Rock felt the familiar hollow feeling, brought on by terror beyond his control. It was 'Nam all over again, and it terrified the hell out of him.

The wretched bitterness of rage overwhelmed Rock's sense of taste. He took a fleeting glance at Vic, calmly sitting at his post. What he saw was a cool and collected young man, tense as a spring and ready to uncoil his wrath at the first sign of his old partners. He also saw the image of a little boy and his brothers playing with so much joy, a picture of an innocent time long past. His thoughts raced on. Rock knew firsthand how silly things pass by your mind in the confusion of destiny and heat of combat.

Seconds changed to torturous minutes that only a true hunter could fathom. They waited, searching and listening for sounds and signs. They were near; Rock could feel it, and with the wind could now smell them as well. Rock's eyes turned to Vic to give a silent signal. He wondered, *Is there a chance for this kid, or is he forever committed to a life of wrongdoing?*

With sudden urgency, Rock's ears confirmed that his sixth sense had been correct when the faint rustle of long dead leaves disturbed by a slight wind was made more alive by the footsteps of a living adversary. Three marauders crashed through the brush as one. All thought ceased. Rock's total energy focused on the new threat. As if in lock step to do as Rock surmised, they crashed through the partial clearing, not seeing their immediate danger hidden from their view. The sun rising in the east blinded them; they clearly lacked common sense.

Rock's reflexes took over. He aimed his barrel at the first menacing target, bursting open the chest of his unsuspecting victim. The bullet's impact at close range was almost as loud as the gun's recoil. It dissected the marauder's heart as neatly as a surgeon's knife. The quizzical look of surprise was etched forever on the dead man's face. His eyes remained wide open in his last gasp of sight as he fell sprawling to the ground, never knowing what hit him.

Vic's pistol sang out, ringing its echoing sound three times opposite Rock. A marauder went down, wounded but not out, as he sprayed a burst from his automatic weapon. Nevertheless, it appeared to hit Vic. The last marauder hit the ground and fired in Rock's direction. Rock felt the sting and instant burning sensation as the bullet cut a path along his arm, exiting into the soil behind him. The desperate man's automatic fire was high due to the sun's interference. In intense pain, blood flowing from his wound, Rock instinctively lifted his rifle, quickly sighting it. He put aside the intense hurt and squeezed a 30/30 slug square through the top of his adversary's head—it split like an overripe melon.

Vic's adrenaline took over as he pulled off two nine-millimeter shots at his wounded ex-partner. It was over almost before there was time to think.

Rock's arm began to sting like fire. Ripping a strip of cloth from his checkered shirt, he wrapped it as best he could. Leaping up as fast as his old bones could take him, he ran to see if Vic was all right. With only a glance, he knew his grandson was badly hit.

Vic stared with glazed, unfocused eyes at Rock, who started to talk. His voice seemed far away, almost too low for Vic to hear.

Rock could see that Vic was going into shock. Blood pulsed out of his right leg like a fountain. Rock had lived this horrid scene many times in 'Nam.

With unforgotten, trained precision, Rock took off his belt, making a quick tourniquet, and pressed on the flow to stop it with what force he could. Blood was everywhere. It appeared, though, that the bullet had passed through Vic's leg, which gave him a chance.

Rock had to move quickly to get Vic to shelter. If Vic lived, it would save the pain of telling Joe about his son's death and his foul past. The distance to the house, a good football field away, seemed like forever. Rock glanced at the gore and blood flowing freely in the little clearing as he began to drag Vic. *I must get a grip*, he commanded his soul. *In less than an hour—3600 ticks of that old clock—I have killed three men.*

Rock, though always ready to take action when necessary, was not a violent man. He always paid dearly for his calm after the storm, when the adrenalin dropped to normal. Now was no exception. Now he had the shakes. His adrenalin ebbed and all he felt was regret for what had just happened.

He pulled Vic, who was slipping in and out of consciousness, by his shoulders, dragging him with difficulty through the tall brush to the house. Once there, he took care of Vic's leg and then his own wound. He'd bury the vermin later as best he could once he rested a bit. He understood without remorse that he must erase the evidence of this encounter, and quickly.

Rock deliberated, saddened for what had become of his once great nation. He couldn't explain why thoughts returned to a desperate editorial he wrote several years ago. Then he tried to vent his sentiment and give reason for concern, but most who had read it thought it too radical. *Too late now, folks,* he thought. *Sometimes, especially like now, it hurts to be right. God, how I wish I could have been wrong.*

In desperation, Rock placed Vic on the couch in the rustic expanse of the living room, saying softly, "You hang in there, boy. You *must* live, you must."

At the doorway, he glanced off to his right and saw in the distance the silhouette of a lone hawk circling in majestic freedom, unaware of the current destruction below. "If only I could soar like that hawk above all this turmoil," he said as if talking to the bird. He closed the door and returned to aid his grandson. He felt faint as the burning pain from the wound in his arm seared through his body. Somehow he must suck it up and put it aside just like he did long ago in a faraway jungle when fear was a constant and unwelcome companion.

Since reason is the only sure guide which God has given to man, reason is the only foundation of a just government.
—John Locke

CHAPTER SIX

May 19, 2020—Prosper, Republic of Texas

The early evening cast a gloom on the joy of returning to Prosper. When Justin and Taylor reached what was left of their home, they found only remnants of what had been. Although most of the exterior of the two-story brick structure was untouched by war, the interior was ransacked. Many prized possessions were missing; all provisions were gone.

"Taylor, at least our beds are still here. Let's hope that Mom and Dad took the valuables."

"I wonder if we'll ever see them again. Things aren't worth much these days, compared to human life."

Justin stood at the entry of his bedroom, once his haven in a loving home. He stared angrily at the disrupted linen and debris everywhere. A few pictures were untouched. His desk and chair remained in place; its drawer and contents were scattered on the floor along with the meager remnants from his dresser. The closet door had been torn from its hinges, its interior in total disarray. It didn't appear that anything of any value, other than sentimental, was left. Justin picked up his model of a 2002 yellow Ford Thunderbird. The model brought back fond memories of riding in the actual car with his grandfather. *Boy, Papa sure loved that car. I wonder if it still is in one piece.*

Taylor rushed into Justin's room, too deep in anger to slow his stride.

"Damn, Justin, it looks like a freaking cyclone hit here. It's pretty much the same in my room."

"I really doubt it's much different than the way you left it, Tay. With or without vandals, your room was always a mess." Justin's sarcasm softened. "It would be nice to go back in time, to your peaceful and forever messy habitat."

"Whatever, make fun all you want," Taylor mused. "At least the water's still on, and I've got dibs on the first shower, cold water or not. That's a miracle in itself."

"What, you taking a shower?" Justin laughed.

Justin observed the remaining belongings of his boyhood scattered throughout the room. "Whoever has been here last didn't think much of my memorabilia." He looked with love at his baseball glove, thrown with abandon to the floor from its perch on its shelf. He and Taylor had talked about tossing a ball every now and then when off duty. He wondered if a general would seem foolish tossing a baseball or even a football. "Well, I guess," he mumbled, then smiled, "a general can do just about anything he wants."

He would make room in his knapsack for the glove, even if it meant giving up a can or two of food. He shouted out, "Taylor, why don't you look for your glove? Maybe someday we could get a game going at HQ. Did you see a football anywhere?" He spoke as he continued his futile search. "If you find one, let's take it along."

After they inspected their home, there wasn't much else to do except rest. Sleep was a welcomed respite. But both slept poorly; it was not what they had envisioned.

After waking about 5:00 a.m., Justin wondered if their so-called R&R was worth the pain of staying in the ruins of their happy past.

After a meager breakfast of C-rations and beef jerky, the brothers set about straightening out what they could. There were no valuables worth the worry, so they spent the majority of their time securing the home from the weather in hopes that it would remain in better shape than they found it, should their parents return.

"Taylor, the real reason we came here was to see if we could find out anything about Mom and Dad. It feels crummy to be here now. There are so many good memories, and somehow seeing the place like this just ruins them. Why don't we leave? There's only one day left anyway, and I'm not sure I care to stay here."

"I'm with you, Justin. Remember, though, the memories will never fade. This old house's spirit will always be here no matter what. With our extra time let's look up Becky and see how she's doing."

"That's not a bad idea. When we stop at Celina to pick up the Humvee, we'll ask around where Becky's unit is. Oh, before I forget, did you find your glove, or do we have to do some scavenging ourselves to find one?"

"I found it, General, Sir," he taunted. "Once we find a bat, it'll be fun striking you out again."

"In your dreams, Lieutenant."

"Tay, see if you can rustle up a baseball."

"I've got one." Taylor felt a sting of reality, fidgeting with his hands as he spoke. "It's that Nolan Ryan signature ball that Dad gave me when we were little. Remember, he said it was worth over 100 bucks. I guess right now no one has any money for collecting luxuries. Hell, let's use it. Not much else left for us to do here, is there, Justin?"

"No, Tay, afraid not. Sure isn't the same anymore."

"No, everything about this war seems to mess things up. Hell, with no TV, no electricity, no communications, no phones, and no computers, we've returned to the 19th century."

"Taylor, I suppose that's what happened. Wars change things, but it doesn't need to change us. We still have each other," Justin said, as he stood to face his brother.

In a show of emotion they grasped each other in a brotherly hug that said it all. Never could they do this in front of their men; alone, here in the privacy of their boyhood home, it seemed right.

"Justin, do you ever wonder if what we're doing is worthwhile? I often think hard on the number of men I've killed, or caused to be killed at my age and somehow ... " Taylor started to choke up, "it doesn't seem right. I know they're enemies, marauders, intruders, whatever, and it's our duty, but it eats at me, Justin. It eats at me and it won't let up. I sometimes think I can't go on much longer or, worse, that I'm going nuts."

"Look, Taylor, what we're doing is for our family, our country, and us, in that order. After what we've seen, it's what we believe. It's also right. How can we get freedom unless we pay a price? For me, it's the combination of a lot of things. Most of all I'd like to see this mess over as much as any reasonable man."

Justin grasped his brother's arm. "It won't end easily. For some reason our generation's been chosen, for this quest for revived freedom. If we're lucky and live, we'll be able to look into our future children's eyes and let them know how we fought for their freedom. I hope and pray this will be the last time any generation will have to go through this. Can we do less?"

Justin looked deeply into Taylor's eyes and then smiled. "Come on, Tay, let's go see if we can find a beer and stir up some activity before we leave."

"No, Justin, as stupid as it sounds, I'm ready to return to our post. Being here for a short time has been good medicine for me. It's reminded me of what we've lost and the difficult work ahead of us. I'm with you. Let's get on with it."

"Well, little brother, you show signs of a future general. Becky's unit is probably somewhere north of Sherman. It should be on our way as long as the war doesn't move in a different direction."

Justin closed the door and locked it, though it didn't matter. It just seemed the right thing to do. Symbolically, the bolted door temporarily secured a piece of their past. Justin, with a feeling of regret, wondered if he'd ever see his home again. They had come to Prosper in need of familiar roots and some rest. Instead they found sanity in the moment and in the realization that there would never be true respite until freedom was won.

"Taylor, take a good look and let's go. Unless the final battle is won, we may never see this place again." Justin shook off the dread of that kind of future and moved on.

Justin's mind involuntarily wandered back to happier times spent at their grandparent's ranch in Sherman, riding horses, rounding up cattle, and doing the fun-filled things Texas boys do so easily. Now he truly appreciated how special those times were. Suddenly he stopped, turned in mid-stride, and ran back to the house, his abrupt action confusing Taylor.

Justin unlocked the front door and reentered the living room. Initially his intent was to take one last look. He really couldn't explain why, but his eyes were drawn to the family portrait on the mantle, taken during Easter break his freshmen year at Texas A&M. Taylor followed his brother and watched as he took the eight-by-ten picture from its frame.

"Taylor, this was a happy time, and no, darn it, I'll never forget." He placed the photo gently into his knapsack.

Then, he began to thank God for this day and its opportunity. After all, he reasoned, he was alive. Taylor knelt with him in silence on the living room floor. Justin prayed openly, something he hadn't done in a while.

"Dear Lord, please watch over our scattered family and let us live through this journey to see the freedom and independence we desire for this troubled land. And please, Lord, let Taylor and me always do what's good and right in your eyes." Justin stood up, took one last, longing look, and left the room. Taylor was not far behind.

Justin slammed the door and checked its lock. This time he did not look back. Taylor watched him from a few feet away, noting the new determination in Justin's step. Both men remained quiet, respectful of each other's feelings as they walked past their worthless borrowed Jeep, not knowing what lay ahead. For the moment they were two Rebel brothers walking side by side, stepping confidently into their future.

With lessened concern for the past, they walked north toward Celina to recover their Humvee. If need be, they'd commandeer a ride, but for now their legs would provide transport. Rebel officers seldom enjoyed the privileges that Federal officers took for granted—Rebel success was needed for that comfort.

Sunday morning had the quiet veneer of a warm spring day, except in Prosper it was just another day of the week in another forgotten city and battlefield.

Walking past Prosper High School's sports field, Justin observed, "The grass needs cutting."

"Hey, Justin, you thinking what I'm thinking?"

"Not sure I know where you're coming from, Bro."

"Well, Justy, old boy," Taylor snickered, "I was thinking of that day you struck out four times, right there across the street, all the time trying to impress a girl. Who was it then—Joan, Bess, Annie? You always had too many girls to impress."

"You're jealous, and anyway, you would go and remember that day, you Federal ass-kissing Rebel. It seems, I recall, you struck out a few more times than me in your career, and you didn't have a pretty girl watching to make you all nervous. And for your information, dumbass, it was none of those girls. It was only one girl, Angela Michaels, that I was trying to impress. She sure was a looker. I wonder what's happened to her."

"Pitchers aren't supposed to be as good at hitting as center fielders." Taylor snapped.

Justin laughed and gazed up at the peaceful sky. He felt good, for the moment; he was happy to be away from his post only a hundred miles north. Like old times, he and Taylor bantered back and forth like brothers should.

Justin's brief reverie was interrupted by Taylor's excited shout. "Justin, there's a truck coming. Let's stop it."

They waved the truck to a halt. The driver slammed his brakes, unwilling to take a chance with two heavily armed Ranger officers standing in the middle of the road.

"We need a ride to Celina, Soldier. Our vehicle broke down."

The driver, a militia private, saluted smartly from his truck seat and spoke nervously, "I can make room Lieutenant, General, Sirs, jump in and welcome."

May 20, 2020—Celina, Republic of Texas

Sergeant Rodgers looked up from his desk, surprised to see the two Ranger officers returning so soon. He stood at attention listening to Taylor's request to see Captain Long, but his concerned look alerted Justin that something was wrong. The sergeant reached for his crutch and led them to Captain Long's office. It appeared less cluttered than at their first encounter.

The Northcutts approached Captain Long. He acknowledged them and then offered them seats. "What can I do for you today, General? Didn't you have at least a couple more days leave before we were to see you?"

Justin responded, "Yes, Captain, we did, but circumstance dictates a return earlier than planned. We've come for transportation to our unit. Has our Humvee returned?"

"Sir, it hasn't left yet."

Infuriated, Justin stormed, "What do you mean, it hasn't left? Captain, an explanation is in order."

"Sir, if I may, most of the men in this post are walking wounded and invalids. We have few able-bodied men. Orders require two personnel to deliver the packet. I've been working on doing just that, as well as finding enough diesel fuel to make it to the front."

"That's horseshit, Captain. You mean to tell me you couldn't come up with two men from a whole goddamned brigade? You were entrusted with this assignment, and I'll have your head before this is through. You'll be reporting to buck privates when I'm finished." Justin's fury was only beginning.

"I'm sorry, Sir, but I did the best I could with what's been given me to work with. We need every man we have, and there are so few 'complete' men at this post."

"Where's the courier packet?" snapped Justin.

"I have it secure in the HQ safe, Sir."

Justin's anger was not restrained. He slammed a fist on Long's desk, scattering papers just as he had during his first visit, and rattled off his request. "I suggest you get it, the necessary fuel, a rocket launcher, a machine gun mount with a .50 caliber machine gun, and one whole man to accompany the Lieutenant and me. I want it all here within the hour. Am I clear, Captain?"

"Yes, Sir, it'll be done." Long almost wet his pants in fear. He leaped up, stopping at Sergeant Rodger's desk to give instructions before leaving the building, wondering all the while if this crazy Ranger general would carry out his threat. Rodgers left shortly thereafter, limping and in a hurry.

In truth, Long had only half-carried out Justin's orders, figuring the Rangers would not return to Celina until the next day. Then he could truthfully say the Humvee had not returned. His plan envisioned them finding replacement transportation, leaving the Humvee at his disposal—spoils of war. Usable vehicles were difficult to come by. *Damn, I hope I won't be demoted. Rank, even in this wretched unit, means a lot to me.* Rank gave him power, something he had never enjoyed in his meager civilian job working for an accounting firm.

Lieutenant Jackson arrived, saluting the Ranger officers as he entered the HQ. Rodgers had found him in the mess hall. Long's office and its drab walls served to underline the poor condition of the Celina command.

"Sirs, I hear you're back early," Ed remarked with a knowing smile.

Justin, too angry to reply, ignored the lieutenant, but Taylor, happy to see a friendly face, quickly figured that Jackson might be able to update them on the location of Becky's unit. Taylor reached out his hand and grasped Jackson's firmly.

"Good to see you again, Jackson. Is there some way you can determine where Becky's unit is? I believe it's the 77th."

"Actually, Taylor, after you left yesterday, we had a supply truck come through. It dropped off another invalid replacement. He said the 77th is in Denton at the high school campus."

Taylor beamed. "That's good news. Maybe with some luck, we can pay her a visit. It should be on our way. We decided to volunteer to deliver the courier pouch."

"I heard. That's why I'm here. Long sent for me. I suppose there'll be hell to pay." Jackson knew Justin's intensity and didn't feel sorry for his captain.

"You've got that right; I don't appreciate my brother's order not being followed. I hope your captain's ass gets fried." Taylor deliberately snarled as he spoke.

Jackson was taken aback by Taylor's openness, not knowing what to say. On the one hand, he was talking to friends and fellow officers from his old unit. On the other, the captain could make his life miserable. He decided to keep his mouth shut.

"Jackson, screw reporting to Captain Long," Justin demanded. Long, just entering the headquarters, could not miss hearing Justin's remarks. "I'm ordering you to take us to your commanding officer.

What's his name?" Justin's anger was boiling. He no longer had any patience, and he needed results.

"Colonel Lewis, General. Please follow me." Jackson, still a Ranger at heart, was not ready to disobey a superior's direct order.

Justin and Taylor entered Colonel Lewis's outer office. It was just a shade less drab than the captain's. Lewis, overhearing the lieutenant introduce the Ranger officers to his staff sergeant, came to his office doorway. "Good to see you, General Northcutt, it's been a while since A&M."

Justin returned Lewis's left-handed salute. He hadn't immediately placed his old acquaintance and would never have recognized him in any case. Along with a missing right arm, the right side of the colonel's face was badly disfigured. *God! Will Taylor or I end up in one of these miserable ambulatory units? Will we be lucky enough to survive, unharmed?* Silently he preferred death.

Forcing the unpleasant idea aside, he spoke. "How're things going with you, John, or do you prefer to remain formal?"

"Screw formalities, Justin. What brings you here?"

Justin sat down, not waiting for an invitation from the colonel. "I thought it'd be a good idea to fill you in on some problems in your command. I know I'd want to know about any bad eggs in my unit. I suppose you'd feel likewise. While it's not my place to overstep you at this post, I figured you'd want your own opportunity to correct things." Justin carefully explained his experience, sparing no details.

After listening to Justin's complaint, Colonel Lewis stood, reached across the desk with his left hand and said, "I apologize for the mess up, Justin, and appreciate your willingness to deliver the dispatch and take it off my hands. You'll have what you need, and I'll handle the captain."

Motioning, he turned his direction to Lieutenant Jackson. "Jackson, check how far Captain Long's gotten on the general's request, then see to completing it yourself. Place one of our MPs at General Northcutt's disposal. Advise Captain Long he's to report to me at once. Wait for a moment while I say my goodbyes."

Turning back to the Rangers, showing the strain of command, Colonel Lewis gave the visible sigh of a man who has seen too much.

"Justin, you understand, for the record, I'll need to write up orders transferring the detail. I hear you hope to look up your sister. Say hello for me when you see her."

"Thank you, John, I will. Do whatever you need to do."

Lewis remembered Becky with fondness. He had met her many times when she'd visited Justin with her parents at College Station. She was a bubbly teenager, seeming to enjoy her brother's college friends. He remembered how Justin, acting the big brother, was always so damn protective of her. Now he wondered in dismay if she would give him a second glance. Feeling sorry for his bad luck, but not showing it, Lewis looked at Justin and Taylor, commenting sincerely, "Thanks for retaking this mission, gentlemen, and good luck. I need to make arrangements to cover what we just discussed. I'd better get on it, with your permission."

Justin waived his agreement to end the meeting.

Returning to formalities, Lewis addressed Lieutenant Jackson with further instructions. Jackson saluted and turned as smartly as he could without two good legs, leaving the tense room to do his colonel's bidding.

Justin noted Lewis's handshake remained firm and was gladdened. Quietly, Justin was electrified at the thought of seeing action again. At the same time he also felt dread.

Outside the HQ building, he turned and whispered to Taylor, "It sure looks like we're about to return to war, brother. Are you ready?"

Taylor, suddenly serious, answered, "As ready as I ever was, General. Battlefields have been our only home these past several months, and it seems we've already had a lifetime's worth of fighting. I suppose this is the proper thing to tell a general, even if he's my brother and full of shit. I'm ready. But as your little brother, and my blunt true self, I'm not really looking forward to it. If it's assurance that you're looking for, I can't give it. Sorry."

Taylor pointed to the Rebel flag, high on its pole about twenty yards off. "Justin, my enthusiasm right now is about as limp as that flag on this stifling, still day."

Justin did not comment; rather, he chose to change the subject. "Lieutenant, I seem to recall it was you who took me up on my desire to return to duty before our appointed time."

"Rub it in, General, rub it in!" Taylor said jokingly, but as he looked at his brother, a stern look crossed his face, arousing Justin's interest. "Oh, by the way, when do you think an adjutant to a general can become a captain? If I die for the cause, I'd like to die a bit higher in rank. It's the snob in me, you know."

"Oh … let me see," Justin paused, enjoying teasing Taylor since it was a rare opportunity to top him. "I was thinking that a sergeant would be the rank I needed to follow me around like a hound dog instead of a meddling lieutenant, especially one from UT. I suppose a captain, though overkill, might do. Where do you suppose I might find an adequate captain, Lieutenant? Do you know of any?"

"Give it a rest, General," Taylor pleaded, sorry he had brought up the subject.

"OK, *Captain*! Have it your way. I was going to wait until we rejoined our post to announce your promotion. But I'll tell you now instead. I'll handle the formalities after we return to the front."

Justin pulled a box from his fatigue pocket containing captain's bars he'd been saving. He handed them to Taylor, who had a suppressed, cocky smile glowing on his face. "Here, pin my old bars on and make it official." Justin saluted his brother and then passed over the shiny bars. "I still want my little brother to get his due at our HQ. You earned it, Taylor, not because you're my brother. You're a damn good officer."

Lieutenant Jackson arrived to advise that all was ready. Noticing the change of rank on Taylor's uniform, Jackson smiled and saluted his acknowledgement.

Introducing Corporal Rhodes as their temporary gunner, Jackson went over the details of his successful salvaging mission. "General, the Humvee is fueled and ready, including a mounted .50 caliber machine gun and rocket launcher with five rockets stowed in the back, as requested."

Looking at his watch, Justin noted only fifty minutes had elapsed since he had given his order. He happily said to Taylor, "Let's get something to eat and roll out in thirty minutes!"

Taylor stepped forward to shake his friend's hand. "Thank you, Jackson. Both you and Rhodes meet us back here in thirty, so we can go over the equipment."

Jackson, saluting the Ranger officers, said, "Taylor, I hope you get to see Becky. If you do, please send my regards."

Four MPs walked by with Captain Long in custody. Justin saw them but said nothing.

Taylor, who was not of the same mind, wasted no time. "Looks like John didn't let any dust settle on that turkey. I hope he's broken down to private and sent to our unit."

"No, Taylor, I don't have any use for the son of a bitch. He'd only manage to get good men killed." Justin abruptly turned, walking across the street to the officer's mess.

Taylor, shaking his head in consternation, ran to catch up with his brother, hunger replacing his desire for revenge.

Vision, when 20/20, is considered a blessing. Clarity into the dark reaches of the future could be a curse.
— Jim Damiano

CHAPTER SEVEN

May 6, 2020—Adirondack Mountains, near Tupper Lake, New York

Rock opened the cabin's back door to a new day, inhaling brisk mountain air to clear his mind and focus on something, anything, other than the burning pain he felt in his arm. The sky's darkening hue gave notice of an impending change in the weather. Cloud patterns entwined in darkened fringes, framing the beauty of the place like a fine painting. Towering blue spruce trees swayed in the wind, their branches reaching out in majestic dance. The day was a poem waiting to be written. But Rock did not feel the poet.

Vic's wounds would take several days to heal, and only if Rock could get him medical attention. The bullet had passed through his right leg. Gangrene lurked in the shadows. Rock applied his minimal knowledge along with the sparse rudimentary supplies he carried. Vic needed more. The cabin contained no first aid supplies, and the marauder's vehicle provided only a little bourbon and rubbing alcohol. Vic had slept through the night in a deep stupor, thanks to the bourbon.

Rock figured he'd better bury the dead before the weather changed. He must get them under dirt before they began to rot, and more importantly, while he still had energy. He opened the front door and, feeling his age, gingerly walked down the stone porch steps. He wished there was some bourbon left.

The old tool shed was a few feet from the house, nestled on the edge of a clearing. Rock had seen shovels there on an earlier search. With some luck he'd get the bodies buried before the pending rain.

Rock decided to stay here until Vic healed or, worse, died. Then he planned to return south towards Utica to scout things out, hoping to see if it was safe.

The shed was overflowing, but organized. Like him, the missing owners appeared to be meticulous creatures of habit. He surmised they were in their late sixties from pictures he had seen in the house. He hoped they had escaped to a safe haven.

Rock had heard that many New Yorkers had taken refuge in Canada. Those fortunate to have friends or relations there appeared to be welcomed openly by what remained of the disorganized Canadian government, which was having problems in their province of Quebec. All others were turned back at the border. Some refugees were rumored to have been jailed or even shot. Rock felt this was nothing but a ruse concocted by the Canadian government to scare off would-be exiles.

Canada prospered from the unfortunate state of affairs of its southern neighbor. Its commerce flourished with each sale of exorbitantly priced war supplies to anxious Rebels. Some even speculated that the Canadians were in league with the Federals, but it was only speculation.

Rock singled out a well-worn spade and a pickaxe. They would do. After all, he didn't plan on digging any deep holes. His painfully burning arm would prevent any such notions. He planned to give them a Christian burial, but no more than would serve to keep wild animals, and more importantly, the smell, away. Natural terrain provided plenty of rocks to serve his intention. The pain in his arm increased with every movement when he began to work. He dreaded the thought of moving the bodies.

It was by chance that Rock looked up. There, framed in the changing sky, the hawk he had seen earlier appeared, soaring freely. Rock never failed to stare in wonder at a hawk's graceful flight, high above life's turmoil, seemingly looking down upon man's ceaseless plodding and plotting. It gave him courage to continue shoveling through his pain.

The bodies were strewn across the clearing, frozen in their last grasp at life. Vultures had to be scattered, their nasty work evident. He wrapped a cloth around his face, but it didn't reduce the rancid smell. He noted they were beginning to deteriorate; rigor mortis had set in. The moss-covered ground was soft, making the sandy soil easy to dig. Despite this unexpected luxury, each shovelful caused a sharp pain. Digging ambitiously only caused it to worsen. After about an hour of toil, he had dug a satisfactory six-by-eight-foot trench about three feet deep. Another half foot or so and he'd drag the five bodies to their mass burial. It'd be tight, but his strength couldn't hold out much longer. In his fatigue he didn't give a damn.

Rock forced himself to think pleasantries to keep his mind from his gruesome work. Each shovelful, though, brought more anger his way, forcing him to relive the horrible moments of the previous day. He wondered at how abruptly life can change in a second's flash. One moment you're in hiding, safe and content; the next you're fighting for your life. He looked at the five lifeless bodies. This unmarked mass grave at the edge of nowhere emphasized his point.

Dragging the dead with difficulty, one by one, he laid each in tight formation in the hole—it was not pretty work. The smell choked him, temporarily taking his attention away from the searing pain. In frightful flashes, Rock remembered a similar work detail fifty years earlier in 'Nam. Life wasn't worth much there, either. Back then, all high command seemed to care about was the body count of the Gooks, as the GIs disparagingly called the Viet Cong. Their burials, if done at all, were inconsequential.

Then his mind shifted to more current affairs, and he chuckled. *Would the environmentalists approve of my work? I wonder how they are stopping this war from hurting the environment.* Rock caught himself. This wasn't humorous, so why was he laughing almost hysterically? Perhaps he was going crazy in his advanced years. Finally, the last mangled body fit with lucky precision in the remaining space. Rock got an old blue tarp from the shed, covered the bodies, and rolled several rocks on top of the tarp. *Almost done.* He gave a deep moan as mounting pain radiated throughout his body. He shoveled the dirt and leveled it with the shovel. Then he spread the nearby moss as ground cover, trying to make it difficult to see its disturbance. A little over three hours had passed.

Rock walked down to the driveway, covering and washing away the blood from the first two dead men. He emptied the vehicle, removing the few valuables into the cabin, hiding the weapons and ammo in the basement. He gathered the tools and headed toward the shed just in time to see a military column winding with slow precision up the mountain road.

Oh shit, he thought. *Someone's bound to see that damn Humvee in the drive, and it's bound to raise curiosity.*

The column, too far away to determine if it was Federal or Rebel, flew no flags or familiar emblems. And since most Rebel vehicles were stolen, confiscated, or taken from Federal forces, they gave no clue to the unit's identity.

Rock quickly placed the tools in their proper place in deference to their owner and walked as fast as his tired old legs could take him to the temporary safety of the cabin. Rock preferred to avoid a confrontation. Moving was the only wise thing to do in his estimation. It would be difficult, but he must rouse Vic, gather what he could, and get into the deep woods to hide. Rock's well-planned escape proved fruitless. The column's scouts had already seen the cabin, and its advance vehicle appeared before Rock could take a deep breath.

Rock knew it would not do any good to hide. Taking the next best course, he somehow summoned his strength and walked out onto the front porch, both hands held high, acknowledging their presence and his vulnerability. His eyes focused on the briskly waving Rebel standards fluttering on their perch on the lead vehicle's front fender, and on the young sergeant with his gun at the ready.

"Whose vehicle is this, old man?" he shouted.

"Not mine, Sergeant. Some marauders thought they could get the best of Rock Rinaldi and his grandson. They found out they were wrong."

"Where in the hell are they now, old man?"

Rock waved his good arm in the direction of the marauders' mass grave, pointing up the hill, deciding quickly to tell the truth. Silently, he hoped it might protect them from a quick execution if the sergeant thought him a marauder, too.

"Wait a minute! Did you say your name's Rinaldi? Do you have a son in the Rebel forces, old man?"

"As a matter of fact, I do. My son and two grandsons are in the First New York. And stop calling me old man, goddamn it!"

"Sorry, Sir. But you're in luck, Mr. Rinaldi." The young MP sergeant's voice turned friendly and polite, though guarded.

"How's that?" Rock queried.

"Well, Sir, your grandson, Sergeant James Rinaldi, is but a half mile from here, down at the column."

Rock couldn't believe his good fortune, but then he figured he was long overdue. Now, if he could just convince them Vic had always been with him.

Rock, with practiced calm, shouted to the sergeant. "What's your name, son?"

"Jerry, Sir, Sergeant Jerry Tomasi, of the First New York Volunteers, 121st Division, 7th Regiment, Company N, Scouts. I'm from Utica."

"I say, Sergeant, you are a sight for sore eyes. James's brother Vic is in the house. He's badly wounded from our fight with the marauders. I'm hit too, but I'll live. I sure hope you've got medics with you."

"That we do, Sir." Tomasi turned, "Corporal Hanna, get down to the column. Report what we've seen and get permission for Sergeant Rinaldi to come on the double to I.D. his grandpa and brother."

"Got yah, Sergeant. Anything else?"

"Yes, see if you can get a doc or a medic up here, pronto."

Turning to face the cabin porch, the young sergeant said, "Now, Mr. Rinaldi, we'll just wait, but for the heck of it, please show Private Vickers where this here mass grave is."

Rock showed him the spot. It was evident that the ground had been displaced. After hearing Private Vickers' report, Tomasi asked Rock to explain how it was that two men managed to kill all five of the marauders.

"We were just lucky, I suppose. We both got hit, but hiding in the woods on familiar ground was to our advantage and their downfall."

"Sir," Tomasi asked, "were you ever in the military?"

"Yep—saw action in Vietnam, though I try to forget it. It wasn't a favorite time in my life. The last day or two has brought back horrible memories that I thought I'd put behind me."

"Grandpa!" James's shout could be heard a mile away as he ran up to Rock and hugged him, lifting him off the ground. Rock's eyes misted as he took in his grandson. James looked leaner and taller than when he last saw him. His eyes were familiar, though not in a family way. He'd seen those same eyes years ago. They were the eyes of a man forced to see horror and its awesome terror. It was surely more than God intended.

"Jimmy, how are your dad and your brothers?" Silently, he wondered if James knew about his mother's death.

"Grandpa," James said, and looked away as if to avoid the hurt. "Billy was killed a few days ago in the battle for Utica." James felt his grandfather's pain and saw it turn to tears in the old man's eyes. "I guess you know that Mom died a few days before Bill. Was it you who buried her?"

"Yes." Rock thought upon his daughter-in-law Betty's needless death. How would he lessen the pain for her son? "I guess her heart couldn't take life anymore, Jimmy. I'm so sorry." He wiped a tear from his withered face. "Is your dad OK?"

"Don't know. He's somewhere with the First—haven't seen him in weeks. We're heading to the border. I expect he's up ahead. I don't think that he knows Mom and Billy are dead."

"I hope Joe's OK; I don't think I can take another death." Rock's love for his only son pushed him to believe he was alive. It was all he could manage for the moment.

Acknowledging the need to pull everything together and go on existing, Rock's old war experience took charge. Right now he had at least two grandsons alive. He must remain alert to their needs and while he was at it, keep praying for Luke's safety.

"Jimmy, your brother Vic's in the house. We fought and killed a group of bandits yesterday belonging to that vehicle in the drive. He's hurt bad and needs attention. If he doesn't get it soon, he'll probably die. I did all I could. Now it's up to your people."

Smiling, James fondly squeezed Rock's uninjured shoulder, then rushed past him into the cabin, shouting Vic's name.

Vic had been listening to the banter through the old home's thick walls. He was too weak to go to the window to listen. When he heard and then saw his brother, he didn't know what to expect. He hadn't seen James in months. Did James know he was a marauder? He waited in baited silence as his brother knelt at the couch that served as his bed.

James grasped his younger brother's hand in his, smiling. "You're in good hands, Vic. Help's on the way. Damn it, I'm sure happy to see you, Runt. It's been too long. We've got a lot of catching up to do."

"Jimmy, I'm sorry for being such an idiot, for hurting Ma. Such a damn fool ..." Vic's voice trailed off. He was white as a sheet and had fallen unconscious.

James instantly understood he may have found his brother too late. He'd always suspected that Vic's vocation might be unsavory, but for right now he'd play it by ear and keep quiet.

Later in the early evening, Vic's pale features announced his dire condition to the Rebel doctor's keen eyes long before he gave his official diagnosis. Vic's pulse was low and his chance of survival slim. Mass infection appeared to have settled in, and large doses of medication would be needed to keep him alive. The drugs were available, but according to the doctor, it might be too late. Vic needed to be in a hospital, and the column was leaving. The doctor felt moving Vic would be the same as signing his death warrant, so with some reservation he left a small but adequate supply of antibiotics, some morphine, and a list of instructions for Rock. He also treated Rock's wound and gave him antibiotics and medication to stave off infection.

"Remember, don't let him get up for a couple of days, and then for no more than five minutes at a time to relieve himself. It's imperative for him to build up his strength."

"I read you, Doc. Will he make it?"

"Mr. Rinaldi, he's young, in fair shape, and his will to live is strong. I feel he has a very good chance. If he does live, I strongly suggest you talk some sense into him or all my good work will be for nothing."

Rock looked at the doctor with new eyes, reached out his good arm, and grasped his hand in thanks. "I appreciate all you've done, Captain, and thank you for your directions and advice." Rock's wizened smile was returned in kind.

James stood close by listening to the exchange, keeping his own counsel, well aware of the doctor's suspicions. A healthy young man Vic's age was usually in the army, a deserter, or a marauder. It didn't take a genius to figure out which category Vic was in. Vic's semi-believable story, according to Rock, was that he had been looking out for his elderly grandfather, aiding him in his journey to safety, before he joined the Rebel Army and the rest of his Rebel family.

"Grandpa, I must catch up with my unit. We're heading for borderguard duty somewhere near Plattsburg. When Vic heals, try to talk him into joining my unit as a recruit. He'll live longer as a soldier than a marauder. And Grandpa, please think about this; your many talents are valuable to the cause. There are quite a few older vets from your war in our division. They're not in the field fighting but serve in valuable areas behind the scenes, planning strategy, plotting, and working in supply. Your grocer's profession, your strong historical background, and your overall know-how would sure be helpful. And your knowledge of these mountains would be especially helpful."

James's smile warmed Rock's weariness. He looked fondly at his eldest grandson, feeling a pang of sorrow. It could be their last goodbye. "I'll give it some thought, Jimmy. You're right, though. It's not like I have Rinaldi's Italian Grocery to run any longer or a house to keep up. The last time I looked, the store was ransacked and my house burned." Rock's eyes trailed off as a small tear fell. "But, you know, Grandson, stores and houses are replaceable things. What's most important are the things we do and what good we leave behind. I'll consider what you say, if these old bones allow. You can count on it."

"Grandpa, you're in better shape than half my men. Hell, you're fifty or more years older than most of them. When this freaking war is over, you can count on me, if the Lord lets me, to help put a roof over your head. So please be careful and look me up when you can. More importantly, though, kick some sense into my wayward brother once he heals."

"I will, don't worry. I'll influence the little pain. He's a good kid. He'll listen. I'll send him to you, even if I have to drag him."

With the column's departure imminent, it was time to say his goodbyes to James—and to the bandits' Humvee. "I'm sorry you'll have to walk, Grandpa, but my corporal brought you three week's rations. I better go. I love you, Grandpa."

Sensing his grandson's discomfort about leaving him, Rock tried to put his fears to rest. "Thanks for the food, Jimmy. I can still hunt, so we won't starve. I love you too, Grandson. You be careful."

"You can count on that. I'll try to send a message if we have a courier coming in this direction. I doubt I can ever get away to visit. It's about seventy miles to where we're headed and we don't seem to ever stay put anywhere very long."

"You don't need to explain war to me, Jimmy. Don't worry." Rock hugged James. Watching him leave, he reflected that James looked every bit the soldier. He had no doubt he was a good sergeant, though surprised he wasn't an officer. Jimmy had always been a reluctant leader, a shy, quiet, intense boy. He would lead eventually even if he chose otherwise, for it came naturally to him and those around him felt it. Rock knew James never fully understood his abilities: always a thinker and plotter, traits critical for war. A good commander would no doubt recognize this strength in good time.

Rock watched the column disappear into the distant mountains. Walking into the house he spoke aloud. "Me, a soldier again? No damn way!" Rock laughed at himself and at the thought. In 'Nam, he couldn't wait until he got out of the army, counting the days and minutes, praying to live through the terrible, jungle-rotting, dirty experience. But back then he had a young wife to return home to. For now, he'd nurse Vic back to health.

Then suddenly, with the swiftness of a raging storm, Rock realized he had a purpose and a good cause; he decided to take James's suggestion and see if the Rebels wanted his service. *Well, maybe I can be of help with supply. After all, I am a grocer. Living like a hermit has its disadvantages; it does give little value to my existence, though. There's little to lose, even if I have to peel potatoes.* He felt good about things for the first time in months. He felt needed again, and that pleased him.

x x x x x

Later the next day, Rock confronted Vic with his decision. Vic's response was predictable, especially from a boy who'd been living in selfish abandon for the last two years.

"Grandpa, don't be a fool. You won't survive. You know how cold the North Country gets, even this time of year. It's tough enough for men forty years younger than you." But deep down Vic knew it was futile to argue with Rock once his mind was set. If Vic inherited anything from his grandfather, it was his persistent and stubborn disposition.

Rock walked over to Vic's bed. "Look, Vic, I understand your concern. Sometimes there are things a man must do, no matter the cost. This is one of those times. And you, Grandson, need to wake up. How long do you think you'll last leading the life of a bandit? We're going to be forced to put up with each other for a few days 'til you heal up, and I intend to convince you to change, even if I have to kill you to do it. I'm going to join, and I'd like you to come with me. Your brothers' unit is made up mostly of boys from Utica. Fighting for freedom with those boys will do us both good!"

"You're sure about this, Grandpa?"

"Yes, I'm sure about it, and about you. Remember when you were a boy and I used to take you and your brothers to the historical sites around our state?"

"How could I forget? It was one of the best times I had as a kid. I never cared much about history, but loved being with you. You made it come to life for me. Why?"

"Remember how I'd talk about the historical significance of this place or that battle, and you'd always ask, 'Why does it matter, Grandpa?' "

Vic looked up from his bed, a smile upon his face. "Yep. You'd say, 'We study the past to learn, not only about what's happened, but also to learn from our mistakes and from our victories too.' And you said history sometimes has a way of repeating itself."

"Well, I'll be damned, you were listening after all. I'm proud of you, Vic. And that's exactly why I must do this. It seems our nation didn't learn from its past and some things never really change. They just repeat and this is what's happened to our country. The same damn mistakes made by the British, before our first revolution, have been made again by the government I once served and defended. It causes us to find ourselves right here, right now, in the middle of a conflict that no one can avoid. So I figure it's time to join in and do my part, however small, so that my family someday will enjoy the real freedom I once knew."

"You know, Grandpa, I remember the infamous letter to the editor you wrote to the Utica paper a few years ago. I never read it; it was too damn long, and you know how I hate to read. But it sure stirred up Dad. He was worried that you went too far. I even recall him saying that your day in the paper had made life miserable in some of his classes."

Rock laughed aloud. More so because he was surprised that Vic had paid any attention to his ill-fated attempt at freedom of speech and pontification. He looked directly at Vic. "Joe's always been a worrier. But he was wrong. Nobody paid attention to it, least of all his students. Shit, most of them are like you when it comes to history. They're just occupying a seat to get a grade and forgetting everything once they leave the classroom. Anyway, it was over most people's heads. They just figured me for a complainer and a windbag, though your grandma would say that they were partially correct, as far as the windbag statement." Rock chuckled at the memory of his sweet Rose. How he missed her.

"Hell, if anyone gave my editorial a passing glance, it was only that. I figure it was used to line the bottom of birdcages more than anything else. I'm pleasantly surprised you even remembered that I wrote a political piece."

"Oh, I remember. Not any of the content, only the excitement surrounding the letter. It appears you can now say, 'I told you so,' to me at least. You don't think much of the average citizen, do you, Grandpa?"

"No, as a matter of fact, I don't. It's been the indifference of the average citizen that's gotten us to this place in our history and most likely to the end of a great country. I often wish I wasn't so goddamned right. You know it's a burden sometimes to be able to look into the future. Being a student of history can drive you crazy if you let it because in truth you can't control anything. We see the parallels where others see only newscasts and media bias. I can get on my soap box and talk endlessly, but it'd only bore you."

"Not really, Grandpa, go ahead and bore me."

"You're tired and need to rest, but you can sleep on this if you're searching for a valid reason. When special interest groups and lobbyists got so firmly planted in our political system, people began to lose interest in their right to vote. The country got some pretty poor excuses for candidates and elected officials. People began to realize that it didn't matter who they voted into office because the politicians all turned out the same. When this happened, the elected politicians, those damn leeches and mistaken servants of the people, once in power, exercised a limitless ability to manipulate. Unfortunately, this has happened frequently in the last twenty years. People began to think that their vote was a total waste of time. It didn't matter if they were Democrats or Republicans. I could go on but since we'll have several days to spend together, we'll have a lot of time to talk and ruminate."

Vic pulled his body, trying to sit up in bed, but he couldn't manage. Rock motioned for him to lie still. He forced himself to speak slowly. "Grandpa, you give me no course," he winced when he moved. "I will follow you and look out for you after I heal. I suppose I'll have to join my brothers' Rebel cause just so my conscience won't be compromised in worry over you. It can't be any worse than what I've been doing."

Still Vic hoped his statement would slow Rock's determination. Instead, he saw once again that bright, beautiful smile he remembered most about his grandfather.

Rock, very pleased, didn't hesitate to show it by giving Vic a very careful hug, ruffling his black hair. Nothing more needed saying to bridge the two generations. Vic now had a solid reason to heal quickly and Rock had his motivation to go on. War is a strange bedfellow. It was no exception for the Rinaldi family.

Looking at the moonlit northern sky, James was trying to say a prayer. Words came hard. He gave up and slowly returned to his tent. Once there, he lay restless on his sleeping bag. Worry about his family hung heavy upon his mind, making needed sleep an impossible task. He tried to wipe away all thought but found it impossible. Leaving his shelter he went out to check sentry posts. It was better to stay occupied. No matter how hard he tried, though, he could not erase his fear for the living or his grief for the dead.

In the distance, James heard the hoot of an owl. Its call seemed to warn him of some unknown, an eerie unknown he'd rather not contemplate.

Ideas are like stars; you will not succeed in touching them with your hands, but ... you choose them as guides and following them, reach your destination.

—Carl Schurz

CHAPTER EIGHT

May 20, 2020—Celina, Republic of Texas

The Humvee was parked in front of HQ under heavy guard. Newly promoted Captain Taylor Northcutt surveyed an old but dependable .50-caliber machine gun mounted on the roof and an additional five-gallon can of diesel fuel strapped to the rear bumper. Unseasonably warm, the cloudless day would not offer the best conditions to travel open roads with the skies still owned by Federal pilots.

"Captain Northcutt, Corporal Rhodes reporting back for special guard duty, as ordered, Sir," Rhodes saluted.

"Carry on, Corporal. Check our fifty. I'll see about the gun mounting."

Justin, carrying the dispatches, briskly walked down the HQ steps. Colonel Lewis, walking with difficulty, slowly followed behind.

At the bottom of the stair, Lewis addressed Justin. "Be careful, General. I've just received a report advising the sky's active with Feds today."

"Thanks for the heads up, Colonel. We'll keep to the trees where possible. With Corporal Rhodes watching the skies, we'll be OK."

Sergeant Rodgers limped to the Humvee, his load heavy. He carried a hand-held missile launcher and four rounds. "That's all I could find, Sir. Let's hope you don't need them."

Taylor, happy to see the launcher, gave a nod of agreement. Looking directly into Rodgers' eyes, he said with a smirk, "You're not so bad after all, Sergeant, thanks."

"Watch your backside, Sir. Sorry we got off on the wrong foot." Rodgers reached out his hand in friendship.

"All's forgiven, Sergeant. You take care," said Taylor. He put a friendly hand on Rodger's shoulder as he turned to speak to Justin.

"General, from what Colonel Lewis said, we'll have Corporal Rhodes glued to the fifty."

The three men climbed into the Humvee. Taylor took the wheel, Justin sat shotgun, and Rhodes perched up by the fifty. The cab's interior was intense with the built-up heat of the day.

Leaving Celina's historic square, Justin turned to Taylor. "What do you think, Captain, take Old Preston Road?" Justin rolled down his window. It didn't help.

"I believe it's best, Sir. Surveillance advises that the enemy continues to patrol Old Highway 75 and the Dallas-Oklahoma toll way. We might be sitting ducks if we take the easier route. And don't forget, refugees flood most roads going south, so I suggest we make it a slow twenty-to-thirty miles per hour to preserve our fuel and allow reaction time to any altercation."

"That seems like a good plan, Taylor. Any suggestions you'd like to add, Corporal Rhodes?"

"None, Sir." Rhodes wasn't about to express his opinion to a general. He was old regular U. S. Army and not used to the casual Ranger behavior. He'd heard they were a bit loose on decorum; now he saw it firsthand.

Justin turned, shouting at Rhodes' legs. His body protruded through the roof as he manned the machine gun. "For the record, Corporal, we're a bit less formal than you may be used to. This will probably be an all-day trip or even longer, so you're commanded to be at ease. You may have heard that the Ranger bite is worse than its bark. We still believe in the spirit of the old Ranger axiom—each man is expected to be a leader, if he sees an opportunity for the good of the unit."

Rhodes pulled his whole body into the cab to give full attention to Justin.

"That's better, Rhodes. Sorry, I should have realized you couldn't hear me, even with us going so damn slow. To repeat, in the Rangers every man from private to general is an individual. As such, each Ranger must always perform in the best interest of their unit. So while with us, you're expected to use your own judgment. Am I clear, Corporal?"

"Yes ... General, Sir ... very clear, and thank you." Rhodes stuttered when nervous. "In that case, Sir ... " Rhodes was not sure how to take Justin, but his instincts told him to go with his heart, " ... I believe your plan to go twenty-five-to-thirty miles per hour is a bit ambitious."

"How's that, Rhodes?"

"There's massive damage on the roads north. The Feds destroyed everything in their retreat, Sir. I suspect we'll find craters and no bridges most of the way, with the road crowded with refugees."

"Thanks, Corporal." Justin returned his attention to Taylor, who had been listening to the exchange. "Captain, you've some rough driving ahead. Get to it."

As Rhodes had warned, Preston Road was filled with refugees, craters, and obstacles. Most refugees were Oklahomans, all heading south. Nothing pushed them harder than hopes of escaping the rage of war. Justin studied the harried faces of the tired, beaten people. They were mostly women with children, the old, or the infirm. Their familiar look of despair was a rerun of scenes he had witnessed all too often. Burdened with the weight of their paltry possessions, the masses of unsung civilian heroes moved in a never-ending line—trying to survive.

"General, I don't recall so many refugees when we came south a few days ago." Taylor let out a long, low whistle.

"I'd guess the battle for Oklahoma's gotten pretty hot to cause this exodus. Something big is happening, Taylor. Stop. I need to see what we can find out. Corporal, stay alert for anything unusual. These people are frightened enough. Make no unnecessary moves."

Taylor pulled the Humvee to a halt at the edge of the road's tarmac opposite the long line of refugees. Justin opened the door and walked across the road. He stopped by the first refugee he reached, an elderly man whose face was streaked with mud and sweat, emphasizing his weariness.

"Sir, can you give me any news of what's happening north of here?" asked Justin.

The old man eyed Justin's shoulder, noting his star and Ranger insignia, fear showing in his eyes. "General, it's all a big mess north once you cross the Red River. When I left two days ago with my daughter and her children," he nodded in their direction, "it appeared the hot spot was in Durant, our home. It was in flames, Sir." The old man's voice trembled.

Justin looked at the man's family, meekly huddled together. An old woman, probably younger in years than her unforgiving appearance suggested, stood with a younger woman of about forty. Two teenage girls, both beautiful and definitely related to both women, stood listening.

"Thank you, Sir. I don't have to tell you to be careful, but I will anyway. You should be safe once you reach Waco, but by foot, it's a long way."

"You're welcome, General. May I ask your name? Mine's J. T. McKnight. This here's my wife Dora, and our daughter Irene and her daughters—Julia, she's the oldest, and Jessica." McKnight beamed proudly at his beautiful family.

Justin nodded his hello to them, stopping short when his eyes met the captivating smile of Julia McKnight. He'd remember this dainty, green-eyed, beautiful brunette anywhere. He felt temporarily scatterbrained in her presence, though he managed to speak. "I'm Brigadier General Justin Northcutt. It's a pleasure to meet y'all. It's going to be rough on you no matter where you go. Do you have enough food? It's mighty scarce in Texas. Many people are starving."

Julia spoke then. Her words were honeyed with a dreamy smile; her voice sounded like sweet music to Justin's ears. "Sir, about all we're carrying is food and a change of clothes." She pointed to the wagon she was pulling by its handle. Roped boxes bulged over its sides, and what appeared to be an old tent was tied securely on top.

"Be careful, Miss, and good luck." Justin felt tongue-tied and confused. The young girl, no more than his sister's age, had both captured and stirred his young imagination. Slightly embarrassed, and without saying another word, he walked quickly to the Humvee. "Let's go, Taylor. I sure don't know how all these people are going to make it. Texas certainly isn't ready for them."

"Its part of the price of war we'll all pay. It's another responsibility for us to be concerned with now," Taylor responded, restarting the old diesel engine and pulling forward slowly.

"You're right, Tay. We've figured how to organize an army and keep supplies moving after a year of disaster and hard learning. We've even overcome several major defeats. Now we'll have to figure refugees into the equation. Our government's become better structured, but this'll be a real test of whether we're as good as we think we are."

Justin took another look south in the direction of the McKnight family. He wished he could do more. He sighed in silent despair at his helplessness. Her captivating smile haunted him, causing him to jump to action, and perhaps even to act his age and listen to his heart. Justin's shouting scared the hell out of Taylor. "Stop the Humvee!"

Justin opened the door and jumped from the vehicle. He ran to the old man, giving him a few K-rations from his knapsack. "Mr. McKnight, here's at least one extra meal. It's not much, Sir, but I want to help. Welcome to Texas." Justin's smile was not missed by Julia.

Running quickly behind his brother, and on seeing his purpose, Taylor returned to the Humvee to retrieve some of his rations. He had seen into Justin's heart—he seldom, if ever, missed his big brother's moods.

They made ten miles the first two hours. Obstacles appeared everywhere, and the human horde filled what little road there was left to traverse. Everywhere the blight of war showed its ugly side: destruction and terrible disarray.

Standing at the machine gun, looking out the open roof, Corporal Rhodes had a clear view of the sky. It gave him small comfort. He fully understood that a Federal chopper could come in faster than he could react. It didn't unnerve him, though.

Justin, looking ahead, shouted, "Captain, pull over, looks like the bridge is out ahead. We need to investigate how we can get through."

Corporal Rhodes, who knew the road, spoke up. "It looks like a recent problem, General. Our boys will need to get some people up here to fix it, so's we can keep the supply traffic going."

As they pulled over to the side of the road, a sentry appeared from nowhere, emerging from the brush, gun raised and aimed at Justin's chest. "Who goes there?" And what's the password?" he demanded.

Justin, seeing at least three additional rifles, quickly called out, "Zero 2000, what's up, Doc?"

"The nature of your business, please, Sir."

"Couriers, Private, for Command of Texas forces at the front. Soldier, we need fast entry through here."

"No problem, General, just pass about thirty feet to the east. You'll find a dirt road that'll go down a steep incline. Your vehicle shouldn't have any problem getting through; the water's not very high."

Justin asked, "Are there more problems you're aware of north of here?"

"No more bridges out that I know of, Sir, but watch out for heavy enemy reconnaissance and scouting parties. I'd be careful with the sentries from here on out. You'll be stopped when you least expect it, about every four to five miles or so. The boys are pretty trigger-happy right now. There's been a lot of infiltrating by the Feds, dressed in our uniforms, and since we all talk and look alike, it's hard to tell the good guys from bad."

Justin chuckled, waving to the private as they passed, thinking, if he only knew what we've seen, he wouldn't remind this Ranger about infiltrators. He'd spent several months hunting down many, and he hoped this part of his duty was behind him. He smiled and sighed deeply, thinking how old the private, about sixteen, made him feel.

Driving as directed through the creek, it became clear that any enemy coming through there would be blown to kingdom come. Two 105mm howitzers and three Bradley tanks, hidden in the bush, would make entry deadly.

"General, it looks like the Fourth Texas Volunteers occupy this sector," Rhodes yelled. He was familiar with this unit, which had done its basic training near Celina.

"Corporal, isn't this one of our Home Guard units made up of teens and elderly men from Grayson and Collin County?" Justin turned, shouting up to Rhodes standing at the roof turret.

"Yes, Sir!" Rhodes snapped smartly, forgetting his earlier directions. "Youth or old age, I wouldn't want to cross their path. This area's filled with irregulars and a few southern Oklahoman militias." Rhodes adjusted his goggles as a large ugly bug impaled itself on his face.

About five miles south of where Preston Road intersects Texas Highway 56, Taylor's sharp eyes were first to spot a rapidly approaching Apache helicopter about a mile to the north-northwest.

Rhodes, also seeing the approaching nemesis, shouted, "I think the bastard saw us!"

"That's a roger!" Taylor shouted as he roared the Humvee to the side of the road into the cover of several large live oak trees.

Taylor felt his adrenalin pumping. "I'm sure he nailed us dead on, Justin. Let's bail the hell out of here and get to cover."

Taylor grabbed the missile launcher and his backpack. Justin and Rhodes grabbed their packs and M-16s, running about fifty yards from the Humvee. The helicopter came in fast, firing two rockets, obliterating the Humvee, now a ball of flaming debris.

Justin felt for the courier packet safely over his shoulder. It was still in one piece. Everything else, except for what they carried, was gone.

Without thought, Taylor's wrath took charge. He slammed in a round and adjusted the hand-held Stinger launcher. He took dead aim at the chopper's backside exposed to his heat-seeking missile. The chopper, searching for more easy targets, exploded before its pilot or crew knew what hit them. Several nearby refugees who had been crouching in fear raised an uproarious cheer.

"Damn, Taylor," Justin shouted in excitement framed with alarm. "Good shot! But you should've let the bastards go."

"Why?" Taylor looked at his brother in disbelief.

"Because, Captain, if you'd missed the son of a bitch, we'd be burnt meat. We don't have a chance against a chopper down here with three rifles and a Stinger."

"You forgot one thing," Taylor said with a cocky air. "I never miss, so there's no sense in worrying about it now, General." He smiled. "Let me see, where do I mark a notch for a chopper on this useless launcher?"

"Captain, you're one hell of a cool bastard. You realize that?" Justin, amazed at his brother's calm under fire, didn't know what else to say.

"Yeah, General, I guess so, but I don't know what else I could've done different. Don't I have to live up to our reputation of being slap-happy, gun-toting Texans? So what's next, General?" Taylor saluted in his taunting smart-ass way, a grin from ear to ear, hiding his inner relief. His adrenalin high had slowed to a crawl as the moment's excitement drained away. He felt temporarily deflated.

Justin turned to both men, directing his answer to Taylor. "Brother, I suppose we just pick up our gear. Since you're so attached to the rocket launcher, you carry it. We need to start walking. I'd guess it's about thirty to forty miles to wherever our damn HQ is. Hopefully we'll be able to commandeer a ride."

"Oh crap!" Taylor laughed in nervous abandon. A germ of an idea hit him simultaneously with the relief he felt. "I guess most Texans aren't used to walking, so before we make it a habit, let's look up Granddad's ranch. It's not far from here, and there were at least a dozen horses the last time we were there."

"Good thinking, but better than horses, Tay, there's that John Deere Gator Granddad uses to work his property. Maybe we'll be lucky and find it. He'd never leave it where it could be seized."

Corporal Rhodes quietly kept his own counsel. He studied the two brothers, happy for their quick action, though he was beginning to wonder if they'd ever make their destination. However, after seeing them in action he now knew that if anyone had a chance to succeed, it would be these two.

"Do you think all's OK at the ranch, Justin?"

"It's far enough off the beaten path and a bit out of our direct route. Maybe the Feds missed it in their hurried retreat, and what would anybody want with horses anyway?"

"Horse meat's edible, Sir." Rhodes thought of his family farm as he spoke. "Not many horses left on the farms and ranches surrounding my hometown of Gunter."

"Good point, Corporal. Let's get going. It wouldn't hurt to find out if the ranch has anything we could use. Maybe we'll get lucky on this trip yet."

x x x x x

It was only 4:00 p. m., and the heat had soared to ninety-five degrees, making progress slow and dusty. Their energy was about depleted when they saw a vehicle crawling south, dodging the continuous line of refugees.

The old Ford F-150 came to a sudden stop. Its driver had little choice—Taylor stood in the middle of the road with the Stinger aimed directly at him, literally scaring the shit out of the young driver. Refugees scurried to the side of the road trying to avoid any potential altercation. The truck halted.

Corporal Rhodes approached slowly, his M-16 aimed at the driver's head. Calmly he barked out in a commanding voice, "Halt! Soldier, you're about to be commandeered."

The young soldier, shaken with surprise, asked, "What's the problem, Corporal? I've got orders to deliver this vehicle to my General, up the road a piece. We're on the same side, aren't we?"

Taylor came forward then. "Aren't you Andy Taylor?"

"Yeah, and you're Tay Northcutt, aren't ya? I always remember you having my last name for a first name."

"I recognize you have an assignment, Andy, but we need a ride and you're convenient."

"Where y'all goin' to, Captain?" Formality returned along with the private's respect for the Ranger officers blocking his vehicle.

"We'll drop you off at the next sentry stop. Where we're going's no concern of yours."

"Beggin' your pardon, Sirs, this is General Maxwell's vehicle. He commands the Fourth Texas Volunteers. I don't reckon he'll think too highly of you takin' his truck."

"How will he ever find out, Private, if we choose to eliminate the evidence?" Corporal Rhodes waived his M-16 in a menacing manner. It worked.

"Enough, Corporal! Private Taylor's my grandparent's neighbor and family friend," Justin interrupted. "Andy, we have urgent need to deliver a courier packet to the front. It has top priority. General Maxwell will understand. Do you have a CB radio in the truck?"

"No, Justin, I mean Sir, those kind 'a luxuries stopped several months ago." Andy wanted to comment that the enemy could monitor a CB, but he chose to remain silent.

Justin continued. "Then, Private, take us to the next sentry post. We'll see if we can get transportation." Justin hesitated. "On second thought, we need you to take us to Granddad's. I'll let the sentries at our next checkpoint notify your general that his vehicle's on temporary assignment to me."

Taylor turned to Andy, concern on his face. "Andy, have you seen our Granddad? What do you know?"

"Taylor, uh sorry, I mean Captain." Andy shuffled from foot to foot. "The last time I saw 'em 'twas about six months ago. They was headed south with just about everyone else from here. Haven't seen 'em since."

Justin jumped into the conversation with a question he dreaded to ask. "How's the ranch? Is it in one piece?" Andy's family lived about a mile from their grandparents' home.

"I do believe some friends and neighbors have stayed on in the area. They're few and far between, though. Justin, sorry, I mean General, I doubt there's much left if the Feds stumbled on the place. You probably heard the Feds lived off the land as they skedaddled."

"We were there, Andy, chasing their sorry tails." Justin fumed. The vivid memory of that poor little girl came back, haunting him, rekindling his pent-up anger.

Taylor cut in, "Those horses were thoroughbred. So I guess the Feds ate expensive horse meat if they found the ranch."

"Let's get going. We lost too much time and need to saddle up." Justin turned, speaking directly to Andy. "Private Taylor, I'll give you a note for General Maxwell to cover your backside. Hop in back, or stand here watching our exhaust." Justin climbed into the cab, and Taylor, jumping in, took the wheel. Rhodes and Private Taylor went into the bed. Rhodes kept his rifle at the ready.

The drive to the ranch was quick and uneventful. Taylor turned off a remote dirt road leading to the 300 secluded acres, once part of a 20,000-acre ranch in the 1800s. Granddad Northcutt bought the ranch in the early 1980s and built an Austin Rock, 5000-square-foot home. It stood proudly on the top of a steep rise, overlooking a greater part of the property. Taylor parked next to the barn.

Private Taylor pointed out two horses grazing in the field north of the ranch house. "It appears the Feds didn't take all of the horses after all. I do recall about two dozen."

"Yes, at least that many, and about forty head of cattle, the last time we were here," Taylor replied.

Corporal Rhodes quickly assessed the horses from afar. The ex-farm boy shook his head. "Sorry to say, Sirs, those horses are too skinny to eat and wouldn't last ten miles at a walk."

"I agree," said Justin. He scanned the waving grass surrounding the abandoned property. The fragrant smell of warm spring air fell upon them, and brilliant wildflowers dotting the pasture made them feel welcome. He could almost, but not quite, imagine the many joyful times he'd spent here. *War*, he pondered, *often dulls the senses, though thankfully not good memories.*

Taylor's perceptive eyes had been searching the familiar landscape. "Justin, the place looks pretty run down. I wonder if anything of value's left."

Justin turned to his brother. "No, Taylor, I'd expect any items of value are gone."

Granddad's old Ford truck was where they expected to find it, but it had been ravaged for parts and offered little help for their current needs. The '57 and 2002 yellow Thunderbirds were missing, too; both tractors and the old John Deere Gator were nowhere to be seen. Fortunately, they managed to find two five-gallon cans of diesel fuel tucked away in the far corner of the barn, half buried under scattered hay.

Suddenly, Taylor had an idea. He turned and shouted across the barn.

"Justin, are you thinking what I'm thinking?"

"Sorry, Taylor, I'm losing you."

"Granddad most likely took the tractors for his trek south. His trailers are missing, too. I've a feeling that the Gator may be in the old line shed. You remember that shed? As I recall, it's well hidden by the pecan trees and brush along the creek. With luck, it might not have been discovered. It would be like Granddad to hide it if he couldn't take it. He liked that Gator almost as much as his old T-Birds."

"It's worth a try. Let's go." Justin turned and called to Andy. "Private, you hang here for a few minutes. See if you can find some jumper cables."

"No problem, Sir. There's a pair of cables in my truck." Andy smiled, happy to be able to help.

"Thanks, Andy. I knew I could count on you." Justin waived Rhodes over. "Corporal, you and the private rummage around the barn and the corral and see if you can find anything else we can use."

The brothers found the green John Deere Gator nestled sweetly in the shed in all its glory. Justin lifted the driver's seat to view the fuel gauge. It read half full.

"I'd guess it's been left idle for about nine months. It's no worse for wear. Can we start it, Taylor?"

"No, the battery's run down. It does have about a half-full tank. Hopefully Granddad treated the fuel."

"Hell, Taylor, you know he did," Justin replied.

"I'll need to cross some wires, but I can get her started," Taylor said. He reached under the controls, and in a minute he got contact. "Now I'm hoping all we need is a jump."

After a rough drive down to the shed in Andy's truck, they jump-started it. When they returned to the barn, Justin handed the truck keys to Andy. "Thanks, Private, here's your note to General Marshal. You better get going." Justin shook the private's hand, saying, "Thanks for the help, and take care, Andy."

Private Andy Taylor saluted, happy his mini-ordeal was over. Justin returned the salute. Andy jumped into his truck, waving his goodbye.

"Let's get this show on the road," Justin shouted. "Get those cans of diesel and a canvas for cover. We may need to camp out tonight. It looks like rain."

Taylor said, "This six-wheel drive may come in handy. Unfortunately people will hear us coming a mile away, and we can't go very fast. I recall top speed's about seventeen miles per hour."

Justin laughed. "Yeah, Tay, that's with the wind at our backs. Let's look for a tow rope when we get back to the barn." They drove slowly back to the main house to pick up Rhodes.

Before leaving, they walked into their grandparents' home for the first time since the war started. Justin had purposely put it off to the last. It was hard to look at the home without emotion. When they arrived, it had been necessary to stay focused on finding transportation. Now what he needed was the courage not to break down at what he fully expected to find inside.

It was in shambles. Windows were broken, everything thrown about, and any remaining contents destroyed. Justin, outraged and hurting, shouted to no one in particular. "Damn, is all this pillaging necessary? If people in my command do this to anyone's home, be it Rebel or Fed, I swear I'll have them shot, so help me God." Justin spewed out his anger, giving it full vent. "Still, I've got to say that those Fed bastards who did this do more for our cause than we could ever do. But we sure as hell don't have to follow their lead."

Taylor picked up a broken vase he recognized as one of his grandmother's favorites. "Grandma will be sick over this."

"Taylor, all I hope is they're alive, and live to see it. That's all I care about now. When this freaking war is over, we can come back here and help them get everything back to normal."

With a bit of pessimistic sarcasm, Taylor expressed his feelings openly. "You know, Justin, we may not live long enough to make your wish come true. If either of us does live to see peace, we'll need to make life right for all our family."

Both men turned abruptly, walked out, and closed the door behind them.

With a grunt and a spit, the old Gator pulled out of the dirt drive, with Taylor at the wheel, Justin at shotgun, and Corporal Rhodes sitting in the dump bed with the tarp, knapsacks, weapons, and fuel. Justin's feelings were frazzled; his home in Prosper was wrecked. His grandparents' home sat in ruins. Everything he valued most, both people and possessions, seemed cast to the whim of the winds.

There was little left for Justin except to complete this seemingly endless mission and, hopefully, reach his new brigade. He vowed to himself, *I'll keep at it as long as I draw breath.* He looked at his brother driving—his rigid grasp on the steering wheel. Justin knew his brother's torment. The past few days had done more to disturb Taylor, and him, than had the last several months.

Taylor is the insightful sibling, gentler than this war allows, not the hard case his persona projects. He kept his own counsel, but Justin knew he was hurting. Taylor's inner rage usually built up until it was too late to control. Yet it was Taylor's anger that Justin feared the most. This war had allowed Taylor to vent his wrath upon the enemy, but in doing so, he hurt himself even more. Justin feared Taylor would break if he did not get away from the killing fields. Taylor would eventually need help to work his way out of his emotional dilemma. Until then, Justin planned to help him by keeping him too busy to think.

After a hard night's sleep in a drenching rain, they drove patiently northward. Sentry stops became annoyingly frequent. About two miles outside Denison, they were directed to follow a motorcycle trooper through difficult terrain, taking care to avoid enemy infiltrators. To their disappointment, they realized there was no longer time to look for Becky.

The Gator performed well, thanks to their grandfather's routine loving care. It navigated the rolling hills and deep ravines with ease.

When they reached the Red River, they were directed to go two miles upstream to a submerged pontoon bridge that had been built to elude air power. Once across the bridge, they were in Oklahoma. Within thirty minutes, they were back on old Highway 75. About nine miles up the road they hit another sentry post, where they were pleased to see the familiar arrow patch of the 36th Division. The Ranger MP, upon seeing their insignia, saluted smartly. After receiving the proper password, the private escorted them to his company commander, Captain Anderson. Justin's first glance took in the unkempt appearance of the post; it angered him.

"Captain, I'm General Northcutt. What unit's this?"

"Sir, Charley Company, Third Regiment, 1st Ranger Brigade."

"Well, Captain, you're addressing your commanding general. After we take care of my business, I fully expect you to police your command for a field inspection at 0800 tomorrow."

Captain Anderson, unfazed by Justin's hard exterior, knew his reputation. It was common scuttlebutt that Northcutt was a stickler for order. However, the word on Justin also claimed him to be a leader whose good judgment gave his men confidence. "I'll escort you to Major General Phillips when you are ready, Sir. Sorry we don't have a vehicle we can give you." Anderson snapped a very military salute.

"Captain, this green workhorse got us this far, I suppose she can take us the distance." Justin returned the captain's salute. "Let's go now, Captain, the sooner I report and get rid of these damn papers the quicker I return to my command."

Four motorcycles escorted them through some of the wildest country they'd seen on their two-day ordeal. Each was armed with a machine gun manned by a trooper sitting in its sidecar. It would take them about two hours to reach headquarters with the cycles having to slow down to match the Gator's speed.

"Corporal, where'd you come across these cycles?" Taylor asked. He loved motorcycles.

"Let's just say the Feds had them and we took 'em. And well, Sir, we put them to good use, don't ya think?"

"That you did." Taylor chuckled. "OK, like the general said, let's get going. We've kept General Phillips waiting long enough."

Taylor started the Gator after Rhodes added the last of the diesel fuel and tossed the empty can back into the bed. Above the drone of the Gator, Taylor asked, "Justin, what's in these papers?"

"I have no idea, only suspicions. Whatever it is, I'll be happy to be rid of the responsibility."

In about forty-five minutes, they approached the beginning of an active front, the terrain rugged and rich with rolling hills. It looked like a suitable place for battle.

"What's the name of this place, soldier?" asked Taylor.

"I don't know the exact name of this here ground, Sir. We're about two miles south of the city of Durant, Oklahoma, or what's left of it. We had to pull back about thirty miles after the Feds kicked our butts last week. We fought our way back to this shithole and have been at a standstill ever since." Taylor recalled that the people he and Justin had given their rations to had come from Durant. He understood why they left.

Major General Steve Phillips's field headquarters was two miles from the active front in a manmade underground shelter once occupied by Federal Command. After exchanging pleasantries and taking delivery of the packet, Phillips asked Justin to give an account of their trip, his view of the war, and its toll on the countryside and citizenry.

Complying, Justin wondered silently if it mattered. Tired, he asked, "General Phillips, what can I expect? What do I need to know before I return to my command?"

"Justin, we're fighting daily skirmishes without a major encounter since our fallback. Intel advises that the Feds have received replacements, though not as steady as they're used to. Two weeks ago the enemy caught us with our pants down and pushed us back to the Red River. It got a bit hairy for a while. We counter-punched and pushed them back to Durant. Durant has changed hands four times. It's been a close shave ever since. They hit us like they did at the beginning of the war with a big one-two punch of air power, Bradleys, and Arty. We had several hundred casualties and they lost aplenty too."

General Phillips stood, letting out a deep exasperated breath before continuing. "The sons of bitches' air power almost did us in. Thankfully, we received timely reinforcements, mostly from Mississippi, Arkansas, and Louisiana, and even a few from Oklahoma. Word is we're getting help from all across the nation. Our allied states are taking on the Federal Army in the South and most of the Southeast. The Southwest's almost in our control, all the way to the Nevada border."

"Sir, does this mean we're gaining ground in all the states?"

"Yes, I'm told we're seeing a lot of progress." General Phillips stopped talking as Taylor entered. "Hello, Captain Northcutt."

Taylor saluted and stood at attention.

"At ease, Captain Northcutt." Phillips waved for Taylor to sit. "By the way, Taylor, congratulations are in order on your promotion. I've heard good reports on your performance, young man. Keep up the good work."

"Thank you, Sir. My brother gave me his silver bars. I'll do my best to fill his shoes." Taylor immediately felt foolish; he had meant to praise Justin, not schmooze. It wasn't his way. It didn't matter, though; they understood.

Phillips turned his attention back to Justin. "General, your new command is presently in our reserve position a few miles from here. Your unit's responsible for the protection of our supply line and the two hospital units about one-half mile from your command post. The 36th is holding a ten-mile front, along with three other Texas divisions. Joining us are five divisions: two from Mississippi and three from Louisiana. We enjoy a force of about 50,000 troops. Our little army will soon include an additional armored division. It's on the way to reinforce our three tank battalions.

"We also have some permanent air power of our own. Our air jockeys revisited the Tucson, Arizona reserve depot and managed to put together a fair number of fighters that will work with our limited fuel supply. They're mostly old prop planes used in the Korean and Vietnam era. The air jockeys feel they're best suited to this war since jet fuel has all but disappeared. Command tells me it's just a matter of time before we have air parity with the Feds. That's about it. Any questions?"

"General, I stumbled into my new command on our way here. I believe I have my work cut out for me," Justin replied.

"Don't be too hard on them, General. They've been through a lot since you went to Austin. That's why I placed them in reserve. I gave them to you so you can do a little of your magic, and I have full confidence in your ability to pull it off."

"Thanks for the confidence, Sir."

"You're welcome. Now get busy. I have a pissload of work to get back to."

Justin and Taylor saluted their new Division Commander and returned to their Gator. Under his breath, Taylor whispered so Justin could hear, "Thanks for your confidence, Sir. Thanks for nothing but more headaches."

"That's enough, Captain. One can't be heard or seen mocking one's superior."

Taylor just beamed his sarcastic smile, which only Justin could appreciate and recognize for what it was—pure brotherly love.

About halfway back to their post, their motorcycle escort ran smack dab into a Federal patrol. Luckily the Feds didn't have the patience to wait for the full column to be exposed. They took out the lead scout's cycle, killing both soldiers. These were the first casualties of Justin's new command.

With quick thinking and precise, if not lucky, reaction, Justin's guards responded rapidly, taking out the Federal patrol. One lone enemy soldier waved in surrender, shouting to stop the firing—his war over.

"Three enemy soldiers dead to our two. What a senseless waste of life all around," Taylor grumbled to no one in particular.

"I know, Taylor. Welcome back to the war."

"General, may I request a word with you?" Rhodes came forth, saluting.

"Sure, Corporal Rhodes, permission to speak."

"Sir, I'd like to request a transfer to duty with your unit, Sir, if you'd have me."

"Welcome aboard, Rhodes. I'll do the paperwork. But why? You've got a pretty good post now. This will be more action than most would want, and a lot more risk."

"Thank you, Sir. You see, it's like this. After riding with you for two days and seeing your persistence and spirit, there's no place I'd rather be, Sir, than where this war will be won. And Sir, at least with the Rangers, I'll see it firsthand."

"With that explanation, I believe we'll have to live up to our lofty reputation and see if we can arrange an end of this war for you. Glad to have you with us, Corporal. Welcome!" Justin gave Rhodes's hand a firm welcoming shake.

"Captain, after we get to our post, locate Becky's hospital unit and send word to her to request permission to visit 1st Brigade. Send Corporal

Rhodes—no, correction—send *Sergeant* Rhodes with an escort to bring her to us for a visit."

Taylor was not surprised at Justin's impromptu promotion of Rhodes, knowing he'd need to surround himself with men he could rely upon. He walked over to Rhodes. "Congratulations, Sergeant. Any man who has the courage to join the Rangers deserves a promotion." Taylor saluted Rhodes and then shook his hand.

"Follow me, Sergeant. I'll see if I can get you set up with some proper Ranger gear, and of course, you'll need our illustrious patch and badge."

Rhodes left with Taylor, feeling good about his decision.

Jim Damiano

It is the character of a brave and resolute man not to be ruffled by adversity and not desert his post.

—Cicero

CHAPTER NINE

June 10, 2020—Saint Lawrence River, Canada/U.S. Border

The 121st Division of the 1st Corps of New York Volunteers was part of a vast line defending the northern border that New York state shared with Canada, a stone's throw across the St. Lawrence River. The 1st Corps was thinly spread over several miles, covering Rebel territory from Buffalo, New York, and crossing the state's border to within a few miles above Burlington, Vermont.

Maine lingered in Federal control, while New York and Pennsylvania militias held territory in a line stretching tenuously from Buffalo to Pittsburgh across to Newark, New Jersey, bypassing New York City. The line turned north up the Hudson River to Albany, New York. From there, the Rebels held most of New York state, including areas contiguous to Vermont. The 15,000 veterans of the 121st Division included two heavy artillery batteries, three light infantry brigades, and a tank battalion. Its headquarters were centered at Plattsburg, New York.

The old St. Lawrence Seaway formed a natural border for the majority of the defended landmass. The only exception lay at the northernmost border opposite the Province of Quebec, which was now a free republic. They had withdrawn, without a shot, from the Canadian Union. There, New York was protected by the will and determination of its militia.

The Rebels had held an uneasy peace with the new Quebec Republic. The tension became thick enough to force each to strengthen their borders for possible invasion when Rebel intelligence suspected a possible alliance between Quebec and the Federal government. The Rebel forces were eye-to-eye with the Canadians along their northern line. Everywhere else the Rebels faced Federal units.

At the beginning of the war, the rebellion had endured one large mistake from their leaders followed by another. For once, though, blundering politicians and the Rebel Command were correct. Federal leaders, fearing the Canadians would see Rebel control as a sign of weakness, were taking advantage of the unrest.

Cities in war-torn areas were in disrepair and various stages of decay. The lifestyle formerly enjoyed in the 21st Century was now nonexistent. The government had universally and routinely neglected to establish emergency war plans shelved after the Cold War ended in the 1990s. Civil Defense, once a stout organization, was a fond memory. Cities, thrust back into 18th century conditions, faced dire concerns over energy, water, waste treatment plants, and other functions once thought necessary for everyday life. The countryside, filled with starving refugees seeking shelter, added to the mass confusion. Migrating civilians, a major concern for opposing armies, were often caught in the crossfire. In this atmosphere, most Canadians were reaping the rewards of neutrality.

The 100-plus-mile front, though thinly defended by the New York 1st Corps, was reinforced when threats appeared imminent. Every available unit of Freedom Fighters from the 1st and 2nd New York Volunteer Corps, totaling ten divisions and 200,000 men, was sent to the region. Pennsylvania's Militia sent a division to help near Buffalo, marking the beginning of Rebel unity on the northern front.

The strategy against the Federals had initially been simple. First, fight a guerilla war until Vermont, Pennsylvania, and New York could link up with the balance of the southern Pennsylvania militias, including West Virginia, Virginia, and Maryland fighting northward.

Second, in the west, Michigan, Ohio, Indiana, and some Kentucky units were fighting their way east, pushing to combine with fellow Rebel forces. The overall strength of these loosely tied units was just under one million men and women, approximately forty Rebel volunteer divisions comprised of combat and support personnel.

This, in short, was the northern Rebel's strategy to unhinge the Federal forces on their way to forming a new United States.

Sergeant James Rinaldi glared across the St. Lawrence River, wondering expectantly when the next chapter of ruin would begin. Tired beyond his endurance, he tried to concentrate. All had become one confused muddle. He needed to stay alert. His uneasy post stood in the way of the menacing Canadians patrolling across the river. Occasionally a Canadian soldier would wave or even speak; they were that close.

James stood stretching as he studied one of the many magnificent locks on the old Seaway. It was a cool, late spring morning, hazy and pleasant. The musty smell of the river floated to his nostrils, reminding him of happier moments. His squad's position was gloomy, not the best place to daydream about fishing for pike.

He was hungry, tired, and reluctant all in one moment; the reality of his worst fears enveloped him.

His platoon was at the ready, but a month's guard duty at the front line has a way of numbing the mind. No one in his small command was as sharp as they should be. Nor could any soldier, especially the New Yorkers, understand why the Canadians were a threat, especially James, who had made several Canadian friends while he was a student at Syracuse University.

Vic ambled up to James, holding a freshly brewed pot of coffee liberated from the coals of the cook stand. He limped noticeably, favoring his healing leg. "Well, Jimmy, things sure look the same as always. I suppose you'd call this posh duty, considering what's going on elsewhere. Sort of like watching paint dry." Vic laughed at his own joke.

"Someone's got to do it," yawned James. "Heck, Vic, this is grand duty—enjoy it while you can. I'll take boring detail anytime over street fighting. But I agree boring can sure be tiring."

"Jimmy, do you think it's worth it—this friggin' war?"

James still grieved Billy. How good it would've been to have three of the Rinaldi brothers together. He almost wished he could forget the cause. Like so many, he was caught, a captive of the war's rage. *But I cannot forget why I'm here.*

133

James put his right hand to his forehead, trying to think of an appropriate answer. "You know, Vic, at first it seemed so right. Now, with all the killing, I sometimes wonder if anything is worth this, even freedom. Whatever, it's too late to worry about what you can't control. Like so many, I was appalled when the revolt started in New York City. Then, when rioters protesting the killing of demonstrators in Dallas were gunned down, I felt it was time to take up arms." James's face tightened as he remembered. "The war took a wicked turn; militias came out of places nobody ever thought of as pockets of rebellion. Now, Vic, it's simple—we're in it up to our ass, and we can't look back. What I don't understand is the worry over those boys across the Seaway."

"Jimmy, if Luke's still alive, he's probably killing Rebels. Would he kill us? Could we kill him? How will he feel when he hears Billy was killed in action? God, Jimmy, all this thought of fighting our own brother hurts. Now, don't get me wrong. I don't mind killing those frog eaters across the way, but I thought it's the goddamned Feds we're fighting." Vic looked haggard. He really hadn't fully recovered.

"Man, you're full of questions. You OK, Vic? You look like shit."

"Yeah, I'm fine. But have you looked in the mirror lately, you butt-ugly pain?" Together they laughed, and it felt good.

James changed the subject, talking with his hands—a family trait—pretending to slug his brother. "Wasn't it just like our grandpa?" James smiled. "Rock sure is the one with posh duty. When he volunteered his services, General Smithson wouldn't have him in the infantry."

"Boy, I'm glad it was a general that told 'im he's too old. I hear he was close to tearing the General's stars off his shoulders!"

"I'd have loved to see that moment. How's it that they made him a major? He was only a sergeant when he was in 'Nam."

"Probably his experience. And you know what a mind for detail Rock has. As far as I'm concerned, his freakin' experience is where it belongs—on the HQ staff of the 121st, not in one of these damn foxholes looking at the Canucks. Not to mention the fact he's a mere seventy-five years old, although we have older men and women on the line."

James wondered aloud, "You know his prior military experience never got stale with all the camping and hunting he did. This war's no different. He's a natural for this shit. So—when did you last see him?"

"About a week ago in Plattsburg. He looked great. His arm's mending nicely. I can't remember seeing him happier, since …"

James broke in, "Since Grandma was alive! I know—I saw the change too. He's needed now. It's amazing how a little civil war can make some of us feel better."

"Yeah, sure! Do you mean 'better' like in those flakey hemorrhoid advertisements?" Vic jested, making an exaggerated look of pain as he sat down.

Suddenly, Vic shouted, "Jimmy, what the hell's that?" as he pointed across the river at a huge column of tanks roaring out of the morning mist, firing devastation in unison across the international border.

"Incoming!" James shouted, pulling Vic to the safety of their foxhole, while shells flashed, in surreal order, their insincere song of death.

The brothers crouched in terror, clinging like moles to mother earth. The hillside behind them disappeared into clumps of broken rock, dirt, equipment, and human body parts. Bloodied from the remains of unfortunate comrades, they knew immediately their platoon was devastated.

The specter of his fears, past and present, brought a sour taste to James's lips as he slapped at the disemboweled earth coating him. He reached on impulse for his field phone, shouting into it in a controlled anxious voice, "Attack, northeast sector, Post 15! Heavy tank and light infantry at river's edge. About to be overrun. Please instruct. Over!"

"This is Captain Rivera. Who am I addressing? Over."

"Sergeant Rinaldi, Sir!" The deafening noise made conversation almost impossible.

"Hold tight, Sergeant, Command is receiving calls from most sectors in about a twenty-five-mile perimeter. Hold tight, repeat, hold tight. Reinforcements are on the way. Acknowledge!"

"Message is to hold, clear. Over," James sighed and then shouted to the unseen enemy, "Yeah sure, we'll hold. Hold freaking what!"

x x x x x

To James's right, Vic lay unhurt, looking like a ghost from all the dirt and dust and gore. Vic's angry eyes signaled his determination to put up a fight.

"Looks like we've been skunked, Jimmy. What's next?"

James sarcastically replied, "We're to hold our ground."

"Shit, Jimmy, I couldn't hold onto this ground any harder than I am without hitting oil. I've dug as deep as my bare hands can."

"Vic, stay put. I need to check if Larson and Battaglia are alive. I'm hoping the Canucks are just testing our resistance. It seems like their firing has leveled off some."

James embraced the earth as he crawled to where most of his platoon should have been. The awful smell of death and sulfur reeked around him; he found only ripped body parts scattered everywhere. James tasted bile, an all-too-familiar reaction. In a short distance, he found five men alive, huddled in earthen shelters. With the quick precision of a battle-wise non-com, he arranged for the defense of their position, posting the one remaining .50-caliber machine gun to its best advantage. He instructed his men to dig in, wondering why, knowing their picket defense in this whole sector was probably devastated. With communication gone, all that was left was speculation

The next phase of the Canadians' one-two slam came as the New Quebec Air Force started strafing and bombing runs to feel out the Rebels' remaining strength; planes were followed by helicopter gunships. The veteran New Yorkers were ready for them. They hit back with their improvised air force and hand-held Stinger rockets.

The Canadians countered with paratroopers and infantry. Their synchronized moves cut off the forward Rebel units. James realized they were surrounded and ordered his men to hide.

The Canadians hadn't figured on the Rebels' lightning-quick response. The seasoned Rebel veterans, fearlessly rushed in to counter, answering the Canucks' uninvited visit with ruinous devastation. Unlucky Canadians, caught in the Rebels' crossfire, did not escape their wrath.

This day, luck was with the Rebels. Federal forces, unable to react, were too far south to take advantage of the Canadian aggression. Massive Rebel forces merged to reinforce the perimeters facing the Federal Army. In two hours it was over. The Rebels pumped in two full divisions to reinforce their line and began their counterattack, systematically stopping the Canadian onslaught dead in its tracks. Casualties for both sides were high. The Rebels took Canadian prisoners by the thousands; their momentum was thwarted, and they could not recover their initiative.

Quebec, expecting to find an unprepared and easy foe of unseasoned and undisciplined men, was surprised to face a force as regimented as the old U.S. Army. The furor of the New Yorkers and their Allied Free States was devastating. It's often difficult to kill fellow citizens in a civil war. It's another matter to kill foreigners.

To a man, the Rebels wondered why a friendly nation like Canada, even the recently independent Quebec, would have attacked the New York border. Many wondered if the French Canadians were bent on retrieving the property in northern New York they had lost to the British in the 18th century. An explanation would soon be forthcoming, but only to a select few.

James's devastated platoon made it through the two-hour ordeal by playing possum while Quebec's shock troops rolled over their position. James knew deep down if this had been an attack by seasoned Federal troopers, scattered bodies would have been shot to make doubly sure they would not fight again.

It still wasn't safe to come out of hiding. Waiting until the day turned to dusk, James's depleted platoon did little effective fighting; instead, they survived.

"James, are you all right? Answer me, damn it, answer me!" Vic pulled himself from the bowels of the earth. His disheveled appearance confirmed his ordeal. His first introduction to conventional war was that of a frightened spectator, not a participant. He had played dead about as long as he could stand it. Every part of his body was numb from fear and lying still for hours. Yet he was alive, and glad of it. He pinched his arm to make sure.

Quietly, James answered, "Grab your piece and be ready to use it. It'll be dark soon. It's time we return to the living."

The few survivors of James's platoon grabbed their weapons and slithered like snakes seeking their prey. Scanning the immediate area, James found visibility difficult. The area was still; signs of death encircled them.

"Vic, I think we're secure. God only knows where the hell we are, though. For all I can tell we're in the middle of the enemy's position."

"Well, I'm not sure I needed to hear that. I guess there's but one way to find out," quipped Vic, his bravado forced.

"You're right, Private," taunted James. "How about you crawling around a bit to the west. I'll take the east. Does your watch still work?"

Vic answered, "Yeah, Mickey's arm is still moving."

"OK, Charlie Brown!" James whispered, "The rest of you, stay here 'til we return."

"Ready?" asked Vic. The brothers moved out at a crawl.

"Remember, Vic, be back here in thirty minutes. Bring anyone you find who's on our side back with you."

"Roger that. You mean you don't want any Canucks?"

"Only dead ones, dipstick. Now move out," James whispered.

Both brothers returned as planned with four more Rebels in tow, all from other displaced platoons.

"Vic, did you see much?"

"All I saw was devastation, big craters in the ground, and bodies, or what was left of bodies, everywhere. These guys were moles like us."

James eyed a large knife hooked to Vic's belt and pointed to it. "Where did that pig poker come from?"

Vic's toothy grin gave James a chill. "Let's just say that a Canuck won't be needing it anymore."

James turned to the others. "Men, we better get out of here while we can. I figure we covered about a quarter mile. We saw no one alive. It appears we may have retreated."

A ragged private came forward. "Then why in hell aren't there any enemy patrols, pickets, or anything else for that matter? Why haven't our guys returned to this strategic point? Sarge, it makes no sense."

James looked with appreciation at the private. "It beats the crap out of me, soldier. My guess is, whoever won, if anyone actually did, hasn't had time to regroup. I'd suspect both sides are licking their wounds. Hopefully, we're not in the Canucks' backyard." James reached for his field phone still attached to his web belt. I'm going to break silence and see if the radio still works."

Vic put his hand on the phone to stop him. "James, do you think that's wise? Who knows who might control the receiving end? Begging your pardon, Bro, is it worth the risk?"

"Good thinking, Vic. Men, there's little reason to stay here. We're leaving this death trap and heading south." James waved his arm in that direction.

Quietly, eleven ragged men formed a single file, walking and occasionally crawling cautiously southward, slogging five exhausting miles before hearing movement.

"Holy Hanna, I believe it's our guys, Jimmy," Vic whispered hoarsely in his excited fatigue.

James grabbed his brother's leg, pulling him down, waving to the others to do the same.

"Yes, it's our men, but I expect they'll be jumpy. We'll wait till dawn to make our presence known. It's safer."

June 13, 2020—Plattsburg, New York, First New York Headquarters

"Sergeant Rinaldi, you're wanted at Command."

"Thanks, Corporal. What's it about?"

"They don't tell me, Sarge. I'm just an errand boy."

James's tent flap opened to a brisk morning accompanied by a solid mist of rain, thankfully covering the stink of death. He stretched, getting the kinks from his body. A haggard colleague said that the Rebel army had, with efficient ease, regrouped their assets and swiftly organized the counterattack. It remained a mystery how, or more importantly why, the Canadian armor had crossed the St. Lawrence. *Intel will solve the puzzle in time; right now my only concern is breakfast, not Regimental HQ.*

"Jimmy," Vic grabbed at his arm as he was leaving. "Before you go, I've been wondering. Why didn't the Fed army take advantage of the confusion and attack us when we were most vulnerable? It just doesn't make sense even to the likes of me. Hell, I would have cut us off at the balls if I were them scums."

James, thinking the same thing, replied, "Vic, you always were the quizzical one of our brood. Perhaps they're in league with the Canadians, or maybe wanted to see what damage the Canucks could do without risking their chicken-shit necks. Whatever happened, it won't reach us foot soldiers anytime soon. Maybe one day we'll know; right now I'm thankful for another day on terra firma."

James pondered for a brief moment, "We can count on Rock to let us in on what he may know." Vic nodded in agreement.

James looked at the remnants of the Quebec flag he'd found while scavenging. He dropped it, purposely grinding it with his foot, pushing it into the mud. He brushed the rain from his face and turned to address his corporal, Tim Rockwell. Tim had been separated from their squad during the attack and had just returned. "Tim, watch things here while I'm gone. And get the men together. I suspect we'll need to go over a few things when I get back."

Tim moved closer to James, walking with him toward HQ. "You know something we don't, Jimmy?"

"Only this, Tim. You survive by anticipating, not waiting for things to happen. If I've learned one thing in the past year, it's been to constantly be aware and to be ready to adapt."

The command tent for 7th Regiment was musty and dark, and it leaked. The smell of smoke and sweat permeated the air; several unwashed men filled its stuffy confines. Colonel Marshal, the regimental commander, had been killed in the battle along with his second. The battle had reduced the regiment's strength to fifty percent. There were voids in all the ranks. Rinaldi's company captain, John Allen, was missing in action, probably one of the blotches of obliterated soil that mercilessly impersonalized the dead.

James was particularly affected by the captain's death. Allen's sister Debby was the love of his life. He missed her and was saddened that he couldn't be with her to comfort her.

All the men were standing as the 7th Regiment's newly appointed colonel adjusted his glasses and started talking. "Men, you're aware we've suffered heavy casualties. I've been assigned to command the 7th. For those who don't know me, my name's Bert Danzer. At this moment, I'm a brevet colonel, but my formal rank is captain. I'm old regular U.S. Army. Because of the holes in our ranks, I'm obliged to promote several men."

When Danzer announced Charley Company's new commander, Rinaldi found himself staring in the face of his biggest dread. He was now a company commander, with the rank of first lieutenant. James's emotions were mixed. He'd been dodging the responsibility to lead from the beginning. Unfortunately, his cool, calm ability to carry out orders had been noticed by command. He couldn't dodge any longer. To remain a noncom, which would be his right, would not be patriotic, and his sense of duty wouldn't allow it. Nevertheless, it pissed him off to be promoted.

Danzer continued, "Men, I'll discuss any special assignments privately after this meeting. Right now we need to get prepared for our next campaign, which begins in two days. The 121st will take part in a massive assault on Federal forces. Our objective is somewhere in Pennsylvania, and will be conveyed to us at the appropriate time. It appears our intent is to link up and assist Rebel armies from other states."

Rain intensified and Danzer brushed the water leaking profusely from the tent's canvas roof away from his face. He smiled, but spoke in a clipped voice. "It appears this rain has better aim than the damned Feds." This drew a reserved laugh. "I've been told we will eventually link up our combined forces, maybe by year's end with the Texans. They are presently linking with forces from several Midwestern and Southeastern states. It's really a simple plan on the surface. All we're asked to do is furnish the fighting and the bleeding. And the brass," he hesitated, "well, I suppose we'll let them continue to do the thinking."

James quietly wondered if Rock was somewhere in the mix of these plans.

"Any questions?"

Newly promoted Lieutenant Edgers raised his hand. "Sir, what about the border? Are we leaving northern New York to the Canadians? Are we allowing them to take some of their old territory without further fight?"

"That's a big 'no,' Edgers. Only our 1st and 2nd Volunteer Corps are leaving. The rest of the army will remain. I suspect a greater portion will be going into Canada to finish what the Canucks foolishly began. We'll miss that fun. But we'll be showing the world our army is capable of a two-front war. It should serve to warn aggressors we won't tolerate their interference. Don't lose any sleep over the wrath we'll spring on the Canadians. I'm told they're about fought out anyway after the severe beating we just gave 'em. Intel doubts they'll last much longer. Any more questions? If not, prepare your men to leave with full gear and supplies. Edger, Lance, Jefferson, Vicaro, and Rinaldi, stay here for your assignments and your new bars."

James returned apprehensively to Charley Company. His new lieutenant's bars shined brightly on his dirty, rain-soaked uniform. A noticeable outline where his sergeant's stripes had been quickly ripped from his frayed tunic matched his disposition.

The first man he saw was Corporal Dillard, who did not miss the new lieutenant bars. "Corporal, its official. Company C's now my command. Please gather the squads. Have them assemble here in thirty minutes."

"Yes, Sir." Corporal Dillard saluted James for the first time. A quick field promotion was nothing new to him. But it was still too new to James, and it felt a bit uncomfortable.

James kept his meeting brief. He laid out the upcoming marching orders and promoted three corporals to sergeant: one, Dillard, whom he trusted without thought; another, his capable boyhood friend, Tim Rockwell; and the third, Julius Jones, a fast-thinking, street-wise Harlem kid who'd shown leadership qualities numerous times. He promoted four men to corporal, including his brother. Though Vic was new to the First Squad, his ability to lead was readily apparent. His natural skill at foraging would be a plus for the upcoming campaign. Anything of value rarely escaped Vic's eye.

The initial march south was uneventful. Most of the way, troops were happy to take in the serene beauty of the Adirondacks, still mostly untouched by war. The full bloom of late spring lightened their step, making progress easy. Their column stretched for miles, snaking under the forest's canopy from Plattsburg to Utica, then south to Binghamton, where the first crucial test of the campaign awaited them.

Federal forces were waiting, firmly entrenched, cutting off direct progress. The Federal commander knew he was outnumbered but hoped his bluff would work. Rebel Intelligence, directing the army's path, outflanked the Federals after a forced march under cover of darkness, surprising them. The maneuver was reminiscent of Stonewall Jackson's Shenandoah Valley campaigns 160 years earlier. James's company, taking part in the flanking movement, started calling themselves Foot Cavalry, the time-honored nickname for Jackson's men.

The Feds, surrounded and outnumbered five to one, surrendered without a shot. Over one third of the Federal soldiers, when given the opportunity, joined ranks with the Rebels. The rest were stripped of their weapons, supplies, uniforms, and shoes, and were left on their own to make it back to their lines. Faced with the prospects of a long march with no shelter, clothes, weapons, or food, another thousand or so developed a sudden urge to join the Rebel cause. Those who joined took off their shirts to avoid being shot accidentally.

Two heavily armed Rebel companies escorted the new recruits north to join the border guard and the potential battle with Canada. They'd be allowed to kill Canadians to prove their worth and then be absorbed into the Rebel army. Once at the border they would be issued some semblance of uniforms and weapons.

James spoke out loud in disgust to no one in particular, "If this had been us, we'd have been shot."

"Then why don't we just shoot the bastards?" Vic agreed.

"I'm told we need men and supplies, and maybe they'll remember someday that we could've killed them. I'm sure they're aware our prisoners are shot more often than captured. And anyway, who has time for prisoners or the bullets to waste on 'em?" James replied.

Rebels jeered at the Federals choosing to remain loyal as they moved out in their skivvies and bare feet. The notorious New York black flies, anxious to dine on every orifice, tormented them.

Despite his strong feelings, James did not jeer. He ordered his men in a sharp voice, "Stop taunting them. They're being true to their beliefs. You have to admire that, even if you hate their politics!"

A few miles south of Binghamton, the two New York Corps joined a division from New Jersey, adding 10,000 men to the column. At Harrisburg, units from Ohio and Kentucky, along with additional Pennsylvanian units, raised the Rebel force to around 100,000 men. The Kentucky units brought in heavy armament taken from Fort Knox. They'd captured it along with the fort's gold reserves, badly needed in this new era where currency had lost all value. Ohio divisions brought two field artillery battalions. The Rebel Army was suddenly a force to reckon with.

It came as no surprise to James when the advancing columns, now forming three massive parallel lines, each separated by five miles, turned toward Washington, D.C. *So this was the plan.* James felt it but didn't dare voice it. He wondered if their numbers would be enough.

Around Gettysburg, historic turning point of another war, the three columns joined with several Pennsylvanian militia units now supplemented with regiments from several New England states. Approximately 200,000 men and women, encompassing over fifteen full divisions, were ready to attack D.C.

The Rebel Army didn't have long to wait. The Federals, forced to retreat in the face of the Rebels' unexpected threat, consolidated their lines and called for their reserves. The swiftness of the Rebel buildup had surprised them.

The Federal Army would hold its line and defend Washington ten miles south of Gettysburg. Their reserves formed near Frederick, Maryland, with orders to move north to Thurmont, Maryland. Within a short walk from Gettysburg, the Federal Army massed thirty divisions by bleeding posts from Florida to Maine, leaving them undermanned in a grand gamble to end the Northern revolt in one major battle.

Both armies headed for a major clash near hallowed ground already steeped in the blood of 19th-century patriots. By chance or destiny, Gettysburg might again witness a clash of titans attempting to change a great nation's future. Vultures, said to inhabit this area since the last great battle, spread their ugly black wings, patiently awaiting their feast.

"Lieutenant Rinaldi, you're wanted at Command, Sir." The courier saluted, leaving before James could answer.

James moved with the swiftness of youthful legs, hardened by a year of campaigning. He arrived to find the command tent filled with anxious men.

"Gentlemen," Colonel Danzer began, "we're part of a great force about to be tested beyond, I fear, the very boundaries of our endurance. Only our willingness to persevere will carry us through. The Federal Army has amassed about thirty divisions spread over a fifty-mile front. They have formed a giant defensive curtain from here to the Maryland border. The nation's capital is our target. We aim to get it. We're advised they have about five divisions in reserve a few miles south of here. Our job's laid out for us. We're to go through them, depending on our artillery and tank corps coordinating with our choppers and air force. It's thought the enemy still has air superiority. The good news is we're getting some air support from the Texans. Also, it's said we have parity with the Feds in the Midwest."

Danzer's determined face was lined with sweat. He wiped his neck with a dirty handkerchief and continued. "We must coordinate with the combined air and artillery assaults expected to begin at 0600 tomorrow. I'm told our regiment's been given the honor of holding our division's center. We'll not let the 121st down. We go forward at 0630. Please fix your watches. I have 2015.

"Any questions?" Danzer looked around. He saw Rinaldi's anxious look and nodded.

"Sir, how can we be certain the Texans will be there, with communications as they are?"

"Lieutenant Rinaldi, we can only believe that they'll show. They're coming in from Missouri in three waves. They know it's desperate, and even with surprise the Feds will have the edge. The brass feels it's our first chance to change the direction of the war and to save lives in the long run."

"Sir, are you implying defeat is expected?"

"No, Rinaldi, I never intended to imply that. We haven't hit them this hard yet. In my opinion this is more of a show. It's time the enemy knows that we're able. A sort of wakeup call to let the bastards know we're not going away. Hopefully we'll weaken enemy civilian support and encourage more recruits for us."

Another officer spoke up, "Sir, I realize both opposing air forces are reduced to fighting in pre-Vietnam-era craft. Can they make it here with their limitations?"

"It doesn't matter, Captain. In conventional warfare it always boils down to us foot soldiers doing the job. With the infrastructure destroyed as it is, we may actually be as far back as the late 19th century. Our primary strength is our belief in ourselves and in our cause. With resolve we'll prevail."

Danzer eyeballed each officer and non-com in his tent and then spoke loudly. "Return to your units and prepare your men. They'll need your guidance and assurance more than ever for what we are about to ask of them. Rabbi Benjamin will lead a nondenominational prayer service at HQ for anyone who wants to attend at 0500 tomorrow. This meeting is now dismissed. Good luck men, and God go with you."

James felt the uneasiness of the coming battle. The terrible sour taste returned once again. Even if his men could not comprehend, he knew. This would be his first real test as an officer. He returned to his men with mixed anticipation, wondering if surprise, as suggested, would play a factor. Deep down, he doubted it would.

The Federal Army thoroughly knew its predicament; it had been retreating since Binghamton, while continuing to consolidate a response to the Rebel drive. *Tomorrow is June 20th, and many good men will not live to see sundown.* But he was now firmly committed. Vic ran into his tent moments after he returned.

James spoke quickly but quietly, "Vic, shit's about to hit the fan. It's up to me to do what I can to lead these good men. Somehow, I must. Corporal, have all officers and non-coms here in ten minutes."

x x x x x

The men gathered around James would lead his company's three platoons, comprising nine squads. James knew from personal experience that his sergeants had the real job of moving the men to his timetable.

James faced them. He looked at each one openly, assessing the moment. "Men, tomorrow at 0630 we attack the Feds." He pointed to their position in the upcoming battle on the map atop a stump that served as his field desk. "Be certain your men have adequate supplies and ammo. Have the men hit the sack by 0900 and up and ready at 0400. Questions?"

When none came, he went on. "Then do what's needed and good luck. I'll see you all at 0400."

After the others had gone, Vic nudged up to his brother, concern on his craggy face. "Jimmy, do you think we have a chance tomorrow?"

"We've as good a chance as any. I wonder, are you aware we're just a few miles from Gettysburg? I can't believe we're about to fight another battle here, of all places."

Vic looked at his brother, confused. "Jimmy, what's so special about Gettysburg? Seems like it's only another place to fight or die."

James looked fondly at his brother, another good example of the country's failed education system. "Vic, it's just like you not to remember anything about American history, you meatball." He laughed, and it helped ease his uncertainty. "Don't you have to get ready, Corporal?"

"Yes, Lieutenant, and screw you, too, Sir." Vic turned, somewhat confused and pissed at his laughing brother. "I'll ask someone else, and yes, one of Mom's meatballs sounds pretty damn good," he mumbled, grabbing a ration from his backpack.

The morning came, cool and abrupt. The brooding silence was broken only by the nervous clatter of men checking and rechecking weapons and supplies, each man trying to breathe in life, keeping his own counsel. Some appeared overly jovial, while others, with serious demeanors, calculated their chance of survival. Across the open ground only four miles away, the Federal Army waited. It planned to strike at 0730, unaware that Rebel plans were about to trump them.

James's men were too far from the prayer service to attend, so James led his company in prayer. About 150 men kneeled or stood as James gave voice to his hope. "Lord, please watch over us this morning. Let us do our best. Protect us from harm, and should You desire our presence in Your kingdom, please take us into Your loving arms to comfort us in our journey to Your celestial home. If you don't want or need us right now Lord, then grant us the courage to do what we must. Amen."

After a moment of silence, James shouted, "Men, form up! Lock and load."

Company C's platoons were linked at three-foot intervals with other platoons of the 7th. Lying upon the ground, the waiting seemed endless, the curse of the foot soldier.

The barrage went off as planned, except that the Rebel Air Force was late by five minutes. It arrived in time to counter the Federal Air Force, though. The dogfights at several thousand feet were reminiscent of World War II. James, aware that the Rebels could only fight a limited air battle, watched excitedly as the feisty Texans took on the Feds, disrupting their battle plans. Then, almost as soon as the air battle started, the Rebel planes, their work accomplished, disengaged. Their fuel was at dangerously low levels, and several good planes fell from the sky before they were safely home.

At 0630, the whistles blew and butternut-clad men moved forward. The battle lasted through the day and early evening. The opposing armies sent over 500,000 men into harm's way, all to no firm conclusion. In desperation, the Federal Army dug its heels into the rich Pennsylvania soil. Men died by the hundreds, then the thousands, satisfying the carnal tastes of the hovering vultures waiting patiently for the killing to end. The initial air battle had been a draw, but it prevented Federal airmen from doing a lot more damage to the exposed Rebels. Surprised Federal leaders realized their air superiority was now a fond memory; the Rebels were catching up swiftly.

Charley Company lost ten men killed, with twenty wounded, and five missing. It was an expensive day. The Rebel Army's numbers fared no better, with total losses at around twenty percent. The real test for the Rebels' newly allied army was its performance against well-trained Federals on even turf. With three-to-two odds against them, they had held their ground, performing better than hoped.

Even with the battle a virtual draw, the Federal government realized its worst fears had come to roost. Dire predictions from its pessimistic leaders and Intel came to fruition. Skip Newman, commanding general of the Federal Armies, ordered his forces to pull back to Frederick, Maryland, to secure defenses for Washington. Even though, he thought that the Rebels would never bomb the capital, since it was considered sacred ground by all. For the time being, he was right.

President Rex Collins called an emergency meeting of his chiefs of staff in the protected tunnels below the White House. The revolt was now totally out of control. Drastic measures were needed to stop the Rebel onslaught.

The next day, James awoke to the warmth of a summer's day and its lovely yet eerie quiet. The Feds had moved their positions away from further immediate confrontation. Temporary relief settled in his chest as he received orders to pull his company back to regroup.

The Rinaldi brothers stood outside James's tent, currently being dismantled by two of his privates.

"What's up, James?" Vic asked.

"Vic, your squad did well yesterday. I'm proud of the way you handled things. It seems the Feds are not looking for a fight. We want to oblige them and lick our wounds, too. We're pulling back to the Allegheny Mountains."

Vic unhooked his backpack, enjoying the temporary release from its burden. "I can't say that I'm upset about that news. Until yesterday's carnage, I thought I'd never see Satan until I died." He laughed. "After what I've seen, this here second Battle of Gettysburg was sure hell on earth. I'd suppose it makes the real place—you know, hell—look calm by comparison."

"Vic, how the dickens do you know how hell looks?" He laughed, surprised at his brother's wit. Then he wondered aloud, "Lord, was all this really worth it?"

James grabbed his pack and rifle and started his men south, unaware that the 1st Corps had received orders to march to San Antonio to reinforce the Texas Army and help with its border problems. Texas was in trouble, its manpower depleted after a year of daily battle. James thought he was marching to the protection of the cool mountains and the Shenandoah Valley. Texas was the furthest thing from his mind.

He yelled to one of his sergeants, "Form a better line and spread out. What do you think we're on, a picnic? Move it, soldier!"

A few feet behind him, Vic shouted, "Hey, Lieutenant, I remember about Gettysburg. It was one of those Civil War battles Dad and Rock talked about." Vic couldn't see his brother's broad smile.

In the distance, a lonely hawk screeched. James looked up to see it disappear into the overcast sky, its wings spread out, seeking a hidden thermal, as if wanting to rise even further above the disarray below.

Our way of living together in America is a strong but delicate fabric. It is made up of many threads. It has been woven over many centuries by patience and sacrifice of countless Liberty loving men and women.
—Wendell Lewis Willkie

CHAPTER TEN

July 20, 2020—Command Post, 1st Brigade, 36th Division Near Del Rio, Ten Miles from the Texas-Mexico Border

The sun's rays beat relentlessly upon the 1st Brigade's HQ tent. Inside Justin felt like a loaf of bread baking in the heat. He searched his mind, attempting to solve his command's dilemma. His 6,000 troops were almost surrounded by a strong force of Mexican Nationals. Intel predicted that as many as 50,000 were in the area closing on his command.

After Rebel success in Oklahoma, the 36th was ordered to patrol the southern border, which had been quiet. The transfer was intended to provide the division with a much-needed R&R before actual police duty started.

Chance had favored both the 1st and the 4th Brigades. Just prior to executing their orders, they split off at Del Rio. The 1st had been preparing to go east for its assigned 50-mile perimeter. The 4th would go likewise to the west. Both were to spread out in thin lines, loosely patrolling the Rio Grande. The Mexican attack came one day too early, allowing the two brigades to form in strength near Del Rio.

If fate had allowed their intended dispersal, the Mexicans could have massacred them at their leisure. *Now,* Justin thought sharply, *they'll get to slaughter us all at once, if help doesn't come soon.*

Justin sent an urgent call to Austin, pleading for Texans and allies to come to his aid. Like Colonel Travis's call for help from the Alamo in 1836, he too appealed for reinforcements. His message boldly stated that his command "would fight to the end to defend Texas and its borders without surrender." Like Travis and Bowie's arch nemesis, General Santa

Anna, the Mexican commander, General Jesus Rivera, didn't see any necessity to take prisoners. Fighting like bearcats was not an option for the Texans—it was the only way to survive.

Justin's Rangers didn't intend to surrender or to take many prisoners either, not after the reported slaughter six days earlier of a homeland border battalion posted east of Del Rio. This outrage clearly demonstrated what the Mexicans had in store for their adversaries.

Justin had received distressing news the day before of the Rebels' draw with the Federals at Gettysburg. He read solemnly that the Federals were calling it a great victory. However, Rebel Intel reports claimed optimistically that with more manpower, victory would have been theirs. Now, Justin's small command faced an Alamo-like situation. It forced him to think about retreat, or worse, a valiant last stand. Current intelligence cautiously advised that retreat was no longer feasible. Justin beat his brain trying to think of a way out of the mess he had unintentionally walked into. Another Alamo disaster for Texas was not an option.

While border squabbles were commonplace, the Mexicans' prolonged attack had been a complete surprise. Mexico's government usually stayed out of the deadly conflict between their gringo neighbors to the north. Faced with the threat of strategic nuclear warheads aimed at them, as well as the economic loss should they interfere, Mexico took a cautious position of neutrality. Feuding Americans wisely thought that Mexico was just waiting with patient indifference for the outcome, like most of the rest of the world. Then they would see who'd end up buttering their tamales.

The Republic of Texas would never go nuclear on Mexico. Too many Texan citizens fighting for the Rebel cause were either of Mexican descent or had family in Mexico, and more importantly, prevailing winds would cause almost as much damage to Texas. So, Texas continued to trade with Mexico for food, clothes, arms, and oil. Since the war's beginning, a pitiful Texas economy forced compromise with principle. It was a reconciliation only as solid as the Mexican government. Mexico—past and present—did not include a reliable government in their equation of common sense.

x x x x x

Whatever the reason for the invasion, Justin, with feigned joy, found himself thrown in command of two brigades by virtue of the date of his promotion. To him it was an unwelcome responsibility. The frightful reality that this invasion might become the biggest single disaster to face the young Texan National Army made it even worse. However, neither Justin nor the Mexican general surrounding his unit knew or realized the tenacity, perseverance, and sheer stubbornness of the young Aggie general from Prosper, Texas.

If the invasion was not enough pressure, he had only to look east. There across the desert-like terrain, Becky's 77th hospital unit was precariously stationed a few short miles away in Uvalde. His two Ranger brigades were all that stood between them and disaster.

Justin always enjoyed spoiling his little sister. Yet despite her pampering, she was strong-spirited. He chuckled at a recent memory. It had not surprised him when she had stepped in to intercede for a Federal prisoner who was slated for Huntsville. It was obvious that Becky was fond of this Fed sergeant, whom she had helped nurse back to health. She had encouraged and then pleaded with her big brother, through Taylor, to use his rank to intercede on Rinaldi's behalf. When he and Taylor talked to the prisoner, they liked him instantly. His manner was infectious. Justin pulled rank and made things happen. Accepting Rinaldi's word, but not without reason or intense investigation, he gave him freedom so he could join the 36th.

Justin had learned that Rinaldi had received excellent training in the old Federal Army before the outbreak. His request to enlist in the Rebel Army was believable when intelligence advised that he had three brothers in the First New York Volunteers, two alive, one an infantry captain.

While interrogating Luke, Justin was impressed with the New Yorker, especially his sincerity. Still, he initially placed Rinaldi where he could watch him. His old command, Company B, 2nd Ranger Regiment, needed a sergeant and Rinaldi was available. What sold him most was Luke's candor and his statement: "Look, General, I made a mistake, and now I'm back alongside my brothers. Even if it is only for a short time, I need to do this. Please, Sir."

It was also no surprise to Justin when Becky volunteered for the 77th hospital unit sent to accompany the 36th. Her hazardous duty term had expired, and she could have enjoyed an easier post. Justin wondered if he could keep the young lovers alive long enough to realize their romance. A sickening feeling made him gasp for air.

Currently, Justin faced a major internal problem. General Harrington, the 4th Brigade's senior officer, was feeling put upon—outraged at Justin's appointment to command the besieged brigades. Justin's patience was beginning to wear thin and the 99-degree temperature didn't help matters. He shouted across the bunker for his adjutant. "Captain, where's General Harrington? I sent for him over an hour ago!" Justin glared at his brother as he paced the tent's dirt floor.

"Sir," Taylor answered unfazed, "he was addressing his command and said he'd be here soon as he could."

"Taylor, what's your take on this man? Is it insubordination, or is the bastard on a misguided mission?"

"Justin, I'd say he's pissed. You know he's old army and, well … you're probably an Aggie upstart irritation to his ego."

"Captain, if you must, go and grab the old fart by the collar. Take the MPs with you. *Get* his stubborn ass here on the double." Justin slammed his clenched fists together.

Taylor appreciated the urgency of the situation. He had been present during the last intelligence briefing a couple of hours earlier. The report wasn't pretty. Harrington had been mysteriously unavailable then as well and had also missed the scout's report reconfirming their precarious situation. It was urgently apparent that drastic measures were needed. Presently, the only obvious alternative was to develop a rapid defensive position since escape no longer seemed a viable option. Precious time to develop a comprehensive plan was wasting.

On Taylor's stormy, unannounced arrival at the 4th Brigade HQ, he witnessed activity heightened to a fevered pitch. The short half-mile walk had left him winded. He was not in the mood for any crap. He saluted the guards at the entrance of Harrington's tent, walking in uninvited. Captain Marseles, Harrington's adjutant, intercepted Taylor.

"Captain, may I help you?" he snapped.

Taylor ignored him, and with controlled anger, walked up to General Harrington. "Sir, General Northcutt respectfully requests your presence at once. You are needed on the double." Taylor waived in his MPs.

Harrington did not try to hide his anger. He had been a major in the regular U.S. Army before the war began and didn't appreciate that Justin, an ROTC Reserve second lieutenant, was now his commander. Harrington's irritation came to life. He leaped up, shouting angrily, spraying spittle at Taylor. "I'm ten years older than Northcutt. I cannot accept the idiotic mistake that he outranks me by a few f-ing days. General Sinsome's choice to pick him must be an error."

Harrington sat down, glaring at Taylor. "Sinsome and I served together. What the hell is Command thinking? Captain Northcutt is it? Well, Sinsome's not here, and until I officially hear from him, in writing, confirming this absurdity, I will not accept your brother as my commander."

Taylor, clasping his hands so tightly that they hurt, tried to remain calm. His eyes gave him away.

Harrington continued, spraying venom with every word. "Captain, tell General Northcutt I'll meet with him when I'm ready to meet with him, and no sooner."

Taylor spoke coolly, though in a vivid, strained voice. "Begging your pardon, Sir, but there's a state of urgency requiring your presence. General Northcutt will not be left waiting." Taylor wanted desperately to call his guard detail into action. Nothing frightened him any longer. With patience expired, it was time, but before he could act, his brother's angry entrance upstaged him.

Justin's eyes glowed with rage. He flung the table in front of Harrington across the room, ripping the tent. Harrington, startled, reached for his service revolver. Justin's hand was too quick. Justin slapped the gun from Harrington's hand while pointing his own Colt .45.

Only Taylor had ever seen Justin this angry. Taylor knew that anyone nearby had better look for shelter.

"Everyone out! I will converse with General Harrington alone." Several subordinates left the tent. "No, Captain Northcutt, you remain. You, Captain! What's your name?"

"Marseles, Sir—adjutant to General Harrington."

"You stay, Marseles. I may need a witness!"

In a measured tone, Justin spit out his rage. "General Harrington, you have purposely kept me waiting. Worse, 6,000 men now depend upon me. General, you are holding up our progress in a traitorous manner. I didn't ask for this command. The 1st is enough for me. But your BULLSHIT so far has convinced me that not only are you out of line, you are not the man you think you are. I won't tolerate your insubordination now or ever, and certainly not when we're about to be in a fight for our lives."

Justin took a deep breath trying to control his fury. It didn't work. The cold steel in his blue eyes emphasized his anger. "I don't regret that I command by the virtue of a promotion that predates yours by four f-ing days. Live with it or be placed in chains. I'd arrest you now, but we need every able and experienced man. But, General, if you stand in my way again or disrupt my command, I'll have you shot. Count on it. I'll pull the goddamned trigger myself. So don't waste my time giving me measurements for your damn leg irons. All you'll need is a hole in the ground. Better yet, a toss to the coyotes. Am I clear?"

Harrington hadn't counted on Justin's rage. He noted Taylor's eyes—they were determined. Taylor's M-16 was aimed at his heart. He feared, correctly, that the young officer might not wait for Justin's order for a firing squad.

Harrington did not doubt Justin would carry out his threat if it became a military necessity. If Harrington was anything, he was first a soldier and a realist. With sudden awareness, he felt naked and foolish before the young brigadier and the two adjutants.

He took a deep breath, slowly expelling the uncomfortable air before speaking. "General, please accept my apologies for my insubordination. I was out of line."

"Apology accepted, General!" Justin's retort sounded like the snap of a braided whip on wood. "Be at my tent in thirty minutes. Bring Marseles with you." Neither his expression nor his tone changed.

The brothers, without saluting, left. Taylor, relieved, still had a thought or two he needed to get off his chest. "Justin, why'd you let that scum off the hook? He may cost us yet."

"Taylor, the man has old army pride. Let him alone for a few minutes to stew on what I said. He's really a good soldier. Always remember this. That son of a bitch and many like him want and enjoy this shit. Unlike us slobs, who are mostly thrown unwillingly into the responsibility of command, he actually likes it. Let's aim them in the direction of the enemy, and worry about their ilk later. Right now I've a crisis to manage."

Returning to his headquarters, Justin noticed a camouflaged tanker truck parked in a newly dug protective bunker. It hadn't been there when he passed a few moments earlier. Something stirred him about the soldier leaning at its wheel. He looked familiar. Taylor also noticed the soldier. Smiling to himself, he walked up to the private. The private's helmet fell off as he stood to salute the young captain. Justin wondered what had distracted his brother. The young, boyish-looking private's uniform was about two sizes too big and not very soldierly, even for a Rebel.

As the private stood saluting Taylor, Justin realized he was a she. Females were on active duty in all ranks. The Motor Pool was almost an all-female branch. Still unfazed, Justin figured his brother was on the prowl.

Suddenly he recognized her—she was the green-eyed, brunette beauty he had met a few weeks earlier on the road north to Oklahoma. He silently mouthed the name he had not forgotten, Julia McKnight. His stare was interrupted by Taylor's comment. "It's nice to see you again. Your name's McKnight, isn't it?"

"Yes, Sir, Private Julia McKnight. We met a few weeks ago on old Preston Road. You and your general," she nodded in Justin's direction, "gave my family some badly needed food."

"Yes, Private, it was General Northcutt." He pointed to his brother standing within hearing distance. "And I'm Captain Taylor Northcutt," he said with emphasis. "When did you arrive?"

"Sir, I delivered fuel a couple of minutes ago. Sir, I'm very fatigued. I've been hauling for the past eight hours. Please forgive me for not standing when you walked by." Julia fidgeted, thinking she must have broken

157

some military code. She continued speaking nervously, "I'm told our convoy is the last to get through and that I'll need a weapon and instructions on using it. May I ask if it's true—we're not getting out soon?" Taylor nodded in the affirmative.

Justin walked over, a rare smile on his face, acknowledging her salute with his own. "Private, how's your family? I truly admired your grandfather's spunk."

Julia lowered her eyes, embarrassed. She was shy and fearful of addressing a general. Or could it be something else? She shuddered at her inner feelings.

"Sir," Julia's face showed the pain of memory. "My grandfather died on the trip, right after we met you. Our refugee column got caught up in some crossfire between Rebel militia and a Federal helicopter. Grandmother and Mom are at a refugee camp with my sister in Waco. I joined the Women's Army Corps to be useful. Anything's better than that camp They only trained me to drive this rig, but it appears I'm stranded without a weapon."

"Private McKnight, I'm very sorry to hear about your grandfather. This war's been cruel to everyone. Captain Northcutt will see that you're assigned a weapon and given proper instruction. As we speak, there's a new company being formed of soldiers in the same predicament. I'm afraid you drove badly needed diesel in at the right time for us, though the wrong time for a round trip. Still, I'm very happy to see that you're OK, Private." Justin smiled openly—a love-starved schoolboy, feeling inwardly foolish.

A few yards from the rig, Taylor poked fun, "You've got it bad. I saw how you looked at her. She is beautiful. I'd pursue her myself if there wasn't a war going on and you weren't interested."

Justin frowned. Taylor smiled. "Taylor, you find someplace safe for her. I don't want her in the middle of a fight. She won't stand a chance."

"I'll see what I can do. Though I think any lady that can learn to drive an eighteen-wheeler can take care of herself. You know, you can count on me, Bro. Truthfully though, is any place safe? Oh, and by the way, don't worry about what you did to Harrington. I'll be there for the meeting to shoot the bastard myself if you want me to. And I'm not kiddin'."

Justin watched his brother leave to work his magic. Life seemed so fragile now. *Hell, war doesn't invite love. But it just showed up without warning.* He resolved to enjoy every moment God allowed him because now he had another major reason to survive and to worry. Somehow he'd make her a major part of his life.

Taylor entered Justin's command tent late; Harrington and Marseles had already arrived. He found himself focusing on Justin's desk askew with papers. It was unlike his brother. Justin stood to start the meeting.

"Harrington, it appears we're totally surrounded and will have to make a stand. It's not a place I'd have chosen, but we'll have to make do. General, disperse your brigade and dig in on the north and west perimeters. The 1st Brigade will cover the east and south." Justin walked to the map pinned on the wall, pointing to the areas.

"We have eight howitzers, four 105s and four 155s, and four tanks, not much to oppose what the enemy's amassing against us. Thankfully, it doesn't appear they have any ordnance greater than ours. It's strange that they have only infantry, when you consider their numbers."

Harrington interrupted. "I'm guessing they figured fast travel is more important to them. They probably didn't plan on two Ranger brigades in their path."

Justin, relieved at Harrington's voluntary participation, continued his overview. "Intel figures they planned to overrun the Home Guard Militia and waltz north to San Antonio. We're told they've hit our forces near Brownsville and El Paso and are also attacking near Nogales, Arizona. Their shenanigans appear to be a three-pronged attack with Texas taking the brunt."

"Are we to expect reinforcements?" Harrington asked, settling into his secondary role.

"We've had some local militia get through. It only amounts to about two full companies. There's rumor that some New York troops are on their way. They're a couple of light infantry divisions deployed to San Antonio for R&R and border duty. They're part of the units that fought off the Canadians in New York last May and who recently fought at the Second Gettysburg. Command advised they've been fighting nonstop for a year and are northern Rebel shock troops."

"Some R&R," Harrington said sarcastically. His humanity caught Justin by surprise.

Justin brushed away a pestering fly and dropped his notes. He picked them up and continued. "The last we heard they were near Austin. We need to let our men know there's help coming from seasoned veterans. They have about 15,000 men, though I doubt that'll be enough. Let's hope they can get through."

"Do we still have that helicopter gunship?" Harrington asked.

Justin paced. "Yes, I'm about to order it on what will probably be its last mission. That's if we can rustle up enough fuel. I need it for courier service. We've got to see if we can rush the New Yorkers and maybe get our meager air force down here. Strangely, the Mexicans haven't used any planes. Again, dig in deep and have your men fed in their foxholes. No more two-hour shifts; every soldier must be at the ready until adequate reinforcements get through."

They spent the balance of the meeting on details and dispositions of men and material. In the background, rumbled the sounds of entrenching tools and a couple of bulldozers. The diesel fuel Julia had delivered was making the difference, enabling the quick and necessary dirt work needed for their defense.

Harrington saluted as he took leave. "May I say, General, I hope you know you can count on me. I'm sorry we got off on the wrong foot. I'm regular army. It can get in the way sometimes. I clearly see you know your way around."

"Consider it over, General, and good luck! I'm for leaving our fighting for the enemy. I'll be in touch soon."

The brigadiers found a new mutual respect. Justin watched Harrington leave. It was men like Harrington who helped win battles.

July 20, 2020—San Antonio, Texas
First New York Voluntary Expeditionary Force

James Rinaldi inspected his men's gear, readying them for the forced march to Del Rio. Since Gettysburg, three weeks earlier, the 121st, along with the Ninth New York Division, had been traveling in a southwestern direction. Commanders were told that only two Texan Ranger divisions could be spared to cover a 1,200-mile border. The New York shock troops were determined to make a difference.

They initially moved under the cover of darkness along the old scenic Blue Ridge Highway. For the balance of the journey they kept off main roads. Federal Air still dominated the sky.

They marched dog-tired into San Antonio with little fanfare. Most of their transport vehicles turned north to return to their two divisions.

All available trucks plus those left behind had immediately been dispatched to transport James's regiment, along with two others, to Del Rio. All they were told was that they were to reinforce two Ranger divisions dispersed along the border. It reminded James of Canada. His unit was the closest to Del Rio, and by chance, would be the first to relieve the besieged Texans.

He had mixed emotions; he'd heard that Luke had been fighting in Texas. An uneasy feeling crept into his thoughts. *Where is my brother in all this mess? Far to the north, I hope.*

James's regiment rolled out at 1900. They headed west slowly, filled with uncertainty. Finally, they were told it was a rescue operation against the invading Mexicans. Del Rio was being touted as a "Second Alamo."

Vic caught up with his brother and jumped on the assigned truck. Relieved to be riding, he looked with renewed interest at James. "Jimmy-boy, it seems like we're always going to some second battle. Let's see, the second Gettysburg, the second Alamo, and the second Bullshit. What gives, Jimmy?"

"Not sure, Vic, all I know is we're the advance force of 2,000 men. The rest of our guys will probably march. I suppose you can say we're lucky."

Vic's face soured. "You know, Bozo, this is one time I'd rather walk."

"You sure turned regular grunt awful quick, Bro."

"Survival, Jimmy, survival." Vic hugged his rifle like it was a curvaceous blonde.

Del Rio was about 150 miles due west and a twenty-mile-per-hour convoy crawl; they would reach their destination in eight hours. The column moved past endless cacti to the slow roar of the trucks' engines and road vibrations. Behind his vehicle, dozens of trucks in every conceivable form followed to supplement the New Yorkers' service vehicles: eighteen-wheelers, six-wheelers, confiscated rentals, cattle and hog carriers—you name it, the Rebs had put it together into a workable troop convoy.

James was told to have his men ready for battle at dawn. Texan Militia accompanying their column would alert the Rangers of their presence. Total Mexican strength and disposition was unknown. Every move was a gamble. Their linkup was intended to be coordinated with an air attack at 0500. James closed his eyes, trying to think pleasant thoughts.

At 0230 the convoy came to a halt. Orders to dismount and form up were given in careful whispers. James stirred his tired company from their lethargy. Many groaned when orders came to move out. A nine-mile march awaited them along with probable battle. Feelings for loved ones and fear of death consumed many. The heat was unbearable. Their threadbare uniforms clung to them.

James looked over his shoulder at the empty convoy heading east back toward San Antonio. They would refuel and pick up another load of men who were currently marching west. Though not a part of strategy sessions, he knew from briefings and hard experience that this was a desperate mission. As they came closer to their destination, they were told that over 50,000 Mexicans surrounded the Texans. Even if the full complement of New York's two divisions reached the besieged Rangers, their combined force would remain severely outnumbered. James shuddered; a feeling of dread overwhelmed him.

x x x x

Justin called an impromptu briefing. His new, hastily built bunker was crammed to capacity with officers. General Harrington stood to his left. Justin had a disturbing thought. *A lucky Mexican artillery round could render us leaderless.*

Justin spoke hurriedly. "Men, we just received urgent news. A relief column of about 2,000 men is only ten miles away. There are about 8,000 more following closely behind. They're hoofing it and not expected for some time. We'll need to hold out until they show and then include them in our plan to break out after they've rested some.

"Our air support will start bombing runs on the Mexican positions to the east, north, and south. They'll leave the west alone and open for the New York boys to get through. Air will hit at 0500. Our job's to provide cover and distraction. We'll need to move half our men to the western perimeter. It's a valid risk we must take. We'll start artillery fire at 0430 and stop at 0455."

Justin reached into his pocket for a rare piece of hard candy. He opened the wrapper, popping the candy into his mouth, crunching it. It calmed him. Seeing some of his men look longingly at the wrapper, he took the bag from his backpack, offering it to his men.

"Any concerns, ideas, questions? Yes, General Harrington."

Harrington stood to speak. "General, if we can secure a nearby dry creek, I think we could run the relief in through it. It's a deep-cut channel called San Felipe Creek. I used to play in it when I was a kid. At least it'll provide some cover. We can have a company go there under cover of darkness—get them in position. It's chancy, but I believe it'll save lives."

Justin smiled; he felt vindicated for not having Harrington arrested. "I like your idea, General. Go for it."

Taylor stepped forward. "I'd like to volunteer to lead that company, General." Justin, not surprised but damn proud, reacted quickly to approve his brother's request. To deny him would not look well in front of his command.

"Yes, Captain, you may have that honor. Take your old company in Second Regiment and prepare to leave immediately. We'll get word to the relief column of the change." Justin grasped his brother's hand, looking into his eyes. Worry and pride showed on his face. "Go with God," he whispered. "And Taylor, be careful."

"Thank you, Sir." Taylor saluted confidently.

"Men, get to your posts. We have a lot of work to do."

Taylor's old company greeted him warmly. He was pleased but not surprised when First Lieutenant Appleton, latest commander of Company B, readily turned over command to him. "Baker Company is ready to do anything other than dig, Sir."

With blackened faces and minimal gear, the company's 180 Rangers crawled to the unmanned position near the creek bed. An occasional horned toad interrupted their anxious push past the endless brush, sage, and mesquite trees ripping their already tattered uniforms.

"It seems too quiet, Lieutenant. Maybe the Mexicans are puffed up thinking their superiority is all they need," Taylor whispered. "Damn." He pulled out a thorn from his hand, licked his wound, and kept crawling through the brush.

Appleton answered, "I don't like it either, Taylor. Something's not right."

The Texans did not know that the Mexicans had been advised by their intelligence that any Rebel reinforcements would be too few and far between to arrive in time. They were also told the surrounded Texans were spread too thin to present a formidable defense, let alone a viable counterattack. This overconfidence allowed Company B to secure its strategic position on San Felipe Creek.

At 0430 the Rebels' main perimeter opened up with steady, calculated, diversionary fire. The Mexicans, temporarily confused, fired back sporadically, thinking it a small, remote skirmish. Neither side had good targets. Universal night vision equipment was a memory.

At 0500, two wings of Texan air power totaling ten prop planes came in low with napalm and took out several artillery pieces exposed by the flares sent up by the Texans. Still, the Mexican Army showed little concern. They expected some resistance. At the same time, Taylor's unit made contact with the first of the New Yorkers, who were carefully guided to the Rebel lines.

Suddenly intense fire erupted on the western perimeter. The Mexican Army finally understood that Rebel reinforcements were arriving and opened fire in the area opposite Company B. Taylor's small force returned fire. With the cover of the creek bed and the early morning darkness, the Rangers held off the Mexican onslaught, while the New York regiments quickly traveled the creek beds to the Rebel lines. The last company came through, its officer finding his way to Taylor.

Taylor quickly stepped forward, saluting. "Captain, you sure are a welcome sight."

"Glad to be here, Captain. We're the last of our relief. Captain James Rinaldi, at your service! Where can my men help?"

"Good to meet you. You can help best by getting back to our main lines quickly." Taylor paused. "Did you say 'Rinaldi'? By any chance do you have a brother named Luke?"

James looked at Taylor, extremely surprised at hearing his brother's name. "Yes, how do you know him?"

Taylor quickly answered. "He's a sergeant with this company. You can have a reunion when we get back to safety."

James felt numb. "I'll be damned, I'll be damned." He looked to his left. Seeing Tim Rockwell, he shouted above the gunfire, "Tim, did you hear? Luke's here. He's safe."

Tim stepped forward; his blackened face formed a smile. "That's great news! Hopefully he'll have news about Bobby." Suddenly, Tim brushed a large furry-like presence off his shirtsleeve. "What the hell is that?" Tim shouted.

A Ranger sergeant walked bent over laughing, "Just a tarantula, soldier. Welcome to Del Rio, and watch out for the freakin' cactus. It's all over the place."

The sergeant was about to say something else when they heard, "Incoming!"

Enemy mortar shells rained close to Taylor's location, laying a carpet barrage over the area.

Taylor shouted, "Let's get the hell out of here. We can talk later. Move out." The company pulled out, while firing into the darkness.

With an urgency that prevails when faced with the need to survive, the remaining men snaked their way to the safety of the encircled trenches, visible in the light of early dawn.

Courage is almost a contradiction in terms. It means a strong desire to live taking the form of a readiness to die.
— G. K. Chesterton

CHAPTER ELEVEN

July 21, 2020-1st Brigade Encampment, near Del Rio, Texas
Ten Miles from the Texas-Mexico Border

With the infusion of the New Yorkers and the few local Home Guards that somehow made it through the Mexican siege, the surrounded Rebel force now numbered around 10,000. Justin found himself responsible for a force of highly motivated, mostly seasoned combat veterans. With little time for doubt, the young brigadier faced a monumental task. New intelligence estimated the surrounding enemy force to be near 90,000 combatants. What Intel didn't know was this was one-third of the Mexican forces jointly attacking Rebel-held positions along the southwestern United States border.

Taylor, alone with Justin in the command bunker in a moment of deep reflection, spoke, breaking the silence. "Some things don't add up in this equation. If Intel can't fathom why the Mexicans attacked, how in blazes can we? Heck, don't they have a faltering economy, dependent upon trade with us? How can we—lowly rangers—figure why they'd suddenly turn on us without cause or provocation?" Taylor threw a punch into the air.

"Taylor, maybe there are deeper implications. We and our allies do have the Federals on the run."

"You mean you think there's more than opportunism drivin' Mexican ambitions?"

"Taylor, politics can make strange bedfellows, and so can opportunity. You'd think the Mexican government would stand on the side of the Rebels, not the Federal government."

"It'd certainly be in their best interest to side with Texas. Damn, we're next door, major trading partners with the bastards, and largely populated with Mexican Americans." Taylor spat out each word.

"Maybe they want to take back Texas, now that we made something of it." Justin smirked, nodding—his subtle signal that it was time to return to military formality. Several staff officers entered the Command Bunker.

When everyone was assembled, Justin looked directly at Taylor and said, "Captain, you did well last evening. What's the final casualty report?" Justin had covered this earlier. He needed to include his staff.

"General, three men killed, with seventeen wounded; three seriously. We're fortunate General Harrington's quick thinking allowed us to use the cover of that splendid creek. Our scouts report, though, that avenue is now history."

"Captain, here's my order to divide reinforcements between the 1st and 4th. Advise the New York commanding general and his three regimental commanders I'd like to review our position with them in thirty minutes. Send out Sergeant Rinaldi to inform the Home Guard commander and the regimental commanders of the 1st and 4th to be here post haste."

Taylor sent Rinaldi and another man to do Justin's bidding. Turning to Justin he said, "Sir, can you spare me a couple of minutes?" Justin dismissed his staff with a wave of his hand.

Justin, impatient, turned to his brother. "Barely, Captain. Out with it! You have a minute."

Taylor was quietly amused by his brother's control of the situation, in particular his strong desire to remain aloof, even with him. It marked his developing personality and his evolution into a remarkable officer. Taylor remained thankful for his subordinate role.

Fearing his brother's anger, Taylor spoke rapidly. "General, there's a Captain in the New York 4th Brigade's 7th Regiment you might want to meet. He's Sergeant Rinaldi's older brother. Since Becky's so keen on our Sergeant Rinaldi, I thought you'd want to check him out. Also, I'd like to add that Sergeant Rinaldi handled his men in excellent fashion last night. He's too good a man to remain a sergeant. I'll keep my eyes on him.

I fear we'll have several openings to worry about if any of us survive this fiasco."

"Thanks for the heads up. Rinaldi sounds like he's working out. You know, I never doubted Becky's judgment, so I'm with you on this one. Send Captain Rinaldi to me, ASAP. Intel and my personnel investigation say he's a good soldier. The Rinaldi clan sure appears to support our cause. Have they had a reunion yet?"

"I'll get them together this morning after your meeting." Taylor strapped his helmet on as he began to leave. Justin gestured to wait.

"Taylor, how about Becky's hospital unit. Any word yet?"

"No, not really." Taylor took his helmet off. "Only that they pulled out and headed farther inland. Some of their doctors volunteered to stay. They arrived with the New Yorkers. There's no word Becky was among the volunteers. I'm hoping she moved inland with her unit. There are enough Northcutts in harm's way."

As Taylor left, Brigadier General Michael Holt, a middle-aged, tall, dark-haired, serious-looking man entered the command post. Saluting, he introduced himself and his three regimental colonels from the 5th, 7th, and 9th New York Volunteer Regiments. His wizened face showed the strain of the past year's campaigning. He was pure regular army.

Justin reached out his right hand in a clasp of welcome; Holt took it in a vice-like grip. "Thank you for pulling all the stops to get here, General." Justin tightened his grip as he spoke. "You're a welcome sight. Your veterans will fit in nicely with my boys.

"I'll get right to the point." Justin motioned for Holt to sit on one of the improvised crates. "We're surrounded and in desperate straits. We'll probably see action from the enemy at any time. Hell, if I were in that Mex general's shoes, I'd have attacked by now. My guess is he's working on regrouping his scattered units so his boys can walk over us by the sheer weight of their numbers."

"What exactly is the disposition of the forces surrounding us, General?" Holt asked as he walked to the small map on Justin's desk.

"From our patrols and infrequent intelligence, it seems the enemy has amassed about 100,000 men." Holt sighed deeply. Justin continued.

"Some are already, I'm sorry to say, beginning to call this the second Alamo. I'd like to draw a distinct difference to put a rest to this faulty analogy. The last Alamo had what history believes were about 180 men surrounded by around 4,000 Mexicans. In 1836, there wasn't an organized or experienced military in Texas. There is now, and we will not give them an easy victory. Like the original Alamo, we don't intend to let them take us without rendering a horrific cost. We still have some air power and more on the way. With your men, we now have four heavy artillery batteries and ten Bradley tanks. Dug in like we are, we have significant firepower to hold them back for some time. You'll find, General, that what we Texans lack in numbers, we make up in esprit de corps."

"Yes, General," Holt smirked, his distinct Yankee accent underlined with playful sarcasm. "I've also heard that one Texan can take care of any ten Mexicans."

Taking the bait, Justin countered. "Well, you heard right, General. And we plan on living up to our reputation."

Holt added, "I know a little bit about your Texas history. It seems you're about the same age as the legendary Colonel Travis of the first Alamo." Holt's amused stare caught Justin off guard.

"I guess that may be right, General. What of it?"

"Nothing intended except for the irony, General. It seems like history's repeating itself. Only this time you have three regiments of New York's best, fresh from Gettysburg, here to help make the difference. Did I hear correctly that the sons of bitches aren't taking prisoners?"

"You heard right." Justin eyed each of Holt's colonels, speaking directly to them. "Fill your men in. If it gives as much incentive to piss off your boys as it does mine, maybe they'll match my men in that ten-to-one category," Justin smirked.

Holt rose to the challenge, his friendly laugh invigorating the moment. "Why, General, my boys recently put down an invasion of French Canadians. Where we come from we're known as the 'Canuck Killer Brigade.' Your boys are now in good Yankee hands and can count on us to do our fair share of killing and dying."

Justin stood, reaching across his improvised desk, to shake Holt's hand, signaling the close of the meeting. "General Holt, as far as the no prisoner crap, I suppose the Mexicans fear taking captives will slow them down. If that's the way they want to play, then so be it. It'll serve to harden the resolve of my Rangers, and heaven help the enemy if they do manage to overtake us. They'll have a terrible price tag for any victory they enjoy."

Holt, now standing, nodded his agreement.

During the next hour, all possible tactics were covered and regurgitated over and over by Justin's officers. At the same time, recon patrols continued to feel out the Mexican strength, confirming the enemy's continued buildup. Justin's next decision would be his most difficult. He felt like a cornered lion sitting and waiting for the hunter to strike. With this in mind, he reluctantly concluded that his force would have to make a coordinated, highly concentrated attack to distract and divide the unwary Mexicans. He hoped the temporary confusion would allow the meager Rebel air support an opportunity to help them divide, conquer, and break out of their entrapment. He reasoned it was the only practical option. Taking the offensive seemed more desirable than waiting to get hammered. Surprise would have to serve as their only ally.

Justin's strategy meeting ended. With little time for niceties, he asked General Holt to wait after appointing him second in command of the combined Rebel forces. General Harrington took the disappointment in polite stride as he fell third in line.

Dismissing everyone, Justin faced the New Yorker. "General Holt, I prefer we address each other on a first-name basis. May I have a moment?" Justin liked this man. It was time to break formality.

"Certainly. How can I be of service?"

"Mike, I understand you have a Captain Rinaldi under your command. His brother Luke's a sergeant in Company B, 2nd Ranger Regiment."

"Yes, Justin, I heard about the coincidence. Captain James Rinaldi's a fine officer. He commands Company C, 7th Regiment. He won't stop at Captain if he survives." Holt hesitated. "For that matter, if anyone survives."

The tension was telling on Holt's troubled face. He didn't like the interruption for what appeared to be personal matters. Respect for

Northcutt and his strict West Point training made him listen and respond accordingly.

Holt continued, "Rinaldi's my reluctant leader. His men respect him and will follow him into hell. He's risen from the ranks, but he should have started as an officer instead of a private in the first place. He's a college graduate, cum laude from Syracuse—was well into his master's when he joined us."

"Mike, he sounds like a warrior; it must run in the family."

"He's a warrior but a hesitant one. I'd say he's here only out of sense of duty. But I'll say this for him, he'll not shirk responsibility. I'd hate to be his enemy." As Holt's description unwound, Justin felt himself relating to Rinaldi's traits.

"I'll send Rinaldi right over to see you," Holt said. "Getting back to your plan, Justin, I'd like to recommend sending my 7th and 9th regiments to fall in next to your 1st brigade. I believe it will enhance our position on that perimeter."

"Thanks, General." Justin smiled, pleased to have Holt's experience. "Move forward with your recommendations. Perhaps with two Rinaldis together, we'll have a force to be reckoned with." Justin grinned. "By the way, General, off the record ..."

Holt nodded agreement.

"Luke Rinaldi and my sister Rebecca seem to be very close, so I'm also a big brother checking out my sister's friend."

"I was wondering why the sudden interest in my New Yorker."

Justin beamed and said, "I wonder when we'll start thinking of ourselves as Americans again. Not Texans or New Yorkers. Someday soon I hope." Holt's smile reflected agreement.

Taylor entered the command bunker with Sergeant Luke Rinaldi in tow. Both saluted as Justin gave each a warm handshake.

"Sergeant, I hear your brother, Captain James Rinaldi, arrived with reinforcements. He's on his way. We've arranged it so you can have a brief reunion."

"Thank you, Sir. The last I heard, he was a corporal. It's been at least two years since I've seen Jimmy. It'll be good to catch up. You know, Sir, I didn't even know if he was alive."

Justin smiled warmly at Luke. "Sorry about the short time you'll have to visit. By the way, my brother here thinks highly of you and advises you have potential. I must admit I've been a skeptic, but our sister seems to have placed a lot of faith in you."

"Sir, may I be frank?"

"Yes, go ahead, Sergeant."

"Well, Sir," Luke paused, clearly uncomfortable, "I'm very fond of Becky, though her feelings for me seem a bit baffling."

"Sergeant, I doubt anyone knows what's in our sister's head. I'll tell you this, though; she wouldn't give you the time of day if she didn't like you. You can be assured of one thing; an ex-Federal sergeant wouldn't be in a front-line Rebel unit if we didn't value Becky's judgment."

"Thank you, Sir. That's a relief."

The sound of artillery fire echoed in the distance as Captain Rinaldi entered Justin's bunker, interrupting the conversation. A smile from ear to ear showed his pleasure upon seeing his brother. Following closely behind Captain Rinaldi was a grinning Vic. Even with a scrubby beard he looked like Luke's mirror image.

"General, Captain, Captain Rinaldi and Corporal Rinaldi reporting as ordered, Sirs." Both James and Vic stood at attention while introductions were made. The Northcutt and Rinaldi brothers shook hands.

"Shit, I didn't know there were two of you," Justin remarked. "I'm surrounded, it seems, by Rinaldis. Gentlemen, I'm sure you know we're in a difficult situation here. I figure I can give you about fifteen minutes in the privacy of my bunker. You might have guessed the Mexicans have little interest in family reunions."

James began. "It's damn good to see you, Luke. I heard from Captain Northcutt you were badly wounded. He also filled us in on how you came to join us Rebs. I suspect she's one beautiful girl to change your stubbornness."

Luke laughed at his older brother's familiar directness.

James didn't just play the big brother, he lived it. The joy on his face spoke unsaid volumes. He looked at each of his twin siblings grasping each other in a bear hug. Both had tears in their eyes.

"James, Vic, I didn't realize how much I've missed you lugs." Luke's eyes fixed upon Vic—they were beyond close. The years they lost suddenly rushed into this steamy hot hovel as they quickly caught up on news and family.

Vic's gaze on his twin was thoughtful. *How he's aged. Do I look the same?*

Luke hugged his brothers again and thought sadly, *There may not be a tomorrow. How in the hell did we all end up in this dusty Texas border town, surrounded by an overwhelming enemy?*

They spent their short time filling in the blanks, good and bad. It troubled James deeply to hear of Bobby Rockwell's death—more so because he'd have to break the difficult news to Tim, especially before a battle.

When Luke heard of his mother and brother's death, he became distraught. He wiped away a tear. "It seems all so damn pointless to me."

"I know, Luke, it is. But somehow we still have each other. You know, Grandpa Rock and Dad are somewhere near San Antonio. Hopefully, we can see them soon with the good news about you."

With this, Vic came forth exuding his streetwise wisdom. "You know, fellows, this may be our only reunion, so I want you guys to know that I care about you, no matter what. Even if you are all shitheads. There's a reason for all this, you know. Like why we're meeting like this, even if it took a pretty Texas girl to make it all happen. By the way, Luke, does she have any sisters, or is she really stuck on you even now that I'm here?"

"Afraid not, Vic, you'll have to hunt down your own Texas rose. She's off limits, even to you, little brother." Luke, fifteen minutes older than Vic, enjoyed reminding him of his seniority.

The brothers reluctantly parted with purpose in their step, fully aware of the uncertain future their family faced.

An hour after the brothers' reunion, the Mexicans made a concentrated push at the Rebels' northern position, testing the strength of the Texas 4th

Brigade and the New York 5th Regiment. The Rebel position, providentially reinforced minutes earlier with 1,000 Home Guard militia, held firm.

General Harrington's men dug in deep and withstood the pounding. Strangely, it didn't seem as if the enemy desired to attack any other position. Yet no one could be certain of the Mexican commander's goal, knowing full well he had the time and the manpower to do as he pleased.

With intuitive resolve, Justin ordered three companies to reinforce Harrington's perimeter, along with a field battery to add firepower.

Their lone Rebel gunship found fuel for another sortie in time to make good use of its temporary superiority. It was put out of action by the Mexicans, but not before the heroic action of its crew had devastated a Mexican battalion caught out in the open. The situation looked precarious for the besieged Rebels as the seemingly unstoppable offensive made its way toward the reinforced Rebel defenses, almost breaking through the advance line.

Suddenly, when all seemed lost, seventeen beautifully restored World War II vintage P-51 Mustangs roared in low and deadly. Panic ensued in the charging ranks of inexperienced Mexican soldiers. Inspired, the Rebel defenders witnessed the old birds strafe and firebomb with legendary precision. The planes left almost as quickly as they had arrived, their firepower expended, their mission a success.

General Harrington looked up, waving along with other admiring foot soldiers at the Mustangs, watching them return to their base in San Antonio. Several pilots dipped their planes' wings in salute and recognition. Harrington knew his well-entrenched troops were lucky this time. Rebel casualties were low, but the enemy's assault had cost them a horrifying toll. He figured enemy losses to be in the hundreds from the napalm and concentrated machine gun fire. But this, he reasoned correctly, was only the beginning.

With a blissful lull in the action, Justin quickly called for a briefing of his commanders. It was time to introduce his desperate contingency plan before all their options expired.

The commanders arrived, each carrying his own silent worry. "Men," Justin said, looking directly at each officer in turn, "we've just experienced the enemy's first thrust at our defenses. We were very lucky this time. The Texan Air Force wasn't intending to stop an all-out attack. Its mission was only to harass the Mexicans."

"They sure as heck did that, General!" a Colonel from one of the New York regiments shouted. Everyone yelled in agreement.

Justin's smile was guarded and stern as he spoke. "That they did! Their timing was perfect, but not part of our plan. I guess God was looking out for us this time. We probably won't be so fortunate in the future. I figure their intent was to feel out our defenses. They probably won't be so timid now that they know our strength.

"As I see it, surprise is the only option left us. By our best calculation, they outnumber us ten to one. Right now they're spread out, giving us a brief but viable window of opportunity. I seriously doubt they'd expect us to attack. In any case, I've sent several encoded messages to command asking for more troops. The response is not encouraging."

Justin paced the bunker's plank flooring. "Austin has advised we're on our own for perhaps as many as fifteen days. It seems the reinforcements they've sent can't get through. About 8,000 men are in place; most coming from the New York 121st Division, along with some Home Guard units only ten lousy miles to our north awaiting orders. I have proposed an offensive move to General Sinsome. He concurs. I grant y'all, this is a desperate gamble … but one we must take. I'm hoping for the elements of shock and surprise."

Justin spoke slowly, pointing to his map. "We'll move out at our northern perimeter. It gives us the best opportunity to link up with our reinforcements. Our air support will hit in a concentrated effort on the southern perimeter, with some, but I emphasize, *very little*, attention given to the east and western defenses. It is my hope that this will cause a diversion, especially when we fully utilize our artillery and the ten Bradleys. I anticipate our violent thrust will disorient the enemy enough to cause temporary mass confusion. Hopefully that's all we'll need. I'm banking heavily on Intel's information that the soldiers opposing us are mostly untrained, untried militia—recent draftees."

Justin looked squarely into the eyes of each man, seemingly speaking to each one individually. "Any questions so far?" No one responded; many were simply too surprised by his plan to have an opinion.

"OK, then we hit them at 0600 tomorrow with everything we have. I'd have preferred to go much earlier, but our air force is not as sophisticated—the flyboys need daylight. So, gentlemen, we go with what we have and pray we're right."

Justin picked up a pencil, using it as a pointer. He walked back to a larger map on the wall. "We'll leave a minimal fire team guard of 100 men on all perimeters but the north. All units must move with extreme silence to positions in our northern defenses at 0400 tomorrow. Leave all gear, taking only weapons and ammo. Have the men eat as much as possible beforehand. Further rations will be served only if we're successful. Remember, victory depends upon our stealth. Emphasize this to every man. I can't stress this enough. Questions?"

Colonel Jameson stepped forward. "Sir, how many men do we leave in the corporal's guard, and won't they be sacrificed?"

"Good point, Colonel. Once the air moves in, move those men out as quickly as possible, but I emphasize again, with secrecy. The enemy must be led to believe we're there in full force. Expect a lot of casualties tomorrow. But it's certain to be worse if we sit here and wait for them to hit us."

As the commanders were leaving, Taylor got his brother's attention, uneasiness apparent on his sweat-filled brow. "Justin, ah, I mean, General," he corrected. "Do you think this'll work?"

"Surprise is the key, my little brother. It's our only hope, and it's the only plan we can possibly use under the circumstances."

"Then, with your permission, I'd like to rejoin our old unit."

"Taylor, I appreciate your reasoning, but I need you with me. Things may move rapidly out of hand, and I need your good judgment, not only as my adjutant, but as my brother."

"OK, General, I roger that. May I make a suggestion?"

"Go ahead, you'll do it anyway."

"This could be the last time that I get to say this so don't get angry. I've seen you whenever you're around the McKnight girl. I know you really like her, so while you've got a few spare minutes, why not move your ass and go to her. Let her know how much you care. And Justin, I know you care!" Taylor put emphasis into each word. "I've seen it in your eyes."

"But, Tay, I hardly know her. My feelings may just be capricious fantasies." Justin stood fidgeting nervously.

"Well, my dear brother and gallant General, when the hell in this very busy war will you ever get the right time for anything unless you make life fit the moment. At least let her know you think about her." Taylor turned abruptly to leave. He needed to set up coordination for the morning attack.

"Wait, Taylor." Justin called him back. "Thanks."

"Think nothing of it." Taylor slipped out of the bunker into the night.

With Taylor gone, Justin comprehended his brother's meaning with sudden, noticeable shock. He ran out of his bunker and shouted to Taylor a few yards off. "Hey, Captain, where's McKnight's post?"

Taylor grinned and retraced his steps.

Justin's orderly drove him in an old beat-up Jeep to Julia's unit in the center of the fortified camp. The ground literally shook from the activity and turmoil of the defensive preparations.

"Sergeant, I need to see a Private McKnight. I'm told she's temporarily assigned to the Home Guard aid station."

"Sir, follow me. I'll take you to her post." Julia's deep green eyes and winning smile had already mesmerized the sergeant. *What is the commanding general's interest in this beautiful private? Damn, officers have all the freaking power*, he sniveled.

Julia sat busily preparing medical supplies and rolling bandaging for the coming battle. She had never been in combat and didn't know what to expect. Outwardly she was very calm; inwardly, she was scared to death. She reasoned there was little she could do to change her circumstances, so why worry? She promised herself not to show fear.

The sergeant called out, "Private McKnight, you're wanted on the double. General Northcutt's here to see you."

Julia now combined her inner fear with the confusion she felt. *What could he possibly want with me?* Her thoughts raced as she straightened her uniform and her scattered hair.

She neatly saluted Justin as he approached, meeting her halfway. The cover of pending darkness did little to hide the softness of her essence, despite the awkward circumstance of the meeting between a lowly female private and a general, a definite no-no, even in the more casual Rebel Army.

"Private McKnight, may I have a word with you?" Justin did not know where to begin. He hadn't planned this moment like he had the upcoming battle. It was unlike him to be so unprepared. And now here he was tongue-tied, standing with his heart exposed.

He quivered as he looked at her standing in front of him, vulnerable and beautiful and disheveled. Justin did not notice nor care about her non-military appearance. He knew he was hooked the first time he'd met her. Seeing her again sealed it for him. Somehow he must convince her of his good intentions in short order. *Is this what they call love at first sight?*

Julia immediately felt his commanding presence. She also saw a side of his personality reserved for another life in a far friendlier world. "Uh, yes Sir," she stammered, "at your command, Sir."

"Private, may I be so bold as to call you by your given name?" Justin removed his helmet, holding it by its strap.

"Yes, Sir, you may." Julia smiled; she noticed how uneasy and fidgety he was. He wasn't the image and strength of presence he'd been when she had first laid eyes on him. Something was pleasantly different in his demeanor.

"Julia, when we first met, I would've moved the world to get to know you better. Duty forced me to make a hasty advance to the northern battlefront while you and your family chased refuge in the opposite direction. Julia, you don't know me from Adam but, well, I'd like to get to know you better. If you'd see fit to permit me, I'd like to get to know you once this mess of a war's behind us. I understand it's wrong for an officer to fraternize with enlisted personnel, but quite frankly I don't care." Justin rattled on in an amusingly clipped tone.

"General, I'm flattered, but I hardly know you."

"I understand, Julia. Please call me Justin. You see, my mom always told me when the right girl comes along … " he stammered. "If you only knew how foolish I feel." Justin had proven he could lead a brigade without hesitation, yet this slight young woman had him stumbling. "Well, when the right girl comes along, Mom said I'd know, and while you may not have this feeling yet, my desire is to convince you otherwise." Justin stumbled over his words. "I hope in time you'll feel like I do."

Justin fidgeted with his hands, clumsily dropping his helmet. His pride was ruffled; his muffled words emphasized his struggle. "You see, Julia, I may be way off base with this approach, especially because I'm an officer. But you see, I may never be able to express my true feelings to you if I don't do it now while I still have the courage."

Julia was not really surprised. She had felt Justin's piercing eyes when he first looked at her. "Justin, I'm pleased to hear your feelings for me. I can't say I'm as certain as you. Perhaps if we live through the next few days we can see where it takes us." Looking at the tall, blue-eyed Texan, Julia knew deep down she wanted it to work out.

"That's all I can ask. Thank you Julia." Composed now, Justin smiled, and his eyes penetrated her soul. "I only wanted you to know I had a desperate need to see you again. I didn't want to hold back what my heart's feeling. Go with God, Julia McKnight." Justin looked intently into her green eyes. "I promise if fate allows I'll see you again, and soon."

Julia fidgeted with her hands and spoke hesitantly. "You're welcome, General." She smiled, still uncertain about using his given name. Although unsure about what had just transpired, Julia was excited and happy.

Yes, General, thanks for coming here to me for God and all to see. I know you could have ordered me to you, but you didn't. That means I'm special to you, and it means the world to me.

Watching Justin leave she sighed. "Wars do have a way of giving rise to shortcuts," she blurted in a quiet whisper to herself. Then a bright smile lit up her face.

x x x x

Dismissing his driver, Justin chose to take a brisk walk to review defenses. He was pleased at what he saw. Upon arriving at his command bunker he found Taylor industriously reviewing details.

Slipping into the office, he startled Taylor. "What's up?"

"Oh, you're back," Taylor said with a start. "I've been setting up the troop alignments you asked me to do. It's about ready for you to review."

Justin dropped his helmet upon his desk. He motioned Taylor to join him. "Great, we'll get right on it."

Taylor noticed a change in Justin. "Boy, you sure look pleased with yourself."

Smiling, Justin responded. "Yeah, I suppose I am. I met with Julia, and though I feel a bit foolish, actually more like an idiot, I'm really happy I took your advice."

Taylor stood up from the worktable, his right index finger pointing skyward as if checking off a point. "Ah, wait ... I need to record this moment for posterity. Did I hear my big brother say he's happy about my advice?"

"Now wait a minute, squirt. Don't go and get a big head. I didn't say your advice was that great; I felt like a complete jerk. I'd rather charge into overwhelming odds than go through that again. But I've got to tell you, it was worth it."

Taylor suddenly got serious. "The way I see it, with your radical plans for tomorrow, you may have that opportunity all too soon."

Justin, now all business, said, "No kidding. Look, Taylor, after we're finished here, please get her into a safe place. As safe a place as you can under the circumstances. I plan to marry Julia McKnight, even if she doesn't know it yet."

Taylor was still surprised by his brother's sudden, unusual penchant for jumping blindly into a situation. He saluted as he started to leave to do his brother's bidding. "Justin, you can count on me. If I have to, I'll put a guard around her to keep her safe. Heck, I knew there was something between you two when you first met; and I was certain after I saw it in your eyes the second time you looked at her. If I had any doubts before, your face just erased them forever."

Justin could hear his brother's happy chuckle as he raced to carry out his orders. *Now the only real plan is to live through tomorrow.* Fitfully he thought, *It will not be an easy task.*

Taylor wondered if his boasts about doing Justin's bidding could really save Julia from harm. Looking across the open field, he visualized hundreds of unseen enemy fires dotting the open field, all no doubt circled by resting enemy soldiers waiting to kill his future. Taylor's nerves were raw and his feelings difficult to suppress. "Tomorrow, I may die," he muttered. "But damn it, I won't die cheap. You can take that to the bank, you taco-eating sons-a-bitches!" Taylor shouted curtly into the bleak night as he walked to his destination.

His shout startled a Home Guard soldier trying to catch some sleep. "Shut the hell up!" Too late, he saw Taylor's captain's bars.

"Don't worry, Private; I'm letting off some steam."

"Does it help, Sir?"

"You can bet your sweet ass it does. Sorry, soldier, go back to sleep or whatever you were doing."

"Thanks, Sir. It was a bad dream anyway."

Taylor continued to walk, wondering how many men were having bad dreams tonight. The lingering smell of the enemy dead penetrated his nostrils, reminding him of today's reality. It didn't help his restlessness.

James Rinaldi stared hard at the clear, star-filled night. It wasn't as hot after the sun went down, and the slight breeze felt good. *Perhaps*, he thought, *Jennie might be looking at our homing beacon, the North Star.* At least that was what they promised each other on that last blissful evening together, so long ago. *Yes, she's looking.* He closed his eyes to blot out his concern. It didn't help.

Act quickly, think slowly.
   —Greek Proverb

CHAPTER TWELVE

0400, July 22, 2020—Rebel Position, Del Rio, Texas

With silent thunder, the encircled Rebel forces formed at their northern perimeter for their desperate attack upon the unsuspecting Mexican Army. Justin aligned the battle-hardened Texas 1st and 4th Brigades in the forefront of the advance. Once again they were called to play their relentless role as shock troops, driving what was hoped to be a ragged wedge into the Mexican line. The veteran New Yorkers would follow directly behind, with the Home Guard trailing in reserve to give cover if retreat became necessary.

Justin selfishly chose his Texans for the forefront. He knew his Rangers' abilities and had full confidence in their giving a good account. In truth, the Rangers sought revenge for the numerous atrocities the Mexicans had committed and needed to dish out some Rebel violence of their own. Justin hoped to give the enemy regulars a basic lesson in war's subtle hell using his den of cornered, Texas killer-wildcats as his hammer.

Justin's commanders gathered in his bunker for his scheduled 0500 meeting. Their mood was outwardly optimistic. His officers knew they had little choice.

Justin raised his hand for quiet. "Gentlemen, you're all aware of the urgency of our current position." Justin looked haggard; he hadn't slept. All night he had run options until they were fixed in his mind as a go.

"All but one of our patrols made it back. Nothing has changed. Some of our Hispanic comrades were able to infiltrate their lines. The Mexicans apparently feel it's a matter of time before they defeat us upstart Texans and get back glory for Old Mexico." Justin watched to see if his words had any effect. They did.

"They see this as history repeating itself. Another goddamned Alamo—my emphasis, not theirs. I seriously doubt most of the enemy soldiers ever heard of the Alamo. Our spies report that all they talk about around their campfires is how it's going to be easy pickings to have a victory against the gringos and *rape* our women.

"Patrols confirmed our relief column is poised and ready to move in concert with our breakout. They have 8,000 veteran troopers and are confident they can link with us within an hour of our advance. They'll coordinate their move forward with the air diversion's arrival."

Justin pointed to their positions on his wall map, rivulets of sweat gathering on his brow. "Furthermore, the New Yorkers have deployed their tank brigade along with three heavy and one light artillery battery to cover our retreat north. Here's where it gets hard. All we must do is cross five miles of open ground to get to the protection of their cover." Justin heard some strained concern coming from his men. "At approximately 0500, two wings of the Texas Air Force, about ten Mustang planes, will hit the Mexicans, hopefully to the west where flares will direct them. I remind y'all, it's mostly a diversion, and the best we can do with the minimal air power we have available."

"So, gentlemen, let's review the game plan again. Our primary hope is for our attack to cause massive and momentary confusion within their untried ranks. If all goes as planned, the order will be given for the Rangers to swing west, where recon shows the enemy to be weakest. Once there, we'll harvest the mass confusion amongst the Mexicans and destroy as many as time allows. Then we turn back north to regroup with reinforcements who should've linked with the New York regiments and the Home Guard units. Remember, we don't have a moment to spare. All depends on speed and coordination. Are there any further questions?

"If not, then remind your men once more that we're desperate, but we have a chance. I doubt it'll come as a surprise. This f-ing enemy doesn't plan to take prisoners. Remind the troops we're Americans first, and that sitting here only invites certain death. Our only option and hope is to perform the unexpected. Either way, we probably will die. At least this way we'll take a lot of the Mex bastards with us, and on our timetable."

Several officers nodded in approval. Others remained quiet, lost in their own thoughts. Justin's jaw tightened. "Last, as I speak, there are an additional three divisions coming to reinforce us, including the balance of the New York 121st. If they link up in time, the Mexicans will wish they had stayed on their side of the border. However, I must remind you all that it will be a good seven days or more before they show. Hear this and hear it well: we are buying time for our country." The impact of Justin's words hit the room with a sense of foreboding.

Justin stared purposely at each man. His eyes seemed to be on fire. "Gentlemen, we all know we don't have a week and I don't believe anyone in this bunker wants to see another Alamo-like massacre." The second mention of the Texas tragedy didn't go unnoticed.

In a quick, sideward glance, Justin caught Taylor's concerned eyes and immediately wished his brother was miles away, safe from harm. As long as they were together, the chances that neither would survive rose with each firefight.

He purposely turned his attention to Taylor. Others in the hot bunker waited in silence. Justin wiped his brow as he spoke. "Captain, I need you with me. If any regimental commander is hit, you take that command. So I'm promoting you to major to avoid confusion. Are our runners ready?"

"Yes, Sir, as ready as the good Lord allows," Taylor responded excitedly, his face and uniform drenched in sweat.

Justin turned and shouted passionately, "Get them moving then!"

With precision, Taylor set the wheels of Justin's plan in motion.

At 0600, during the early light of dawn, the Rebel Mustangs hit their targets as planned, causing the anticipated havoc and confusion. The Mexican Expeditionary Force, in its belief that they had the Texans surrounded and at bay, did not rush to its defense as quickly as prudence dictated. Feeling secure in their overwhelming odds, they completely underestimated the strike capacity of the Rebel Air Force due to inferior intelligence, mostly received from faulty Federal American Intel. Too late, the Mexicans reacted with blind abandon, as if on script. Today, their government's secret fifteen-day alliance with the Feds was of little help.

The Mexican troops were dished their first plate of total war. So far, all they had confronted were untried, outnumbered Home Guard units. Now they faced a determined and cornered enemy, an enemy who would not be denied its rightful share of the coming battle's blood. Initially, about 4,000 Mexican soldiers paid the supreme price for their country's ignorance; the air attack caused chaos and prompted several desertions.

The Mexicans' supreme test came when the Rebel Americans opened up a devastating barrage from two directions with their combined artillery and tanks. All firepower was aimed at the northern Mexican positions. From the south, Justin's beleaguered troops aligned their firepower with that of the New York 121st Second Artillery Brigade's 155m howitzers that poured wrath from their position four miles off. It took several minutes before the Mexicans could regroup and retaliate. As the Rebels hoped, the response was slow to nonexistent in all sectors.

Once past the initial shock, the Mexican commander unleashed a major counterattack on all sides. He quickly learned, but still too late, that the Rebels were only facing him in the north. By then, valuable time had been wasted while Rebels attacked in concentrated force against a badly scattered Mexican Army unable to give a rapid response. To use his neatly calibrated artillery would wipe out many of his own troops; the Mexican field commander was not ready to risk reducing morale any further by doing so. He keenly felt he could still defeat the badly outnumbered enemy once his forces regrouped.

The Texans held a different view. They pushed their concentrated charge into the startled enemy. Screaming the Rebel yell and sounding like banshees, they gave chills of fear to those on the receiving side of their wrath. Shouts of "Remember the Alamo" echoed across the bloody field.

Many Mexican soldiers were confused by the Texans' war cry. "What is this Alamo?" some cried out. Many would ask a comrade, seconds before a Rebel bullet or bayonet ended their confusion, wondering why a cottonwood tree was used by the Gringos as their battle-cry.

The Mexicans, despite their disorder, gave a good account of themselves. They still outnumbered the attackers by almost three to one in the breakout area. That gave them some false and temporary courage.

The New Yorkers then joined the fray shouting, "Kill the Mex bastards!" It left no doubt as to their intent. In terror of the combined forces, Mexican resistance collapsed along with its line of defense. The Mexican Army retreated in the only direction it could go, north, into the waiting sights of the advancing relief force.

Taylor didn't have long to wait for a command responsibility. Only ten minutes into the fight, word was rushed to him that both the colonel and major of the 2nd Regiment were down. Justin reluctantly released him to his destiny. Taylor immediately left with Sergeant Rinaldi to find his new command.

Taylor looked anxiously at Luke, who was drenched in blood which, thankfully, was not his own. The breakout had slowed. The enemy began to regroup, and Taylor's new regiment was directly in its way. It was up to his men to break the impasse. Luke shouted above the din, "Major, I'm proud to serve under you and, Sir, good luck."

Taylor fixed the bayonet on his M-16. Shouting to Luke, he pointed to the enemy. "Let's give them some Ranger justice, Sergeant. Lead the way."

The two young men quickly exchanged the kind of knowing looks that only men in combat notice. Taylor arrived at his command. He quickly scanned the Mexican nemesis directly in his path with the skilled eyes of a veteran. Understanding the predicament, he shouted above the roar to Luke, now his temporary adjutant, "We have to eliminate that machine gun nest or we'll all be buried here. Sergeant, have Charley Company charge obliquely to this point on the map. I'll lead Able Company on the left. The balance of the regiment is to be held in reserve until I say."

"Yes, Sir!" Rinaldi ran, crouching low, hugging the earth like a lost lover, with bullets chasing his every move.

The two companies did Taylor's bidding. Several men fell in a hail of concentrated fire. Within eighty feet of their objective, dozens of hand grenades were launched, devastating every living thing in their explosive path. Blood and gore scattered in all directions.

With little hesitation over their brief success, Taylor continued his regiment's charge, cutting a path of Ranger destruction. Casualties were heavy, but there was still a lot more killing to be done. Taylor, during a moment's reprieve, realized that Able Company was reduced to platoon strength. He was running out of men.

The Rebels' avalanche of anger unnerved the enemy. Many Mexicans broke ranks, mostly running to the north, into the waiting guns of the advancing New York relief column, which raced south to hook up with their besieged comrades. Realizing with sudden relief that the northern Mexican position was routed, Justin turned his small force to the west as planned. It worked—his units wreaked havoc and fear in the bewildered enemy.

Hand-to-hand combat was at its pinnacle. It was at this moment of battle that the Rangers' full wrath was unleashed. It was payback time—a slaughterhouse. Justin tried to call back his men from further senseless killing. It was a momentum difficult to stop and one he was inwardly reluctant to check.

The enemy now learned the hard way that war is like a double-edged sword, able to slash either direction. By the time it was over, the Mexicans had turned tail for the border, leaving over 30,000 casualties. If they had had the skill and organization to regroup, they would have won the day. But it was not their day to win. Subsequently, they paid a terrible price for starting a war with their northern neighbors.

The two Rebel columns met as planned, reforming ranks. They moved out in an orderly fallback motion, turning east to join the reinforcements expected from Dallas. They watched the Mexican retreat, having no energy left to give chase. Now it was time to regroup and await the next strategy from Austin and General Sinsome. The rebellion had a new look with Mexico's involvement added to the mix.

The Rebels had survived this day, but the borders were not yet secure. Though outnumbered, they would not be denied a victory. Many had died defending Texas, and like the Alamo defenders of 1836, they had not died in vain. It was an expensive day for Old Mexico and a new rallying call for the Republic of Texas. Why the Mexicans had decided to invade their northern neighbor was still a mystery but one that would soon be solved.

x x x x x

Taylor caught up with his brother near dark as they encamped near Brackettville. "Justin, it's good to see you alive." Taylor's uniform, covered in blood and mud, gave him the appearance of a figure from a horror movie.

Justin noticed and smiled. He spoke, his voice lacking energy. "You too, Captain. By the way, I'm executing orders to move your temporary rank of major to that of Brevet Lieutenant Colonel. You're now officially in command of 2nd Regiment."

Taylor responded in a saddened, weary voice. "What regiment? It's more like a battalion. We've had so many casualties. But thanks, Justin, I appreciate it."

Standing, Justin placed his hand on Taylor's shoulder. "You'll get replacements soon enough. Good work, Taylor."

Taylor sat on the ground, too tired for formality. "You too, brother. Your bold moves saved the day."

Justin joined him on the hard ground. His body ached in places he never realized had feeling. "No, Tay, a lot of luck. I doubt the Mexicans will take us lightly again. Now I fear we're in for a real test."

Taylor pulled an apple from his pack, slicing it in half and offering a share to his hungry brother. Food supplies had not yet caught up with the column. Justin beamed at the sight of food, however meager. "I suppose you're right as always," Taylor said. "Say, what's this place? It looks like an old fort."

It was another irony of life that they would camp within a mile of the replica of the Alamo. It was used in several movies in the past century; the most famous was a 1960 John Wayne epic.

Taylor was not initially fazed by his second promotion in one day, only happy to be alive. He'd deal with this surprise later, after the full impact of the day was behind him and he had time to think. Taking a bite from the mushy apple, he smiled. "General, I thought you'd like to know that your Oklahoma girl is fine. She's safe somewhere to our rear. The sad news, though, is that General Harrington didn't make it, and it looks like the New Yorkers lost General Holt and half of their regimental commanders."

Famished, Justin finished his piece quickly. Hunger still lingered. "Yes, I know. We lost a lot of good men today, Colonel." Justin emphasized Taylor's new rank with pride.

"You called me 'Colonel,'" Taylor said in surprise.

"Oh, so you noticed. I just remembered that a colonel, not a lieutenant colonel, commands a regiment. I guess I'm a bit tired. You earned it today, Taylor. And I need your leadership now more than ever."

"Thanks, Justin. You can depend on me."

"I hope it was worth it. But honest, right now, I don't give a damn. We'll regroup as quickly as humanly possible and move out quick as we can. My best guess is our command will receive orders from Austin advising we're formally at war with Mexico, pounding their collective chests like this is news. So we better brush up on our Spanish."

"Sí, mi general."

"That's bad, Taylor. You never could master Spanish in high school." Justin smiled. "Thanks again for looking after Julia."

"No problem, Justin. Before I forget, Becky's beau did well today. In my opinion, we can't afford to let Rinaldi remain a sergeant. Despite his past, we need good officers. The ones we had are dropping like flies."

"I agree. What do you have in mind?"

"Well, I've got several dents in my regiment and could use a company commander or two. I'd suggest we make him first lieutenant of Charley Company."

Justin unintentionally sighed. The stress of the day was beginning to take charge. "Put all your suggestions in writing for my review. You can assume all will be granted, but don't you think Luke would rather fight alongside his brother in the 121st?"

Taylor didn't hesitate to respond. "No, Luke Rinaldi, by reason of insanity, is already a Texan. I believe you can thank Sis for that! And I kind of like him as well. I'd prefer he remain with my unit if you don't mind."

Justin answered, "OK, if that's what you want. Now, let me get to this paperwork. Justin smiled at Taylor and began the dreadful work of going over his casualty reports.

Taylor stood to leave. "Thanks again, Justin. I better see to my regiment, but before I do I think I'll explore Brackettville's version of the original Alamo."

Jim Damiano

The shortest and best way to live with honor in the world is to be in reality what we would appear to be.

—Socrates

CHAPTER THIRTEEN

July 30, 2020—White House, Washington, D.C.

President George (Rex) Collins's six-foot-three athletic build didn't show his seventy-one years. He stared with keen blue challenging eyes at Skip Newman, his Commanding General of Armies. Newman, exhausted from shuttling daily from his headquarters in Philadelphia the past month, did not look forward to today's meeting. The humiliating Second Battle of Gettysburg had humbled the once mighty Federal Army. Skip felt fortunate that his combined forces had managed to fight the outnumbered Rebs to a draw.

Newman sensed his commander in chief's foul mood. He was astute enough to keep his thoughts to himself. The atmosphere in Washington was chaotic. Federal forces had suffered defeat after embarrassing defeat at the hands of the Rebel militia's informal alliance. The mood in the Oval Office was somber; President Collins's attitude was pensive.

"General, I expect the Point taught you our history. What tune did the British band play after their defeat at York Town?" asked President Collins.

"Sorry, Mr. President, I haven't the slightest idea. I do know the year of the battle was 1781. Don't recall the tune." Newman's mind raced. *What bullshit is he feeding me now?*

President Collins replied, his face livid, " 'When the World Turned Upside Down,' damn it. It was 'When the World Turned Upside Down.' "

"What's the point, Mr. President? I don't follow."

"Simple, Newman." The frustration visibly showed in Collins's demeanor. "British General Lord Cornwallis couldn't face Washington. You do remember *him*, don't you?" Collins's sarcasm stung. "So, General, he gave his sword to a subordinate and asked the regimental band to play this damn tune to express his true feelings. Cornwallis felt the tune fit the occasion when his king, that imbecile George III, the leader of the greatest nation in the world at that time, surrendered to a rag-tag rebel army. Worse, included in the drama was the colonists' ally, the despised French. Of course, that was when the French had balls, not like now." Rex noted that Newman openly rolled his eyes.

"Not only did Cornwallis cravenly give his sword to a subordinate to hand over in surrender, he commanded him—I forget his fool name—to give the frigging sword to the French commanding general, Rochambeau. The French commander refused to accept it and directed Cornwallis' second to turn the sword over to Washington. Washington, not to be outdone in this, his moment of glory after enduring eight long troubling years of trial, directed the frustrated British subordinate to hand the sword in surrender to his subordinate. I think General Green."

"Yeah, I'll bet that sword needed to be polished after all that handling." Newman couldn't resist poking fun at Collins's history lesson.

Collins's eyes bugged out in anger, and his voice rose. "General, I don't intend to hand this government over to that damned rag-tag Rebel Army, which is now only sixty miles from this city. You, Sir, will have that distinct honor. Do you get my drift?" Newman returned Collins's glare without feeling.

Newman was not fond of his president, nor did he hold much respect for him. He knew Collins for what he was: a spineless bag of wind, but the S.O.B. was also the commander in chief. If Newman respected anything, it was military protocol. "May I ask where this is going, Mr. President? I don't see us surrendering anytime soon, or ever, if I have a say in the matter. And I don't carry a sword." Newman couldn't miss the president's scowl.

"Hear me, Newman, and hear me well, for I won't say this in the staff meeting." Collins's face skewered to make his point. "You make pretty stout talk for a commander who is losing battles. Newman, do you recall that Mr. Lincoln fired most of the Union generals early on in the last civil war?" Collins scowled, a tenuous hold on his anger. "I relied on your judgment. I find it wanting."

Collins pounded his desk and went on. "General, we've lost, for the most part, New York, Vermont, northern Pennsylvania, Ohio, Illinois, Michigan, Indiana, Florida, Georgia, Alabama, Mississippi, Missouri, Louisiana, New Mexico, Arizona, Oklahoma, Colorado, Montana, and my home state, Texas." Newman tried to control his emotions by clasping his hands together as the president rattled off each state. To Collins it was a litany for the dead.

"Damn it, man, that's nineteen, count them, nineteen states or part of them that now declare themselves free and clear of this Union. We also have turmoil brewing in North and South Carolina, Tennessee, Kentucky, West Virginia, Virginia, Minnesota, Wisconsin, Washington State, and Nebraska. Not to forget Idaho, Iowa, and Kansas mixed in for good measure. When the hell are we going on the offensive? We must consolidate our forces and start taking back our lost states before everything is gone. Newman," Collins spit Newman's name out as if it were an unwanted seed, "do you have any good reason why I shouldn't can your ass right now?"

"Ah, no sir, it's a mess and I could try to transfer the blame, but I ... "

Collins interrupted before he could finish. "You what, Newman? Out with it! My patience is running thin!" Collins stood and paced like a prowling tiger.

Newman hesitated. Thinking he'd be fired anyway, he didn't see the point in arguing. Getting sacked was his first and only intuition for the urgent summons he'd received earlier to report to the White House. It would almost be a relief, but Newman had too much to do to just give in to Collins's whim.

"Newman, you're my raging bull," the president ranted on. "I point your sorry ass, and you do what I say. You're brutal, brilliant, and a bastard all in one convenient package. Yet you let that son-of-a-bitch Sinsome and others like him kick your butt every time. And you've let their traitorous militia tear your hide almost daily during the past six months with their goddamned guerilla warfare. When do you plan to put some life back into our army?"

Newman desperately tried to control his desire to strangle Collins's worthless neck. He thought, *How can I say what I must so this idiot will grasp what's happening?* Regaining his composure before he spoke by counting to ten, he thought, *This subject won't please His Royal Majesty King Rex Collins, but I didn't get to where I am by caution alone. And I won't lose this opportunity.*

Newman broke the silence. "Sir, at the risk of being insubordinate, may I bring up what I believe is our best solution?"

"Yes you may, and try to surprise me while you're at it."

Sarcastic prick. "Well, Sir, I know this isn't new. The world is totally screwed up. Europe, in particular, Sir, has unemployed military seeking a home."

"Goddamn it!" shouted Collins with such force that his voice carried beyond the Oval Office. "You want me to hire mercenaries? What little loyalty we have left will be lost to the Rebels if we do that. What kind of fool idea is that? Is this really your best?" Collins thought, *Yes, Newman, keep talking. This is what we need. I've been working on this for some time. But I need you to be the one to suggest it so that if it fails, you'll take the fall, not me.*

Newman silently contemplated before he spoke. "Mr. President, if we don't do something soon, whatever loyal military personnel we have may desert or die. Damn it, Sir, more men are lost to desertion than in actual combat!" Newman shouted, losing his composure for only a moment. His voice regained its calm. "Mercenaries should have little problem shooting deserters, Sir. For them, taking orders to pillage, burn, or even to shoot Rebel prisoners is a given. Plus we'd be able to rebuild our army on promises to pay with confiscated booty and Rebel land."

Newman looked at Collins's face to measure his reception to the idea. Collins showed nothing of what he was truly feeling.

Newman continued, "Once this mess is over, we can politically and politely tell them how to catch the nearest boat back home. Perhaps we can also have our loyal Federal soldiers convict them on trumped up war crimes. Then we simply keep whatever share of Rebel wealth they might expect. Keep it in the family." Newman's cackle unnerved Collins.

"Newman, don't you think your approach invites more citizens to join the revolt?" Collins asked, his voice several notes higher than before.

"I can't answer you on that, Mr. President. I sure feel it'll give us hope and help us win this ridiculous war. If you can find another way to get me more troops who'll stay and fight, we won't need the foreigners."

Collins's eyes squinted, as if he were trying to focus on the idea. He was a good actor. "Won't there be a language problem?"

"Mr. President, right now, as you're aware, Sir, over twenty-five percent of our troops are unable to speak English, thanks to a piss-poor system that felt no need to push our chosen language the past thirty years. We also have an overabundance of aliens and immigrants in our ranks, many promised citizenship when drafted. Others who are citizens now don't understand or can't read English. For want of common dialect, many die needlessly. Their worthless lives depend upon increasing our troop strength. Sir, our survival may depend upon it as well." Newman slammed his fist into his palm, his voice raised to make his point.

"The Rebels don't seem to have this problem," he continued. "It's almost funny. Their damn 'Black George Washington' leads the greater part of the Rebel forces. What an irony. It's beginning to look like a race riot in reverse, mostly English-speaking Rebels against our grand mix. The commonality feeds the Rebels' cause. I think mercenaries can neutralize our dire weakness. Mr. President, they can bolster our already mixed bag, without hurting our cause."

Collins's lips formed into a sneer, "I seem to recall, Newman, that Sinsome, the damned 'Black Washington' as you call him, was first in his class back at West Point in 1999. If only we could have persuaded him to join our team in the beginning!"

"Or had him assassinated like I suggested." Newman couldn't resist reminding Collins about that mistake.

Collins shook his head in dismay. He knew something drastic must be done and soon, or all would be lost. He loved being president—he loved the power, and he didn't want to be remembered in history as the Jefferson Davis of the old United States. He decided quickly, taking his own counsel. The Rebels must be destroyed at all costs. He'd freely pay the piper in the future after all was won and full power returned. Of course, he would feel it his duty to declare absolute rule once those fallen states were returned to the fold. He snickered to himself at the thought.

I'll never return to those days where I have to kiss ass for every cause, whether it be social security, health insurance, tax loopholes. You name it, when I'm in total control, it'll be history.

"General Newman, I agree. We have little choice. There's very little left to discuss regarding this issue. If we don't move soon, there'll be no tomorrow to worry us." Collins stood. "I'll call an emergency session of my cabinet this afternoon and get things rolling. With my war powers authority, my decision is a foregone conclusion. Yet, for the record, I'd like history to see how we discussed this issue. You know, for the good of the country's future, blah, blah, blah. Do you have any particular mercenaries in mind?"

"Yes, Mr. President, I do. My staff has been making inquiries with foreign governments favoring our cause. We can obtain about one million mercenaries in addition to the few unsolicited personnel who previously volunteered. They'd come from several countries. The majority are available from Germany, France, and Russia. Since I've anticipated your answer in the positive, I can have as many as one and a half million trained foreigners on our soil in thirty to forty days."

"Skip, how long have you been working on this behind my back?"

"About six months, Mr. President." Newman looked pleased.

Collins was suddenly concerned, though not for the reason Newman thought. Even though Collins had been steering Newman in this direction, it bothered him that Newman had taken it upon himself to look into this pivotal question. "What's to prevent them turning against us?"

"Well, Sir, I don't like this any more than you, but I need men. *I also need to lead this army. I can't get fired now*, he thought. "I don't intend to place them all together in one unit. I'd disperse them around the country to supplement our forces. I'd also recommend putting the largest concentration in the Midwest, especially in northern Kansas, where your loyal Lone Star state is anticipated to hit us hard. We'll test them out as potential shock troops before they've had time to dust off their boots."

Collins's sinister smile foreshadowed his reply. "That's why I like you, Newman. You're one devious bastard."

"Thank you, Mr. President." Newman's thoughts raced, his cunning concealed beneath a feigned smile. *You have no idea how devious I can be.*

July 30, 2020—White House Cabinet Meeting

President Collins finished his presentation to his cabinet. It was evident to all in the meeting room that the decision was made and the gathering was just a matter of protocol.

"Does anyone have any questions?" Collins scanned the table, eyeballing each member.

"Yes, Mr. President, I do, Sir."

"Speak please, Secretary Sparkman."

Harris Sparkman, the secretary of state, was too new to realize when to keep his mouth shut. He had yet to understand that only yes-men were tolerated in Collins's cabinet. Like the long-dead Franklin D. Roosevelt when war broke out in 1941, Collins's presidency took on an almost dictatorial demeanor, using the war's emergency as his excuse. Unlike FDR, though, Collins was not a patriot. He followed the Constitution loosely, if at all, and only when convenient to his purpose.

Sparkman began, his pencil keeping time with his remarks. "Sir, 1.5 million mercenaries will be very expensive. I realize you covered this fact, but I'm talking a non-monetary price, one I fear may cripple our nation after we win. Won't these people decide they want to stay? And worse, can't they take up where the Rebs leave off? How in God's name can we control an armed force of cutthroats from gaining power?"

The strain on Sparkman's face matched the crumpled white shirt and tie he'd thrown on for this emergency session. "Sir, I realize my Rebel turncoat predecessor, Mr. Loxland, once took this same position regarding the first mercenaries we took on. Despite my predecessor's current traitorous political persuasions, I find myself agreeing with his earlier, unpopular posture."

Collins's immediate dislike at being questioned for his actions was overridden by his desire to be understood for posterity. *You fool; I'll do whatever it takes to be remembered as a statesman who pulled all stops to save the Union in its darkest hour.*

Remaining silent, Collins's eyes scanned the cabinet members awaiting his response. *Screw them,* he thought, *I'll speak when I'm damn ready.*

Pondering further, he smirked. Most of the cabinet members noticed. They couldn't know that he was laughing at General Newman. Unknown to anyone, Collins had been looking into the mercenary issue from the war's first day. Even then he knew things might get desperate. Difficult decisions often require orders that might prove thorny for American citizens to carry out.

Finally, Collins broke the silence. "Secretary Sparkman, I honestly concur with your concern. That's why we're meeting today. Let me take another step to outline our predicament in the bottom-line terminology you appreciate."

Sparkman grew restless, fidgeting as he became the focus of the president's attention. Collins continued, "First, to maintain our nation, we must neutralize the Rebel forces. Next, we must recapture what's been temporarily lost. Last," Collins pounded his fist on the broad table for emphasis, "after peace is restored, we'll have swift and severe justice for thousands of our Rebel friends."

"Pardon me, Mr. President, for interrupting," Army Secretary Abraham Levy intervened abruptly. His bluntness was taken for granted by all in the room who knew his booming personality. "Sir, isn't this very un-Lincoln-like of you? Shouldn't we be willing to pass the olive branch to encourage reuniting the nation?"

Collins's smirk was deadly, his reply measured. "I know how much you admire that other great Abraham in our history." The cabinet members all laughed politely. "Abraham, screw the Rebels and get with it. This is the 21st century, not the goddamn 19th. Lincoln, pardon my unpopular opinion of our illustrious 16th president, was a fool. Honest Abe got himself assassinated because of his ass-kissing intentions. Yes, and never forget this." Collins stood and again slammed his fist down on the conference table, knocking several papers to the floor. "We need law and order first. To accomplish it, we must kill or hunt down every political and military leader of these damn Rebels. We'll save most of our real wrath for those Rebels from my own home state, including my dear demented sister."

Collins continued. "While I feel we're putting the cart before the horse to talk about this issue now, let it be known to all that it's my intention to feed their Rebel carcasses to the dogs and leave what's left to the vultures. As far as I'm concerned there's simply not enough punishment we can dole out to them to suit me. God, this rebellion has already cost over four million lives."

Collins pointed his finger accusingly at his army secretary. "It's good to see that you have a heart, Abraham. Save your generosity for our fellow Americans trying to hold on to this Union. They, Sir, have suffered too long at the hands of those who commit treason!" Collins's reprimand did not go unnoticed by those members, all hand picked yes-men, who might be foolishly inclined to think for themselves.

"Here's the recap of the plan the Joint Chiefs of Staff put together. General Newman has worked out the details, and he'll brief you later today, though a few of the specifics are still being ironed out. This time we do not plan to fail!" Collins shouted. His renowned anger startled no one.

Collins's determined air took on a frightening aura as he continued. "OK, I'll give it to you all straight. Here's the bottom line and a glimpse at the real world. That little skirmish down in Texas was set up by our security council and the boys over in the CIA. It was a failure. Under my authority, they set up and recruited about half a million Mexican Nationals. It was a secret alliance with the Mexican Government to invade Texas, New Mexico, and Arizona. It was to take place from three points. We were going to pick up our counterattack in the North at the same time. We held in reserve over 250,000 Cuban and Brazilian forces. They were ready to follow up on the Mexican invasion as soon as it proved successful. It didn't." Collins's face registered his disappointment.

"It was a gamble and it almost worked. You all know the disturbing details as well as I. You also know how I hate the Rebel bastards. Yet, I'm still a Texan, and I've got to admire their resolve. Outnumbered ten to one in Del Rio, they defeated those worthless Mexicans and pushed them back across the border, and the attack on El Paso never got off the ground." Collins looked each cabinet member in the eye to assess his or her reaction. What he saw was both surprise and shock.

"Yes, I negotiated in secret and promised that they could keep southern Texas up to San Antonio, most of New Mexico and Arizona, along with part of southern Nevada. The agreement only applied if they were successful. Since they failed, all bets are off. Still, it may turn out better for us in the long run. Forcing the Texans to concentrate on their borders takes away their momentum. More important, we still have our alliance with Mexico. They, along with the Cubans and Brazilians, are still waiting in the wings. Let the Texans spread themselves ragged. Maybe they'll even take over Mexico. Then when the time is right, our allies in South America can come to the rescue and help fight our war for us." His chuckle turned to a raucous laugh as he said, "Sort of a liberation campaign to free the poor Mexicans, much like the debacle in Iraq back in '03."

Sparkman was not convinced. "Mr. President, to give away part of the Union, even to establish a creditable ally, could be considered an impeachable offense, even during frantic times."

Collins sneered through his answer. "It's like this, Gentlemen. As I said, all the agreements were made in secret. Of course, if anyone shouts about it, it must be denied. If our casual friends and allies holler too much, they may find themselves a casualty of our war." The threat was finally out, obvious and unveiled. "After we take back full control of our country, we'll have about four million well-trained troops under arms. We figure about one third will most likely be mercenaries. Some, those who speak English, we'll reward with land grants and such from Rebel holdings. Not the best land, mind you. The best we save for ourselves, like the carpetbaggers of the last civil war. Such are the fortunes of war, Gentlemen. Don't look so shocked. As a goodwill gesture, most of the mercenaries will be given the persuasive option of more conquest and booty."

"Are you proposing to continue this war after we beat the Rebels?" Sparkman could not resist asking his question.

"Certainly. It shall be our new Manifest Destiny for the 21st century. Oh, and before I forget, y'all are aware of that little episode where the Free Quebec Army failed in northern New York. You're right if you figured by now that incident is similar to the southern Texas fiasco." Collins, smiling demonically, could see that his words were sending chills through the cabinet members. It was almost like he was a comic book character, though he was dead serious and fully three-dimensional.

"Next, we'll direct our new mercenaries, under our leadership and guidance, in precise, systematic order to take control of every country or territory and principality in North and South America. Once we're done, even the island nations of this hemisphere will be conquered, particularly those bothersome Cubans. I do like their cigars, though." Collins's cackled viciously. "When it's all done, I'm proposing we be known as the Grand United States Empire. It'll be the best thing that's ever happened to this hemisphere, and definitely a way to retain our way of life, especially from those damn Chinese commies."

Sparkman, unnoticed, looked upon Collins in disbelief.

"You all must agree that the time is ripe, if not overdue. That is why the mercenaries are such an important part of the mix. We'll do this hemisphere a good deed. It'll be a better world after we hunt down and destroy all drug kingpins running those bothersome banana republics in the Caribbean and South and Central America. With this accomplished, we'll restore the western hemisphere. Then we can isolate our side of the world from the chaos on the other sides of the Atlantic and Pacific. Right now the rest of the world is waiting around like vultures, hoping to pick clean whichever side wins. This will never happen as long as I have the bomb. It'll take time, but time will be ours once we destroy the Rebs."

"Mr. President, I'm confused, Sir. What about the citizens of all these sovereign nations? They surely won't just sit back and be taken without a struggle." Sparkman was beside himself but hid it well. He particularly didn't appreciate the idle threats Collins had thrown his way. He was determined to play this out to get Collins's full meaning. *I'm sitting in the room with a madman—a time bomb about to explode.*

Collins, tiring of Sparkman's emotional outbursts, knew he would have to do something. In fact, Sparkman's appointment to the cabinet was beginning to look like a mistake. Always the statesman, Collins, for the record, attempted to appease Sparkman. "Here again, you appear to have missed the point, Mr. Secretary. Our combined forces, increased by each conquest, should be welcomed as saviors. The present desolation in those nations can't get much worse. If you think we've been thrust back into the pit of the 19th Century, I suggest you look at other countries. South America, Europe, and Asia have returned to medieval times. Damn it, man, we bring them hope!

And hope, Gentlemen, makes it easier to force our bitter pill down their collective, shallow, ignorant throats. It'll become a simple question of fight, be conquered, and die for their resistance; or be grateful, join us, and live. This country should have started on this road back when we first whipped the Mexicans in the 19th century. Hell, we took everything we could from the Native Americans, only we stopped when we were most hungry."

Collins stood and began to pace the small room. Again, he looked carefully at each member of his cabinet. He slowly circled the table, continuing his strategy. "I'll give them the opportunity to be a part of a first world nation. And relief from their third world status or from their tattered democracies, especially where our Canadian friends are concerned." Collins's voice became a hoarse whisper, emphasizing his fearful resolve.

"As for Canada, their aggressive actions of the past few weeks will give us cause for our declaration of war against them. Covertly, plans are in place for the demise of the Quebec ministers who worked on our alliance. This necessary act allows us to deny its existence.

"Gentlemen, our objectives have merit and purpose, and we'll have our way. And by the way, lest you forget, we need Canada's wealth to help pay for this Godforsaken war!"

If anyone was stunned by the president's admission, they hid their feelings, despite misgivings. Collins's cabinet sat in collective, eerie silence. The conspiracy plan was out, leaving little doubt about Collins's dictatorial ambitions. If the U.S. Federal government retained power, future historians would view Collins's move as brilliant and Caesar-like, if not somewhat devious. If it failed, it would go down as a huge blunder in the trash heap of time.

Collins broke the silence enveloping the room. Many were fearfully considering the days or minutes their lives had remaining. "Gentlemen, are there any questions? Yes, Mr. Coates?"

Gregory Coates, the attorney general, was a lonely man. His thankless job now stepped constantly upon the very Constitution he so loved and had sworn to defend. "Sir, what about Hawaii? So far it has stayed out of the mix, but we're hearing that the Japanese may be showing some signs of aggression."

"That, Mr. Coates, is why we have our nuclear subs in the Pacific. If the Japanese even come close, I'll resume where President Truman left off in 1945." Collins blew a cloud of smoke from his Havana cigar; his practiced, vivid exhalation resembled a mushroom cloud.

"Gentlemen, I trust everyone in this room understands the necessity for secrecy. No one but you and very few others know of this plan. If it gets out, it can have significant repercussions for our secret alliances and potential new ones, and would strengthen the resolve of our enemy."

Some cabinet members looked stunned, while others appeared visibly hurt. To a man, most were friends who had supported Collins, both on his climb to his presidency and throughout his two-plus terms in office. Now, it was clear Collins intended to make himself an emperor.

If the meeting was somber at its beginning, it was funereal by its end. Each member appeared to take a brief moment, unintentionally, to look at the other. Each man needed a moment to reflect on this day, which would change life as they knew it.

Silently, Sparkman, a loyal Pennsylvanian from his grand state's capital at Harrisburg, could not see how this grandiose plan could possibly work. He thought in fearful frustration without showing his emotion, *My God what a madman we've created by our silence. What we need now is a statesman. We have a demigod. Damn, where do we go from here?* Sparkman, a student of Jeffersonian history, thought of an ironic statement Jefferson had made two centuries earlier. The third president's prophetic statement was underlined by the moment at hand: "Professional government unfettered can lead to tyranny."

Secretary Sparkman left the cabinet room unsure of his next move, knowing he could no longer blindly walk Collins's tightwire.

Across the hall, General Newman watched the cabinet leave. He nodded briefly to Sparkman: as their eyes met he sensed they shared the same concern. As the members filed out, no one had seemed jovial and only Sparkman had acknowledged him.

Collins watched Sparkman leave, knowing what he must do.

He returned to his office and picked up his phone. A devious smile forecast his thought to the silent walls of the Oval Office. *Oh well, another casualty of war.*

Not gold, but only man can make a people strong; men who, for truth and honor's sake, stand fast and suffer long.
—Ralph Waldo Emerson

CHAPTER FOURTEEN

August 2, 2020—Rebel Base of Operations, El Paso, Texas

Windswept streets cast a dusty haze over a once bustling city. Desert winds do not bestow favors upon men. They just blow when the need arises. Such was the situation this hot summer day on the Texas border. With war about to be declared on Mexico by Texas and its allies, the southern Rebels, like their northern counterparts, now fought on two fronts. It was not an ideal situation.

Rock Rinaldi was tired and parched. The past weeks had been a hard ride for men half his age. The last time he had felt this uncomfortable was during Vietnam. Up until now, he had been in the rear echelon, providing assistance with supplies. Rock, now a colonel, headed procurement. At the moment this task was proving difficult.

His responsibility included feeding the New York 121st and 20th Infantry Divisions, both stationed at old Fort Bliss. A side benefit of this post was the opportunity for an occasional visit with his only son, Joseph Rinaldi.

Several Rebel units had rushed to defend the Texas border along with his own New Yorkers. Through sheer will and determination they had quickly filled the gaps caused by the Mexican three-pronged attack.

Unexpectedly, El Paso was spared Mexico's wrath. Rebel command considered it a prime target at this early stage of the newly extended war. However, with the Mexican army currently regrouping a few miles south of the Texas border, both adversaries enjoyed needed rest from the mad passions of the past few days.

It had been nine months since Rock had seen Joe, now serving as intelligence major to the 20th Division. Rock paced patiently, waiting to see the "Professor," his pet name for his son.

Joe arrived punctually, which did not surprise Rock. He always teased Joe that he could keep time by him. Both men beamed at the sight of the other. Hugging in unmilitary-like fashion, Joe was amazed at his father's strength. His age didn't prevent him from almost squeezing the breath from his son's slight frame. Rock thought to himself, *It's good the boy's in intelligence. He'd never make it on the line. He's grown frailer than I remembered.*

"Dad, you look great. It seems army life agrees with you."

"Joe, it's not a picnic, though it does keep me occupied. You look tired, Son!"

"No, Dad, no more than anyone else. We had our plate full without the Mexicans placing their shit into the mix. And I feel out of my element down here in this God-forsaken place."

"I know what you mean. I miss my mountain. You know, I never really had a chance to tell you how sorry I am about Betty. I loved her like she was my own daughter."

"She loved you too, Dad. It eats at me how she died. I keep telling myself little could have been done under the circumstances. Yet, I'm still plagued with regret for joining the cause when I did. Maybe, just maybe, I could've made a difference for her if I had stayed."

"Joe, you need to stop second guessing. We did all we could. Without proper medicines, you couldn't have changed the outcome. And," Rock paused, as a tear dropped on his weathered face, "there just wasn't any medicine to be found. I tried and would've killed for it."

"Thanks, Dad. I know you did all you could. I can't stop missing her. These damn lulls bring out the sadness. I often wish for action so that my mind can escape the pain the heartbreak brings." Joe's eyes pleaded for relief.

"Joe, we still have the boys, even though they're all in harm's way. We need to live for them."

"Yeah, I know. We all seem to be in God's hands." Joe saw his father nod in agreement. He shuffled his feet, still upset. "Dad, I wish I could've seen Billy one more time. I'm so damn proud of him. He was such a good kid. Somehow I know he's with my Betty and Ma in a better place than this hell hole."

Rock motioned Joe to sit. He saw the pain on his son's face. "Professor, what do you think about this place? Do you Intel boys think it's defendable?"

Joe sat on a crate near his father's. "Dad, I doubt we'll be here long enough to find out. It's rumored my unit is needed to help set up new local governments in Mexico. To my way of thinking, this means we plan to invade. Right now, I don't envy your mission to find food."

Rock took a ration from a nearby box, opened it, and offered it to Joe. "Here, eat!" he intoned, smiling a toothy grin. "You're thinner than the last time I saw you. You need to eat more. By the way, Son, can we really invade Mexico with the Feds still breathing down our backs? They sure haven't been licked by a long shot."

Joe took Rock's offering, momentarily ignoring Rock's question. "Thanks, Dad. I am a bit hungry." He took a bite, then considered. "Your question is not easy to answer. I'd say it's a gamble we must take. Look at what we've seen on our long trek here. Our country's in a shambles. Refugees and food shortages are everywhere. Life, as we knew it, is over. Heck, Dad, Morse code is being taught again so we can improve our communications. There's even a horse cavalry unit in the works."

Laughing, Rock responded, "Joe, we still have a lot of the modern luxuries. It's not that bad."

Joe, ever the serious son, answered, "Sure, but most of our electric and even solar power sources have been compromised. Everything is unusable as long as generators don't have fuel."

Rock opened another ration, handing it to Joe as he answered. "Yeah, about every available diesel truck has been converted for military use. It's amazing how man can improvise when he must." Rock's mind raced to visions of his motor pool.

"Dad, we've no choice. The longer this war goes on, the more the debate slides back in favor of the Federals. If they manage to prolong things, it'll become easier for the populace to embrace a life with fewer freedoms. Hunger and desperation aid the enemy's position."

Rock, his mouth full of C-ration peas, retorted, "Professor, we caused a lot of this mess ourselves." Rock loved to debate his son. He had missed this most when they were separated. "You know firsthand the education given the average American was lacking in basics and never stressed common sense. We've lost our values and therefore, it became easy to rebel. I'd guess only about half those rebelling really understand why. For many, it was just something to do. For others, especially those who were drafted, it was fight or the firing squad, and for many, it's been wait and see."

"Dad, aren't you oversimplifying things a bit? Although, as ever, you're mostly on target. No matter how we got here, we find the country we both love torn in two and unable to return to its former glory without drastic measures. The Federal government won't ever acknowledge our concerns. I grant you the seed of change is firmly planted and will not die easily no matter how little it's watered." Joe stood, wiping the sweat from his face.

Rock, his mood turning pensive, continued, "Joe, what do you think will happen if our cause prevails?"

Joe stood posturing like he was back in front of a classroom. It felt good. "Right now it must. If we fail, a lot of us will be tried as traitors and killed. Others will lose their land, wealth, and everything else they hold dear. We have little choice now but to stay united in our resolve. So, first we need to put a firm base back under the Constitution and change some of our laws. If not, all this will repeat itself. You know, Dad, it would take a semester of lectures for me to get to the meat of your question."

"Joe, I don't have time for a semester nor the class fees. What must we do? What do you Intel guys think?"

"Hell, Dad, it's anybody's guess what Intel thinks; they're all over the lot. Here's what I think, though it might be a bit simplified. When all this is over, assuming we win, we must educate all citizens to understand our government and persuade them to participate in its functioning. I recall quoting Daniel Webster in class; he once said, 'The general education of youth forms the firmest security of our liberties.' I firmly believe this is where our former nation first failed its citizens."

"Now who's oversimplifying things?" Rock smiled.

"OK, Dad, remember at the turn of the century when the Catholic Church was in crisis over all the sexual abuse business?"

"How could I forget? Your mom was furious and crushed. It was the first time I ever saw her angry with the church. It was crippled by the scandal. I stopped giving our pledge, and only after your mother made me feel guilty did I pay it. It took the church a long time to overcome that setback."

"That, Dad, was just a part of the overall puzzle. Among many other events, it started an unraveling of ethics that went on for two decades, leading us to El Paso and this horrible heat."

"Damn, Joey, I don't follow your reasoning." Rock stood to stretch. The dry heat did help his arthritis but not enough.

"Dad, religion's existence depends on the social contract between it and those whom it serves. When trust was betrayed and then hidden conveniently under a theological rug of regret, the church lost many of its most loyal followers. Even unthinking people saw through the scandals, wondering why the church couldn't change its course. Worse yet, they wondered how much more was hidden. It seemed to many as though God left the formal church, though it was really the church that left God. As the church went, so did our government in its path to ruination. You know as well as anyone that while the Founding Fathers kept the church out of the state, they never intended God to be excluded from the hearts of those who were governed. Now, ignoring God seemed to help give power to those politically-correct crazies."

Rock, appearing confused by the subject, paced as he answered. "Joe, there are so many events and issues leading to this war. All events appear innocent at first. Each one became kindling for the fire now upon us. I sincerely doubt that any one issue caused this mess."

Joe looked respectfully at Rock, absorbing his subtle wisdom. "I agree. But, Dad, one thing's certain, we won't solve this puzzle today. If we prevail and survive, I'd like to write its history, if only to help sort it out before I teach it."

Rock pointed his finger to his son's heart. "Professor," he said, "instead of fretting, you need to start putting some of this stuff down so you won't forget it. In your free moments, why not start outlining a history of events leading to this crisis and how it's been fought? With the staff of educators, businessmen, attorneys, politicians, and over-educated guys you have in Intelligence, I'd expect you'd have a good sounding board. Sometimes I find it's good to put down what ails you, if for no other reason than the peace of mind it brings."

"Dad, that's an excellent idea. Let's hope we win, though. As you've often told me, the losers never seem to write history." Joe beamed with the seed of another thought. "I'd even start my lecture with another gem of Webster's: 'Our honor requires us to have a system of our own language as well as government.' The Revolution had forced the people to accept new ideas. Webster saw, over two centuries ago, the need to establish a national language to unify our then-new nation. He knew things wouldn't last unless we had a fundamental commonality in most everything."

"Professor, here's another quote you can put in your arsenal. It was Lincoln who said: 'The people are the masters of both Congress and courts, not to overthrow the Constitution, but to overthrow the men who pervert it.' Doesn't that fit right in to what has happened?" Rock smiled.

"That's a good point, Dad. It does go deep, doesn't it?"

Joe continued to pace, his voice in lecture mode. "The last three decades have seen our nation go from the English language as its primary tongue to having it become politically correct to allow other languages an equal footing. For political reasons and votes, we allowed the newcomer minorities, whether legal immigrants or not, to dictate our policy. All the do-gooders pushed for this. Damn it, votes became more important than the country's values." Joe was really into his dialogue, moving as he talked, to the amusement of his father.

Joe continued, "I really believe the original intent behind allowing for diversity in language was right. I also firmly believe it helped weaken us as a nation. We lost our identity and strength in our oneness. Here Mr. Webster had it right." He removed his soiled cap, moving it briskly to stir the air.

Suddenly, the germ of an idea hit Rock. Animated, he interrupted. "Son, one thing I'd recommend would be to emphasize how we gradually began to lose our freedoms, one by precious one. Remember back in the early days of the war on terrorism, when American citizens were arrested and many were charged, but never indicted, with betraying their fellow countrymen?"

"Yeah, my first reaction, as I recall, was that I would've liked to strangle those traitors myself."

Rock saw his turn to lecture. "You and most of the country felt that way. But several do-gooders didn't. They meant well, and they were on target, even if for the wrong reasons. Because any U.S. citizen charged with a crime has the constitutional right, or at least they once had, to a speedy trial. As I recall, the second President Bush waived civil liberties, using the excuse that we were at war. Eventually, as time progressed, people caught saying the wrong things were put in jail for the duration of the war on terrorism. Since that war has never ended, many are still incarcerated, at least those we haven't liberated. This was all based on the president's unilateral judgment that they could possibly be part of an enemy force that might do harm to our country." Rock's voice rose as he spoke.

Joe's eyes beamed in recognition of Rock's ploy. He delighted in the exchange; it enlivened him. "Dad, I see where you're going with this. By presidential decree, we slowly abandoned the Constitution's system of checks and balances for nothing more than a promise of security and that our president was correct. In short, we created a monster in the name of a War Powers Act that got out of hand. Some of those people were probably guilty." Joe hesitated to make his point. "But by refusing to give them their rights as American citizens, we were guiltier than they. For what are we without our freedoms? That's what made our republic the greatest experiment in democratic government the world's ever known."

"Joe, don't get me wrong. I'm not saying it was immoral to detain anyone, foreign or domestic, who would harm our nation. But if you make one exception, often you get more exceptions—grant an inch, lose a yard. We risked the rights of many to catch the few who would harm us, and in so doing, we lost sight of our founding principles, letting the terrorists win in the long run."

Amused, Joe tried to hide his smile, not wanting to give Rock the satisfaction that once again he was on point. "OK, I'm beginning to see where you're going with this. It would seem you're saying our old government began to lose its legitimacy when it eliminated the court's ability to challenge its conduct." Joe, for a moment, forgot the sweltering heat.

"Yeah, hot damn, you're getting the picture, Son." Rock was on a roll. "Don't forget the government gee-haws also limited the lawyers' ample access to those they chose to detain. It was here I feel we first veered into tyranny. We took on the appearance of a kingdom where once stood a republic. We let it happen, one little piece at a time, and it slowly but surely made our old nemesis communism look timid." *Boy, this feels good.*

Joe's face gave away his need to leave soon. Responsibilities waited, but it had been months since he'd talked to his father. "Dad, as always, you've made me look deeper into myself. Thanks. I've got to be leaving soon, and you haven't told me anything about yourself or what you've been up to."

Rock sat down, grabbing at the spasm in his aching back. He didn't complain. "I'll try to be quick, but you know me, Son, that won't be easy. In short, it's a mess in my neck of the woods and most likely will become a nightmare. So far, we've been lucky. Any American who served in Vietnam will tell you that the biggest reason we won all the battles but still lost that war was our inability to find and then round up the full Viet Cong force and bring it to a pitched battle. We had a few chances at parts of their army. When we did, we kicked their ass to kingdom come. But we never had a decisive battle to force an end. You know the British had the same problem with us in the first revolution. Now that we Rebels are so well organized, we have slowly lost our ability to disperse into hiding. We're too goddamned big now, and that makes us more vulnerable." Rock showed concern as the lines on his face stretched. "I sure hope the Feds continue to take their time in realizing it. To stay stronger, we need to develop better supply lines if we mean to carry on this war as a conventional one. This is our Achilles heel."

Joe quizzed, "Do you think we can put together a supply line in time?"

"As you know, Son, it's become a major challenge to supply the army since the Mexicans put in their two centavos. We did receive a good deal of our provisions, from guns to butter, from our new enemy. Now that rumor has it we'll invade, I'm not sure where we'll get adequate supplies unless we carry what we can and take it from them as we invade and conquer the bastards."

Joe, ever the history professor, interrupted, "Sherman did that to the South in the last civil war. In his infamous march to the sea, he took what he needed from the countryside and burned the rest. He moved lightly, with little provisions and a lot of gall." Joe again removed his cap to wipe his sweat-soaked brow.

Rock retorted, "That's all well and good, but what if the Mexicans burn everything before we get there?"

"I suppose that's the chance we take. Intel feels the Mexican citizens are not for this war. They're impoverished. It'll be difficult for them to burn their food stores. Dad, I agree we're in a mess right now. Our army's poised as far north as Kansas. There, the Fed Army is at us like loose tigers. I've heard they're also threatening our eastern strongholds. We do hold the south from Georgia to Kansas. The rest of the country is still split with guerilla warfare. To the north, Quebec, and now the rest of the Canadians, are still a major threat, and here we're facing Mexico and who knows what. The wild card is still the far west and that deck is short a couple cards."

"Joe, we've little time." Rock seemed excited to share his news. "So to change the subject, did you hear that the Rebs in Mobile, Alabama got the old *USS Alabama* working again? They even got her 16-inch guns and all her weapons operational. Our people did likewise with the *Wisconsin* in Norfolk. You know how I love those old battlewagons. I was told once that the navy has the right to re-commission any warship, even museum craft. This began after the Federal Navy reactivated the *USS New Jersey* and several decommissioned destroyers and cruisers. I still can't believe we have the ability and the manpower to reactivate them. However, all this serves to do is neutralize commercial shipping, though it also widens the overall scope of things. It sure makes my job more difficult. You know, Joe, things don't always come in to fill the void in supplies when ships are sunk or captured."

Rock wiped his brow as he continued. "I also heard a few days ago that both sides still have active nuclear subs and that last month a couple of Fed subs had mutinous crews that went over to our navy."

Joe responded animatedly, "Dad, then you'll enjoy this bit of news, knowing how fond you are of the *USS Missouri*. The big news around Intel yesterday was she's being fitted out for service by the Feds at Pearl. Word is Japan has eyes on Hawaii."

"Boy, I'd like to see that ship in our hands, but keeping the Japanese at bay serves us in the long run."

"I agree, but I don't see us making many inroads in the 50th state. Most Hawaiians have remained loyal, and the numerous military bases there are still very strong. If a man wants to desert over to our side, it'll be a long swim. Unless some guerilla action takes place, Hawaii stays Federal. And the enemy's too strong there to allow that to happen."

"Joe," Rock looked at his watch, "you said earlier you had to go soon, and now it looks like I've run out of time and have to get back to work. There are over 25,000 men my group needs to feed, and this old grocer has got to find some food. I wish we could continue this discussion, perhaps soon."

Joe looked fondly into Rock's eyes. "We will, soon. Good seeing you, Dad. Keep low and stay out of trouble," he chuckled.

Rock hated seeing his son leave. For a brief moment it was like old times back home, discussing world and local events. Rock wished for a return of those happier days. With a raspy voice he spoke, trying to hide his emotion. "I love you, Joey. You take care now, hear? If I see the boys, I'll let them know you were thinking of them and see if I can send them over."

"Thanks, Dad. I love you too. I'll try to get some time to look them up." Joe left the old man reluctantly, shedding tears hidden from his father by his exit. Rock had a way of lifting Joe's spirits and bringing the best out of him. It forced him to reflect and amend. Joe thought, *Life sure has changed from the free and easy '80s and high-flying '90s of my youth. Now it's all a distant blur, lost I fear, forever.*

"Goodbye, Dad," he whispered.

July 28, 2020—Near Santa Fe, New Mexico

Trey Northcutt reached into his pocket for the pear he had hoarded to abate his constant hunger. He could do little, however, to eliminate the recurrent pain; his arthritis had worsened. The past months had been one relentless search for safety and food.

Donna Northcutt, slim and petite, hid well her fifty-plus years, but after long days of drudgery, her eyes began to give away her secret. After her parents' violent death at the hands of marauders, she had hardened to the cause for freedom. Until then, she had been an advocate for peace, despite having three children serving in the Rebel Army. Her restless days were filled with prayer for her offspring when they were not dominated by the relentless need to survive.

She hadn't heard from any of her children for several months. There was nothing she could do to verify they were alive. This was difficult for a person who liked taking control. She was in the beginning stage of a breakdown.

Her father, David York, had arrived in Prosper several months earlier. He had driven his big John Deere tractor, towing two trailers and many of his valuables. She and Trey reluctantly joined the caravan of refugees fleeing the rampaging Federal peril arriving daily from the north. Several friends and neighbors had already fled south, despite the Texas Army's success driving the Federal hordes back north.

Neighbors foolish enough to voice opposition to the Rebel cause were killed by ever-increasing mobs seeking revenge any place they could for the atrocities visited by the Federals.

When Texas was made secure by Rebel victories, her dad recommended they return to his ranch near Sherman, Texas. Trey had unsuccessfully tried to join the Home Guard, but was told his disabilities only made him a liability. Frustrated, he accepted his father-in-law's offer, taking with them the few valuables they could carry. A few miles from the York Ranch, marauders unsuccessfully attacked their column of anxious refugees, killing David and Mary York in the encounter.

Donna's father was a crack shot and fond of his little arsenal; luckily he carried it with him. Though his weapons saved many, they did not save him. Donna smiled, remembering her father's bravery and that of her husband. Invalid or not, Trey had stood his ground and could be proud of his conduct during the skirmish.

With everything lost and no hope in sight for a normal life in Sherman, they decided to try to reach relatives in New Mexico. They were truly refugees now, moving on what seemed an endless trek, seeking comfort where they could find it. Sadly, they were not alone; millions throughout the torn country were in the same sad state.

"Trey, how much farther do we have to travel?"

Trey carried a blanket tied around their meager possessions. The Rebel Army had seized his father-in-law's tractor and equipment several days earlier. The few valuables they'd managed to carry away with them were gone, sold for food. They were dependent now upon Providence.

"Honey, let's go on until we see some life. I think we're about five miles from Santa Fe. It may be safer to camp near people than out in the open. Maybe with some luck, we can find some food and cover for the night." Trey dropped his pack, momentarily relieved. He was tired and ready to stop.

"Do you still believe we'll be safer here than home?"

"Donna, I don't know!" Trey's weary face showed anxiety and all of his sixty years. "With the Mexican threat in Texas, and probably here too, we may be better off to head for the Rockies. Hopefully, my cousin is still in Santa Fe. Let's pray he'll give us some help and rest before we continue."

Trey's cousin, Jack Petry, had moved to Santa Fe in the late '90s to get away from the population explosion in Dallas. An artist drawn to the Southwestern culture, his work was well received by tourists, giving him and his wife Christina a moderate income and a good but simple life. Donna and Trey last visited in 2013 and had last heard from them during Christmas 2018, just prior to the start of hostilities the following April.

Donna, a resilient person, would not allow herself to be discouraged by the war. She had an enduring hope based upon a deep abiding faith, and still retained the youthful determination that had initially captured her husband's admiration. Trey loved strong women, and Donna, as hard-headed as he, matched his own need to be in control. Their marriage often resembled a battleground, but most of their battles were settled in compromise—they were two dominant people who thoroughly loved each other, beyond any doubt. Their children were a fine blend of their personalities. After losing all his worldly possessions, Trey rejoiced with fatherly pride in his only worthwhile wealth—his children and his solid union with Donna. His thoughts wandered then to a concern he could not shake. *Have they managed to survive?* The constant dread plagued him.

Looking at her now, he couldn't help but notice the worry in her face too. "Here, Donna, have my pear. It's all we have left, but it'll hold off hunger for a few minutes."

"Thanks, but you eat it. I'll survive." Donna's willingness to sacrifice was an integral part of her stubborn, strong personality. It was the side of her that Trey both admired and sometimes detested most. Her comment did not surprise him. Still, he knew she must be as famished as he.

Trey reached into his ragged pocket and pulled out his old Boy Scout knife, now chipped with age. He cut the pear in half, compromising with her for the moment out of necessity. "Here, and no 'buts.' We'll both eat and pretend it's a feast." Both knew it was a very temporary relief for their hunger.

"Trey, I can manage a few more miles if you can."

"I'm with you, Honey." Trey lifted his load and continued to walk, forcing himself to put one foot after the other.

They arrived on the outskirts of Santa Fe a couple of hours from sundown. The landscape appeared untouched by war except for the hundreds of refugees wandering aimlessly, crowding the roads. Otherwise the scene was so serene that one would never think that a war ravaged the country.

Trey followed his rattrap memory to the street where his cousin lived. It was a few blocks off the historic central square of Old Santa Fe. It seemed that the frantic times had yet to touch the city. Trey noted in wonder the absence of bullet holes, blood, and destruction. They even had electricity. To Trey it was a grand step back into a happier time.

Donna interrupted his contemplation. "Do you think your cousins will let us stay for a while?" Her tired eyes spoke volumes.

Smiling, he answered, his lips barely visible through his beard. "I don't know. These are tough times, and I suppose food is scarce here too. We can only hope for the best."

They reached the Petry house, a haven of peace in the midst of a tumultuous country. At first glance, Trey saw the house needed paint; it didn't surprise him. His cousin, the consummate temperamental artist, never was much good at the upkeep of his home when he lived in Garland, Texas. Why should he change here? The porch creaked as they stepped carefully up its stair to the entry. Trey knocked. A curtain was slipped aside just enough for the occupants to see who was intruding into their domain during curfew.

Trey, too late, thought anxiously about his unkempt appearance. His scraggy beard hid any familiarity; his cousin might not recognize him. His concerns were unfounded; the door opened slowly, and a hand beckoned them to hurry inside. The door was quickly shut and bolted after their entrance. Jack Petry threw his arms around Trey, and Christina gave Donna a warm embrace.

"Trey, of all people. I'm flabbergasted! Why, we were just talking about you two only a moment ago!"

"Life sure can play tricks on you, Cousin." Trey looked into Jack's deep grey eyes. What he saw was concern and worry. He opened shyly, "Jack, we're desperate and need shelter for a day or two. Our endurance is played out, and our bodies need rest. It's hard for me to ask, but do you think you can put us up? Please don't feel you have to say yes. We'll understand if you can't."

Jack looked at Christina for assurance as he hugged Donna. "Christina and I'd be happy to let you stay as long as you need. We can't offer much in the way of hospitality, though. If you're willing to scavenge with me, I think we can all make do."

"Hell, Jack," Trey said, tears of relief falling freely, "I've been scavenging for months now. You can rely on me to do all I can to hold up our end."

Christina started for the small kitchen off the parlor. She had a worried look on her face, and she wanted to hide it from her husband. She wasn't as pleased as he to see unexpected family. She had always been fond of

Trey and Donna—company would make a nice diversion, but they had so little to share, and Donna looked so fragile. Feeling a pang of guilt she busily heated water and then reentered the living room with cups of tea. Suddenly, the electricity went dead.

"Oh, don't mind. This happens about this time every day. It will probably stop altogether soon enough. With all the shortages, we've learned to cope."

Christina put the cups down on the coffee table and took Donna's hand into hers. "How are you two? Donna, you look so tired. Finish your tea and come with me. I'll draw you a bath while we still have some hot water."

Donna left with Christina, a broad smile on her face as she imagined the pending bath she had only dreamed of during those days of endless walking and hiding.

"Trey, Donna's still as beautiful as the day you married her. As your best man, I feel I can still say she remains too good for you. You dog, you." Jack playfully jostled his cousin's balding head. "How about scraping off some of that beard, or do you want to join me in my nonpaying profession? You sure look the starving artist with that beard."

Trey laughed deeply. It felt good. "I suppose I could play the part, Cousin, but I don't think the world is ready for my illustrious talent."

"Trey, I still can't believe you're here. Fill me in on what's happened. Was there any news on the road?"

"We haven't heard much of any interest. I can only fill you in on what's probably old news. It appears the world, as we knew it, has turned upside down. It's thought the Mexican government has in mind to take back what it lost in the Mexican-American War, way back in the 19th century. When we left, our army was beating them back across the border. On the road, we heard the Rebels are planning to invade Mexico. It looks like it's now a three-front war." Trey drew a deep breath.

"Yeah, with the Federal Army and the Canadians up north, it seems the Rebel cause has bitten off more than it can chew."

"Jack, I don't expect anyone thinks this'll last much longer. Yet in my limited experience, war plays awful tricks on common sense. So, Cousin, what's the situation here?"

Jack placed his cup down as he spoke. "As you can see, we're sort of in the middle. Neither the Federal Army nor the Rebs have a presence here. Our state has supplied men to both sides, so it's still best for people to keep their mouths shut and their thoughts to themselves. I don't think it'll be long, though, before the shit hits the fan."

"Jack, I was really surprised to see the electricity; it's been a long time since I've seen any. How're food supplies and the infrastructure?"

Jack gathered the empty cups, talking as he walked to the kitchen sink. "The state supplies as much food and water as it can. We have running water, but it's rationed. We're in a serious drought, so everyone's saving water in every available container. Our garden is poor, and we are low on food. Sewer and treatment plants still work when we have energy, but that's sporadic at best. A lot of people have left town, only to be replaced by refugees. It seems most of them come from Texas and Oklahoma."

The room's light slowly faded to pitch black as the evening sun dropped out of sight. Donna carried in a candle while Christina brought out some homemade bread and preserves. The meager fare constituted the night's supper. Donna and Trey felt like they were at a banquet in heaven.

"Tell us about your kids. How're they doing?" Christina asked.

They could see the worry on Trey's face as he thought of his children's safety. He sighed. "Their welfare is in God's hands. We've no idea what's happened to them." Trey slumped deeply into the sofa's inviting comfort. It helped to ease his hurt.

"Not any of them?" Jack asked.

"Yes, it hurts me to say, not a one. It's been months since we've seen any of our children." Donna choked out her words. "The last we heard, Justin and Taylor were still with the Ranger Division."

"You mean the 36th Division? I heard they practically saved Texas all by their lonesome." Jack had been following the unit by the bits and pieces of news he'd been able to gather.

"Well, I'd suppose that's a bit of an exaggeration, but they are a top fighting unit of the Texan Army. Our sons are officers," Trey said, beaming with pride. "Our Becky is a nurse's assistant serving in a hospital unit. We haven't had any letters in months, so we don't know. ..." His voice trailed off.

Christina's smile showed sincere concern for the Northcutt children. "I'm so sorry; I'll continue to pray for their safety and your peace of mind."

The Petrys couldn't have children, and they had never adopted. In Texas, they had enjoyed spoiling the Northcutt kids every chance they could. "Remember," Christina hugged Donna as she spoke, "they're good kids, and smart, too. They'll be OK, I'm just sure of it."

"You know, Trey, there's a way you can send a letter," Jack said, having just thought of an avenue that might work. "I happen to know of a secret Rebel mail service that goes out to our New Mexican boys serving with the Rebs. I hear that most times the messages do get through. You know, a lot of our boys are serving with Texas units. It's iffy but worth a try. I'll check into it tomorrow. There's some paper and a pen on the desk if you want to write letters. You know, just getting words on paper sometimes can help rest the soul."

"Thanks, Jack." Donna's smile gleamed with hope, her blue-green eyes showing happiness for the first time in weeks. "Yes, I'll write to my children. I just know it will get to them somehow."

Trey didn't share the same optimism his wife enjoyed, but he couldn't burst her enthusiasm. "Sounds wonderful, doll; leave a few lines for me."

"Trey, they're alive. I want to believe they are."

She closed her eyes for a moment; the glistening of a long line of tears gave away her feelings of faith and joy that had remained hidden by fear for so long. She walked with deliberation to the desk, placed a small candle Christina had provided for light, and began to write in her clear and delicate hand.

"Dear Justin ..."

Jim Damiano

A TIME TO STAND

Clouds of war thicken the sky,
Signals of life passing by.
Time to stand, or time to hide,
Men and women forced to decide,
A nation in turmoil, a carrion feast,
But war's fury is the real beast.
Revisited sites, where men once died,
Fighting for beliefs, now denied,
Triumphs for freedom now long forgot,
Trampled by posterity and left to rot!

—Jim Damiano

PART TWO

OVERVIEW

Total war envelopes the divided nation, as brother must again fight brother on a scale never before seen. The conflict carries its wrath to worldwide proportions. Neither cause has much energy left, nor envisions the desperate path each must take to bring the struggle to conclusion.

Jim Damiano

There is one quality that one must possess to win, and that is definiteness of purpose, the knowledge of what one wants, and a burning desire to possess it.

–Napoleon Hill

CHAPTER FIFTEEN

August 8, 2020—Capitol Building, President's Office, Austin, Texas

Barbara "Babs" Collins-Smythe did not need to force her presence upon anyone. She was six feet tall, yet her statuesque figure was not the reason behind the impressive fact that she led one of history's largest rebellions. As soon as she made somebody's acquaintance, that person was immediately struck by her commanding presence and her charm.

It was clear to her followers that she was the right person for the turbulent times. Like her brother, she was trained from birth for her current role. There the similarities ended, for the sixty-five-year-old grandmother was not anything like her brother, except in a very few good ways. She did possess the strong Collins persona and political tact. While her brother was devious and cunning, she was charming and brutally honest. Where he was viciously efficient, she worked by persuasion and example.

The Rebels universally accepted this gray-haired woman who refused to color her hair. They felt certain she'd guide them to victory. Many would die trying to accomplish her wishes for she wasn't just their president; she was everyone's nurturing grandmother.

Underneath her genteel veneer was a steel magnolia. She was clearly unafraid to lead citizen soldiers to independence. If she had one weakness, it was her calculating disposition. She seldom listened to or followed advice, even from those she trusted. As the Rebellion's president, she seldom sought any counsel but her own.

Raif Sinsome, however, was the exception. A trusted adviser, he stood patiently at her desk awaiting her direction. Today she sought his valued opinion, needing to ease the monumental distress of the moment. She could be a very private person, but she knew her limits. Now was not the time for bravado.

Babs looked up briefly from her work to acknowledge Raif's presence. "Have a seat, General. Please excuse the delay. I've a couple of items to put to bed, and I desire to devote my full attention to our meeting." She returned to her scattered papers without looking up. If she had, she would have seen Raif's broad admiring smile.

"Thank you, Madam President." Raif sat, resigned to watching her work.

"There. OK, Raif, I'm finished." Babs, all business, skipped the niceties. "I've called an emergency meeting of our security council and my cabinet for five o'clock. Representatives from several of the eighteen freed states will attend the first meeting to discuss our proposed formal alliance."

She fidgeted, looking for the right words. "Raif, the historical significance of this meeting needs no explanation. So it must run smoothly." Babs stood as she continued.

"As you're brutally aware, until the past few weeks, almost all fighting was piecemeal and within the confines of the old United States' borders. The lone exceptions were a few minor naval engagements on the open seas and in the Great Lakes. Now our allied forces find themselves on the receiving end of unprovoked attacks by the Canadians in New York, and the Mexicans in Texas, New Mexico, and Arizona." She pointed at the map on her office wall, frowning as she did.

"I had originally thought, and hoped, that rogue segments, eager for power and expansion, were out to retake territory lost to the United States and Great Britain in past wars. It's become abundantly clear there is more to the evil acts than Intel originally realized. Until now the unwritten but vocal alliance between my brother and me had made it known to the world at large that we would jointly use whatever means were at our disposal to destroy any nation that interfered with our war."

Raif listened intently, folding his hands tightly, appearing worried. "I had hoped this alliance of convenience with Rex was sufficient to keep potential assailants at bay. Obviously, I now have doubts. Up until now most of the rest of the world have chosen to sit on the sidelines, let us slug it out, and wait for the results."

Raif nodded, listening, taking notes, wondering what was expected of him. "Raif, I know the mindset of my devious brother. I don't take anything he says at face value. With that in mind, I sent out spies with instructions to find, at all costs, the true nature and intent behind the invasions. It took some digging, a lot of payoff money, and a few IOUs. My 'deep throat' confirmed this discovery. What's been uncovered isn't good."

Babs returned to her seat, brushing her hair back as she did. "Diplomats and politicians are all the same, no matter their nation. So now, with our already strained treasury down several million dollars after these payoffs, we've learned the full extent of the Federal-Quebec-Mexico secret alliance."

Babs laid out all the disruptive details to Raif, who continued to listen intently. She didn't know that her report was partially familiar to him. Raif, a quiet but controlling man, had his own sources and spies.

Raif did not come across as someone who commanded over one million men. It was another irony of the war that Raif's exact opposite and chief adversary, Skip Newman, was once his best friend and West Point classmate.

"Raif, you appear very upbeat, even after all the sour news. Why?"

"Madam President, if I appear optimistic, then you have caught me; I'll explain."

A day didn't go by without President Collins-Smythe thanking her God for the genius of the little general sitting before her. A rabid student of history, she'd often commented to confidants that Raif thought and acted like the great General Robert E. Lee. Like Lee, he had the unconditional respect of his men. He had cleverly maneuvered his troops throughout the conflict, always outnumbered and mostly on the run. Yet he never sacrificed his men unnecessarily. Raif had often said there was neither pride nor worth in winning a battle only to lose the confidence of his troops.

No one thought of Sinsome as black, only as a man. People who met him saw a leader they could trust unconditionally, proving that this war was not burdened by racial bias, as were previous conflicts. Oh, it would have its racial problems, but opponents trying to say otherwise were few, though nevertheless vocal.

"Raif, why aren't you boiling over angry, especially over what I just revealed?"

"Madam President?" Raif feigned surprise.

"Please cut the formality, Raif. We're alone. I prefer to believe we've been through too much to be formal."

"Yes, Madam." Raif caught himself, his military training interfering with his president's wishes; her glare reminded him of his mom. "I mean, Babs," he stammered. "I'm not as disturbed by it as you are. You've seen what just two Ranger brigades did in concert with our New York allies and our Home Guard. And the militias from Arizona and New Mexico held their own as well."

Babs, not convinced, stood to ease her worry and her lingering indigestion. "Raif, I understand all this. I couldn't be happier, but a three-front war isn't in our best interest."

"I can't disagree but, Babs, we beat them back. Outnumbered at Del Rio and surrounded, we hit them hard. My report says that two brigades of our 36th made their desperate charge to the cry of 'Remember the Alamo.' We couldn't ask more of our fighting men. With this historic victory, our cause has a new spirit and a national hero. He's a true example of what a patriot is supposed to be."

Raif's personality lit up as he spoke about his protégé. "Our young General Northcutt and his brilliant strategy was a stroke of military genius. I'm damned pleased the Congress agreed to promote him to major general of the 36th."

"Yes, Raif, I know all this. Still, I ask why you're so positive when we're about to get sandwiched between two armies?" Babs felt a sudden, sharp, frightening pain in her chest. She compressed her lips to hide it.

Raif noticed and stopped talking. "Are you OK?"

"Go on, Raif, it's nothing but the remnants of a bad breakfast."

Nodding, Raif continued, "Babs, now that we understand the true reason for the attacks, in my opinion, we have the option to declare war or, at minimum, hostile conditions against our northern and southern neighbors. I grant you, it's not an ideal situation. It is, however, an opportunity to neutralize this threat, especially the one to our south."

Raif stood and walked to the wall map behind Babs's desk. "I'd like permission to unleash the 36th as my lead unit, along with the Texas 1st, 5th and 7th Volunteer Divisions to take a large piece of northern Mexico for no other reason than to show them we can."

"Are you serious, Raif? Didn't we give them sufficient reason to rethink any further invasion? All we'd accomplish is to stir up a hornet's nest we don't need and can't control." Bab's concern filled the room. "I understand your wrath and desire to teach them a lesson. Realistically, though, how can we spare the forces and supply such an expedition?"

"That, Madam President, is the beauty of all this. We can't allow them to think they can cross our borders at will without terrible retaliation. The enemy particularly fears the Ranger Division. Remember, the 36th was merciless in their six-month defense of our borders the past year. In my opinion, we have no choice. We must find the forces and ask help from allies."

"But Raif, except for Del Rio, what the Rangers did was against marauders and petty thieves, not the whole Mexican army."

"Babs, if we unleash our shock troops—the crazy Norte Americano Rangers, as the Mexicans like to call them—we will no doubt have the proper effect on their local populace."

"And that is?" Babs's quizzical look amused Raif. It reminded him of one of his tough West Point professors.

"This, damn it, is our war! If they want a piece of it, we'll be very happy to oblige. Vultures will be insufficient to finish the carnage left by our men." Raif's determined eyes met Babs'. "I, for one, have buried far too many good men to Federal treachery. We must retaliate, and fast."

Raif raised his voice, which was a rarity for him. "I suggest, diplomatic crap aside—pardon me, Madam President, for my choice of words—that you tell Mexico City that unless they want their capital in Austin, they'd better stay on their side of the border. I plead with you to let my top divisions loose before you do anything diplomatically. I'll show them how quickly, and at will, we can take 100 miles or more of their northern states." Raif's eyes showed his determination. It strengthened Babs's resolve as she began to speak in earnest.

"Do you really think you can accomplish all this?"

"Yes, I do." Raif was emphatic. "Mexico is in big enough trouble without our scrambling their lives. Sometimes shock therapy is the only method to put things right after a mental breakdown. Babs, what the Mexicans did was nothing short of idiotic."

"Raif, I see where you're headed in your argument. The Mexican attacks caused terrible civilian casualties that need payback. I'd expect our Rangers' feelings are running high towards revenge. Is it wise to set those boys loose on northern Mexico? I don't want to see Texas' legacy in its quest for freedom compromised by atrocities on innocent enemy civilians, or ours, for that matter."

Babs took a deep breath, trying to collect her thoughts. She continued, "Raif, I'll put forth my best effort to get what you want approved, but only on the condition you give me your word there'll be no unnecessary pillaging or atrocity."

Her experienced eyes looked intently for Raif's commitment but saw reluctance. She pressed on. "I want enemy civilians to be spared at all costs. Can we carry out this retaliation without creating long-term reasons for continued hatred? You know we'll have to return to normalcy some day. Raif, promise me this, and you'll have my support."

Raif was silent. He wasn't sure he could hold back his Texans. He'd seen the bloody work of his Mexican adversary; worse yet, so had his Rangers. It would not be easy to put aside their lust to kill without thought. His president was being naïve, and he didn't know how to tell her that nor did he want to. He knew that war could become a personal hell that only those who live within its immediate torment can understand. He would not hold back his men just yet; he couldn't, and retain their respect.

Undeterred, Babs's alto voice raised an octave "Can I count on you to use restraint, General Sinsome?" She doggedly asked, returning to formalities.

"Madam President, you've my word as a true Texan, I will follow your desire as best I can under the circumstances, given the confusion battle sometimes bring."

"OK, then, who do you suggest to lead this campaign?"

"I suggest Lieutenant General Hollingsworth, with Major General Northcutt his second in command, and Major General Cortez next in line."

"Whatever you want or need in reason, General. You know you have my support, but isn't General Northcutt a bit young for such responsibility?

"Madam President, he may be just a couple of years removed from college, but at twenty-four he leads like a Moses and fights like a Patton. Leaders like him don't come along very often. We're lucky he's on our side. He'll do just fine, even if he's the youngest general officer that we have. His men will follow him, and that's what counts."

Babs momentarily let her guard down. "I didn't realize he's our youngest general. I fear before this war's over, we'll have many more boy generals. Raif, this all has to end soon so we won't have to promote more children to positions beyond what any seasoned mortal, let alone boys, should endure."

"Madam President, I couldn't agree more. Yet, every day, I get on my knees to thank God for placing young men like Northcutt in my command. He makes me look good." Raif smiled, showing a rare side of his personality. "And sometimes that can be difficult."

"Well then, General Sinsome, may God grant you make it all happen for us. I think, though, I'll need much more ammunition to help me persuade the first new United Congress we can fight on so many fronts."

"Madam President, I believe if we move quickly, we can assure our success on a wider front. I'd recommend we use one-third of our Texan forces along with equal numbers from other state units to first devour Mexico and then swallow it whole. On the Kansas front, we're holding in check all that the Federals can throw at us. When we neutralize the Mexicans, and our allies in the north contain the French Canadians, we'll be in position to force your brother to divert his assets to prevent our success."

Raif waited to see if she followed his reasoning; her attention and gestures gave him confidence to continue. "When he does, he'll be meeting us on our terms. Offense is better than waiting for them to act. All I need from this Congress is the movement of men and supplies to accomplish our plan. I suspect we'll be living off the land as we go. It'll also serve as a training ground for all the free states to act in unison and give us the organization needed to beat the Federals. I'd much rather our army faced the inexperienced Mexicans than seasoned Fed veterans. We have some precious time before Mexico catches up with our experienced troops and learns the art of war."

"General, I'll do all I can to get what you need. I am, though, leaning towards your latter idea for a full offensive rather than your original plan to stop after a few miles. I'll keep that plan in reserve. It's good that almost every free state is represented. It'll allow me to garner the full support we need. We must not fail." Babs slammed her pad of notes firmly upon her desk. "Raif, we have no alternative. After they hear my opening statements, everyone will understand why we have only this course of action."

The momentous events and the tremendous weight they implied showed on Babs's strained features. Her determined, deep-set eyes burned with a tenacity General Raif could not mistake.

"Any other suggestions you'd like to add before I put to paper what I'll say to our allies?"

"No, Madam President, not at the moment." Raif's resolve was infectious.

Raif, recognizing the meeting's end, smiled and stood. "Madam President, I've some papers to get to and orders to draft. With your permission, I better get on with it. I'll anxiously await the outcome of the Congress."

"Thank you, General, and good day. You can be assured that I'll convince our fellow patriots of our plan, though I expect the new Congress will not be as easy a pushover for your ideas as I. You will be called as soon as we have something, but Raif, I honestly believe this dog will hunt."

Babs watched him depart, silently saying a prayer. The republic's future, an awesome burden, lay in her hands.

x x x x x

The afternoon's emergency session went more smoothly than expected. Most of the debate was spent over who would command the invading army, which included 200,000 of Texas' best young men, along with a like amount of troops pledged from other free states. It was argued Lieutenant General Ralf Hollingsworth was certainly the most qualified man on paper, while Major General Justin Northcutt, the hero of the Second Alamo, was the more popular. In the end, General Sinsome's suggestions prevailed, and Hollingsworth was appointed to lead the southern invasion into Mexico. It would be the first formal military expedition of American forces into Mexico since 1916 when General Black Jack Pershing chased Poncho Villa all over southern Texas and northern Mexico.

Plans were also worked out for the northern theater. The combined D-Day for all fronts was to take place in thirty days, depending on availability of helicopter gunships, air, and artillery recently liberated from Federal armories in Kansas. The mobilization of the necessary troops and the logistics would test the Rebel Army to its limits.

As Babs left the meeting of the First United Congress, she could not release her concerns. She felt a sharp pain in her chest but again passed it off as indigestion. She turned and walked back to her desk and poured a cool glass of water. She took a deep swallow, thinking, *We must prevail. Can we?* She tried to erase her doubt but couldn't. She was too well groomed in her political education to throw common sense to the winds.

A few yards from the president's window, a red-tailed hawk seemed to be staring intently at Babs before it lifted its powerful wings and flew from its perch, screeching as if in defiance. Babs, staring out her window from her desk chair, did not miss his ascent. She stood mesmerized, watching his flight, transfixed, wishing, *If only I could just catch a plane, fly above all this, and leave this heartache behind.* Babs stood to close her curtain on the outside world and then returned again to her desk to attack the mountain of paper awaiting her attention.

At this point, Oklahoma was totally under Rebel control, as was most of Kansas. The depleted ranks were being filled with conscripts from newly reestablished state governments, increasing the Rebel manpower. The nineteen liberated state governments pledged an additional combined 400,000 men, consisting mostly of untried draftees, for each of the two new fronts.

The conflict had slowly evolved into a full-scale conventional war relying heavily on the foot soldier. Shortages of fuel, parts, and everything necessary to carry out campaigns plagued both sides. Air power was used sparingly—it became universally obvious that before the war ended, each opposing air force would be gone.

Men learned to ride horses and joined cavalry units that were formed out of necessity when modern communications broke down. They would become the eyes and ears of two opposing armies rushing toward extinction.

The one thing over which you have absolute control is your own thoughts. It is this that puts you in a position to control your own destiny.

—Paul Thomas

CHAPTER SIXTEEN

October 10, 2020—At Sea, Gulf of Mexico

Taylor, deep in thought, leaned upon the ship rail looking blankly at a blustery ocean. The ship cut easily through the waves that were seemingly indifferent to its course, aimed in a southerly direction.

The *Crystal Harmony* had started service as a luxury cruise ship sometime in the '90s of the last century. Now past its glory days, the ship was still a lady to be admired. Confiscated for Rebel use when hostilities began, it now served as a troop carrier. Its current mission was to transport 4,000 Rangers of the 10th Brigade, 36th Division.

Taylor's thoughts raced to home and peacetime, both of which were becoming rare visions. It had been three months since the Battle of Del Rio. Much had happened; most of it he preferred to forget. The war refused to let him. There had been too many battles. Mexico was not the easy victory the Rebels had hoped; yet victory was close.

As the newly appointed brigadier general of the 10th Brigade, Taylor tried fruitlessly to analyze why they were being sent to the old resort city of Cancun. He figured his brother, the newly appointed commanding general of all Rebel forces in Mexico, knew. Justin had signed off on Taylor's orders to set up defensive positions for the city, with the emphasis on the seaward side.

It was not as difficult for him to imagine Justin as the commanding general as it was to think of himself a brigadier. Promotion meant only one thing—another poor soul had died or been maimed, and he was the next in line. Promotions had come with extreme rapidity for the

Northcutt brothers. For Taylor, it was not welcomed, but he would not shirk his duty.

The war had become a confusing picture he could no longer grasp. Yet, he calmly thought, *It's impossible for anyone to actually comprehend the complete picture, even if that person was president.* Taylor's doubts were not unfounded.

October 24, 2020—10th Ranger Brigade Expeditionary Force Texas Army Defense Works, Cancun, Mexico

Taylor carefully walked through the ragged rock to within a few feet of the splashing waves on the beach below. This was not a defensive position he would have chosen. While his men enjoyed the place, he would have preferred to be in the States as far away from this country as possible. He never liked Mexico, even as a child when they vacationed, ironically, at this very resort. But orders were orders.

Taylor attempted to guess why his unit had been ordered from Galveston to this tiny peninsula. As soon as he had arrived in Galveston to take command, orders were issued to embark. It was his nature to second-guess everything. Once given command, though, he had little time to think.

The area appeared to have little military significance other than a good place for R&R. It was miles from any action or reinforcements.

His ordnance included two helicopter gunships, with limited fuel, to help in the defense. The three destroyers that escorted his brigade's convoy had left port yesterday. It would have been comforting to have the Navy remain on duty in the area, but the Navy had its own agenda.

A destroyer captain had advised Taylor in idle conversation that the magnificent battleships *Alabama* and *Wisconsin*, part of the escort, had gone on to assist in shore bombardment assignments further to the south. He had never seen either magnificent battlewagons because they cruised parallel, several miles away from the *Crystal Harmony*. Taylor supposed mopping-up operations were underway by now. He had no way of knowing how wrong he was.

Reviewing his defenses, he wondered how 4,000 men of the 4th Brigade and 100 unassigned sailors could hold off any possible invaders. With their three destroyer escorts gone, they now faced an awesome task. But having the Navy boys out to sea made overall sense.

Taylor's rookie brigade had accomplished much in the fourteen days since their arrival. He inspected several mortar and machine gun emplacements and the series of trenches and tunnels his men had dug to connect their defenses. On the beach, men carefully placed land mines, while artillery officers plotted and re-plotted fields of fire. Looking to his right perimeter, he decided to assign two additional rifle companies to defend the artillery units.

The artillery battalion from 3rd Corps under Colonel Samuel Marquez had arrived three days earlier. Its ten 175-millimeter cannons and ten gun-howitzers, along with its 300 officers and men, were a pleasant surprise. Yet Taylor was inwardly doubtful that the defenses before him would be enough against a determined enemy.

What plagued him most, though, was the gnawing question, "Why here?" Like his brother he had inherited his stubborn nature from his mother. Yet any good soldier using common sense would realize this place was defensible only for a short period and only against a poorly trained and inferior enemy.

Taylor kicked at a lizard that crawled over his boots. *Sometimes it is easier to follow an order when you know the purpose.* Yet high command saw no reason to inform its new brigadier. He doubted even his brother would do so until the time was right for him to know.

Intuition born of combat led him to believe that 10th Brigade was here as bait, to draw a fight. He knew other units were working their way, battle by bloody battle, southward. There hadn't even been a minor skirmish when they arrived here; civilians had abandoned the city to the Texans. The few Mexicans brave enough to remain quickly found they had nothing to fear as long as they behaved. Standing orders to all expeditionary forces had come directly from President Collins-Smythe, stating explicitly not to provoke the enemy civilians and to avoid unnecessary confrontation. Taylor's men followed the president's order.

x x x x x

In the late summer, Texans and their allies were initially ordered to take 100 miles of northern Mexico south of the old U.S. border. In an overwhelming, concentrated effort, the Rebels, under General Hollingsworth's command, quickly subdued the Mexicans' minimal resistance. There was only one major engagement in the first three weeks of the campaign. In that battle, Taylor's regiment distinguished itself and he was promoted to brigadier general. The original plan—to neutralize the Mexicans and teach them a lesson—seemed to work. Taylor had hoped the invasion force would withdraw to Texas and the main conflict. They didn't.

For political reasons, never explained or understood by the common soldier, it was decided to conquer Mexico. Taylor could not fathom the purpose. The country did have its beauty, resources, and good points. But to him Mexico was not worth the bloody price. And more importantly, their expeditionary force was needed for the rebellion at home, which was far from won.

Justin was one of the few who knew about the discovery of the covert Federal Expansion Plan to conquer all the Americas. The hemisphere was now in total war.

Once it was revealed, in appropriate diplomatic arenas, it suddenly became fashionable for various countries to choose with whom they would ally. The Argentines and Peruvians allied with the Texan Rebels. Texas had many ties to these South American nations, established over years of trading. The Brazilians, along with the Cubans and Puerto Ricans, sided with the Federals, while several South American countries remained neutral, choosing to sit on the fence until the right moment.

Unknown to Taylor, Austin had engineered a pincer movement to allow the Rebels to meet up with the Argentine and Peruvian armies, which were now marching north, forcing the Mexicans into their own two-front war. Envoys from the alliance had signed secret treaties guaranteeing all countries their sovereignty if they joined in the cause against the imperial designs of the Federal U.S. Government. In the agreement, the Rebels retained the right to control Mexico once conquered. Brazil was to be split between the allies. The fate of Cuba and

Puerto Rico would be determined at a later date. The alliance's hope was to create a massive diversion to disrupt President Collins's plans for a new empire in the western hemisphere.

Taylor fumed, deep in thought. The rhythm of the waves constantly crashing on the rocky shore was hypnotic, making it difficult to concentrate. His command post was on the tip of the peninsula that formed a giant land mass resembling the number seven. The brigade's main defense was at the top of the seven, surrounded by water on three sides.

Other defenses were placed at the narrow portion of the peninsula. Defensive works were constructed to limit the access of an enemy attacking by land and to force it to concentrate its efforts.

Any attack from the sea required a difficult amphibious assault on the shore defenses, since landing craft would need to navigate strong cross currents. Invading troops would have to wade 200 to 300 yards in two to three feet of water. They would make good targets for the Texan guns zoned for the kill. It was a classic World War II defense.

Taylor, now the complete soldier, constantly adjusted and redirected his defenses until they were indelibly printed in his brain. He still didn't feel easy. Even surrounded by a full brigade, he had the hollow, twisting, gut-wrenching fear of being alone, facing the unknown.

"General Northcutt, it seems like another day of the same old thing."

"Yes, Lieutenant Gray, I'd say you're right. I've been doing a bit of daydreaming. The ocean breeze sure helps the blasted humidity. I've about run out of ideas for our gun placements, second-guessing myself all day."

"Sir, I thought I'd come out and scan the eastern side for a while. We should see supply ships soon. They were due yesterday." Gray, one of Taylor's supply officers, was an eternal pessimist.

"Good to see your concern for your duty, Lieutenant. I'm looking to the east for another reason, one a bit less hospitable than food and supplies. If we have any problems here in Mexico's paradise, I figure they'll come from that direction."

"I'm not much of a strategist, Sir. Why?"

"The Cubans, Lieutenant, the Cubans! My suspicion is that we're bait for the Cubans. If so, I shudder at the thought of what a lone brigade, mostly made up of newly trained Rangers, could do against a determined force."

"Sir, in my opinion, and from what I've heard, the Cubans have a boatload of trouble with our Floridian Rebels. Aren't they trying to keep their shores clear of the Cuban-Americans? I should think it would lessen their interest here, even if they do have a pact with the Mexicans."

"Think on this, Alex. When the Federals abandoned Guantanamo Bay, the Cubans became vulnerable. So vulnerable that they'd want to stop an invasion by any countermeasure they could devise. This could be their first stop on that path. Here, we're close to their shores, while to their north they're boxed in by our Floridians. If they can aid the Federals by attacking us, perhaps they would receive more assistance in return. As allies of the Mexicans and the Federals, it's in their best interest to assist where they can."

"I see where you're going with this. The Cuban army wouldn't last long away from their island defenses; they don't have the capacity for an extended war. So, you think it may be their best gamble to pull the Feds back into their defense. It all makes sense now. Sir, do you think we'll see action soon?"

The sudden breeze felt good, "I really doubt they'll come here. It's just theory on my part. What here is worth a battle?"

"Following your reasoning, I agree. You must admit though, this isn't a bad place to be stranded. We could certainly do worse. A lot of our boys like being here at a major tourist trap, even if it lacks all the amenities. A few bikini-clad babes and some tequila or a cold beer would be nice. Or do you prefer margaritas?"

"Cool it, Lieutenant; you're beginning to frustrate my pleasant sojourn in required thoughts of wanton destruction with side dreams of entertainment instead." Taylor felt good to be alive; a little light-hearted bantering was doing wonders for his mood.

He was suddenly jarred into reality, his levity forgotten, as Lieutenant Rinaldi strode onto the beach and interrupted. "Sir, you're needed at HQ. We've received an urgent radio message. It's been decoded and is waiting for your review."

"Thanks, Luke, I'll walk back with you so we can talk." Taylor nodded his good-bye to Lieutenant Gray.

"Luke, how's the leg doing?" Taylor's style of command, out of sight of his older brother, was casual.

"Almost perfect, Sir. Thanks for asking."

"Anything in the message about past-due supplies?"

Luke, as Taylor's adjutant, had quickly become his strong right arm in day-to-day operations. Both were new in their respective positions and learning as they went. Assigning the easy-going New Yorker to aid him was one of his better decisions.

"Not sure, Sir. I was told to get you posthaste. I sure hope there's something about our overdue mail."

"Why, soldier," Taylor chided, "are you expecting a letter from New York?" Taylor smirked, knowing the letter expected was not from home. Taylor was aware that Luke was writing faithfully to his sister, and enjoyed teasing him about it.

Little word had come from Becky since she had volunteered for duty on the Kansas front. "You know I'd sure love to get a letter from her." Luke's pained, lovesick expression amused Taylor.

"I wouldn't worry much. The mails are slow at best, and Becky never liked to write anyway, especially to a no-account like you."

Luke smiled at the dig. Taylor reminded him of his twin's constant kidding. It was a good feeling in a frightening place.

"Don't give up on the letter," Taylor continued. "Heck, I got one from my mom before we set sail. It was the first I've heard from my parents in a year, and it was dated last July, so you see, there's hope."

"How were things at home, Sir?"

"Best news to me was they were alive. Mom didn't elaborate. It's not like her to say anything that'll worry me, but I know it can't be good. She did say her parents were killed by marauders. She said they died in a firefight and that Granddad held his own during the encounter. I surely will miss them. They meant a lot to us in so many ways."

"Sorry, Taylor, it seems there's no end to all this."

"Thanks, Luke. Enough of this, let's get back. There's a war to win."

Jim Damiano

x x x x x

At HQ, Taylor quietly asked Major Jordan why the message couldn't have been delivered to him.

"Sir, I believe once you read it you'll understand." Picking up the deciphered document, the reason was immediately apparent.

> 24 October, 2020   <u>URGENT</u>
> To: Commanding General, Cancun
> From: Captain Dixon, TSS Destroyer Tyler
>
> *Returning to Galveston, ship listing, Destroyers TSS LUBBOCK and ARLINGTON sunk. Relief supply ships all sunk. Cuban Nationals lost two Destroyers and four gunships. One Cuban Destroyer remains, along with eight heavily armed craft. No big guns. All headed your way. Troop carriers, estimated 15,000 to 20,000, REMAIN WITH CONVOY, HEADING YOUR WAY. <u>REPEAT</u> Coming Your Way.*
>
> *Confirmed, we sunk troop carriers with approximate tally 5,000 enemy killed. You have estimated time of twenty-four hours to prepare. Will contact Command Austin on your behalf. Good Luck.*
>
> END OF MESSAGE"

"Wonderful, marvelous," clipped Taylor. "Major, sound a general alert. Get the men supplied with whatever we have available for a siege. Put the men on twelve-hour shifts. We'll feed the men at their posts. We need to concentrate on speeding up reinforcement of land barriers. We're likely to get the Mexicans coming from the land to hit us as the Cubans strike our shore positions. Shit, I'd never pick this place to defend. But we're here, so it'll have to be a good day to fight for Texas. Major, get all officers here in fifteen minutes."

Waiting for his men was difficult. Taylor used the time to focus on what must be done. "Sure looks like a season to die," he said softly to nobody in particular. *What in God's name is command thinking placing my untried boys here?* Taylor felt sick. He realized it would not be any easier to send unfamiliar men to their death. At first he had hoped that it would be simpler to command a new unit. Now he knew different. The bitter pangs of duty took a front seat, interfering with his natural penchant for compassion. He contemplated how many men might die defending this worthless piece of military real estate.

The mood of the men at officers' call was somber. Taylor reviewed the situation, taking the time to evaluate each position and all battle orders until every officer was certain of his upcoming role. "Rangers, we're more comfortable on the offensive. Yet, we're stuck with this defense. So we'll have to make do with what we have. Without naval support, we'll have to depend upon our artillery and two gunships. Let's pray the Cubans were unable to restore any of their old Russian MiGs. We can only hope they haven't found any jet fuel."

"Lieutenant Rhodes, I'd like you to take your company and join newly promoted Captain Rinaldi. Give our Navy boys a quick refresher course on their assigned weapons. Mix the salts with your two Ranger companies to give them some back-up experience. They'll have to learn fast. Spend the next six to eight hours going over everything you can." Rhodes was one of the few experienced men Taylor had been able to have reassigned to his command. Justin had been reluctant to let him go but bent to Taylor's resolve when he pleaded his case for taking some veterans with his new command.

Taylor addressed Luke and Rhodes. "Your men will cover the land defense. Your two companies contain the only veterans I had transferred with me to the 10th. I need seasoned men to hold that position, and I'm depending on you both not to let me down. That gives you about 660 men; I'm sorry I can't spare more."

Rinaldi, surprised at his sudden promotion to captain, didn't show it. Taylor had not told him beforehand. There hadn't been time.

"Sir, thank you for you confidence. You can count on me to do the best I can to earn it."

"I can't ask more, Captain. Now see what magic you and Rhodes can conjure to strengthen the land route. It's our weakest point. I fear it's where you'll see a great deal of action. If I were the enemy, that's where I'd concentrate."

"Let's hope the enemy doesn't think like you, Sir. That road narrows, which makes for limited space for anyone coming at us. Fortunately, we're not encumbered in the same manner, and our men can put out a devastating, concentrated fire."

Taylor was pleased that his decision to place Rinaldi in command of the strategic post was already paying dividends. "Be careful, Ranger. I don't want to send a condolence letter to my sister."

Rinaldi beamed as he saluted, trotting to his assignment. Each man gave a nod, acknowledging the close friendship they had forged.

The twenty-four hours predicted by Captain Dixon proved ambitious. Eighteen hours after the urgent message was received, the Cuban flotilla was sighted twenty miles out, steaming in from the east. A large portion of the Cuban force was heading to positions that would place them to the east and south of Taylor's defensive positions. With timely precision, he ordered over two-thirds of his force on the western line to the east and south to meet the Cuban maneuver. He kept four companies in reserve to fill any breaches.

With the enemy approaching, final preparations were made at all sectors. Explosive charges were set at five-foot intervals along the landing beaches; land mines were set in irregular fashion; floating mines were now within sight of enemy guns; all buildings had been burned or leveled near the main lines of fire.

Taylor ordered his men to take cover. There was little more they could do. Barely had his order been issued when an enemy spotter plane flew in. Withering Rebel fire intercepted it, knocking it from the sky. Cheering Rangers and sailors watched its fiery fall into the ocean.

"I'd hate to be in their boots, coming at us," said Captain Arroyo, an artillery officer, who spoke to no one in particular. "If they get by our water mines and then our land mines and explosives, they still have to hit our beachhead laced with concertina wire and jagged rock. If that doesn't get the Cuban bastards, then they'll have to confront our crossfire from light and heavy artillery, complemented by our mortar and .50-caliber machine guns."

Charles O'Reilly, a young private from East Texas who was standing nearby, spoke. "Captain, I heard rumor that we're bait for the enemy. So help me, Sir, if that is true, I may never fish again. I now know how that poor worm must feel." Captain Arroyo laughed.

Taylor overheard the captain's remarks and responded, "Just the same, Captain, more difficult positions than this have been taken throughout history by determined men. I figure we'll just have to be more determined."

"I agree, Sir. Do you think they'll attack soon?"

"No, if it were me, I'd attack in the early morning from the east, just as they are now positioning. I'd wait to have the sun on my back and in the enemy's eyes. I don't think the Cubans are as poorly trained as we had hoped. Captain, make sure your men get plenty of rest. They're going to need it."

Like clockwork, at 0500 on October 26th, a lone Cuban spotter plane flew noisily over the 10th Brigade, ruining what should have been a pleasant morning. The plane successfully signaled the Cuban vessels before accurate Ranger fire blew it from the sky. The enemy shells came in thick as hail, blowing havoc into the Rebel defenses. It hit several mines, rendering useless much of Taylor's well-conceived strategy. The shelling continued, uninterrupted. It was relentlessly answered for at least three hours. Aside from the horrendous noise, Rebel casualties were light. The Texans' determined fire kept the Cuban flotilla at bay, badly damaging one gunboat, sinking another, and hitting several. Colonel Marquez knew his business.

Taylor ordered the artillery to hold back its rapid fire and wait for the coming assault. He anticipated the pace of his artillery fire would cause a shortage of ammunition if the current rate of fire continued. He also held back his two seasoned Apache helicopters. The Cuban gunships appeared to be vintage Cold-War-era, Russian-built vessels. They were not nearly as capable as the Texans' two repatriated ships. Taylor ordered the two small fighting naval vessels and the helicopters to enter the fight after the Cuban landing craft were launched. He had them concealed and felt certain that today's enemy spotter plane hadn't seen them before it was downed.

The day slowly progressed, with the Cubans taking their time to reassess. Stress and strain started to wear upon the now bloodied ranks of the newly tested 10th, no longer rookies.

At 0900, all hell broke loose. A thirty-minute Cuban barrage shelled the beaches to soften the Rebels for the blow to follow. Unknown to the Texans, the bombardment was limited due to the Cuban shortage of shells. Their encounter with the Rebel Navy had benefited the outnumbered Rangers. Their first assault began at 1000 sharp.

The winds were high with waves from five to eight feet, banging against the shore. The Cuban assault craft came in from the east, the sun at their backs. Like Taylor predicted, the Cuban first wave, estimated at about 2,000 men, braved their deadly assignment, coming courageously toward the Texans on the beachhead.

Above the Cuban ships, still about two miles from shore, hovered five Soviet-era helicopter gunships. Circling like protective eagles above their eaglets, they posed an intimidating image. At the moment of their sighting, Taylor decided he needed a diversion. He chose to risk his two Apaches; it almost worked.

Three Cuban helicopters were blasted out of the sky before they could respond. The same eastern sun they were using to protect their landing force played to the advantage of the Texan pilots. The air victory was short-lived, however, as the heavy, concentrated fire from the enemy flotilla put an end to the Rebel heroes' suicide mission. One last, lucky Apache missile managed to blow up another gunship before it, too, was hit. The diversion had allowed the shore batteries to sink several landing craft circling the oncoming Cubans in protective maneuvers. As the next Cuban wave of human cargo approached the volatile Texas defenses, Colonel Marquez's howitzers and Taylor's pre-planned firepower got a chance to see firsthand how accurate their alignments were. The Texans had little time to correct minor errors, making adjustments as they continued their concentrated fire.

When the Cubans in the second wave approached the shore, they suddenly realized that they were virtually alone. Their first wave, except for a scattered few, had paid the ultimate price for the honor of Havana.

"Glory to Jesus!" An excited Texan defender shouted above the din. "They've got their whole friggin' army trying to get at us."

"Dang, look over there. Our boys **are** being attacked from the land." Another Ranger pointed to the position under Luke's command. "We're in for it if our boys don't hold."

The Texas private was correct. The Mexican Army had timed its assault with the Cuban second wave when it reached within 500 yards of shore. They were unaware that their first wave had been decimated. Taylor's earlier intuition proved correct.

Taylor shouted above the battle's roar. "We must hit as many landing craft as we can and at all costs. Continue firing at will. We'll need to fight off overwhelming odds if we let the bastards reach the beachhead."

The Cubans' second wave was obliterated as Rebel shrapnel and concentrated fire took deadly effect. Cubans lucky enough to make shore were holed up behind ever-diminishing cover, awaiting the respite of the next wave of comrades. Many used their dead comrades for cover.

Over half of Taylor's shore batteries were neutralized by Cuban firepower, resulting in nearly 300 casualties.

When the third Cuban wave reached land, it suffered a similar fate. However, the Ranger artillery now lacked half its heavy guns; 1,500 Cubans managed to set up a defensive perimeter despite intense Ranger fire.

Taylor shouted. "We've got to keep them holed up. If they hook up with the Mexicans, they'll take our weakest point. I figure they have no more than a couple thousand troops hitting Rinaldi. They're obstructed by the narrow passage, just as we'd hoped. If the Cubans loop around, they can join their compadres. We can't let that happen. Have the boys fix bayonets and get their Bowie knives handy. This needs to get personal and ugly."

On the land front, Rinaldi's two Ranger companies and the repatriated sailors were holding their own. By best estimate, over half the Mexican attackers were casualties. It was not a cheap Rebel victory, though. Over

150 dead and wounded littered their defensive position, including Lieutenant Rhodes, killed by a mortar fragment.

General Northcutt ordered a reserve platoon of forty men to aid Rinaldi. It was all he could spare. The balance of the brigade's reserves was sent to the eastern line. Only one company remained to defend the western line; the Cubans focused their fourth wave there. The sun was directly in the oncoming Cubans' eyes when their naval barrage began in earnest, aimed high, trying to avoid hitting their own forces on the eastern shore. However, two errant Cuban shells managed to fall amongst the entrenched Cubans, causing massive destruction. Taylor quickly assessed the situation, sending two companies from his eastern defense to assist the western line. He commanded half his remaining artillery turned to face the newest threat.

It all seemed hopeless. With sudden fury, Taylor realized his men were too few to hold back the onslaught. The battle had reduced his numbers to a little fewer than 3,500. There were at least that many enemy presently on shore, with as many dead littering the land and ocean floor. Yet they kept coming. Destroyer Captain Dixon had estimated about 20,000 in his telegram. It was beginning to look like he may have guessed low. Taylor knew he must do something desperate, or all would be lost.

The Cubans were not known to take prisoners. With that knowledge firmly planted in their minds and expecting no mercy, they prepared to reciprocate.

The Cubans charged the eastern defenses as Ranger marksmen littered the jagged rock formations with Cuban blood and bodies. The range of over three-quarters of a mile gave little protection to exposed Cuban officers and men, who fell to the Texans' accuracy.

Taylor shouted above the din to an artillery officer nearby. "Major, we must get them off our shore before their next assault hits our western flank. Once you set the land mines and explosives, hit the eastern beach with everything you have. At all costs, Major—all costs."

As Taylor turned his attention to the west, his artillery used its dwindling shells on the charging Cubans' eastern assault. The mines and planted explosives had done their murderous work. Now, after the din, Taylor could see the Cubans still plodding toward his defenses.

"The Rangers will not be overrun!" It was the only command Taylor gave.

Vicious Rebel crossfire caught the Cubans full force and many a brave enemy met his maker. Only about 800 had made it to within 90 yards of the main defenses when the Texans' furious counterattack caught the enemy by complete surprise. The Ranger onslaught was devastating to the plucky Cubans who were lucky enough to live through the terror of an amphibious landing under intense fire. Most were in battle for the first time. After a while, many just dropped their weapons and ran back to the beach. Texan snipers perched in favorable positions, waiting patiently for just such an opportunity, picked them off mercilessly. Several more Cuban soldiers met death as they ran into the ocean's unforgiving depths to watery graves, saving precious Texan bullets.

As the Ranger charge on the eastern perimeter broke the backbone of the enemy offensive, Rinaldi's 500 men charged the land-based forces, causing them to retreat to the cover of their reserves.

Seeing the success of those units engaged, Taylor quickly ordered half of his eastern defenses to the western line. He held the few remaining men as reserves should another Cuban wave try to strike again.

The full force of the ocean's pounding thunder went unheard. Texan cheers taunted the enemy to come in sight of their weapons. All that seemed in the way of Rebel victory was the Cuban's western assault.

Taylor knew his men were near exhaustion. He rushed to personally lead the defense of the western line where close to 1,800 of his remaining 2,900 effectives would meet the next assault. His men had been under attack for over twelve hours. They were hungry and thirsty, and ammunition was low.

The enemy appeared to have seven remaining warships. Taylor estimated Cuban losses at about 9,000 troops. It had been a costly day so far for Cuba. Taylor had no intention of letting them win the day. However, the furious, oncoming Cubans looked as if they might not be denied.

Although his continued offensive had been repulsed several times, the Cuban commander was committed to his attack into the sun. He ordered the western assault. It was to be his last attempt to take the beach. He held 1,500 men in reserve. He'd release them when the beach was secured. Too far into his commitment, he was unable to alter his strategy. It was his downfall.

Most of the Ranger's shore defenses remained intact, unharmed by the previous bombardment. The Cuban gunships had insufficient rounds to do much damage to the Texans other than provide some covering fire. By the time the enemy commander's desperate attacking force of 7,000 reached shore, it had been cut in half.

"General, what are your orders?" shouted Colonel Fitzpatrick. "They still badly outnumber us, and we're about out of ammunition."

"I'm not sure they know that," Taylor answered. "We still have good defenses, even though we're low. And their navy seems reluctant to fire on our positions. I'd guess they may be low, too, or even out of shells."

"Hope you're right, General." Fitzpatrick scanned the enemy huddled en masse upon the beach. "They don't appear to want to move."

"Would you?" asked Taylor. "They've lost a good many men with little to show for it but blood." As they spoke, they heard a screeching roar as two ancient Rebel Wart Hogs, with the Texas flag painted on their wingtips, flew over friendly ranks to strafe the beached Cubans.

"Where the hell did they come from?" shouted Taylor.

"I don't know, Sir, but they sure look good to me."

The Rangers roared in triumph as the two planes scrambled to take on the small Cuban fleet. When they approached, the Cuban anti-aircraft guns opened fire, but not before two ships were engulfed in flame. Two more were badly hit before one of the Texan aircraft took a direct hit, exploding into the sea.

"Oh shit, did you see that, General?"

"Afraid I did. Poor brave soul," Taylor said softly, his voice emotional,. "May he rest in peace. Colonel, let's give that flyboy some help. We've got a beach to clean up. Give them some Ranger steel!" Taylor shouted, fixing his bayonet.

The lone Wart Hog tipped his wings in acknowledgement as he returned to base, his ammunition depleted, his deadly work done.

The Ranger's second charge in as many hours had the same devastating effect as its first. Taylor led his men recklessly into the Cuban center. In mid-stride, a bullet tore into his right shoulder, hitting muscle, throwing him painfully and violently to the ground. As he fell, another round tore into his right leg. Captain Rinaldi, who had joined the attack with half his force, rushed to Taylor's aid. His alert reaction saved Taylor from the thrust of a Cuban infantryman's bayonet. Rinaldi threw his Bowie knife with accurate and deadly force into the enemy soldier's stomach, leaving only the hilt protruding.

It seemed the charge was over before it began. The Cubans that didn't surrender escaped to their waiting craft. Of the 7,000 men in their final assault, only 500 made it to safety. Taylor's command had 1,700 able men remaining, with 1,500 killed. The rest were wounded or dying.

Taylor, close to shock, tried to talk while being given morphine. "What a high price to pay for something so valueless." Rinaldi, nodding in agreement, looked at the destruction and litter of human bodies dotting the land and floating casually in the sea. Many enemy bodies washed ashore, grotesque images of man's folly. The blue, coral waters turned red from the blood.

"Medic! Get the general out of the sun! Quickly!"

Taylor had little way of knowing what the victory meant for his cause. He fell into a deep sleep aided by morphine and shock. His outnumbered Rebel forces had not only crushed the combined onslaught of Cuban and Mexican efforts to take Cancun, it helped dampen the Mexican-Federal alliance. This battle was just one of many raging across the entire western hemisphere. The bravery of a few Texas Rangers, and sailors from several states, was another page in the war.

Captain Rinaldi looked at the western horizon. The sun once again began its daily sizzle into the ocean. Looking at a captured Cuban flag, he noted the remarkable similarity it had to his brigade's Lone Star Flag. *But I suppose it should*, he thought. *They once were close to the United States after it liberated them from Spain, long before the dictator Castro and the communists showed their ugly heads.*

But Luke's primary thought reached several thousand miles north to home and a different time. "What next?" he muttered. It had been only six months since he had been wounded. It seemed longer. He wondered what had become of Becky. He desperately missed her.

Off on the horizon, coming in from the west, the forms of several warships could be seen.

"God, I hope they're ours!" a trooper shouted. He saw the coming force about the same instant that Luke did.

"They must be ours, or the Cubans wouldn't be leaving so quickly," Luke observed to no one in particular. He was correct. The Rebel Navy was a day late to save several hundred heroes for the cause of freedom. But the reinforcements and badly needed supplies they brought were not turned away.

The vast and beautiful silhouette of the battleship *Wisconsin* was cheered by all the island's defenders. Its determined 16-inch guns let off a roar in the direction of the fleeing Cubans, ensuring many more would never see home again.

Luke looked down at Taylor lying on the stretcher and shouted jubilantly, "General, help's coming. We're going to make it!"

Taylor tried to get up, but he was dizzy from the pain. "I never doubted it for a minute, Captain." He weakly smiled and closed his eyes. The narcotics allowed him to rest, peaceful in the knowledge that he had done his job, assisted by Providence.

Luke motioned to the corpsmen. "Get the general to shelter." He then walked toward the shore, shouting, "Let's get to work cleaning up the beach. Have the men take prisoners in case they have some info for Intel." Luke instinctively took charge of the mopping up. Blood trickled from a slight wound to his forehead. *What next?* he thought.

A bloodied non-com approached, his arm bandaged. "Captain, was this worth it?"

"Sergeant, I hope so. I read a quote a few years back about the cost of freedom. Damn if my dad didn't make me read it several times. It came from a fellow named Edmund Burke. He said, 'The only thing necessary for the triumph of evil is for good men to do nothing.' Well, Sergeant, I'd suppose we're doing something to fight back. At least we're trying."

"Roger that, Sir!"

x x x x x

Moans from the wounded and dying mingled with the constant pounding of waves striking coral. Victory seemed distant to Luke who walked amongst the carnage, helping medics in their seemingly hopeless pursuit to save as many as they could. They did not discriminate. Rebel, Texan, Cuban, or Mexican, they were now only boys, some barely men, suffering a common bond. Many would not live to remember.

Lying among the carnage was a dead golden eagle, somehow caught in the crossfire. A Mexican-American Ranger, a corporal, gently placed a bullet-strewn Mexican flag over its mangled carcass.

Jim Damiano

The courageous man is the man who forces himself, in spite of his fear, to carry on.

–General George S. Patton

CHAPTER SEVENTEEN

November 15, 2020—Occupied Mexico City, Mexico Headquarters, Texas Alliance Expeditionary Force

The unrelenting stench permeated throughout the still valley just outside Mexico City, covering it with death's shadow. Thunderous echoes of the machines of war deafened those within hearing. Nature's beauty, torn apart with indifference, cried out in vain. These calm meadows, representing the essence of life's gentle fragrance, once welcomed life's teeming dimensions. Now mans' destructive work reduced all to fields of carnage and devastation, a scene played out all too often.

Gorged buzzards circled lazily in endless flight, waiting for opportunity—another free meal—indifferent to its host's politics. Amongst them flew a lone, hungry hawk. In constant flight, he drifted with each updraft, searching for signs of life below, ever searching for a meal of rodent, snake, or bird. But no living creature save man had survived the holocaust beneath its exhausted wings.

Justin Northcutt viewed the aftermath of destruction. His every sense was numbed by days of nonstop fighting, laced gingerly with fatigue, fear, and adrenalin. With disgust he mumbled, "Nothing is worth this terrible scene."

The allied expeditionary force was decimated with most of Justin's proud legions reduced to fodder for barren fields. His old command, the once virile 36th Division, was reduced to forty percent effectives, with 4,000 dead and 8,000 wounded, maimed, or missing. Several Rangers' bodies lay bloated within his view, their terrible stench filling the valley.

Justin gagged, putting a cloth to his nose. Taking a deep breath and gathering his wits, he let out a sigh of resignation and picked up his carbine. *I've got to shake this and regain my will to lead, more so my persistence to continue.*

With thoughts racing into overtime, Justin focused with difficulty on several confusing feelings. His conscience refused to give him rest. *So many good men. So many friends have died and I gave the orders. Why ... why must victory be so damned expensive?* If he could only cry out freely, let out his true feelings—ask forgiveness from the departed. Shaking his head with disgust, he moaned, "But I was their general. My duty does not include showing emotion nor reprieve for my conscience. I try to act like a good servant. I must keep the hurt deep within me."

Since its inception, the 36th Division's casualty list had exceeded 200 percent. This was not an unusual calculation, for every Rebel fighting division had suffered heavy attrition.

And before him lay the remnants of his army and what had been, by far, the largest massed battle since the revolution's beginning. Here, opposing armies threw a combined one million combatants at each other on the extensive landscape below. Only one force prevailed. And though victorious, Justin felt the sting of subconscious defeat, and now he realized that he must pull himself together or lose his mind.

General Hollingsworth had been killed in action during the battle's initial salvo on September 20th. Justin, a few weeks shy of his twenty-fifth birthday, was tossed into command of all Texas forces, and by default, as the most qualified, the commanding general of the Rebel State Alliance in Mexico. No one opposed his control. Only he silently wished it otherwise, and no one was even the wiser.

The invasion was overwhelming for Mexico. Its army was picked apart as Justin's legions, in a series of running battles, overran it in their drive from the north. From the south, the Argentines and Peruvians, unlike the Texans, played by no rules and destroyed everything in their vicious path. Their terror took the pressure off the North Americans, allowing them to systematically reduce Mexican defenses. Like a hot knife going through butter, the Mexicans were forced to split their army to meet the southern threat. They felt the awesome pressure of a war on two fronts.

Supplies were scarce. It didn't matter. The Mexicans provided by default what the invaders needed to carry the fight. Now everything was eerily quiet, giving Justin time to address the dilemma posed by his victories.

Justin Wondered, *What next? I suppose this conquest will soon be a problem for President Collins-Smythe to ponder.*

He had been instructed to set up a military government in alignment with their South American Allies. Its progress was slow and exacting. Men trained to establish a new government structure for the defeated Mexicans were putting in place a system intended to benefit the victorious. Mexico would not be returned to self-rule anytime soon. Its fate rested in the hands of politicians and the future success or failure of its conquerors. Justin about-faced to return to the stark sanity of his sterile HQ.

Justin, anxious to return north to the primary struggle against the Federals, reasoned it was only there that he had volunteered to fight. Mexico had been a necessary diversion, but now he anticipated new orders and wouldn't be disappointed when they came. Just the same, the early morning's magnificent sunrise did little to energize him.

Justin's contemplation was jarred by a sudden interruption filled with static. "Sir, we've received communication from Austin addressed 'Urgent.'" The sergeant's voice came across as a mere warble. The liberated antique intercom did its best to no avail. Justin's temporary HQ, once belonging to a now-evicted enemy government official, had seen better days.

"Bring it to me at once, Sergeant."

"Right away, Sir! Also, Sir, General Taylor Northcutt is here, reporting as ordered. He asks permission to enter."

"Great news, Sergeant, send him in with my message."

It had been several weeks since the brothers had seen each other. On first sight, Justin was taken aback, surprised at his brother's ragged appearance, though not as shocked as Taylor was at the physical change in Justin. Taylor's eyes did not recognize the brother he remembered. The haggard man before him had turned middle-aged. Justin's dark hair showed signs of gray and the strain of command showed in his deeply creviced eyes. Taylor felt shivers of pain in his shoulder and leg, a vicious remnant of his victory at Cancun. It added to the shock of his brother's shattered appearance.

Taylor, coming directly from an award presentation ceremony, wore the Texas Medal of Honor draped over his neck. Its colorful ribbon stood as prominent, visible proof to anyone who cared to take note of his heroic act.

Justin looked upon his brother with caring and sheer delight. Though upset with himself for being unable to attend the brief ceremony, he knew Taylor didn't require an explanation. They were too close for that. Like him, Taylor never shirked responsibility.

Reluctantly, Taylor wore the medal, only to please his brother. He did not feel proud to have it, feeling certain that many had done more than he. His mind leaped to Cancun and the memory of the two unnamed Wart Hog pilots, one of whom gave his life to turn the battle. *That pilot was the real hero.*

Upon entering the austere room, Taylor walked, a stout cane supporting his wounded leg. He nodded to Justin's staff scattered throughout the room. Several faces were missing and he wondered if they, too, were wounded or worse.

Justin stepped forward to meet Taylor, reaching out with a firm right hand. "General, welcome back. The 36th has missed your ugly face. Sorry, I couldn't attend your decoration ceremony, but I want you to know I'm damned proud of you."

"Thanks," Taylor replied anxiously.

"Taylor, take a seat." Justin pointed to a chair opposite his desk. "Let me read this communication, and we'll get to the official reason for your visit. Before I do, though, how're your wounds mending?"

With a wave of his right hand, Justin sent a signal to his staff that he wished privacy. They left the office, several going out of their way to salute the rebellion's newest hero.

The room emptied, Taylor answered. "Both wounds are improving daily, no thanks to Command—setting my boys up as bait for those god-be-damned Cubans. If it weren't for Rinaldi covering my backside …

You know, I owe him my life, and I thank the day Becky got interested in him. He's more of a Rebel than the two of us combined."

Justin shifted nervously in his chair. "Someday, I'll explain all that fuss in Cancun when the time is right. I needed someone I could rely upon. You will never know how difficult it was for me to choose you. But you, Tay, were my best chance for success." Justin's concerned look spoke volumes.

"I'm happy your wounds are improving," Justin said, his demeanor softening. "For my peace of mind, I want your stubborn butt to see my personal surgeon as soon as we complete our discussions. And that, my little brother, is an order."

"Yes, Sir!" Taylor snapped, teasing. He was happy for the reunion and elated to see that despite his brother's disheveled appearance, he was as sharp as ever.

Taylor watched, wondering, *What next?* as Justin silently read the brief communication and then with a sigh of relief, began to read it aloud to his brother.

URGENT: 15 Nov. 2020 – 0700
To: Brevet Lt. General Justin Northcutt
Commander-Alliance Expeditionary Force

HQ Alliance Expeditionary Forces-Mexico City

General:
You are herewith promoted to full Lt. General, Texas National Army, effective at once. You are to report to First Army HQ in Salina, Kansas to command newly-refitted unit of Alliance 1st Corps. Texas 36th and New York 121st Divisions are to accompany you to Kansas to be re-outfitted with supply and personnel and to join with the First Army. Troops remaining in occupied Mexico are hereby under command of Lt. General Spencer, who will take command at 0600 hours on 16-11-2020. You are ordered to depart for your new post no later than 18-11-2020.

Approval granted for recommended promotions as follows: Brig. General Taylor Northcutt promoted to Major General, Commanding TX. 36th Division, Brig. General James Rinaldi, promoted to Major General, Commanding NY 121st Div. Congratulations to all for a job well done.

R. Sinsome, Commanding General TX National and Free State Forces"

END OF MESSAGE

"Good God, Justin. Did you ever think you'd command five divisions? I know I sure as hell never expected to command the 36th. Do we want this?"

"Well, I suppose that by default I'm doing that and more right now. To answer you, no, not in my dreams nor worst nightmares would I ever wish this damn responsibility on anyone, let alone myself. However, I don't think there's much left, at least not in this sector, or the rebellion for that matter. Now that we've secured our southern borders, maybe things will slow down a bit."

"That's wishful thinking, Bro. Word has it the Feds have moved the capital to Wisconsin and are anxiously readying for a defense. It all seems such a waste to me, and now with the west coast finally getting really involved, it looks like the killing will continue in earnest."

"Taylor, I don't know how you do it. You always seem to have info one step ahead of me."

Taylor laughed. "Hey, it's a talent. What can I say?" he smirked. "Here's something for you to chew on. Did you hear about Hawaii?" Taylor enjoyed scooping Justin.

"No, squirt, is it good news? You're the best snoop in our family." Justin laughed outwardly.

"Not really," he shuddered. "It appears the Japs attempted to invade Hawaii and take over where they left off in WWII."

"Taylor, when the hell did you hear about this? No one's advised me yet. You'd think a damn three-star has a need to know. The bastards never tell us a damn thing until it's at our doorstep." Justin noticed Taylor squirming in his seat.

"A Cuban prisoner we captured at Cancun spilled the story. He spoke better English than me."

"Tay, everyone speaks better English than you. When did this supposedly happen?"

"I heard it happened several weeks ago. I don't understand why it's so secret. I suppose command didn't want to distract you."

"Maybe the Intel boys didn't want to scare our allies or convenient friends, especially those in Europe who are sitting on the fencepost and not all that tight with the Feds." Justin stood and began pacing the tiled floor.

"Well, whatever the reason, the prisoner, a Cuban colonel, said the Feds formally threatened to nuke Japan with a submarine's warhead. President Rex Collins said he meant it when he warned the world and that it had better comply. I suppose the Japanese figured with the Mexicans and Canadians attacking our borders that they could invade Hawaii."

"Damn it, Taylor, I can't believe they were blind to the secret alliance the Feds had with Mexico and Canada and actually thought Collins would stand still. Hell, I always figured the Japanese were a sure bet to ally with the Feds."

"They must've felt it worth the risk." Taylor nodded, a full grin upon his face as he reached across Justin's cluttered desk with his good hand, taking a cigar from an open box. Justin also grabbed a cigar, lighting it and Taylor's.

Justin continued, coughing. "I would've bet my last dollar the Japanese would have joined up with the Feds."

"I'd say that possibility is kind of gone if you ask me." A sullen look crossed Taylor's bearded face. "I do think it sad that nukes had to come into the equation. It sort of puts a whole new dimension on things. I sure hope we never use them."

"Hey, you'll want to hear more then." Not waiting for an answer, Taylor continued. "Remember when we were kids and we visited Pearl Harbor? Do you recall the battleship *Missouri*?"

"Sure, it was a highlight for me to tour that old battleship, though I preferred scuba diving and whale watching, as I recall. Why?" Justin's thoughts raced back to a wondrous week ten years earlier, filled with beautiful blue waters off the Oahu coastline.

"Well, according to my Cuban ... damn," Taylor paused to blow a large puff of smoke, "this is a good cigar, once you get past the first puff. Let me see."

"Glad you enjoy the cigar, Bro." Justin laughed. He'd never seen Taylor smoke before.

Taylor seemed intent, blowing a cloud of smoke as he stood up. "Sorry, Justin, I've forgotten how enjoyable first-time, simple pleasures could be. Getting back to my story, the old Mighty Mo was reactivated by the Feds just in time to join their task force sent to stop the Japanese navy on its way to take the Hawaiian Islands. The Cuban colonel said President Collins-Smythe sent the *Alabama* on truce to join the Feds on the then-secret condition that nukes would not be used. Together they tore the Japanese fleet apart. According to him, the *Missouri* was lost at sea, but not before its combined salvos, along with the *Alabama's*, blew away the entire Jap fleet. He heard a Jap sub got old Mo. Their rat pack paid a high price when Fed and Rebel destroyers blasted them all out of the ocean. I guess that ended the concern with the Jap intervention."

"Hot damn, it sure seems strange to hear we were united. It has a nice familiar ring to it. Maybe there's hope yet."

"Don't count on it, Lieutenant General," Taylor said with brutal sarcasm. "There's still a lot of fighting going on in the heart of our country, with hundreds dying daily and no end in sight."

"Yeah, but Taylor, don't you see? We stood together and fought off a common enemy by sending the *Alabama*. By the way, did the *Alabama* get away after it was all over?"

"I suppose, but I don't really know."

Justin mused sheepishly, "So all this happened several weeks ago? I still find it hard to believe no one ever told us."

"I'd guess Command doesn't want us to feel good about the Feds, especially with the *Alabama* and her destroyer escorts assisting them almost half way to Japan. Some say that when our president prevailed upon her brother not to use a minor nuke, if there is such a thing, it did more to reaffirm to the world not to interfere. My prisoner, I believe his name is Hernandez, heard our combined forces lost about 2,500 men along with the *Missouri* and two Fed destroyers. The Japanese lost their entire navy and untold casualties."

"But did the *Alabama* return to our navy?"

"Bro, are your ears plugged? As I said, I don't know. I'd think by now she's patrolling the Gulf with the *Wisconsin*, hopefully fully armed and ready to rumble."

"What does this leave us in battlewagons, since you seem to be the old salt of the family?"

"The Feds have the *New Jersey* back together, along with two or three cruisers. Aircraft carriers are now useless with no fuel, and most of them have been destroyed or used for parts anyway. Probably neither of us have much of a navy left, but I'd say we have the upper hand, because word is out the *New Jersey* is a mess."

The intercom crackled, interrupting the conversation. "Sir, General Rinaldi's here as ordered."

"Send him in."

James Rinaldi limped heavily, favoring his right leg. His shrapnel wound was received during the recent Battle of Mexico City. But something more seemed on his friend's mind, Taylor observed.

Justin, smiling, stood up and walked to greet him. "Sorry you're hurting, James." Justin pointed to his leg. "It looks like my key generals can make about one complete man between y'all. How're you feeling?"

"Better, Sir. Thanks for asking. The sawbones say I have some nerve damage, so it'll take a while to mend."

"You hang tough, James. The cause needs you. By the way, I'm ordering you to accompany my brother at this meeting's end to see my surgeon." Justin noted a pained expression on James's face but credited that to his wound.

Justin quickly briefed James on his promotion. Shaking his hand, he said with deep sincerity, "James, your New Yorkers have borne more than their fair share of the carnage. I want you to know their sacrifice didn't go unnoticed and it's appreciated. Please tell your command that I plan on addressing them tomorrow to give them a Divisional Citation."

"Thanks, Sir, it'll please me to do so. Will we be able to obtain replacements for my division?" James's solemn look was unnerving to Justin.

Ill at ease, Justin responded, "James, it's my intent to request fresh replacements for all my divisions before I join my new command, or we won't amount to a very effective corps."

"Thank you, Sir. With last count we're down fifty percent. I may be a new major general, but between Taylor's division and mine, we barely have enough men to equal one."

Justin motioned James to take a seat, offering him a cigar. He declined. "We lost a lot of good men, James. It seems there's no end to it. Worse, I've become numb to it."

Listening quietly, Taylor looked away. He fought the hidden sadness wrenching his troubled heart. He, too, had lost many good men. Somehow the fact they were buried in foreign soil or blasted into atoms increased his searing pain.

"James, I heard your brother Luke saved my brother's rear end at Cancun."

James, happy for the change in subject, smiled and answered quietly, "I'm glad he did. Luke couldn't have saved a better man."

Justin spoke, his voice calming. "James, I've really gotten to know you these last several weeks, and I sense there's something disturbing you beyond your injury."

"Sorry it shows, Sir." James's face was pained. "I have bad news. My brother Vic died of his wounds this morning."

"I'm very sorry to hear that; I didn't know he was hit," Justin replied, suddenly at a loss for words.

"Now I must bury a second brother," James said, but his stoic reserve could not hide his grief. "It all seems too high a price to pay."

James turned to his friend. "Taylor, will you get word to Luke for me?"

"I'm truly sorry, James." Taylor put his uninjured arm on James's shoulder. "You can count on me. Is there anything else I can do?" A solemn silence veiled the room.

"Thanks, Taylor. No matter how deadened this war makes me, I can never get used to losing loved ones."

"How did he get hit?" Justin asked.

"It happened in our final assault. He was hit by machine gunfire when his unit tried to storm their northern position. He never came out of his coma. I don't think he suffered. He's with Mom and Billy in a better place now. I only wish I could have buried him in Utica with them. You understand it's more for me than him though, I suppose." James voice trailed off, turning distant.

Justin walked over to James and put a friendly arm on his other shoulder. "James, I don't have a clue when this war will end. Yet, while this won't bring your brothers back, I feel strongly that they and all those lost will be remembered as patriots and heroes." Justin hesitated, "I promise, if I've anything to do with it, we will prevail. I'm really sorry for your loss. Do Joe or Rock know?"

"Not yet. I'll try to find them today. Dad's somewhere in northern Mexico setting up a new city government and Grandpa Rock's here in Mexico City, probably emptying Mexican shelves of their contents to fill our needs. You know, it was Rock who nursed Vic back to life a few months back after an encounter with marauders. He persuaded him to join up, and while he's real close to all his grandsons," James choked on his words, "Vic …" his voice graveled, "well, he's become something special to Rock, sort of like the prodigal son. You know, Vic is, I mean was, Luke's twin brother. It's not going to be easy for Luke when he hears. Dad's another story. He'll take it, but he'll carry it deep inside until the weight of it buries him. I'm worried most about how he'll handle the news."

Compassion filled Justin's eyes. "General, you better find and console your family. Go bury your brother. I don't need you right now."

"Sir, thank you. Did I hear the order right that we head for Kansas in two days?"

James automatically returned to his responsibility, out of rote, but more so to take shelter from grief.

"Yes. They expect us at the front by December 1st. I'm depending on your combined skills to make it happen." He looked with some real concern at his two wounded generals. "We've got our work cut out for us."

Pushing out of the chair with difficulty, James said, "Thank you, Justin, Taylor. I couldn't serve with two better men." The room grew silent again, neither brother felt like talking.

Taylor, still visibly upset over Vic's death, broke the silence. "Why is it we keep losing our best people? One by one, they fall, weakening our leadership. But so far, thankfully, not our determination and resolve. Luke and I have become close friends, almost brothers. Damn it, we've become part of that band of brothers that only combat can mold. Justin, I feel James's loss as my own, and also I feel a bit guilty. Permission requested to help him bury his brother."

"Permission granted. Do what you have to do. Taylor, as long as there are wars, the best and the brightest will top the casualty lists. It's the fate of the intelligent to fully realize the impact of war and the terrible need to fight it. Losing so many good men will hurt both sides of this conflict. When the final price is calculated, it won't just be their heroic presence denied to us, but the quality of their leadership that will be forever missed."

Justin put out his cigar, its appeal lost to the moment. "I fear the real problem will be in the near future when this nation looks for leaders. The true leaders who died for the cause will be missed then. That, I believe, will be the real cost of this war."

The Northcutt brothers looked at each other through new eyes. Taylor's thoughts raced to Luke, who was about to hear that his twin had paid the ultimate price for freedom's cause.

"Taylor, I've heard it's not unusual for the living to feel ashamed they're alive when friends aren't. Always remember, it's usually a fraction of a second that separates the living from the dead. War has forever taught this cruel lesson." Justin seemed to have read his brother's mind.

Daydreaming, Justin's mind fast-forwarded to a wishful future filled with peace, love, and Julia. Would he survive to enjoy the uncomplicated life he so often imagined? He needed desperately to see her again. At least returning north to the war in the States gave him hope for a reunion. He vowed to himself that he would shamelessly use the power of his command to find her and bring her to him. He rarely abused the power of his position, but now his need for unfettered love outweighed the uneven balance he usually maintained between duty and desire. He needed to see her and know that she was safe. He felt selfish, but, for him, she represented a firm foundation and the real hope for a new future. But first victory must be won and peace restored.

Taylor interrupted Justin's reverie. "Justin, will history remember the Rebel heroes who died?"

"Only if we win, Tay; that's why we must prevail." Justin's face showed new determination. "You know what?" Justin answered his own question. "I feel this war will be different, even if we lose. Whoever wins will have to include the enemy's side to enable all to heal. If we're smart, and I think we are, we'll have to include the whole shebang. We don't need a century of divisiveness like the last civil war. I don't think we can afford the luxury or the meanness of allowing our nation's history to repeat itself."

Taylor answered, "Sadly, Justy ole boy—history has a despicable way of repeating itself."

Justin put his right hand tenderly on Taylor's shoulder. "Go and help your friends bury their brother and send for me when they're ready for the funeral. We'll see that Vic gets a fine military sendoff worthy of his good family."

"Thanks, Justin, and I'm sorry I was angry about the bait."

"Don't worry, it's all forgotten, and … you had a right to be angry. You know you performed a miracle. We never figured on losing our destroyer cover. Your defense helped us gain time and set the trap that ended this campaign about a month ahead of schedule. You also saved untold lives for both sides with your bravery. So you don't need to say you're sorry." Justin hesitated. "But I need to apologize because I almost lost my best friend and brother over it. Only your stubborn resolve and determination got us through.

"I have a confession. I knew about the *Alabama*. Our unexpected truce in the fight with Japan was why we almost blew it, and probably would have except for your action. That's why you earned that medal. Wear it proudly."

"Why you! I owe you one for this," Taylor said, smiling. He was glad he had held back. Now everything fit together, and it helped him to cope with the terror he had seen and still carried. Tomorrow would no doubt bring another story. Taylor looked fondly at his brother and limped away, wondering how much more he could take, and then his resolve stiffened. *Bring it on. I've seen hell and lived.*

Things turn out best for people who make the best of the way things turn out.

–John Wooden

Chapter Eighteen

December 3, 2020—Rebel Army Encampment
New York 121st Division Headquarters, Salina, Kansas

James opened the tattered flap of his tent and walked into the early evening's dimming light. The late autumn moon silently waited to cast its amber glow, trying to give relevance to the clear, crisp air. In the northern sky, a solitary cloud captured his mood. The cloud seemed to float casually over the place where the enemy, according to Intel, was supposed to be. It floated like a sentinel on post duty, guarding hidden concerns and treasure. James shuddered as he viewed the puff of atmosphere. His imagination ran wild as the cloud's ghostlike image appeared to take the form of an avenging angel of death.

The cloud vanished, as if his thought had wished it away, into the far horizon and into the deep recess of James's troubled mind. Since Vic's death, he had kept to himself. The trek from Mexico served largely to occupy him, helping to avoid thinking. Now the quiet surroundings allowed hurt to reenter—an enemy without compassion, refusing him peace. James returned to the safety of his tent.

"Sir, can I get you some more coffee?" James's orderly had walked in quietly, startling him.

"No, thanks, Sergeant. I'm just clearing my head a bit. It's sure a beautiful night. That red sky was something to admire."

"Yes, it was, Sir. If only it could be as peaceful down here."

Taking a sip from his cup, James nodded his agreement. The air had turned a bitter cold. Many in the Rebel Army needed warm clothing and shoes. Everywhere the dire shortage of the necessities needed to keep an army going was felt, even more so here on the Kansas plains. Few provisions had arrived at the front except for some inadequate food and shelter. Something would have to happen soon to alter their predicament, or the Rebel Army faced an unwanted dilemma. James, knowing his men deserved better, felt frustration at his inability to improve their lot. Fighting for freedom had its price, both in men and material. Worse, James feared he was quickly reaching limits beyond his ability to endure.

The northern wind confirmed his conviction that action must resume soon before the weather became a chilling ally of the enemy. Winter's pending arrival was a bad omen, providing justification to move the Rebel Army before the elements succeeded where the Federals had failed.

Mexico's defeat was now a bitter memory for many; its future was now in the hands of the rebellion's politicians. James felt troubled at the thought of the many troopers' bones left there to bleach in the hot sun. For him the cost would always be too high. The crumpled ranks of the army were filled with conscripts who tried with difficulty to fill the shoes of dead and crippled veterans. Time was desperately needed to train them. Time was not an available commodity. Recruits and reluctant draftees were given recycled rifles, many previously used in battle, and a quick, rudimentary lesson in their use. Thusly trained, the new soldiers were sent to replenish the Rebels' diminished ranks.

James's solitude was again interrupted, this time by the welcome sound of his brother's voice. It had been days since they last talked.

Luke correctly saluted his brother, remaining old army to the core despite his unmilitary appearance. His unkempt uniform had several rips and cuts, a couple of buttons missing.

"Luke, you sure don't look the part of a soldier, let alone a full colonel in the Texas National Army. But then I guess few of us look like parade soldiers, if we ever did."

"Well, hello to you, too, General," Luke beamed.

"Luke, sorry to pull your chops. I couldn't resist, especially when I remember how meticulous you once were."

"Yeah sure, I guess some things never change, big Brother. From what I've seen of Federal prisoners, they're no better off than we are, except for the warmer clothes the lucky bastards have been issued."

"So, what brings you to my neck of the woods?" asked James.

"Just making a friendly visit to see how the other half lives. That and the fact I'm bored as hell. It's so damn quiet that it's spooky, particularly after all the action we've seen."

Luke's warm smile made James homesick.

"How're my home state boys doing? Any news you'd like to share?" asked Luke.

James, walking with the aid of a cane, moved to the roaring fire beckoning his brother to follow. "We're beginning to look more like the old U.S. Army rather than just a bunch of Rebel New Yorkers. My division now has a big mix of men from other states. It looks like the war's uniting us again by its own osmosis, whether or not we want it to."

"That's not so bad is it?" Luke, joining James, rubbed his hands together for warmth. "Anyway, it's the same with the Rangers. We get a lot of replacements from other states. Our so-called 'Ranger Mystique' seems to draw some, but the draft gives us most of our recruits. Yesterday, for example, we received about 1,000 men from several decimated Texas Home Guard units. There are fewer men who volunteer," he sighed. "I can't say that I can blame them."

James nodded his head. "Luke, I'd suppose we lost most of our original volunteers in the last eighteen months. We're lucky to be here for that matter. I'm with you, though. We really can't criticize anyone for not volunteering for this frigging holocaust."

"Jimmy, you're the history nut. Do you think things will ever return to the old nation we once knew?"

"I've no doubt some form of government, probably very similar, will develop. The way our freed Rebel states have unified is proof we're on the right track."

Luke moved slightly away from the fire. In the fire's light he turned to his brother. "Hope you're right. It'd be an awful waste, though, if we don't make changes or at least try to reestablish a few things. You know, keep what worked—don't fix what's not broken.

Jim Damiano

× × × × ×

Maybe then we can establish a new and better nation." Luke rubbed his hands together, the cold wisps of his breath evident with every uttered word. Neither brother's threadbare uniform gave much protection from the howling wind.

"By the way, Tex, how's your girl?" James gave his brother a rare, full grin. "Have you seen her? I believe her unit's not far from here."

"Becky's the actual reason I'm here. We want to get married. I've known her long enough to appreciate we're right for each other. Jimmy, I want to live with her for the rest of my life, however long that might be."

"I understand your feelings, Luke. But with all the uncertainty, don't you think it'd be wise to wait? I mean, man, look at us and this Godforsaken place." James made a grand sweep with his arm.

"Big brother, I'd expect that from a logical sort like you. Waiting makes the most sense. You know me, and well ..." Luke paused for effect, "when have I ever used common sense, particularly nowadays? No, we plan to get hitched as soon as the next campaign is over, and Jimmy, I'd like you to be my best man. The way I see it, this war's got to end soon."

"You know, I'd be honored, Luke, but, oh crap! I'm thinking. You know me; I'm the philosophical brother. And being me, I'm sorry, but ..." he hesitated. "What if we don't live through the next campaign, or this rotten war for that matter? Then what, damn it?" James shrugged his shoulders, not wanting to look directly at Luke.

"Jimmy, to answer your question, if I'm dead, I won't get married, and if I die after I get married, at least I'll have sampled life and died a happy man. Bro, I want to feel and see hope. A future with Becky is my hope. I need this. Becky needs it too. Life goes on, no matter what we do. As long as I'm breathing and in the game of life, I'd like to fully enjoy it."

"Damn, I declare you're right. It kinda fits the way you put it. But then ... you always were the practical brother. Shit, after that speech, how could I disagree? For me to say anything else would negate our efforts and dirty our cause. So, yes, you have my blessings and my best wishes for a long, fruitful life together." James looked firmly into Luke's eyes. "Has Taylor given you his blessing and, more important, military permission to marry his sister?"

"Jimmy, Taylor thinks a lot like you and suggested we wait. But he promised not to stand in our way. We'll see."

"Then you're not sure either. Are you having second thoughts?"

"Heck no! There's where you're wrong. I've never been surer than I am about this. I acknowledge that common sense calls for restraint. But Jimmy, I love her, and she loves me, and all this helps make this damn situation seem worthwhile. Becky represents the sane future I figure we're so frantically fighting for."

"Well said, little Bro. Well said! Know this, that whatever you decide, I'll back you." James slapped his brother playfully, but hard, on the back.

"Thanks, Jimmy, it means a lot to us. If you see Dad or Rock, please be sure to pass on my good news."

"You can count on it." James smiled, happy for his brother's joy, somehow found in the middle of chaos.

"Hey, Luke, did you hear? Word came in a few minutes ago: the Panama Canal was destroyed. No one's certain why or who did it. We're apparently not taking credit, but now ships are forced to go around the Horn. That should slow down Federal replacements coming in from Hawaii and the West Coast some."

"No shit!" Luke exclaimed. "Jimmy, I doubt it'll stop them from coming by way of the Rockies—most likely in great force, and before we care to see them. I never believed they'd send troops. California certainly took its dear time to wholeheartedly enter this fray. Word of late, though, is they're coming at us soon, and in large numbers."

"Yeah, I heard more are leaning toward the Federals than us. It seems they waited to test the winds before acting." James's face didn't hide his concern. "Maybe it's easier for them to stay put. Change does suck sometimes. You know, they're not known as the left coast for nothing. Remember, it was California that invented Big Brother state government."

"I never expected them to do otherwise," Luke replied.

"No, I suppose I hoped they'd continue to stay home and protest, like they always do." James's face showed agitation. "It always pissed me off when New York was tied with California as a liberal Mecca. In the upstate areas, we sure didn't act like the people in New York City." He returned to the fire's welcoming warmth.

"Jimmy, any truth to the rumor going around that the Feds have several thousand mercenaries? Crap, all we need now are Hessians to fight in the 21st century."

"I'm afraid the rumor's true. It's just been reported, today in fact, by the Intel boys. Seems like they think the Feds took on about 300,000, presently making their way to our eastern shores. Some are also coming in from the north by way of western Canada. I expect we'll know soon enough when the foreign bastards arrive. Now with the Fed government chased to Madison, we'll probably see 'em before we care to. I figure they must be running out of men like us, and probably desperate to boot. Maybe we're getting close to finishing this freaking war after all."

"Why don't we just blow the crap out of Madison and end all this by killing Collins and all his cronies? It seems like the way to go to me," said Luke.

"You know both sides have refrained from loosing total destruction on our cities, especially after the Feds' blunder in Texas. Shit, if we did that, we'd lose what little support we have in Wisconsin and the states up here. More important, we need formal governments on each side to bring about eventual peace. If all the politicians are dead, who'll structure it, the damned military? God we don't need that accident waiting to happen!"

"Jimmy, damn it, you sure have a short memory. Wasn't it those do-nothing bastardly politicians that got us into this mess in the first place? Do you really think we can rely on them now?" Luke's face showed consternation.

"Darn it, Luke, after we prevail, it'll be your dirty politician pond scum that'll do the final cleanup. You know, filling in all the blanks and stuff. Otherwise, we become a country run by the military. We're not fighting for that, even if it has occasional appeal."

"Yeah, Jimmy, I see where you're coming from. While I'll never have much love for politicians, I know the bastards serve a useful purpose. But I hope we're able to change a few rules when we win so they don't revisit the same mess and let all this crap repeat itself." Luke tightened his tattered scarf around his neck. "It's sure getting colder. It's almost like New York. No, shit, it's worse." Luke shivered as he talked. "These Kansas winds sure cut to the bone."

"Stop complaining, Bro. I've got an extra blanket if you want it." James took a ragged blanket, one of many wrapped about his shoulder, and tossed it to Luke, who nodded his thanks.

"Hey, Luke, did you hear about the Mexican nationals joining our forces? Rumor has it 1st Corps took in a few."

"It's true. Taylor said his brother told him several thousand have joined. It's hard to believe, but we've become their hope for the future. The average Mexican didn't participate in his nation's treachery. And since we didn't wantonly destroy their country like our South American allies, they realized they're better off with us Rebels. That goddamned restraint command forced on us may have paid off. What the hell, I suppose the Mexicans need us more than we need them. If they want to volunteer, I say let them, though I'm not certain I'm ready to forgive the little bastards just yet."

"I'm with you there. It still hurts to think they may be on our side after so many of us died killin' them. I believe I'd just as soon shoot 'em as look at 'em." Luke sneered as he talked, thinking of his dead twin.

"Yeah, it sure bugged me when I first heard. But, Luke, while it was Mexicans who killed Vic, we can't forget it was Americans that killed Billy. Are we to go on hating all of them until we shrivel up ourselves from the hatred? Though it's difficult, I choose to remind myself that the average Mexican is only a small, involuntary part of the overall treachery. Kind of like us."

"Once again, you make it seem to fit." Luke slapped his hands together and wrapped them under his blanket. "Didn't the last civil war leave anger and hatred for about a century? How's this war gonna be any different?"

"You're right, it did. Yet the only path to sanity for our future lies in our willingness to move on. There'll always be lingering distrust no matter what we do. Our job is to find a way to make the eventual transition acceptable for everyone."

"Jimmy, that's wishful thinking, unless, of course, our side comes out on top. So I'm counting on you, General, to lead us to victory."

"Thanks a lot, dipstick."

Luke's eyes locked onto James's familiar brown gaze. "I'd better be getting back. Thanks for the blanket." Luke clutched it close to his chest. "And stay low."

James watched his brother walk until he faded out of the moonlight. His thoughts, racing back to where he had left off, now included a new worry. Quickly, he shook it off.

Warm in his HQ tent, James sat brooding while sipping a steaming canteen cup of weak coffee. Like his brother, he wasn't sure what he'd do if forced to include a contingent of Mexican volunteers into his division. He'd deal with it when and if it happened.

Right now, his chief concern lay to the north, somewhere near Lincoln, Nebraska. There, waiting across the cold, windy plains, a vigorous and determined enemy force was about to merge with reinforcements of Californian militia and European mercenaries. Rebel Intelligence calculated the enemy outnumbered the Rebels even before pending reinforcements. The Federals now enjoyed overwhelming superiority, giving them the opportunity to continue to hold out, and to change the momentum that presently favored the Rebels.

Time is too precious to waste, he thought. *Too many men depend upon me to maintain clarity*. He purposely hadn't told Luke he'd seen their father yesterday. Losing another son was too much pain for Joe to bear. James had seen in his dad's eyes his own mortality. It hurt to see the truth firsthand.

Once again, as if someone was on assignment to better his mood, his quiet reflection was interrupted.

"You sure look in deep contemplation."

"Grandpa, what brings you here?"

"A free moment and no supplies to keep me busy."

"You just missed Luke."

"Damn, will I ever get to see that boy?"

"I could use some supplies for my division. Any hope?" James left the tent to stand near the fire.

Rock joined him by the fire, leaning his old lever-action rifle against a nearby stump. "All I can say is we're working on it. It appears some help is on the way from South America and from China, no less. Luckily our navy has been able to keep the sea lanes mostly open. The good news is the Fed SOBs are no better off than us. Kind of makes you feel sort of sorry for them, doesn't it?" Rock cracked a tired smile.

"Sure, Rock, may they all starve to death on their way to hell. You know better than anyone that this war will be won by the grocers, so we could use a little of your magic." James hugged Rock, squeezing his sturdy frame to his. "Are you doing OK? I still can't believe you're keeping up with us youngsters." He stood for a moment looking fondly at his grandfather. "I see you're still toting your old Winchester."

"Yep, though I don't know why. I haven't used it since I volunteered." Rock playfully punched James's right arm. "And, young man, I'll outrun you kids any day. What's slowing me down is my old fart's mind. All I seem to do is think in overtime, and it's wearing on me. I suppose it's a Rinaldi trait to ruminate about things. I've done too much of it lately."

"Tell me about it. I guess you're the one I get my worrying from. Thanks!" James frowned in jest, amusing his grandfather.

"Well now, don't give me all the credit. There are a few others in our clan that like to worry," Rock laughed. "I've been thinking a lot about Grandma and your mom, and if that's not enough, I've added Billy and Vic. All this death in our little family, in so short a time; well … it wears on a person if you let it. There are times I can't stop feeling the hurt of it." Rock stopped for a moment to fix his eyes on James. He saw the worried face of a man, now a general, much older than his years. He spoke in his soft, gruff voice. "I think it's healthy for us to begin to look forward," he emphasized. "That is, of course, if we plan on surviving."

"I understand what you're saying."

"Jimmy, I only have a minute. I wanted to say hello and I've done it. I need to run, so keep up your good work. And before I forget, Son, I'm damn proud of all my grandsons, and you in particular, Major General. Please tell your brother, the colonel, the same goes for him, when you see him." Rock saluted. "Now I've got to find or steal food for my boys. General Northcutt's sending me to Texas to check on its pecan crop. Those in the know think there may be some left. Justin says it should be a banner crop this year, and we need to get some for the men before it disappears. Anyway, it looks like I better work fast 'cause you look pretty damned skinny to me." Rock chuckled, and with some effort, picked himself up, along with his ancient rifle, and started the long walk back to his post.

James watched his grandfather leave, tears trickling from his eyes. Much of what he was came from that man. He owed a lot to Rock's example: his determination, steady persistence, self-sacrificing nature, and most of all, his empathy. He could see Rock was hurting. It was his way to keep to himself. He'd been very close to Vic, more so since their encounter in the Adirondacks. James knew Rock's casual veneer couldn't completely hide his keen pain at losing another grandson, above all, one he'd brought back from the dead. James always figured Vic had been a marauder, but he kept it to himself. Now Vic would be remembered only as a hero.

With renewed vigor, James returned to the lonely confines of his small quarters to contemplate the new orders for tomorrow. He resolved quietly, *It is one day closer to war's end, if my division or I have anything to say about it.*

December 4, 2020—First Army Headquarters, Salina, Kansas

Taylor's wound hurt, a steady burn made more unpleasant by the cold Kansas weather. His heated HQ bunker was still only forty degrees. *To think*, he pondered, *I thought Prosper was cold in the winter. They can have this place. I swear I'll never complain about cold weather again.*

"It looks like heavy clouds to the north, General; I wouldn't rule out some early snow." Rinaldi had hung back after the briefing in Taylor's bunker.

"God, Rinaldi, isn't it bad enough out here without wishing more grief on us?" Taylor shivered as he sneered.

"Sorry, Sir," Rinaldi chuckled out loud. Taylor had just finished another of many early morning briefings with his regimental commanders. More inaction was the order of the day, but it was necessary. Today they covered the time needed to prepare new recruits and rest the veterans for the inevitable upcoming engagement. They weren't ready for it.

Taylor looked at his colonel. He spoke softly. "Luke, I'm not sure I ever really thanked you for saving my life. I seem to have told everyone but you."

"No need, Taylor. You did. You just don't remember. Morphine does scramble the mind, you know, and anyway, you'd have done the same for me. Worse, I couldn't imagine the thought of bearing sad news to your sister." He smiled, knowing deep down his friend's feelings. "General, is there anything you've heard from HQ that you can share with a mere colonel?"

"Not much that you don't already know." It was amusing to Taylor that Luke always seemed to hear the rumors before he did. It was sort of like his ability to beat Justin at hearing the latest news. It was, no doubt, his old regular army past and his old sergeant's stripes that kept him informed. "If I told you everything, I'd have to slap you in irons. Then my sister would hate me. What's bothering you, anyway? You seem troubled."

"Taylor, this'll actually be the first time for me to face Federal soldiers since I was taken prisoner. I have difficult feelings about it. Some of those guys are friends. Some are relatives."

"Now's not the time to panic. This war's not easy on anyone, Luke. I have friends that went over to the enemy, too, and some who stayed put. We all do what we must to stay alive and to outlast our enemy. I'll tell you this much—this is the largest fighting force we've put together so far. First Army has seven army corps, totaling 36 full divisions, with 540,000 men. The real rub is that half are untried. General Sinsome means business, and heaven help those damn mercenaries if they get in our sights."

"Taylor, do we have any air power?"

"From what I hear, we're on our own. Fuel's too scarce to fly even the old birds like the P-51s. The good news, though, is the enemy's no better off. Most of the flyboys we see on either side will be on reconnaissance in those old civilian single-engine planes or hauling rifles along with us grunts."

"It was sure nice to have the flyboys bail out our rear ends in Cancun and Del Rio. I suppose we'll just have to get used to it and concentrate on eliminating the Feds before they do us in."

"That's a big roger! How did James take to your marriage idea?"

"He said about the same as you, all the trite stuff about waiting, blah, blah. It's a grand dream anyhow. Becky's at least 100 miles south of here. The only way I'll ever get to see her soon, let alone marry her, is if I end up on a meat wagon. As much as I love your sister, I'm not ready to take that route again."

"That I can relate to." Taylor winced as he spoke; his wounds gave constant pain. "I hope Command gets us moving soon before we freeze our butts off."

"Yeah, waiting out here is like watching paint dry."

Luke nodded. "Well, it looks like my prediction of snow was right. Here it comes. Maybe it'll give us something else to worry about."

"See to it that the men find shelter, and get them gathering whatever will burn." Taylor stamped his feet, scowling, searching for warmth. "Rinaldi, you and your goddamn weather predictions."

"I better get on it." Luke saluted, but before he left, he couldn't resist. "You know, Taylor, it's probably sixty degrees in Texas."

Luke laughed as Taylor replied, "Get the hell out of here before I'm tempted to throw you in the brig for making a superior officer's life miserable." Taylor warmly grasped Luke's hand. Their bond said all that needed to be said.

Echoes of artillery rounds shattered the night's surreal calm. Neither man needed the reminder the war was very near.

Follow your bliss. First say to yourself what you would be, and then do what you have to do.

–Epicetus

CHAPTER NINETEEN

December 4, 2020—Salina, Kansas
First Army Headquarters, United Army of the Rebellion

General Raif Sinsome paced the dirt floor of his hastily built command post. He fretted. His next strategic move wouldn't be easy for his ragged army. Now at its apex and squarely under his responsibility, the Rebel legions were divided into four armies. Salina, Kansas, was at present the unwilling host of the Rebel First Army and its 400,000 men. Three other Rebel Armies were scattered on the borders of the freed states, positioned strategically on the eastern front with orders to contain the Federals at all cost.

Raif personally took the reins of the First Army. His plan was to go for the enemy's vulnerability. He held the cause's hope to settle the issue of independence. And it all rested on the high plains where his old best friend and current nemesis, General Stewart 'Skip' Newman, awaited his every move.

A stark realization hit him. *Have I unwittingly placed my army in a precarious position?* It weighed heavily upon his mind. As always, Raif found his army outnumbered but not yet outmaneuvered. The musty smell of newly turned earth and burning wood permeated the bunker, temporarily distracting him.

The small space began to fill with lieutenant generals from the First Army's seven corps. Included in the room was Raif's second in command and protégé, Justin Northcutt, recently arrived from victory in Mexico.

Raif liked Justin. Early on, he had seen untried greatness in him when others saw only a youngster, raw and reckless. But Raif also saw a lot of himself in Justin. He, too, was a boy who had become a man all too fast—a man who would not let present circumstance blind him into not doing first what was right for Texas.

Raif purposely cleared his throat to relieve his congestion brought on by a sinus infection. It was loud enough to draw attention. Silence, except for his raspy voice, filled the room.

"Gentlemen, we're in a dilemma." Raif pulled his soiled overcoat tightly in a futile attempt to keep out the bitter cold. His breath billowed out in wispy puffs, seeming to underline each word. The roaring fire did little to ease the penetrating cold. Clouds of bilious smoke from the poorly vented heater enveloped the room, affecting the meeting's mood.

"I believe we have insufficient intelligence on our enemy's present strength." Raif eyeballed each of his quiet generals for their reaction. They showed none. Each, though, patiently waited to hear what Raif had to say. "I am confident General Newman's Army is receiving reinforcements daily from all points. Enemy traffic is particularly heavy from the west and north. Therefore, we need to eliminate the backbone of their replacement strategy before it gets any stronger. Here's what I plan." Raif paced the small room, speaking with difficulty.

"First, the 4th, 5th, and 6th Corps are to prepare to link up with militia and Home Guard units," Raif pointed to the map behind him. "This operation's goal is to intercept Federal reinforcement columns coming in from the west through Colorado. It's imperative we stop them in their tracks before they make it to Denver. Intel believes we can pick our ground at a position to be determined by the Colorado local militia. Presently we're thinking Vail Pass. General Fox, you're to lead this campaign. You will prepare to leave in twenty-four hours. We'll meet after this session to go over particulars." Raif continued to pace.

"Second, our remaining corps, comprising the 1st, 2nd, 3rd, and 7th, will continue improving defensive positions. You will dig in and wait until the return of General Fox and the additional local militia and Home Guard units he determines can be spared for service with our national force. I've requested from Austin, and have received, approval for the following reinforcements from our National Army."

Raif hesitated. He continued to slowly pace the crowded, hard-packed dirt floor. He privately weighed each corps commander's mettle, wondering which one was his weakest link. Abruptly, he stopped his pacing, startling the hushed generals.

"Men, expected reinforcements are as follows: from Second Army, we'll receive half their force, mostly coming from the Canadian front, which we feel strongly to be under our control. The Third Army, on our eastern front, is doing likewise. The Fourth Army advises they have the southeastern front under control and will send a like number. Two divisions of Mexican nationals and two from Argentina are also expected after they can be acclimated."

The men cheered at this good news. Raif let them enjoy the moment while he silently contemplated whether all of his boast and brag would actually come to pass. He would keep his reservations close to his chest. His men needed good news, if only to give them a moment of hope. Raif raised his right hand to gain their attention. The room quickly fell silent.

"When reinforcements arrive, hopefully within the next ten-to-fifteen days, we should be ready to break out. This means, Gentlemen, taking on Newman's army and capturing Madison." Raif's determined look pierced deeply to the very fiber of every commander.

"Gentlemen, we can't continue the war at its current pace." Raif moved from left to right, looking into the eyes of each man. "I'm confident we have the stamina for one huge but final campaign. Its sole intent will be to end this war before we're no longer able to fight. It should come as no surprise that our resources are dwindling. The only good news is the Feds are in the same boat. Just the same, we can't afford to be idle. To wait is to fail."

Raif stopped pacing. Standing in front of his table, he pounded his fist. His voice, raised to a fevered pitch, crackled, and he took time to cough. "When our armies unite, we will immediately put together a pincer movement. Our goal is to attack from three directions. When General

Fox returns from the operation in the Colorado Rockies, his force will act as our reserve."

The magnitude of his plan took many by surprise. Justin, anxious to ask a crucial question, blurted out, "Sir, when do we attack? More to the point, do we have sufficient supplies at present to back success?"

Justin's interruption of the tempo of Raif's presentation gave rise to some snickers from a few jealous officers. A tense mood encompassed the bunker. Justin also drew some unfavorable glances from older peers, but Raif inwardly smiled. Justin's youthful inexperience had hit upon the core of his concerns—a problem his seasoned officers were unwilling or unable to bring forth.

"Thanks, General Northcutt, I can always rely on your practical questions. As usual, you're thinking ahead of me. Since I was about to get to that, here it is, short and simple. We don't have time on our side to wait for sufficient supplies, which may never come. Our only hope is to stop the enemy before it successfully unites with arriving mercenary and West Coast reinforcements. If we don't stop them before they merge or, worse, train these raw troops, our army is doomed to failure."

Raif reached forward and picked up a paper from his field desk, which he had received earlier. "If you add to the mix the weather we're about to encounter," he pointed to the report, "well …" Raif's worried look exposed his fears. "We don't need a double blow we can't survive. It is believed we have ten days, tops, to get ready, and we need to make the most of it. December 14th will be our targeted D-Day. This, of course, is subject to reinforcements reaching us.

"Now, Justin, to address your question. I'm unable to give a firm answer. Supplies," he hesitated, "now there's the real rub. I'm afraid it's here we have little choice. This is why I'm praying the next campaign will be our last. Simply put, we don't have the wherewithal to feed an army as large and growing as we are, indefinitely. We do have the ability for one good solid thrust at the enemy. We won't attempt to be picture perfect. Don't expect miracles. Due to our lack of everything necessary to carry on the cause, our next thrust will have to be on a personal level. We must destroy the enemies' morale and their will to fight. We must prevail."

"Sir!" General Maxwell stood to speak, his voice polished and direct. "You make it sound like we're on our last leg. Hell, Sir, during the last six months we've won about every encounter we've had with the enemy. Surely, if they're as bad off as you think, why must we move now?"

"Maxwell, your statement is on the mark, except for one thing. We're miles from our source of supply, and those bastards are in the middle of theirs. We'll have to alter our policy and start living off the land where we can. We must do whatever is required to succeed. Gentlemen, I repeat, to do less means we forfeit all that we've sacrificed. It also condemns the many that have died to anonymity. Worse, if we prolong hostilities and are forced to pillage, we'll definitely lose the favor of many here who support our cause. Gentlemen, there simply is no other choice."

Raif paced the room with nervous energy. Inwardly he thought, *Maxwell is a good man, but he moves and thinks too slow. I'll need to watch him.* Raif had been speaking rapidly; the smoke in the room seemed to have increased in pace with his words. He turned to his orderly. "Lieutenant, see what you can do about this damnable fire. It's doing more damage than the Feds." Several chuckled; many thinking of lost comrades wished his comment true.

Raif refocused. "Worse, and here's a real rub to add to my answer to General Maxwell. We lose what little air support we have. I've been told by air command they have one last fight in them. If true, we can't afford to misuse it."

Raif's generals, alerted to the dilemma, couldn't avoid the dire strait they were asked to navigate. Earlier battles had been fought under far friendlier circumstances within more favorable terrain. The Rebel Army found itself spread out along seemingly endless boundaries. Despite the First Army's pending consolidation at the expense of the rebellion's other three army groups, it remained outnumbered, but not outclassed. Sheer determination had brought the Rebels this far. The question on everyone's mind was, *Would its success continue?*

x x x x x

Raif dismissed his men. He watched them leave the bunker, carrying both their open and hidden concerns. He especially noticed Justin leaving alone, seemingly deep in thought.

Justin had mixed feelings. After all was said, he was a realist. The deep grinding in his gut gave rise to his unease. He took a deep, harsh breath of the cold air; his resolve stiffened. His thoughts rambled to Texas, pecans, and Rock Rinaldi.

December 4, 2020—Federal Army Headquarters, Southern Nebraska

"Mr. President, it's too dangerous for you to be here! I must insist you return to the safety of Madison." General Newman peered up in disbelief at his commander in chief, boldly standing before him, resplendent in his fur-lined overcoat.

President Collins needed to be in Madison with his army. He desired firsthand knowledge. *After all,* he reasoned, *I'm the commander in chief. General Newman might run the army, but as the president, I need to see the condition of my troops.* Collins was beginning to distrust the judgment of his commanding general. And no matter what turmoil he might create today, control, for Collins, was an elixir even better than sex.

"General Newman, what's our present effective strength both here and elsewhere? I need an overview to see if your numbers match mine." Rex looked directly into Newman's eyes, seeking the true picture.

"Sir, we're well situated. Intel advises that the Rebs are about three to four hundred thousand strong and 100 miles to our south near Salina, Kansas. That, of course, is not their entire force. As you're aware, they're spread out over four fronts and estimated to number about one million." Newman stood, taking a Cuban cigar from his humidor, offering Collins one. Collins refused.

Newman lit his cigar. Continuing, he blew smoke past the president's face. "Here, we outnumber Sinsome by about three to one. We're expecting 200,000 reinforcements soon from the west coast, along with nearly 300,000 mercenaries coming south from Canada. They should meet with our west coast column somewhere in Colorado, probably near Denver. We have an equal number of troops spread out in western Canada and hold the northeast with at least twenty divisions. All we lack are adequate supplies. Interrogation of enemy prisoners has led us to believe they're near the end of their rope. Supplies, especially food, are all but nonexistent. With his Rebel First Army gaunt and hungry, Sinsome will have to make a move soon or he'll be in trouble. It appears, Mr. President, our damnable rag-tag enemy may have reached the end of its rope and outmaneuvered us for the last time.

"As you know, it's been my continued strategy to fall back in the hope the enemy would spread itself dangerously thin. By all accounts it's working. This time Sinsome has placed his growing forces a bit too far from his wretched supply lines." Newman smiled with an unintentional sneer. "His army is becoming unwieldy and, better yet, very hungry. You should see the skeletal prisoners we have captured of late."

"That's good news, General. Are we still feeding our army?"

"Barely, sir, though more often than the Rebs. That's why I've been in disagreement with your staff. Bringing in more men is foolish if we can't expect adequate supply."

"Then why the hell are you sitting here if we outnumber them in their weakened state?" Collins's voice was raised, and his face wore an angry sneer.

"Because, sir, I believe time's on our side. With the west coast troops finally trained and on their way and mercenaries trooping in daily, we certainly can attack anytime we want, but only, I stress, when the time is right. It'll save lives and that's important in this phase of the war. If we attack too soon, we will run the risk of stumbling into a very able and cornered wildcat that might give more than it takes."

"So when, pray tell, will you determine it to be right?" Collins was losing his patience. Changing his mind, he reached for a cigar.

Newman lit it for him as he answered. "Sir, every time I hit that wildcat Sinsome, as you like to call him, he comes back for more, again and again. Each time we meet the Rebels, they lose men, yet they seem able to replace them even now. When we lose men, we find a need to use foreigners. Our people are tiring of this war. Remember, many of our supporters come from the left—traditionally against war. History is not on our side. Look how they acted in the Iraqi war. Hell, these are the same people who marched against our war on terrorism and then didn't support our troops when we were in Iraq."

Newman spoke with venom at the mention of Iraq. It was a side Collins rarely saw. "The enemy doesn't have our problem when it comes to fighting. By waiting, I hope to let the weather and starvation do what we've been unable to accomplish. If not, I'll let loose our foreigners. Either way we prevail."

"General, I don't agree with your position. We're not tiring. There's still a lot of fight left in our people," Collins said, pounding Newman's desk as he sat down, fire in his eyes.

"Sir, pardon me, but I disagree. I see the desertion reports daily. The citizen soldier you think is not tiring has the sullen look of defeat. Only a major victory, one on our terms, will turn things." Newman contained his inner rage, but his eyes revealed his anger.

"General, I believe your strategy allows the Rebels to get supplies and men and, worse, lets them gain parity with us if we delay."

"I understand your concern, Mr. President. We hope our army will intercept the enemy reinforcements. Even if they do manage to get through, how will they be supplied? Remember, Sir, an army marches on its stomach. This time General Sinsome has bitten off more than he can chew, let alone swallow."

"I hope you're correct, Newman. I appreciate your strategy is to save lives. Heaven knows what little support we have is dwindling. Using mercenaries will lessen Federal casualties and curb the current desire to end the slaughter."

Collins never worried about casualties before this. Now the outcry from his loyalists has given him a sudden thirst for empathy and humanity. What an audacious bore this man is, Stewart Newman thought as he successfully contained his rage.

Newman changed the subject, intent on rattling Collins. "I heard through my sources that you had a parley with your Rebel sister." Newman didn't dare mention Collins's sister by name. No one within hearing distance of President Collins's ears ever did, for fear of his wrath. "Any chance she's asking for terms of surrender?" *See, Mr. President, I have my sources—good, I see it irritates you.*

Collins let out a sinister laugh, almost a cackle. His keen eyes seemed to be calculating what he would choose to reveal and what Newman needed to know. "Yes," he answered his voice in a low growl, "I've talked with her.

"As you're aware, it's necessary to keep open exchanges. She might someday have to beg for terms. How I long for that moment. Then, too, God forgive the thought, I might need to ask for peace." He surprised himself with that mistaken outburst, and then summarily dismissed it as quickly as it had come.

Silently he pondered, biding his time before beginning. His devious miscalculations with Mexico and Canada, Cuba, Brazil, and others had backfired, opening a can of worms with the rest of the world's powers. The results were not as he had bargained. He thought with a vengeance, *The damn disloyalty of that traitorous secretary of state—Sparkman's probable warning to my sister helped foil my ingenious strategy. I really enjoyed having him murdered along with his family as a warning to others.* He turned to Newman, steel in his eyes.

"Our talk was in accord and a follow-up on our joint effort with the Japanese Navy. She was sick over it, yet felt there was no viable alternative." Actually she had said much more, pulling no punches over Mexico, but Collins held that information back. "She also discussed our options in the Middle East. I told her we had to leave that part of the world on its own for now. 'Damn,' I said, 'they've been fighting for three millennia.' She was in a rage. Her sources advised her that Israel was expected to fall and Iraq was again about to enslave that part of the world." What he didn't immediately divulge to Newman was that Rebel submarines were positioned to launch nuclear warheads on Iraq and Iran if they did not heed their joint warning and turn back. It appeared the Arabs chose prudence over annihilation.

Collins spoke after a long hesitation. "My treacherous sister agreed that the threat of using nukes might serve to remind them we haven't forgotten their treachery. She's correct. Whoever comes out ahead in our conflict may find their victory short-lived because those Muslim radicals will have to be severely dealt with. I hope they give me provocation because there is nothing I'd like to do more than blow those rag-heads to kingdom come."

Newman thought that, for once, Collins was right. Even reckless leadership could not afford to shine the shoes of the mullahs of war. He spoke out. "Don't you think the Israelis can hold out?"

"No, Newman, they're beaten. We can only delay the inevitable. They're helpless without our full support, and along with a weakened Europe and Russia to add to the pie, I'm afraid they're at the mercy of the times. Babs," he spit out her name as if it were poison, "though vehemently opposed, agreed reluctantly to the possible need to neutralize things for our mutual interests. She won on Japan; I won't give in on this issue if matters worsen. The situation leaves us no alternative." Collins's determined voice temporarily rattled Newman.

"It seems like you're getting a bit chummy with your sister. But I can see where it's politically expedient to take a stand on the issues you've mentioned. Thanks for filling me in, Mr. President. I believe there is enough on my plate at the moment, so I'll leave the worries of the Middle East to you and the navy."

"It's damned decent of you, Newman," Collins replied, openly sarcastic. "I appreciate your support and concern. You're correct about one thing; you do have a lot on your plate. That is why I am here. Simply stated, I'm giving you fourteen days to see if your strategy of starvation and foul weather works. If not, and I suspect it won't, you're to attack. We, General Newman, are in the same miserable boat as the Rebs. Don't you ever forget it! We do not, I repeat, DO NOT," Collins shouted, dropping his cigar onto Newman's cluttered desk, "have the luxury of time!"

Collins stood, his tall presence menacing. "You will move this army offensively by December 16th. It will be your last chance to vindicate your many failures of late."

Collins pointed his finger at Newman, continuing his intimidation. Newman did everything in his power not to grab his finger and break it. "General," Collins continued, "no one ever won a war on the defensive. We must move on offense before it becomes too goddamned late. I look forward to your daily reports, in particular the one that will say you are on the advance. We'll resume our conversation in ten days. Before we do, you must make preparations to move as ordered. Have your strategic plan on my desk no later than three days from now."

Newman remained silent, steaming.

"Am I clear, Newman?"

Newman nodded, too angry to reply.

President Collins hastily grabbed his stylish overcoat, signaling his Secret Service men he was leaving. He desired to leave quickly. He had once respected Newman's abilities, but that had changed. Collins would not let reason interfere with his compelling need to act, even if that action was accompanied by dire consequences.

Newman watched Collins leave, disdain in his eyes. "Tell me something I don't already know, Mr. President." Newman's hushed, whispered snicker trailed after the shadow of the departing Federal leader who no longer enjoyed the honorary title of Leader of the Free World.

Newman walked back to his desk, opened his humidor, and selected another Cuban cigar. He carefully lit it, looking at its smoke casually rising in ringlets toward the ceiling. "You fool," he quietly uttered, "you'll have my plan in three godforsaken days!" His exhaled smoke covered the silent room like a fog-filled morning, hushed and menacing.

Jim Damiano

Never give in, never, never, never, never—in nothing, great or small, large or petty—never give in except to convictions of honor and good sense.

—Winston S. Churchill

CHAPTER TWENTY

December 10, 2020—Rebel First Army Headquarters, Salina, Kansas

General Raif Sinsome reached into his fatigue pocket for his last stick of gum. He needed this disappearing pleasure to erase the vile taste of his scant breakfast. As he exited his bunker, a cold blast of Kansas wind almost bowled him over. Its sharp wintry bite cut through his rugged frame and invigorated his already keen senses. The day held little promise that the sun would appear.

Raif desperately needed a personal moment, for the day had stirred memories and longings of happier times. The pleasant image of his precocious little girl and his beautiful wife lingered, giving him a feeling of guilt that no matter how hard he tried, he couldn't shake loose. Were they safe in Austin? The fond memory of his wife's lingering, parting kiss, and his three-year-old daughter's possessive hug, punished his peace. The best part of his life was running on empty, and he badly needed a refill of purpose.

How he had hated leaving them. Then a foreboding stirred his lethargy, slamming him back to the real world and matters of war. Slogging along in dogged frustration, he measured the odds for victory, exasperatingly second-guessing them. Despite recent Rebel victories and too many draws to count, the battles he had hoped would bring the war to conclusion seemed to strengthen the enemy's resolve. Desperately, he tried to forget the many battles lost.

But, Raif reasoned, *this enemy is American, so why shouldn't they have determination? Something must give soon or there will be nothing left worth fighting for. The war seems intent upon systematically destroying everything we once held dear.*

Confusion brought on by the dispersal of his forces compounded the dilemma. Forced into conflict on two fronts against formerly friendly neighbors, the Rebels' campaign against the Federals had slowed to a mere crawl, decimating their ranks. Now, with the easing of tensions with Mexico and Canada, the cause was reviving. *But,* he thought with hounding consistency, *is it too late?*

Thankfully, new recruits continued to fill their dwindling ranks. Some did volunteer, though far fewer than in the earlier days. Most replacements came by way of conscription. Nevertheless, the desertions from the Federals that had increased when the Mexicans originally attacked had now slowed. Worse, most of the deserters were the very soldiers who hailed from southwestern states affected by possible Mexican victory. With Mexico defeated, many saw little reason to remain for a cause they once were reluctant to support. Rebel desertions were higher than ever, and now extreme casualties helped influence flight. Raif needed to exhort action before the problem became endemic.

Raif was worried. Sending half of the First Army to intercept Federal reinforcements was, in many military circles, considered foolish. However, he considered the risk worth the reward. It would increase their chance for success if his army prevented Federal reinforcements from linking with the main Federal forces in Lincoln. Recent reports indicated that General Fox's scouts had discovered the enemy column, and that Fox's main army was waiting in ambush somewhere near Interstate Highway 70 at Vail Pass.

Splitting the army was not new to the adventurous Raif. He'd gotten away with it often, despite dire warnings from less daring souls. Raif did not believe caution won battles. Others throughout history had been successful, or perhaps lucky, doing so. At the Point, he had religiously studied examples of historical campaigns, foreign or American, where taking just such a risk had resulted in triumph. Many on his staff, though, were not hesitant to remind him of the hazard. The last such reference, heard just today, was of

Custer and the slaughter of the 7th Cavalry when he split his command in his battle against the Sioux at the Little Big Horn.

His most basic concern this moment was whether his arch nemesis, General Newman, might realize their weakened state and take action before his buildup was accomplished. If Newman's intelligence revealed Rebel maneuvers, he felt certain his old comrade would attack. Sinsome realized the Federals in Lincoln substantially outnumbered the First Army, even before the split. Arrival of reinforcements was several excruciating days away. Everything was held in balance by a thin thread. *Thankfully, Newman's always cautious. Let's hope he'll remain predictable for a few more crucial days.*

Raif's scouts had not discerned any unusual Federal movements. Prepared to retreat at the slightest hint of Federal motion, he would hold on patiently, as long as prudence allowed. Patiently, he awaited word from his advancing re-enforcement columns. Today **he** was encouraged because some replacements were filtering in.

Raif's worrisome ponderings were interrupted by the urgent pleas of a messenger's voice shouting in rage at the general's guard outside his command bunker.

"Hear me, soldier!" the messenger yelled. "I'm requesting permission to see General Sinsome at once. It's a matter of extreme urgency."

"And I told you, Lieutenant, the general is not to be disturbed."

"Look, you damn idiot, move or I'll off you right now." The messenger aimed his M-16 at the sentry's chest, the safety off, his hand on the trigger.

Throwing aside military protocol, Sinsome walked to the entrance of his post and urged the messenger forward. "Put away your rifle, Lieutenant! Now out with it! What do you have for me that's so pressing?" Raif was livid; he did not appreciate the disruption. "This better be good, Lieutenant!"

"Sir, Lieutenant Montemuro." His salute was quick and unmilitary, matching his rent uniform. "I have an urgent message from General Fox." Raif's look matched the distressed countenance upon the disheveled man's face. Montemuro blurted, "Our men have been routed at Vail Pass.

The few who managed to survive have retreated and are being pursued by a determined force of approximately 600,000 Federals."

"Slow down, Lieutenant." Raif was calmer than his rapidly beating heart indicated. "Tell me step by step what's happened. Are you saying our force is destroyed?"

"Yes, Sir, the best I can report, Sir, was we had 'em surprised. Our ambush seemed to work. Then, when we figured victory was ours, out from nowhere came a horde of Feds. We were flanked in a manner we thought impossible, by the full brunt of not just those western Federals we were ambushin', but also by their bloody mercenaries. It was the foreigners, Sir, who flanked us. We gave a good account of ourselves. It was their overwhelming numbers that did us in. General Fox advises we were badly misinformed as to their actual strength, Sir. General Fox was forced to retreat to the south."

"Tell me, do you know why the columns retreated to the south instead of heading for us?"

"Sir, it's as if they were driving us. About two divisions of our reserve ranks, about 40,000 men, were able to get away. They raced toward the safety of our supply reserve post in Hutchinson. I suspect the roads south from Vail gave better opportunity, but you'll have to ask General Fox, in the hereafter, to completely understand. He ordered us south, feeling ... if I may, Sir? ..."

Raif nodded his assent.

"... that it was our best chance. General Fox did say he couldn't let the enemy get between First Army in Salina and Hutchinson. Not with the main Federal Army poised so neatly near Lincoln. I'd say it was the only way he felt we could go."

"Where's Fox now, Lieutenant?"

"Sorry, Sir, sorry, I didn't make it clear. He's in the hereafter. He died from his wounds during our retreat, just after he gave me this message for you. We buried him somewhere near Carson City, Colorado."

"Damn, I'm sorry to hear that. He was a good man, Lieutenant. In your estimation, what's our timing?"

"Sir, I don't think we have any. General Richards took temporary command. He advises respectfully you may want to fall back to Hutchinson where we can consolidate before it's too late. He also suggests that even with remnants of First Army and any reinforcements from Second, we're still outnumbered no matter what and too exposed with our present positions if the enemy forms between us."

Raif paused to take a deep breath before he answered. General Richards had read the predicament correctly. Any imbecile could see their peril. *It's my damn fault*, he fumed.

"Thank you for your concise report, Montemuro. You look hungry and tired. Be sure to get some food and rest, but wait here a moment. I may have some more questions." Raif gestured to the lieutenant to sit on a nearby crate. Montemuro gladly complied.

Raif was shaken by the news. He turned to his adjutant, Major John McKinley, who was standing nearby. "It appears we've got our work cut out for us. John, stand by. I'll dictate my response to General Richards ASAP."

"Sergeant," Raif's voice boomed. "Get General Justin Northcutt here on the double. Gather all corps and division commanders to report in forty-five minutes."

Raif turned his focus to Montemuro. "Lieutenant, regarding the mercenaries, do we know their origin?"

"Not really, Sir. It was a blur. It happened too fast. One moment we were in complete control, the next found us sucked into their trap. We were the hunters, then we became the hunted."

"Were many taken prisoner? A seveny-five percent casualty loss is pretty hard to swallow."

Montemuro's face turned to panic. "Sir, the last I saw they weren't taking prisoners. The killing was done with precision and little mercy. I truly expected we'd all be executed if captured. I'm sorry to say we ran like the Devil himself was a-chasin' us."

"Those sons of bitches!" he said, but to himself he thought, *So this is what this war's come to. President Collins and Newman have sunk to a new low.* "Are you absolutely certain about what you saw, Lieutenant?"

"Sir, should I live to see the end of this war and beyond, I'll never forget that horrible scene." Montemuro's expression reflected the impact of his terror. "It'll haunt me as long as I have life in me. And, Sir, it wasn't just the mercenaries in a killing frenzy. Some of the westerners went out of their way to assist in the butchery. I suppose it's their desperate way, the cowards that they are, to frighten us. Sadly, it worked."

"Lieutenant, again, thanks. You're tired. Go eat and get some rest. You're dismissed. The corporal will direct you to food and shelter. Report back here at 1600 hours."

The lieutenant departed, and Raif called Major McKinley. Just as Raif was about to start his dictation, Justin entered, arriving earlier than expected. Raif motioned Justin to take a seat. "General Northcutt, I'll be with you shortly. Listen to what I'm about to send our president, for it concerns your next mission."

Justin could feel Raif's nervous agitation.

Raif turned his attention back to his adjutant. "John, you ready?"

"Yes, Sir!" John had been Sinsome's adjutant since the beginning of the war.

Justin smiled. He never knew a time when McKinley was not ready.

"Address this to the president, Austin, today's date at," he looked at his watch, "0840, First Army HQ, etc., etc."

Madam President,

> *It is with deep regret that I report of the loss of over forty percent of First Army, or approximately 140,000 personnel, who were killed yesterday in action at the Battle of Vail Pass, Colorado. Their mission was intended to intercept Federal reinforcements destined for enemy units known to be near Lincoln, Nebraska.*
>
> *Intel advised the enemy reinforcements' numbers to be around 200,000, mostly raw recruits from California, Oregon, and Washington state. With that assurance, half of First Army, a force of 180,000, was sent to intercept at a place advantageous. Intel's information was tainted, and I made the wrong decision. I take full responsibility for this defeat, which by its sheer numbers is our greatest loss to date. We encountered an overwhelming force of approximately 600,000 Federals, of which about two-thirds are thought to*

> be mercenary replacements of unknown foreign extraction. Approximately 40,000 men were able to escape and are en route to our reserve post in Hutchinson, Kansas. The force's commander, General Fox, was killed. His second, General Richards, should be in Hutchinson by the time you receive this.

Raif hesitated, took a deep breath to clear his thoughts, and contemplated his next paragraph. What he must say was contrary to his desire and contrary to his nature but necessary to present the proper impact. He continued his measured dictation, keeping his composure.

> While this loss is the most tragic our cause has encountered, even worse, though, is the vivid fact that mercenary forces unleashed upon us have acted in barbaric fashion, executing all prisoners and wounded. I am sorry to report that Federal soldiers, Americans, have joined in this atrocity. This is not new to warfare, nor is it new to this conflict, though we have never seen it at this level. Atrocity happens. Yet, I am unable to tolerate it any longer. I respectfully request you do whatever diplomatically possible to persuade foreign governments from interfering with our war.

"John, underline and capitalize the words 'our war.'"

"Yes, Sir. Got it down."

> I further propose you advise said governments that any of their citizens caught by us in belligerent acts will be summarily executed. Additionally, I appeal to you to contact President Collins through your channels. Of course, I can only give counsel. By the time you receive this missive, I shall, under powers given me as Commanding General of all the Armies of the Rebellion, have issued General Order Number 45, specifically stating that we shall not take any mercenary prisoner. This includes any Federal soldier known or suspected to be a part of this atrocity, wounded or standing."

Raif gave emphasis to the last line. His seething anger began to surface beneath his usual calm demeanor.

> *I am sending the 36th Ranger Division as a vanguard to Hutchinson. I will follow as quickly as stealth and providence provides opportunity. Our position here is tenuous. Therefore, we must link up with expected replacement columns en route. I will only return to Austin when I have secured victory, and no sooner.*
>
> *I remain your trusted servant and ask God to continue to bless our just Cause.*

"Et cetera, et cetera ..."

Justin figured what was next. He didn't need the specifics, though as a subordinate, he had to go through the motions.

Raif, chomping at the bit, turned his attention to Justin.

"Justin, it's bad. Our worst nightmare is upon us. Now it appears we're faced with a war of annihilation and foreign intervention. Now it's our play to show the enemy we'll not tolerate this on our soil without horrifying retaliation."

"But begging your pardon, Sir, won't this make them fight all the more, knowing we'll not take prisoners? I remember Del Rio. We fought like banshees when we realized we'd die anyway."

"Well, I agree, it did encourage our people to fight desperately. I suppose it'll do likewise for them. My hope is, it will serve as a frightening notice and slow the enthusiasm of future foreign adventurers desiring to act as mercenaries for the Federals. Justin, you're to kill any who are foolish enough to surrender. Do you understand?"

"Sir, I'm not sure my boys will give a damn once they get wind of what's happened." Justin, angry and anxious, still felt ill at ease with the turn of events. "Despite the situation, I despise killing prisoners, Sir."

Raif sighed deeply. "All those good men I sent to die. How will my God look at me if I've become like my enemy? I'm only a soldier, not a madman, but I've no choice if we are to win."

Justin received his written orders from McKinley, stopped, and turned to Sinsome. "Sir, you did the best you could with the information available. I'd look into the source of that bad info. That's our real culprit. No one would've acted otherwise."

"Thank you, General." Raif smiled. "I've already done that. And please be careful. I can't afford to lose you. Too many good men have been lost, all superb leaders lost for our new republic. We can't afford any more."

"You can count on the fact that I'll do my best to survive. I'll fill in Taylor right away since the 36th leads the advance. I'll follow closely behind with the balance of 1st Corps as quickly as transport allows. We'll make them pay. That I promise you."

December 11, 2020—77th Hospital Unit, Hutchinson, Kansas

Rebecca Northcutt knew all was not as it should be. Since yesterday, her field hospital unit and its sister unit, the 62nd, were ordered to prepare wounded for evacuation. A massive teardown of equipment took place around her even while she prepared a wounded soldier for the coming ordeal of his move.

"Sergeant, do you have any news on what's happening?"

The sergeant stopped and turned to address Becky. "Lieutenant, I know only we best get a move on, and fast. What few vehicles we have left already started south with the badly wounded. Some stragglers coming into the post said elements of the First Army were routed somewhere in Colorado. Something like over 100,000 men were reported lost. The Feds are coming this way, trying to overtake the remnants retreating toward us. It's said First Army's retreating survivors are a few miles away. It appears they plan to make a defense here when they show."

"Oh my God, Luke and my brothers are with the First!" Becky's panic hit her hard. She reached within her soul, searching for inner strength.

"What's that, Lieutenant?" the Sergeant asked, thinking her mumbling was meant for him.

"Nothing, just a bit rattled, Sergeant. Do you know if the 36th Ranger Division was involved in the battle?"

"I'm not certain. Word's out some of the 36th may be on its way here. Some say they're the advance troops General Sinsome's sending us.

I don't think any of them were in the fight, but ya never know how a general will use his army; sorry Ma'am, some could've been there."

"Thanks again!" Becky, slightly relieved, had hope. Would she see Luke or Taylor? Quickly she surmised it unlikely. If they were coming here, they would have more urgent matters. Besides, she would be moving out soon with the last of the wounded.

Becky's momentary silence was interrupted by the high screeching sound and sudden blast of several artillery shells raining punishment and delivering destruction upon the terrain. Several men laboring to pack the hospital tenting and medical equipment were caught in its path; dozens were killed. The prominent Red Cross flag they flew gave no protection.

Startled, Becky instinctively aided the few wounded lucky enough to escape. She rushed from one fallen soldier to another, saving some and passing on the hopeless.

The sergeant she had been talking to a few minutes earlier grabbed her arm. "Ma'am, we need to get to shelter. The shelling may start off again. You'll be killed out here." He ushered her to an empty bunker while directing the handling of the wounded and the few surviving medics. Their initial priority was to set up a makeshift hospital in the cavernous space. They would deal with their dilemma after they had taken care of the fallen.

December 11, 2020—36th Ranger Division Advance
Two Miles North of Hutchinson, Kansas

Colonel Luke Rinaldi, unlike other reluctant warriors in his division, was anxious to reach Hutchinson. His fiancée was somewhere nearby. His brigade's advance relief column consisted of every conceivable vehicle. The rest of the division was on forced march in the sunny, cold weather of late fall.

Luke's regiment was among the first to reach the area. Once within sight of Hutchinson, the convoys emptied and the trucks returned for more troops. Luke's men were directed to walk the last few miles to Hutchinson, clearly visible in the distance.

General Taylor Northcutt had hoped to coordinate his entire division to arrive in Hutchinson close to the same time, but it would not happen much before tomorrow. Luke and his men were tired and hungry. He didn't know which sensation was greater, his fatigue or his desire for food. Scarce provisions still plagued them. The past twelve hours of forced march without food didn't help to improve dispositions. Luke's stomach growled again as he contemplated his next move. It was not long in coming.

"Colonel, move your regiment to the defensive perimeter about one mile west of this position." The major, directing newly arriving troops, pointed to a sector on the map assigned to Luke's unit.

Luke smiled, noting the area had a Red Cross, indicating it was a hospital staging area. "Major, are hospital units still at that location?"

"No, Sir, they should be moved out by now."

"Damn, you might know. At least she's out of danger."

"Sir, did you say something?"

"No, just talking to myself. Bad habit."

Luke saluted and led his men to the designated area, which, like everything else, was in chaos. Once there, he directed the placement of his regiment and went about the business of fortifying it to his satisfaction, directing machine gun and mortar angles of fire. Satisfied with his effort, he called his second in command, Major Rick Duggins, to his side.

"Rick, take over for a few minutes. I'm reconnoitering over to where the hospital units used to be located. Maybe by some chance my fiancée might still be there."

"No problem, Colonel. I can handle things here. If you see Becky, say hello for me."

The short walk to the spot marked on the map proved futile. What once was there was now gone or destroyed. Shell holes were dominant, leaving great rents in the Kansas soil. Several broken bodies blanketed the field before him. He was about to turn back when he saw the entrance to a bunker. He decided to check it out, figuring it could render possible cover for a future field HQ. Right now it was too far forward of his present position, but in battle you needed to cover all known possibilities. Looking, he figured it might also need to be destroyed to deny the enemy potential use. In any event, it remained too close to his lines to ignore.

Entering the bunker brought total surprise. Amongst the living, medical staff and badly wounded alike, a pretty, disheveled nurse worked diligently to relieve a suffering soldier. Luke waited until she finished her merciful effort and turned, unmindful, in his direction. She looked right past him, not noticing him or his scruffy appearance in the dim light.

"Nurse Northcutt," Luke boomed, "I need your attention here at once!"

Becky immediately recognized his voice. Excited, she shouted, "Luke, you've gotten so thin!" *What a silly thing to say,* she thought. She ran to him, clinging to him for dear life.

"I prayed your regiment might get here before we left. Now it looks like we aren't going anywhere. Luke, it's been awful. You can see our Red Cross affords no protection." She hesitated, and then burst out with what she needed to know. "Are my brothers with you? Oh, I'm sorry for rambling on."

He looked with longing into her gentle eyes. He had missed her so much, and now here she was. "Honey, they're close behind. Do you know Taylor commands the 36th? We're the advance division for 1st Corps. It's now Justin's command."

"Luke, am I dreaming? Are you really here?"

A nearby medic, hearing their musings, shouted, "Becky, he's here."

Luke continued to hold her in a warm embrace. "Honey, I'm here. Believe me, there's no other place I'd rather be. But we have to move quickly. Justin should be a half-day behind us. There's a major battle expected here any minute. We need to get you all out of this place. Our line is about a mile from here, which means this bunker will most likely be in the middle of any battle fought. Besides wounded, what needs to be moved?"

"It's too late for our baggage. The enemy laid a salvo down on what was left, destroying it and our transportation. The barrage killed most of our waiting wounded and medics. We're all that's left of about 300."

Luke shook his head. "Yeah, I saw the mess outside. It's terrible." He grasped her hands.

"Oh Luke!" Becky's eyes showed deep sorrow; she had seen so much death. "Rumor has it they're mostly mercenaries, and they're not taking prisoners. Have you heard anything about this?"

"We heard the same. When all of 1st Corps arrives, we'll have 100,000 vets between the enemy and the rest of the army. We're told we need to hold at least a couple days until General Sinsome arrives from Salina with what's left of First Army. In the meanwhile, those Feds and foreign bastards will face one stubborn SOB when they tackle your brother."

"Luke, what really happened near Vail?"

"I'm not really sure. Some say a feast for Colorado wolves with over 140,000 troops lost. There were very few wounded reported because the enemy killed anyone who surrendered or fell. We think we gave the Feds several casualties and slowed them down some but not nearly enough. Only God understands why they'd turn to this. It's as though President Collins is in league with the Devil."

Becky, restless, saw no better time than the present to ask what had been heavy on her mind for days. "I'll get right to the point because I know time is short. Did you talk to my brothers about us? I see you're still walking and alive," she snickered, "so at least they didn't shoot you."

"Yes, Funny Face, they're cool with us gettin' hitched, but predictably, they think it wise to wait for the war to end."

"Did you agree with them?"

"Nope!"

Becky smiled at Luke's quick and decisive answer.

"Honey, I'd like to talk more, but I've got to return to my regiment. I'll come back with help as quickly as I can. I love you. And don't you go and do anything foolish until I return." Luke gave her a loving kiss to the great amusement of the cheering wounded.

"I love you, too. Please be careful." Becky watched him leave and part of her heart followed. She was no longer alone and in the dark. Her love for Luke made her plight bearable.

x x x x x

Luke returned to find his regiment had been ordered to pull back two miles. This would take it three miles from Becky's hidden bunker. He would have to warn her.

The regiment, before Luke's return, had made the hasty fallback to its new position, in time to meet the next convoy of men from the 36th. It was a comfort to see them. With the regiment calm for the moment, Luke took three men and a confiscated truck and trailer, leaving the regiment under temporary command of Major Duggins. Luke had a deep need to rescue Becky's unit; the major understood fully, being married less than a year himself.

Luke's small contingent reached Becky's bunker. Suddenly, he heard the all-too-familiar and frightening sound of incoming shells. It was possible his vehicle had attracted enemy artillery. He and his men made a running dive into the bunker before the first shells rained upon them. Luke wondered out loud, "Where's our artillery?" He hoped his regiment was safe. He didn't think the enemy knew yet of their recent pullback.

"I guess our scouts saw this coming. That's why they moved us," he shouted above the din, to no one in particular.

Becky smiled, her eyes radiant upon Luke as he rose from his dramatic entrance into the bunker with his men. "Back so soon, Colonel? You really did miss me, didn't you?"

Luke beamed as he gave her a quick hug. It was this wonderful grin she remembered most about him. It was what first brought her to love him, when he was so cynical yet so sure of himself.

Luke turned serious then, putting her at arm's length to look her square in the eye. "Becky, I'm afraid we're in a bit of a fix. All units were ordered to pull back about three miles from here. You're no longer safe. As soon as they stop the shelling, we need to get everyone quickly out and return to our lines."

"Luke, there aren't enough able-bodied men to get the badly wounded out." Becky looked at the long line of soldiers spread on the dirty bunker floor.

"We'll get those we can and come back. With luck, they didn't hit our truck. Maybe there's a chance we can get most everybody out."

Luke continued in a whisper. "Becky, we may have to leave the worst for last. I hate to play God, but I've no choice. I'll decide for you."

"No, you won't, Colonel. Here, I am the authority, and I'll decide who leaves first. I'll stay with them. Someone must, and it should be me!" Becky exclaimed.

"The hell you will, Miss Northcutt," a tall medic nearby exhorted. "Lieutenant, we need you to care for the wounded, not the dead, 'cause that's what you might be if you stay here. I'll stay. Someone expendable needs to care for them."

Becky's look indicated she was not about to give in to the corpsman's suggestion.

Ignoring Becky, Luke said in relief, "Thank you, Soldier."

"With that settled, Colonel," Becky said, starting to respond sarcastically in the negative. Then she fell. The generous corpsman, about to say more, was silenced by the massive explosion outside the bunker's opening.

In an instant, none of the previous conversation mattered. The earth erupted, giving way to mountains of debris. The impact of the explosion killed many. It sealed the entrance of the bunker, controlling the destiny of all those entombed.

Taylor's column stretched for miles. Explosions off in the distance caused him to push his men. Only the gods of war knew what lay ahead. They had to make it to Hutchinson or all might be lost. Somehow everything still mattered, yet he wondered silently, *Why?* He chanced to look skyward out the passenger side of his command vehicle. With talons locked around a captured squirrel, a red-tailed hawk flew above them. *Some things don't ever change. And that's good.* Taylor turned his attention to the artillery harassing his arrival.

Jim Damiano

Courage is resistance to fear, mastery of fear, not absence of fear.
—Mark Twain

CHAPTER TWENTY-ONE

December 12, 2020—Rebel Army Headquarters, Hutchinson, Kansas

The 36th Division arrived piecemeal. Luckily, it was too late to be caught by the Federal barrage that had devastated the remnants of Becky's hospital unit and the Rebel defensive positions, which had been subsequently abandoned. Taylor placed his division squarely at the center of the line and awaited further orders from Command. He was ready for whatever the enemy threw his way.

Taylor lay hugging the dirt works, focusing his binoculars on the scene unraveling before him. Not surprisingly, the overwhelming enemy force approached five miles distant. The field before him lay flat and void of trees, offering a magnificent field of fire. His observation was brought to a brisk halt with the arrival of Major Duggins, temporary commander of his 7th Ranger Regiment.

"Sir, permission to speak."

"Speak, Major. Any news on Colonel Rinaldi?"

"Sir, as originally reported, and now confirmed, we're certain his mission was caught in the enemy barrage. Yesterday he had indicated your sister's bunker was approximately one mile forward of our regiment's original position."

"Do you have an idea of the bunker's position?"

"Not exactly, Sir. He did say it was in the vicinity of the hospital units marked on our coordinates. He showed me his field map, so I have a fair idea of where it is. As you know, there was a massive enemy barrage about the time he should have reached his objective."

"Major, show me on this map."

Duggins pointed.

"Thanks, Major. Until Colonel Rinaldi returns, you will continue temporary command of the 7th," Taylor said

"Very well, Sir. I'll do my best."

Taylor felt ill. The churning in the pit of his stomach gave him little rest, as did his overworked, worrying mind, refusing to give him peace. Could Becky be alive after that intense shelling? Could anyone survive its concentration or, worse, a direct hit? His brain wrestled with repeated questions, all leading to the unpleasantly realistic logic of his training and experience.

Rinaldi had been missing for twenty-four hours. Not a long time, he reasoned. He reluctantly decided he'd wait to advise Justin. The greater demands of the moment lay heavy on him. For now, he and his brother must focus on the responsibilities of command and leave family matters aside. Taylor knew his duty, but it still hurt.

Directly ahead, a few scant miles, lay some 400,000 or more enemy soldiers preparing to strike. The Rebels had little time to adjust their defenses. Taylor's division had reinforced the retreating remnants of the Colorado fiasco and the local Home Guard. The 36th, with fewer than 10,000 men, was below strength. But this was the norm now. Quick preparation in boot camp could not possibly bring the new recruits who were replenishing his ranks to the fearsome ability the Rangers once enjoyed. To reach that pinnacle would take battle experience. It looked like the Federals were about to accommodate them. Yet to a man, Taylor was confident his Ranger division, raw recruits and seasoned veterans alike, stood ready to defend their freedom along with the 90,000 soldiers from several states who were forming on either side of his center position.

Taylor reached for his field glasses, looking to his rear. In the distance, coming south on Route 61, he could see a large column approaching. He felt sudden relief. It must be his brother with the balance of 1st Corps. With Justin's arrival, their ranks would expand to nearly 200,000 troops. This, Taylor reasoned, would certainly help even out the poor odds.

Taylor hoped his veterans were facing mostly rookie Federal troops. If so, it would serve to give them a slight edge. He knew this wish held water only as long as the Federal commanding general stayed in Nebraska with his seasoned troops. *Hopefully, the Vail Pass slaughter will give the enemy false confidence and encourage them to do something stupid.*

A courier carefully wound his way to Taylor, waiting for him to look up. His patience soon crumbled, and he interrupted Taylor's concentration. "Sir, Lieutenant General Northcutt has arrived and requests your presence on the double."

"Lead me, Captain."

The walk was brisk, the sky clear, and the sun bright. It helped lessen the penetrating cold Taylor's ragged uniform could not alleviate. Taylor saw his brother off in the distance. True to Justin's nature, his pensive eyes were scanning Rebel fortifications in his periphery, searching for signs of weakness. Probing for his own army's Achilles heel, Justin was no doubt focusing on the area he'd choose to attack if he were the enemy commander.

Justin saw Taylor's sullen approach out of the corner of his left eye, instinctively knowing there was a problem by the way he walked. He gave up his observation for the moment. He'd let Taylor tell him what troubled him in his own time. He knew his brother too well to do otherwise.

Justin, surrounded by staff, turned to speak. "Taylor, it's good to see you. Is your division in position?"

"Same here, Sir. It's a big relief to see you. We're ready. Is the balance of First Army far behind?"

"They're not coming just yet." Justin spoke slowly in a measured tone, seeing the alarm on Taylor's face. "I'll go over everything after you give me the lay of the land."

Justin put his arm on Taylor's shoulder, leading him to a corner where they could have more privacy. "General Sinsome's given me command of the Hutchinson defenses. General Richards will act as my second. I figure we'll have around 150,000 men. The balance of 1st Corps will be in reserve until they have a chance to catch badly needed rest from their forced march. I plan to place half on the line. The rest are floating reserves until we know what to expect."

Taylor's look turned perplexed. "Justin, please tell me I didn't hear you say the rest of First Army's not coming. Wouldn't they be better off here with us rather than in Salina?" Taylor, incredulous, didn't try to hide his dismay.

Justin tried to skirt over Taylor's question, not wanting to raise his concern. "No, General Sinsome let me know firsthand he spared as many as he could for this defense. He feels it's necessary for him to link up with the Fourth and Third Army contingents coming our way. He left Salina yesterday and is moving south by southeast, making for Wichita, trying to form up sooner. For the moment, Sinsome feels it wise to avoid confrontation with the main Federal Army." Justin talked in clipped fashion, emphasizing every point. Taylor, though disappointed, still marveled at his brother's total control.

"The good news," Justin reiterated, "is that Second Army's contingent is close and is ordered to join us as soon as humanly possible, although it is unlikely they'll be much help to us here. Once we're through with business here, our objective is to link with them and later with Sinsome."

Taylor couldn't resist speaking. "Yeah, and that's if we don't get our asses kicked by that small Federal army facing us. Jesus, Justin, if Sinsome is trying to avoid the main army, what, pray tell, is its strength? Could it be bigger than what's facing us here?"

"Taylor, we will not lose if I have a say about it. But I understand your concern," he whispered, gently grabbing Taylor's arm, not wanting to draw attention. "You can't show open concern to the men. Tay, you're a general officer, now act it."

Taylor stood with a contrite look upon his face. "Yeah, I know, but Justin, we can't continue to be so damn lucky. Look what happened at Vail."

"Yes, Bro, luck's been with us. I'll grant you that. Yet fortune aside, our will to fight got us this far. So, little Bro, let's get positive and back to the business at hand."

Justin's look was hard but brotherly as he spoke. "Word's out the enemy is amassing in Nebraska. Intel thinks they could have as many as one million troops."

Taylor's eyes, seeing the full scope of their dilemma, gave away his concern. "Shit, Justin. Do you have any positive news, emphasis on the positive?"

"Taylor, you must be patient. We'll have something soon. For now, we'll have to make it happen. Simply stated, we can't meet them in Nebraska right now. Sinsome believes, and I concur, that we must do as we've done since the beginning: pick our ground, not theirs, before committing. This means Sinsome's army is in general pullback, except for here. And this is only until our reinforcements arrive, giving us cover to get the hell out of Dodge. We'll see how this plays out. If there's a possibility we'll be flanked, we'll head south and regroup wherever we can."

Trying to return levity to the situation, Taylor could not resist being himself. "Justin, you know Dodge City's not all that far from here," he chuckled. "So I'd watch what I say, Bro. So when can we expect the arrival of Second Army?"

His face showing restraint, Justin replied, "To repeat, not soon enough, not for what we're facing." Justin looked at his brother, whose confusion was evident. He couldn't resist asking any longer. "What's bothering you, Taylor? You seem somewhere else."

"Nothing, Justin! Nothing!" *I can't tell him now. There is so much on his plate and there is nothing we can do to change it.* Anxious to get on with the conversation and to avoid raising his personal concerns, Taylor looked away from his brother's glare.

"Very well then, I'll accept your oblique answer for the moment." Justin continued, "Let's see, where did we leave off? Oh yes, if we must, I'll order a retreat to coincide with Second Army's advance. I've sent several couriers requesting Second Army's forward units to speed it up. I'm awaiting General Joseph's recommended placement of our corps. Since this was his post, I'll rely on his familiarity with the area."

Laughing, Justin pulled a roll of duct tape from his oversized overcoat pocket, surprising Taylor with the sudden turn in the conversation. "Taylor, on the lighter side, my column brought in several cases of captured gray duct tape. You know this is the stuff Dad always used at home. It works wonders to make temporary repairs for shoes and even uniforms. I'll send you a box or two, but I see you can use a roll now," he said as he tossed the roll. "Try to use it sparingly."

"Thanks. Far too many of my men have shoes falling apart. It'll come in handy." Taylor placed his right hand on his brother's broad shoulder. Their eyes met. "Justin, I'll see you soon. Stay low and say a prayer."

Justin looked at his brother again in wonder. Taylor seldom referenced prayer in his conversation.

With General Joseph's arrival, Taylor saluted, excused himself, and took his leave. He walked quickly away, thinking, *When I return to command I'll send a handpicked squad of volunteers to search for that damn bunker. We'll wait until dark.* In his heart, Taylor believed they were alive. He pushed aside his concerns and moved on. Intentionally, he thought of pleasant times. Flashing back several years he saw Becky, about five, playing happily with their new Doberman puppy. "No," losing control of his peaceful image, he anxiously gasped, "please, God, let her live!"

But things were moving too fast and furious, and Taylor had 10,000 men in his command to worry about and a desperate battle to win. Good intentions mean little when the reality of an imminent battle stares a general in the face, and Taylor was not one to shirk responsibility. The squad Taylor sent was annihilated by an advance unit of the enemy Federals positioned for their attack on the Rebels in Hutchinson.

December 12, 2020—Headquarters, 121st Rebel Division Hutchinson, Kansas

A short distance from Taylor, James Rinaldi, tired, dirty, and hungry, looked over newly received orders, wondering what miracle would rescue them. Hunger plagued his every thought. As major general in charge of a division, he could demand sustenance as his due, but he refused to do so. His orderly could not persuade him otherwise. James believed he must feel as his men felt in order to understand their limits. His meteoric rise from the ranks to the command of the 121st Light Infantry Division still seemed unreal—a bad dream. It was true that his promotions had come solely because of his ability to lead, yet the terrible carnage was also a contributing factor. James never allowed himself to forget this simple mathematical lesson of war—only living, vital men lead. And though alive, the numbness of what must be death's sting dug into him with relentless fury. Lately, he quietly went through the motions, just enough to get by. It did little to lessen the pain and worry he carried.

Viewing the activity of the heavy equipment helped underline his sour feeling. The war, out of necessity, had replaced the bulldozer's primary purpose to clear land and to build monuments to civilization. Now its major use, in addition to building defensive works, was digging massive burial trenches for the endless dead. Large mounds of earth continually formed graves for good men like his brother Vic, who died for a cause of which they'd never enjoy the fruits.

It was frightfully true that some men actually enjoyed killing. James never could grasp this freak of nature. As an officer and soldier, however, he was thankful for their existence because the army needed them.

Returning briefly to sanity in an insane world, after his brief pity-party, he thought, *How could a peaceful world welcome these happy, few, killer angels when they were released to a newly rational world?* He thanked God most men wished as he did—a desire and craving for the return of peace and a good life of honor.

Taylor approached. Seeing his friend deep in thought, he reluctantly broke the silence. "James, you seem preoccupied. Should I return later?"

"Hell no, Taylor, I could use a friendly face."

Earlier, Taylor had confided in James about Becky and Luke. Both agreed to hold back on telling Justin, knowing the tremendous responsibility he presently had.

Taylor stepped forward. "I just wanted to personally let you know I've sent a search and rescue party to see if we can find Luke and Becky. I'll let you know when and if."

"Thanks, Taylor; I'm not ready to give another brother to this war. It seems my clan's paid its fair share to the cause. Sorry it shows. It's been hard of late for me to focus; my worry and sorrow has gotten the best of me."

"I know what you mean," Taylor said softly, looking into James's eyes. "We'll find them. Becky's one tough cookie, and if Luke's with her, they'll survive. Sis has always been the toughest of the Northcutts, and after serving with Luke these past months, I can say he's no pushover either."

James turned to Taylor, comfort returning to his face. "In the Rinaldi family we have a saying, 'What will be, will be.' I believe it's in God's hands. Just the same, it's difficult to accept. You know, I truly believe we really don't have much control in life. So if given opportunity, it seems to me it's only by virtue of God's grace that we have it anyway. So, friend, I choose to have faith and place it firmly in His hands."

"Sounds a bit too religious for me, James. Not that we don't need to turn to God, mind you. Heaven knows, my brother Justin's always praying. I just sometimes find it difficult not to place God in all this killing. Thinking of the need for prayer almost made me tell Justin about Becky and Luke. He doesn't need this added to his plate right now. But it bothers the heck out of me, not telling him."

"I know where you're coming from, Taylor, but you did the right thing. I suspect Justin will understand why when it's right to tell him. Besides, what could Justin do that we haven't tried? He doesn't need the distraction. As for your doubts, I can't say I believe God has anything to do with this killing. He gave man free will to do as he pleased. I don't think God planned on the foolish mess man's free will sometimes creates. I honestly feel if we can't have faith in God, then whatever we're fighting for has no meaning, and is a tremendous waste. So I'll keep my faith, if only to retain my sanity." James sat on a wooden supply crate.

Taylor, still standing, took off his helmet. "You sound like my brother. No one can get in the way of his faith either. He says God's not in the middle of war, only that He finds a way to use war for His ultimate purpose. Justin cannot see God as an instrument for evil. All things work, he says, for His good."

James motioned to Taylor to sit on an adjoining crate. Taylor obliged his friend; the wounds he received in Cancun were hurting.

"James, it's mighty good to see the 121st Light Infantry on our right again. Justin's sending orders you'll receive momentarily, saying command will not allow us to take any mercenaries prisoner."

"Yeah, I heard it already through the eternal grapevine we call the rank and file. I'm not sure I'm happy with these orders. All those foreign fools are here for is the booty they expect to amass at our expense. They probably had little going for them back home. It looks like Europe's disarray now comes to haunt us."

"James, as far as I'm concerned, when they butchered our men in Colorado, they threw us both a signal and a warning. This, my friend, is where this here war's going. It's now a fight-or-die situation, and they pushed the wrong unit if they think the 36th will surrender to get butchered. My boys will make them pay dearly. We'll follow those orders to take no prisoners until they're pulled, and James, I suggest you do the same."

"You need not worry. Following those orders will be easier since we've heard several hundred New Yorkers were killed at Vail Pass. If we're going to die, we'll die taking as many of the Euro scum with us as we can. It's not right, but I'm getting used to doing things that bother my conscience."

"I'll send word if we find our kin, James. I expect, though, that tomorrow will give us a lot more to think about than family. You know, it's strange they haven't attacked yet. Surely they know they outnumber us."

"I figure they're probably straggling in from Colorado. Most likely they're resting and taking their time to regroup, figuring their best approach." James adjusted his scarf around his neck, unsuccessfully trying to ward off the cold.

Taylor slowly lifted his sore body from the crate. "I expect we'll know soon enough. Let's be thankful the idiots gave us more time to dig in and prepare for them."

"Amen to that. See you later, Taylor, and keep low."

"You likewise." James firmly grasped Taylor's right hand, renewed, raw determination in his eyes.

December 12, 2020—Entrapped Bunker, Hutchinson, Kansas

The bunker's entrance was sealed by tons of debris. Dust settled, uncaring, on the dead and the living. Luke lay unconscious in an involuntary, protective posture above Becky.

As she came to, Becky's blurred eyes tried desperately to focus in the endless dark. Luke's limp body, wrapped protectively upon her, caused a numb, frightening feeling in her body. She shook him fearfully, thinking the worst, and shouted out in fright, "Luke, Luke, please be alive! Speak to me!"

She felt for his pulse and found its low steady beat telegraphing his life's energy. Becky managed to move his comatose body from her. Crawling around, she stumbled upon a lantern. Reaching for a match in her fatigue pocket, she quickly lit it to assess her situation. In the dim light, she saw wounded and dying all about her. Many were badly dazed. Others would not make it through the next few hours. The air was dank, but the lantern's steady burning gave some certainty of sufficient oxygen. Looking at her watch, still surprisingly working, she calculated she had been unconscious for several hours.

"Luke, please wake up," she pleaded.

Luke stirred slightly, a soft hiss of air escaping his swollen jaw. Becky held the light to his body. From a quick professional glance, his wound did not appear life-threatening.

"Please, Lord," she spoke softly, "let him live."

Luke slurred, his voice a rasping croak.

"Beck, is that you? Are ya OK?"

"Yes, Luke, I'm fine, thanks to you. Stay still and let me see to your injuries." Luke passed out again while she worked on his wounds. He had a concussion. She would need to keep him awake, no matter what.

She looked around her desolate surroundings, finding little solace. The bunker, badly damaged, was mostly intact, but she feared it could cave in at any moment. She called frantically for help; none came. No one could hear her shout. Only the pitiful souls of the wounded and dying entombed with her could hear her voice echoing off the damp walls.

With further scrutiny, she observed she was the only person in one piece. Right now, and by some miracle, she was alive because of Luke. For the moment this was all that mattered. She had one purpose, keeping Luke alive and helping whomever she could by whatever means she could devise. *Help me*, she thought. *Will there be any help for me?* She felt very alone.

The flame in the Coleman lantern continued to burn brightly, giving continued evidence that oxygen was adequate. She searched the ground through the rubble to find a slightly bent flashlight. It was partially buried, hidden beneath a mound of debris. She dug it up, placing it in her fatigue pocket.

The agonized moan from a wounded soldier cried out for her attention. Becky's inner panic gave way to her sense of duty. There was nowhere to run, no way to escape the frightful cries of terror filling the bleak cavern. "Becky," she told herself aloud. "You'll have to take hold and get through this." Her emotions gave rise to a rush of adrenalin; it overrode her fear and pushed her into action.

"What's the racket?" A feeble voice caught her attention.

She crawled in the direction of the familiar, now broken, voice of Luke. His face, badly swollen, caused her less concern now that it showed a happy recognition of the fact that he was alive, and glad of it. Becky felt light-headed; the joy and the stress of the moment were having their effects.

"Luke, listen to me," she shouted. "You've had a bad concussion. You must stay awake. You've taken a bad hit on your head. Do you understand me?"

"Sure do, Nurse Becky. So you're my nurse again!" He spoke painfully and stubbornly, his voice rattled. "You know, Honey, my hearing's still good."

"Luke, relax, I need you. We have a lot of work ahead of us if we're to get out of here. Rest. I've got to help the others. There are so many others. Oh, Luke, I love you."

She kissed him gently on his forehead before going about the grim work of separating the dead from the breathing. She made a silent promise to herself that, come hell or high water, she'd be amongst the living when this was over.

With parched and trembling lips, Becky's shout bounced off the bunker's walls, giving encouragement to anyone who could hear her outcry from within their man-made tomb. "Hold on, I promise I'll help you. Please hold on!" She wished she could believe herself. Words now seemed helpless in this place where only action could make a difference.

She heard a constant rumble above her as dust continually fell from the bunker's ceiling. Its haunting, disturbing presence awakened her senses to new resolve.

Each mortal, in his own time, perfects his meager existence according to a higher schedule.

—Jim Damiano

CHAPTER TWENTY-TWO

December 14, 2020—Rebel Army Headquarters, Hutchinson, Kansas

The cluttered room, dark and solemn, gave little comfort or warmth. Justin methodically reviewed the faces of each of his generals. Their expressions universally showed a hunger and weariness. Each carried the unabashed expectation of the worst. Yet, to a man, their resolve prepared each to accept whatever happened. If the moment's mood appeared somber and quiet, it also stressed the kindling spirit of revolution which still burned brightly.

Justin stood to speak, vaporous clouds rising from his breath in tribute to the cold weather that seemed determined to stay. "Gentlemen," he began, his baritone voice filling the area, its pitch highlighting his extreme concern, "we cannot realistically hold this position as situated. General Sinsome sends word that observers spotted a mass movement of Federals moving south from their base in Nebraska. It appears the esteemed General Newman has finally found the nerve to start an offensive. There is some heartening news, though. All contingents from Second, Third, and Fourth Armies will arrive, meeting General Sinsome as planned, within the day.

"We're still outnumbered; no surprise there." Several in the room laughed, taking the brief opportunity to loosen up. "General Sinsome, as I speak, is turning his force and striking north to harass their advance, buying some time for the reinforcements."

General Rinaldi interrupted. "Are we to join forces with General Sinsome?"

"I was about to get to that, James. Please bear with me." Justin, undisturbed, always encouraged his men to think and speak out. It was one of the key strengths of his command. "It seems we're stuck here. If we leave, we expose our flank and endanger Sinsome's bold maneuver. Intel believes the enemy has 400,000 troops directly in front of us. And they, gentlemen, would like nothing better than to get between us and Sinsome. If they do, they'll destroy us at their option. I ask myself constantly, 'Why the heck haven't they attacked us?' We certainly can't leave. We're too exposed. So to answer my own question, it is most likely they haven't attacked because the fools believe we're where they want us. I thank God for their procrastination."

Brigadier General Owens spoke out. "General, isn't God supposed to be on our side? Perhaps he wants us to feel good about ourselves." This drew more unsettled laughter, but the officer's outburst didn't please Justin. Several men knew of his religious outlook and kept quiet—including Taylor, who, if given the opportunity, would gladly kick the crap out of Owens.

Justin, though uncomfortable upon hearing his God joked about, knew it loosened his worried men some, and chose to ignore the off-handed comment.

"Back to the business at hand, Gentlemen, and I say this with caution," Justin smiled. It was good to see the ease coming back into the room. "The enemy before us is a valid threat. It won't go away without a fight. So be it—if they choose to wait cautiously for their next move, it doesn't mean we should wait for them. Therefore, we will attack the Feds as soon as Second Army's contingent gets within sight of our lines."

"What, reinforcements?" Taylor's blue eyes met his brother's. "I thought we're to be left to ourselves, or at best to fight our way out, and rejoin Sinsome's main army. This change is confusing. Justin, weren't the initial plans for Second Army to direct their columns toward Sinsome and send a few of its advance troops to aid us?"

"Taylor, you're right. That was the plan—plans change. I guess I wasn't clear. Sorry. General Sinsome has diverted the 8th Corps with its six divisions to join us." The news brought hurrahs from the crowded group of men, happy for any positive news. "They should be arriving momentarily. They'll add close to 100,000 men to our defense."

"General, what's our plan of attack?" General Joseph asked from the rear of the bunker. "It appears we're still outnumbered about two-to-one."

Justin's voice rose to the occasion. "Not quite two-to-one, and when the hell did being outnumbered bother us? As for a plan, there's none just yet. I'll have one before the day's end. Until then, we must hold until the enemy believes he has us. Our primary objective is to sucker and stop them from linking with General Newman. If estimates are correct, their force represents about thirty percent of Newman's army. Therefore, they must be held right here, in check—at all costs, to enable General Sinsome to regroup and work out his strategy. If we're not successful here—well, Gentlemen, the proverbial shit will hit the fan."

"More importantly, to insure our success, 8th Corps will need a chance to recuperate before we can implement an effective offensive. They've been on a forced march and pushing their limit for ten solid days. They surely aren't tip-top for an immediate assault. Timing's a factor and also a premium to us right now."

"Sorry, General, I'm confused." James stepped forward. "Why not attack immediately when 8th Corps arrives? We'll have over 250,000 combat veterans, many fresh from Mexico. This is certainly more than a match for those assholes facing us." Rinaldi pointed his arm in the enemy's direction.

Justin instinctively sensed the change in mood, detecting an electric excitement. Officers, good men all about to voluntarily lay their lives on the line, were entitled to a better explanation. He hadn't initially planned to give out everything he knew. Now, despite orders to the contrary, he decided it necessary and worth the risk. His good men deserved to know everything.

"OK, here's the bottom line. James, it's good to see at least one of my generals paid attention. I'm about to include y'all in formulating plans to develop a holding pattern intended to confuse the Feds, while we set our trap to engulf them in their own stupidity. If you, Sirs, are collectively confused, then it's hoped it spread to the enemy. I purposely lied about not having a plan." Men familiar with Justin quickly knew he had set them up. Where practical, he liked his men to play a part in his decisions. It served to get them totally involved.

Justin paced, speaking briskly, "Men, I don't want to be the one that's swallowed up, nor do I like being bait. So here's my plan." Justin's eyes fixed directly upon Taylor's. No one in the room missed the implied message, or the word "bait."

Leaving room for discussion and input, Justin outlined his plan. For two hours they worked and reworked their strategy to a conclusion that Justin could accept with a few tweaks. After several adjustments, the operation was to his satisfaction. Everyone agreed that the strategy, now reduced to paper, was still chancy at best. Under the circumstances, though, it was their only logical option. Simply put, if Justin's force moved too soon to aid Sinsome, it would expose the southern flank of the Rebel Army. As long as there was a formidable enemy force in the vicinity, it must be destroyed or at least delayed to buy time.

Justin stopped pacing, his jaw clenched, eyes focused. "Men, the next move is up to the Federals. Let's hope they follow our lead." *Deep down I give this a fifty-fifty chance, even if it goes according to schedule.*

"If they don't counterattack as hoped, we'll need to revise tactics. We can't hold this line indefinitely, especially without rations. The good news is 8th Corps is bringing a large supply of food. I'm sorry to say it's probably only enough for a couple days' rations. Feed your men well, Gentlemen. It may be literally the last meal for many and definitely the last one until we break out. As you all know, with full bellies and reenergized bodies, men are better able to cope and to face uncertainty."

He turned abruptly to his maps, looking one more time for any black hole in his thought process. It was time to end the planning session. Turning to his men, he said, "Return to your commands to prepare. You'll be informed if I deem another meeting necessary. Thanks for your help. Dismissed."

The room emptied except for a few hangers-on. Justin turned his full attention to General Richards.

"Justin, our strategy appears sound, and like you, I believe we have little other option. Still, what if the enemy attacks before we do?"

"We may be screwed, Vince." Justin stared past General Richards. For a brief moment, his heart was elsewhere. A bright picture of Julia's face with her beautiful smile, framed indelibly within his mind, tossed him a curve. Stealing a brief, silent moment, he prayed for her safety. Those men still standing near him thought him distracted. Justin caught himself and turned his attention back to urgent priorities of the moment. He saw Taylor staring, and knew without a doubt that his brother had read his change of mood.

Recently promoted Corporal Julia McKnight parked her eighteen-wheeler where directed. Her motor pool brigade had been assigned to the relief forces from the Second Army's 8th Corps. The supply of foodstuff on her truck was quickly unloaded, a welcome site for the hungry troops. She had volunteered for hazardous duty, hoping to see Justin, though knowing it was probably a slim chance at best.

"Corporal, move your truck to this intersection." An officer pointed to the location on his worn sector map. "You are to go back south to pick up troops in all haste and return here."

Julia took her map out to highlight the coordinates with her pencil. Her truck was part of a convoy of forty other vehicles of varied description. The Rebel motor pool pressed anything with wheels into service. If fuel held up, it stayed in business. Luckily, Hutchinson had a good supply.

The ordinance officer continued his directions. He addressed the drivers who were standing at attention, awaiting orders to pull out. "You will shuttle all the troopers you can with the fuel available. When done, abandon your trucks as safely as possible and rejoin this unit. If unable to do so, attach yourself to whatever unit your last load carries. In the coming engagement, everyone is expected to participate. Make certain your weapon is in working order; I know you truck jockeys don't pay attention to your arms. Do it now; it may save your life."

Julia didn't need to be told to check her rifle; it was second nature to her ever since Del Rio. She climbed into the cab of her 2017 Mac truck, shifted gears, and moved out slowly in the direction of her assignment. Her truck followed several lengths behind the vehicle ahead.

She had learned to live day-to-day, and this day was no exception. Her body ached from driving nonstop for twenty-four hours, living on coffee wherever she could find it. Caffeine was a lifesaver. She was not alone; the past grueling ten days had taken their toll on her unit. But she understood the necessity of the mission and hoped her personal sacrifice helped to bring the war closer to conclusion.

Julia's hands clutched the steering wheel tightly. She longed for a hot bath and tried unsuccessfully not to think of how itchy and dirty she felt. A stickler for cleanliness, she was privately embarrassed at how badly she reeked. Everyone in the army was in the same fix, though; at least the cold weather helped hide her mortification. Besides, it appeared no one noticed or cared any longer.

Driving, she let her mind wander aimlessly, occasionally falling into pleasant thoughts of running water, warm luxuriant baths, and soft, fragrant soap. These once casual luxuries seemed to possess her. Despite the frustration, it helped her to relax and accept.

The narrow dirt road, hastily built by Rebel engineers, forced her to pay attention to the hazards ahead. Dust cloaked everything, painting it the color of the land she passed.

The cold, crisp day did little to awaken her senses to anything but the rote of driving and daydreaming. Coughing, she expertly reached for her canteen without swerving, cutting the dust from her throat. As she downshifted to slow her speed, she thought, *I'm just another Rebel with a cause, choking to death in the middle of nowhere.* Her laugh was short-lived as she slammed her brakes, just missing the vehicle ahead. Its driver, another woman, gave Julia a look that could kill. She ignored her, too tired to give a damn.

Hours passed before her last load of combat soldiers was dropped near the position held by the 121st Division. Julia knew this unit. It was this division that had come to the rescue of Justin's Texans at Del Rio. She had also heard that it was attached to Justin's 1st Corps. This could mean only one thing, *Justin must be nearby. Well, I'll just have to attach myself somehow to the 36th.* She figured Justin would probably make his HQ near his old division, now commanded by his self-assured and very attractive brother. She delivered her truck to the spot designated and watched as men carefully put camouflage netting over it to conceal it from prying enemy eyes.

Julia walked briskly up to an officer nearby. She saluted. "Sir, could you direct me to the 36th Division?"

The Captain returned her salute, not missing her beauty hidden beneath the road grime. "Corporal, it's to my left, about two miles. Follow the signs and look for the faded yellow farm house."

The Federal attack on Hutchinson came the early evening of December 14th, trumping Justin's offensive strategy by six hours. Its primary objective, as expected, was to coordinate with General Newman's southern advance into northern Kansas. Its secondary effort was to prevent Justin's army from aiding General Sinsome. Raging Federals charged in good order through the darkening fields, now lightly dusted with falling snow. Temperatures fell into the low teens. Unknown to Justin's Rebels, the Federals were on President Collin's schedule, ordered December 10th at his meeting in Lincoln to coordinate with earlier plans to advance the entire Federal Army by the 16th.

Rebel units prepared for the onslaught. Their stomachs, filled with the first warm meal in several days, lifted their spirits. Unfortunately, they had insufficient time to digest the feast.

The first wave included many raw Federal mercenaries, advancing across open, wintry fields. The carefully calculated charge was covered by concentrated artillery fire. Their vicious barrage was met with equal determination by Rebel artillery, furiously adjusting its response with terrible effect upon the untried mercenaries.

Justin, close to the front-line defenses, focused his night-vision binoculars across the open ground. Quickly he realized they were unnecessary. Shells ignited the air with phosphorescent light, shaking the earth's crust. Rebel artillery, at Justin's command, redirected its coordinates. The effect was devastating to any living creature trying to cross in the unprotected fields.

Suddenly, Justin realized with pounding anticipation that the enemy's three-pronged assault was weakest at his army's center. It seemed their immediate intent was to split a wedge into his command and destroy it section by weakened section. "Well," he shouted above the din, "two can play the same motherless game." He signaled for his couriers.

Grabbing one by his arm, he shouted, "Direct General Appleton to concentrate all his artillery to the center of the enemy's attack. I repeat, all. Do you understand?" The courier nodded. "Tell Appleton, do not, I repeat, do *not* fire on the flanks. I want nothing alive in the enemy's center sector!"

"Yes, Sir!" The young boy, about thirteen, left as if on a marathon, his strong legs pumping hard.

Calling two other youngsters, he directed, "Advise Generals T. Northcutt and Rinaldi to advance their divisions at once. You two, come." He pointed out two teens listening nearby, motioning them forward. "Have the 20th and 42nd move in from their reserve positions. They are to back the 36th and 121st in their advance."

To the remaining messengers, he shouted, "All other divisions are to advance in their respective sectors only until it's clear that Rinaldi and Northcutt are successful. Advise each to watch for our signal. Now run like hell's fire, and don't stop till you get there!" *So young, so damn young,* he thought.

Justin's messengers reached their assignments, doling out his verbal orders. Taylor, upon hearing them, read his brother's mind, understanding immediately what he hoped to accomplish. He mumbled, "Hot damn, do exactly what they don't expect. Here we go, once again into the fire, " he said aloud to no one. "Sacrificial lambs …"

Taylor shouted to his adjutant, "Pass the word to each regiment. Have the men lock and load, fix bayonets, and prepare to charge as soon as the enemy barrage lifts."

The Federal troops were now in view of his defenses and vulnerable to friendly fire. He'd give the word to advance when the time was right. Taylor's mind raged. His blood pulsed rapidly. His face tightened with determination. They would not have to wait long for the enemy fire to slow.

To Taylor's left, General Rinaldi issued like orders. James sensed the rising bile in his throat. He felt his only good supper in days about to leave his long-suffering stomach. It wasn't so much caused by fear, but the rapid rise of pulsing adrenalin. The painful thought of possible extinction mocked his body's need for nourishment.

The enemy barrage lifted as anticipated. Federal troops appeared in full view, coming on like shadows in the rapidly failing light. Rebel flares illuminated the sky, revealing thousands of screeching Federals. As one, the entire Rebel front exploded, firing into the ranks of the closely packed, oncoming foe.

In as little as a second, the whole perimeter directly in front of the 36th and 121st Divisions exploded into oblivion. Every available Rebel artillery piece hit the area. When the barrage lifted, Justin's command to advance was carried out as the two light-infantry shock divisions leaped from the protection of their trenches, attacking like disheveled devils in their torn and tattered uniforms, like avenging phantoms. It was complete, conventional war taken to peaks beyond description or man's imagination.

On cue, as if rehearsed, the Rebels screamed, "Remember Vail! Give no quarter!" The clash of the two titans could be heard for miles. One by one, Rebel regiments to the left and right of the two attacking divisions were moved up to join the advance, forming a giant split-V, carving systematically into the Federal attack. Driving forward, in its intended arc, the Rebels stormed in the desired direction, allowing Justin's hasty plan to take on a life of its own. Waiting reserve units filled ragged gaps in the advancing line left by the Rebel shock troops. They waited their turn to be unleashed upon the mostly-foreign enemy infantry.

Early snow now raged into a major storm, blinding the combatants, while earth shook with the clash of hand-to-hand combat. Men fell in every conceivable space, giving the field the appearance of a carpet of fallen, crowded bodies upon the reddened snow-driven earth.

The battle raged for hours. Both opposing armies sent in all their reserves. However, the fury of the Rebel's initial counterattack was never matched. The mercenaries began to understand fully the folly of their venture. Today, the Rebel Army they met was not a group of mostly untried, ambushed Rebels, but a well-organized, disciplined, mean-spirited enemy. It was an enemy giving more than it received, without mercy, venting its voracious appetite for blood. Like angels of vengeance, none of the Federals were allowed to surrender; few wounded were left alive. Somehow these ragged Rebels, though outnumbered, did not know they were supposed to lose, according to President Collins' well-orchestrated plan.

The Federal rookies' minimal battle experience was insufficient to allow them the status of veterans. They faced the Rebel onslaught in terror. They were numbed by their inability to surprise and take advantage of their numerical superiority over the Rebel veterans. To a man, each Rebel realized he had faced tougher adversaries than the foreigners and American Westerners, who were dying by the score before them. Many relished in the killing field; it gave them the chance to even the score for Vail. They killed like madmen until too exhausted to continue.

Before the battle ended, and when it became clear the day belonged to his army, Justin countermanded the orders from General Sinsome to kill all prisoners. He could not emotionally carry out what he felt was murder. They were slaughtering the Federals like sheep. After all was said and done, the Federals were men, like him, who did as commanded by officers, who were no different than he. He felt ill at ease at the comparison.

The enemy began to surrender after realizing that mercy would be given. Justin's action was not solely benevolent, for it also saved further Rebel casualties. His previous order still stood in one regard—no mercy was given to captured enemy officers, particularly mercenaries. Justin ordered the execution of their officers, from lieutenant to general. He could not let them live; he knew he must make an example. After all, he reasoned, as a group they could have shown the same humanity and refused to follow immoral orders. *They made their bed, choosing blindly to carry out orders against the rules of civilized war. Now they will pay. My mercy is greater than that given to our Rebel forces at Vail Pass.*

Justin figured General Sinsome would reprimand him, but for the moment, he really didn't give a damn. When asked for an explanation by Sinsome's observing officer on the scene, he just shook his head and in a clear proud voice said, "Colonel, for thirty hours we killed and wounded over 250,000 enemy soldiers. The blood of my men and the enemy is up to my elbows. This war will end someday, along with the killing. I just couldn't order any more unarmed or disabled murdered. No matter the order. It's not the world I want to return to if and when we are victorious."

Justin, rage flaming in his eyes, stated firmly, "If Raif wants my stars, you tell him they're his to take."

Colonel Edwards, moved by Justin's stand, was unsure how to comment. He chose to speak from the heart. "Sir, it will have to be General Sinsome's call." He smiled, "Sir, off the record, I think you did the right thing, and it's been an honor for me to have seen it."

Justin, for the moment, did not care what anyone thought. He would follow his conscience from now on.

With victory at Hutchinson, Justin moved his once hardy force, now reduced by 100,000 casualties, northeast to link with the main Rebel Army. In the massive withdrawal, he left behind 10,000 troops to bury the dead and escort prisoners. Vultures again were happy and heavily gorged, gliding sluggishly in the wintry air, ever watching from their lofty heights. Justin left Hutchinson, tucking another major battle under his belt, another terror-filled memory to carry forever. But not today—today he was too numb to think. The cold and horror of Hutchinson and now the unknown awaiting his marching army had deadened all feeling.

Justin was still unaware that his sister was missing in action, and Taylor was too far from him to request a temporary leave to look for her. Taylor's division was ordered to leave on the double, and he had not heard from his missing rescue squad. He did the only thing he could. He sent out a platoon with instructions to advise him as soon as they could. But the haste needed to link up with Sinsome's army overrode all his personal needs; he was resigned to his duty, though fear for Becky's safety enveloped him.

Several trucks passed. Justin stood outside his vehicle watching a medical convoy pass slowly by. He'd given them the right of way. The wounded, his wounded, needed care; his march could wait. Then he spotted her driving a big blue Mac truck.

The convoy had gathered its scattered drivers, recruiting new men to replace those fallen in battle. It was now moving wounded as quickly as possible to warmer aid stations to the south. Julia, having done her share of the fighting with the 36th, was happy to be back driving. She wished, somehow, to wash the scent of blood from her memory. She was numb with the horror of watching Rebels shooting wounded enemy soldiers and hearing their pitiful pleas for mercy. Her adopted unit, Company P, 3rd Ranger Regiment, followed their orders to a tee. She couldn't do it, but no one seemed to notice or care. Her one known kill during combat had been difficult enough. At least it was on equal terms of kill or be killed.

"Stop that truck, Sergeant!" Justin shouted, pointing to Julia's mud-and-snow-encrusted vehicle. "I need to talk to that driver."

"Yes, Sir!" The sergeant waved Julia's eighteen-wheeler to a halt. Julia, startled from her unpleasant thoughts, did not need an explanation. She immediately saw Justin standing by the road next to his command vehicle, a late model Humvee, parked in the snow on the road's shoulder. A brisk wind whipped at the falling snow.

She saluted after stepping down from the cab. Standing on the truck's lower step, smiling, she said crisply, "At your service, General."

"Forget rank for a moment, Julia. It's sure good to see you." Justin, with all the tensions of the past days, reached out and held her in his arms, clinging passionately to her. Her love was the only thing that kept him going—it and a future that patiently waited for peace.

Julia's tears flowed freely, causing narrow streaks on her muddy face. Briefly, but not for long, she protested their being so close. In a more pleasant time, she would never have presented herself to someone she loved in such a ragged, unclean state. She noticed quickly that her general was in similar straits. They caressed with the universal energy of young people in love. Passing troops cheered with delight at the couple's embrace, and also for their general's fine choice. Julia unwittingly represented every love left behind by so many of the lonely, tired, and hungry men marching to unknown fates. She became an instant tonic for those fortunate enough to be close, seeing their reunion.

"Sergeant, get someone to drive this truck. I can't have my future wife remain in the motor pool. I'm dismissing her from duty."

The sergeant smiled, and with sudden insight shouted, "General, with your permission, I always wanted to be a trucker. I'll take over if it's OK with you."

"Go ahead, Sarge. When you return, you'll find us somewhere in Kansas. Godspeed to you, and be careful."

He turned his attention back to his beautiful corporal. "Julia, we've got a lot of catching up to do."

"Justin," Julia's eyes were wide with glee and glistening with tears. "Did you just call me your future wife? Is this a proposal?"

"That it is. What do you say?"

"Yes, yes, I'll marry you, Justin Northcutt." The men within hearing broke out in triumphant cheers for their general and his girl. This was not the intimate and private moment Justin envisioned, but it resonated with the same impact. For once in several long arduous months, Justin acted his age, and it felt damn good.

Justin whispered, "Honey, I must get you to safety. Do you mind my pulling rank? I want you to live, even if I might not make it. You are the future, and I don't want to risk losing you any longer, not while I can change things. There is so little we are allowed to control. Let me do this for you."

"Justin, I did sign on as a volunteer, and I feel wrong about taking an easy way out. I want to marry you more than life itself, but please let me decide how I serve my country. If you want to do something for me, ban me from the infantry. I fought at Hutchinson with the 36th, and I don't think I shall ever forget it." Julia looked at him, tears falling, trying to remain cheerful, but the terrible memory made it difficult. "Justin, can you understand?"

Justin looked horrified upon hearing she had seen the slaughter. He wiped away her tears. "I'll try to understand. Let's give it a rest for a while and discuss it after we have a chance to catch up. Right now, I only want to absorb every second I have with you."

They kissed once again, clasping together in the cold wintry morning, oblivious to everything in their peaceful bliss. Only this moment mattered. The war would have to wait a few minutes.

Several yards away, Taylor, amused, observed his brother's happiness. Seeing Julia brought back pleasant thoughts of a pretty nurse he had fallen for when he was wounded in Mexico. Silently, he wondered if it wasn't time for him to taste life.

He pondered for a moment; Julia's sudden appearance had stifled his present attempt to finally advise Justin about Becky and Luke. With the column stopped, Taylor had almost made his way to Justin. They had not talked since before the battle, and he needed to get Becky's dilemma off his chest and share his concerns. But he'd let it pass for now. Though anxious, Taylor would grant Justin a few minutes of peace.

Tomorrow will have to be soon enough. Maybe by then I'll have some word. Taylor turned away, sick with his burden and filled with dread. *Maybe James's search party will get lucky.* With limited hope, Taylor returned to his command vehicle.

You learn that, whatever you are doing in life, obstacles don't matter very much. Pain or other circumstances can be there, but if you want to do a job bad enough, you'll find a way to get it done.

–Jack Youngblood

CHAPTER TWENTY-THREE

December 15, 2020—Kansas-Nebraska Border
Two Miles South of Falls City, Nebraska

A new dawn awoke to sounds of man-made thunder. Brilliant flashes from the mouths of enemy artillery illuminated the early morning's gray-black sky. General Raif Sinsome reluctantly approached the new day, thankful for yet another opportunity to serve. Outside his bunker and happy to be alive, he looked directly into the rising sun, closing his eyes to embrace its welcoming warmth.

Old habits die hard. Raif's daily ritual included greeting each morning with a short prayer, taking time to enjoy nature's peace, no matter the circumstance or obstacle. Today, finding solace was difficult. The enemy had unwittingly disturbed his routine. For a passing uncontrollable moment, he felt weak. He reached into his pocket for another cigarette.

Cigarette smoke billowed in great white whiffs into the cold morning air. With eyes closed, trying to pray, he faced the sun, seeing the red umber of its presence. For a flashing second, he was young again, exploring unknown horizons. He felt peace, recalling wonderful days when the morning sun's inviting rays welcomed a new day, another time, giving ample chance to explore life with his lost youthful exuberance. This morning seemed unlike those others. Yet in his heart he felt triumph very near.

Troubled, he speculated calmly, *Victory, like defeat, could happen in a flash.* The pressure upon him showed its ugly side. Stubbornly, angst remained his constant burden. But the burden was one willingly carried, despite an inner desire to run like hell. Now, with the Federals readying to unleash their most determined effort to date, he'd need more than past magic to stop their determination. He needed God and a miracle.

Melancholy temporarily replaced sound reasoning. He longed for the lost prowess of devoted Rebel leaders who had been killed or maimed. Their sacrifice, forever lost to the cause, haunted him. Trying to make sense out of the confusion, he thought of the many martyrs that got him this far. Now he needed them more than ever. With sickening realization, he feared their sacrifice would be in vain. This vivid, shocking reality revived him, nurturing the strength he needed to ask his army for one last desperate campaign. Sadly, he knew it was all his army had left. The thought unnerved him.

News of victory at Hutchinson both greeted him and simultaneously introduced his biggest challenge—to go for broke and bet it all on one final campaign. Justin's recent success gave him the assurance that the First Army wouldn't be outflanked. Now, though skeptical about his original plan, he was ready to reactivate it.

Justin's heavily damaged force was expected to link up momentarily with the First Army. His 1st Corps, along with the 8th Corps it had absorbed, wouldn't be the factor needed to determine the difference between victory and defeat; they had done enough by anyone's calculation. Intel claimed the Federals continued to retain their two-to-one advantage. If called upon, Justin's surviving 140,000 hardened veterans brought the right stuff needed to tip the balance: Raif hoped they would not be needed.

Raif, contemplating options, decided to place Justin's command in reserve until they regained fighting stamina. He'd call on the 1st Corps' notorious fighting mystique at the right time, preferring to wait until the opportunity for the final act arose. The pride of the rebellion, 1st Corps had done more than its share of the fighting and dying. It badly needed a period of well-earned rest.

Raif reviewed countless reports earlier, but nothing unexpected crossed his scrutiny. It didn't seem probable that General Newman would try to outmaneuver his army—not yet, anyway. *Perhaps, my old friend is licking his wounds over his disastrous defeat in Hutchinson.* Even with Newman's numerical advantage, his actions continued to be predictable. Since

Raif had known him, Newman had never been a gambler. At West Point, he was the cadet who would perpetually contemplate a situation from every angle; his conduct was faultless. However, Newman's caution hadn't played out well in summer exercises. It was here Raif outshined him, often making Newman look bad. *Will Skip continue procrastinating, just once more?* It was the million-dollar question.

"General!" Captain Milton, a staff officer, rushed from the command bunker, excitement in his voice. Out of breath, with the cold air billowing around him, he energized the moment with his youth.

"Yes, Captain, what's got you so excited?" Raif asked calmly.

"Sir, General Northcutt's column is twenty miles south. He respectfully requests, with his compliments, the deployment of his troops."

Surprised, Raif thought, *Justin's made it here already; he must have really pushed his men. Thank God for determined men.*

Raif's mind shifted into high gear, snapping out a reply. "Captain, please advise General Northcutt his men are to be held in reserve, right here." He pointed to a position about five miles south of current lines on the pocket map pulled from his coat. "Advise him to report to me as soon as practical. Right now, his orders are to rest his troops. They'll need to be ready when we call for them."

"Very well, Sir. With this clear weather, my motorbike should get me to General Northcutt in a few minutes." He snapped a smart salute and left quickly.

Raif returned to his command post. He no sooner entered when he was intercepted. "Sir," his aide, appearing badly agitated, said, "the Feds have broken through our eastern line at Pawnee City. They are attempting to flank our 12th Division. It's those damn mercenaries, Sir; reports claim they're shouting 'no mercy.' It's confirmed this bunch of weasels come from Russia."

Raif grabbed the officer's shoulders and shook him to awaken his resolve. Calmly and in measured tones, he spoke. "Major, please, control yourself. I will not allow panic in my command. Send the 10th Kansas to help plug the gap. Aren't they in reserve, about there?" Raif pointed to the map tacked on the wall above his temporary desk.

"Yes, Sir, they are. I'm sorry, Sir."

"Forget it, Major. We've our work cut out for us, so let's get to it. Now, let's see." Raif hesitated before he spoke. "Advise General Holland to pull in his lines to support the 12th Kansas. Inform him the enemy is not giving quarter. Remind him that I expect likewise. Send couriers to pass this on to all my generals, immediately. Now get going, Major. Move it!"

Raif was hot from sudden anger, despite the ten-degree temperature. He didn't enjoy getting down to the new level to which the war had taken him.

Newman's actions convinced him, now more than ever, that the end was near. It was out of character for Newman to move in bad weather. The Feds, no doubt, were as anxious as he, and he mustn't lose sight of the obvious in the midst of the hype. Time was running out and the war turned precariously into a crapshoot. Opportunity and reality hit Raif like a rock.

Excited, Raif called out. "Captain, come on the double." Raif handed him a note. "Take this to General Northcutt. Advise him this rescinds what I just sent. Understand?"

The youthful captain set his jaw, snapping, "Yes, Sir!"

"Grab whatever transportation you can and take two additional couriers. I need to be sure this gets through. Northcutt must immediately send two divisions to our eastern line. I'm requesting, if possible, that he send the 36th and 121st Divisions to fill the gap in our line, right here." He pointed to the break of the line, highlighted on his situation map. "It's fortunate Northcutt arrived only minutes from the breakthrough. Advise Justin to have his divisions travel light, leaving all backpacks and equipment behind, taking only necessary munitions and weapons with extra rounds. We need nothing less than lightning speed from them. Hurry, before you're caught in the crossfire."

The captain raced at breakneck speed to carry out his mission, reaching Justin in less than an hour. Justin's column snaked out over ten miles. Luckily for Sinsome, both the 36th and 121st divisions were in the front ranks. Justin, reluctantly but quickly, sent them as ordered, putting Taylor in command.

Justin gestured to his adjutant, "Major, please have General Richards move 8th Corps to the directed reserve position and prepare 1st Corps to follow Taylor in three hours. Tell Richards I'll return as soon as I can! It appears things are getting nasty." He turned back to the courier. "Captain, lead me to General Sinsome's headquarters at once."

Taylor's 36th Division was the first to arrive at the breach. Half of James's 121st Division arrived minutes later. They had pushed their men beyond their limits of endurance. The scene unraveling before them was not pretty. Like a bad dream, the refuse of war lay before them: men shackled with defeat and chaos. The Federal Army, systematic in its onslaught, left death everywhere in sight.

Taylor grasped James's hand. James could see the deep-set strain on his friend's face as he opened the conversation. "Taylor, what's the situation?"

"James, glad you made it here so damn quickly. You must have flown."

James nodded, saying little, awaiting Taylor's assessment.

"It looks like we've got our work cut out for us," Taylor said. "Our scouts corroborated with officers on the line. They report the Feds have broken a two-mile gap directly ahead. The good news is they didn't immediately follow up their success at the breach, but you can be certain the bastards will do so, and soon. So we've not a moment to spare."

"Sorry, Taylor, I only have half my division here. The rest should be here in fifteen minutes. Is there time?"

"James, we'll have to make due with what we have." Taylor quickly chose his next move. "Place your troops at either side of mine. Have them immediately reinforce what's left of our line that hasn't been compromised. I'm told the gap we need to fill is about one to two miles wide. There's little left of the Missouri 5th. The Kansas 12th still holds some ground in scattered pockets directly in front of our present position."

"Who will we reinforce?"

"James, it looks like your men will aid the Oklahoma 20th on our left and the 1st Louisiana on the right of the breach. I want you to stay here with me as my second until the rest of your division arrives."

"You've got it!" James saluted quickly, leaving to carry out his orders. Taylor's tired but unbeaten men momentarily stood alone, ready to retake the gap.

Without time for further analysis and insane with rage and the pain of unhealed wounds, Taylor shouted to his commanders, "Lock and load, attach bayonets—let's give the bastards a taste of their own medicine! We must retake our lines. Freedom demands it! Victory or death! Move forward!"

James likewise felt a twinge of pain from his leg wound. He could see clearly that their combined attacking divisions were badly outnumbered. Pushing his pain aside, he quickly adjusted his troop movements to coincide with Taylor's.

Taylor's hastily drawn battle plan would drive a sharp wedge through the tough mercenary army's center of attack while simultaneously reinforcing the thinly-held regrouped line of the besieged Rebels, presently holding their own. Their plan of action was intended to prevent the flanking movement currently underway by the Federal Army. The Rebels would need to hold their ground until the balance of Justin's corps arrived. It was a tall order to expect of two battle-weary divisions, but they had no say in the matter and knew what must be done. Defeat was not an option they would tolerate, and disaster waited if the lines were overrun. Fatigue would have to take a short vacation.

Taylor's two columns raced to retake the two-mile gap in the Rebels' crumbling eastern line. Their advance ran directly into the center of the enemy's strength.

The Federals seemed to be playing a game of "wait and see" with the balance of the Rebel line, currently holding the enemy at bay. They sent half their troops, nearly three divisions, into the breach, destroying the badly beaten Rebels holding the crumbling line.

Retreating remnants of the Rebels' Kansas 12th Division refused to follow Taylor's order to rejoin his advance. Panic disallowed its tattered remnants another moment of battle. To Taylor's dismay, the Missouri 5th was overrun and only existed on paper. Its decimated ranks were scattered along the fallen line, unable to give resistance.

The Federals' Russian mercenaries did not expect the ferocity of Taylor's newly arrived shock troops. They received their initiation into hell's fury, soon wishing they had remained in their impoverished *Rodina* (Motherland). The Rebels raked them down as if with a scythe.

Taylor's divisions knew they were in a fight for their lives. Every dog-tired trooper instinctively understood that his or her badly needed rest would either be eternal or after the battle's end.

Never expecting his untried mercenaries to break the Rebel line, General Newman's ploy slowed. Initially his strategy had been to give his newest foreign units their initial trial under fire. He had calculated he'd need them solely to support his veterans and add to his overwhelming odds. The Russians, filled with their temporary success at the Rebel center, zealously went too far into the enemy's works, exposing Newman's veterans to pinpoint Rebel crossfire. Now raging against his Russian and German troops came the legendary 1st Corps' hardened veterans. With bayonets attached, the Rebels screamed, seemingly unafraid. The mercenaries could not possibly know that the hordes of Rebels coming at them were too damn numb to care. The Rebels happily gave the untried mercenaries a horrible initiation. For many Rebels, death, after several long months of constant warfare, would have been a welcome guest.

The battle's rapid fluctuation did not result in the easy victory the Russians had unrealistically expected. Their quest for glory and pillage, already short-lived, was cut in half like the slamming impact of a chainsaw on wood. Taylor's assault ripped a wide hole into the enemy advance, forcing them into the stark realization they were about to die. Panicked Federal troops began to run helter-skelter in retreat, dropping weapons and equipment.

The casualties mounted, too numerous for either side's medics to be of much help. Taylor, unable to hold his emotions in check, recklessly joined his men in the killing spree unwinding before him. Bullets zinged past him, one grazed his right shoulder. Blood oozed freely from his newest wound. It went unnoticed. as his adrenalin kicked into high gear.

Taylor's adjutant grabbed his arm, holding him back. He shouted frantically when Taylor began to sally too far forward. "General, you're more important to your men than the few Federal bastards you might kill!"

The adjutant fell backward, victim to a round that hit his forehead, killing him before he hit the ground.

With difficulty, Taylor held himself back. He took one sorrowful glance and moved on with the charge. Keeping to the rear of the advance, he was again in control.

Directly to his front, less than a quarter mile ahead, his men continued to fight hand-to-hand. He saw clearly the ferocious disdain his men had for the Federals and their mercenaries. It seemed the battle had raged for hours. It had only been a few minutes. Word reached Taylor that the 121st was now fully involved, pouring like hot, avenging liquid into the fray.

Taylor felt a giant surge of relief with James's division fully engaged. He surmised he had approximately 8,000 men left in his force. They could only do so much. Casualties continued to mount to unacceptable levels. James's division helped make the difference. Arriving like the cavalry, they were a vicious presence.

The Rebels' complete tenacity became legend. They recaptured the ground lost earlier and conquered new territory, refusing the enemy its imminent success. Taylor's angry horde hit the enemy like the stink of a dead skunk, making life miserable for anyone it contacted. The Rebels neither gave nor accepted mercy, driving a brutal wedge into the Federal heart.

The eastern line was systematically retaken. The cost was high and intertwined with blood and courage, guts, glory, and cold steel. Near the end of the battle, the two opposing armies clashed in hand-to-hand combat, reducing the ranks of Taylor's two divisions to the strength of one. The Rebels, rapidly regrouping behind retaken trench works, now faced Federal artillery. It rained devastation, killing more Rebels by the score. In a flash, Rebel artillery responded in kind. Their deadly answer allowed Taylor's retaken line to hold while doling out another hard lesson to the surprised foreigners and Federal regulars alike.

Today, Newman's Foreign Legion would not be allowed victory over Americans on their native soil. On this fatal day, their alien allies' presence served only to give spirit to the Rebels. Many a mercenary realized, with a sudden sense of foreboding, that he had been badly mistaken to meddle in the North Americans' family feud.

× × × × ×

Justin snapped, "General Sinsome, Sir, at your service!"

"Justin, thank God you made it. Congratulations on your victory at Hutchinson. Sorry about calling your men off R&R."

"Thank you, Sir; it looks like today brings further saga. Where can I be most useful?"

"It appears you already have. I just got word your men have the eastern breach under control."

"I heard the same, Sir. I already took the liberty to send two divisions to strengthen the position. My verbal report said they have over fifty percent casualties." Justin's matter-of-fact comments did not hide his hurt. "My brother's command was mangled." Justin's eyes were hard and unfocused. He wondered how much more he could handle.

Raif couldn't help but notice Justin's restraint. And he wasn't fooled by his protégé's cavalier attitude. "Speaking frankly, Justin, it all seems such an extreme price to continue paying. I wonder if this is how Generals Grant or Lee felt when considering casualties during the Civil War. Justin, neither side can go on much longer with this carnage. Something must give."

"I agree. It's got to stop soon or there'll be little left to fight for." Justin hesitated but continued anyway. "Sir, I know we've already discussed my unwillingness to carry out your orders yesterday via courier. May I speak on the matter?"

"Yes, say what you have on your mind."

"Sir, I can't and won't murder prisoners. Seeing the blood flow on that snow-covered field with all that carnage was the worst thing I've ever witnessed, and Sir, I have seen so damn much. It didn't seem right to me to kill for killing's sake. It's against everything I hold dear as a Christian and especially against what I believe we're fighting for. Sir, I must personally offer my resignation for my uncontested insubordination. Simply stated, I can't say I won't refuse to follow this order again." Justin, his voice trembling, stood at attention.

"Justin, you won the day, and as far as I'm concerned, the matter is closed. I appreciate the bloodbath you've seen and why you took the action you did. That's why I like you so damn much. You're a man of principle. I always know where you stand. Sometimes in war we don't have the luxury of principle. I realize what you did was out of your humanity and not insubordination. When this war's over, the country will need men like you—men with your vision and values. Off the record, I'm personally sorry I've had to put my men through this. Unfortunately, war, out of necessity, often must be a form of hell, lest civilized men come to love it. Sadly, we needed to reciprocate if we're to survive. I've no choice."

"I understand, Sir. Thanks for seeing my side. I see in all this the Biblical explanation of an eye for an eye, which my upbringing disagrees with anyway."

"Justin, this war reached a turning point this month, and the killing fields are only a part of it. If we don't end this soon, we'll lose. We don't have enough time on our side to go on much longer. This is why I feel the enemy is also on its last legs. I know Skip Newman, and he'd never resort to the merciless killings he's ordering if he or his president weren't desperate."

Raif revealed to Justin a rare side of his personality. His temperament, usually optimistic, could not deny his sincere honesty.

Justin, anxious to change the subject, asked, "Sir, did you hear the Freed States Alliance has called for a constitutional convention? It seems our politicians desire to keep our original Constitution, with perhaps a few changes thrown in. I was told the old U.S. Constitution allows the states to call for a conference of states to discuss amending it when they feel a need for change. I never knew this, did you?"

"Justin, as far as I'm concerned, there's nothing wrong with the old Constitution. Except for all the shenanigans of the politicians, it's darn straight. It's too late to correct that, though." Raif's demeanor changed to scorn. "The country should have done something before this fiasco started; now whatever we Rebels do is up to us. Did you know several states tried for a convention about thirty years ago? They never could get enough state legislatures to agree."

"No, I never heard. Sir, this all bothers and confuses me. I know you're sort of an expert on the Constitution. Why do we want to keep a document that appears to have failed?"

"Justin, that's where you're all-fired wrong. It's quiet for the moment, so let's have a history lesson over a hot cup of something resembling coffee. I'm famished. How about you?" Raif handed Justin a hard roll. He gratefully accepted.

Raif signaled his orderly to do his bidding. Enjoying the moment, he began his lesson. "OK, let me see, where do I start?"

Raif's favorite subject was American history and the Constitution. He relished the opportunity to discuss it. "You see, our Constitution, as written, is a wonderful document that's withstood the trials of time. James Madison, who is thought by many historians to be its author, once said that by virtue of Amendment 10, the Constitution affirmed officially that," he hesitated, "and I quote roughly from what I recall old Madison said, 'the Powers not delegated to the Federal government by the Constitution, nor prohibited by it to the States, are reserved to the States respectively, or to the people.' It was intended even back then that if we ever wanted to rein in the federal government, we could, and this wonderful document gave us a way to do so peacefully."

"Peacefully! That's a hell of a joke." Justin couldn't resist.

Raif casually sipped his weak coffee. "So you think it's funny, then?" Raif laughed openly, feeling good. "When we win this war, we'll change back to the Constitution's original intent, the one expecting the individual states to have more powers than those of the very government we're fighting. We must return our new government back to where it was before the rogue actions of desperate presidents, out-of-control congresses, unsettling supreme courts, media, special interest groups, the failed legal system and the like, have expanded by caveat to create a federal government far in excess of what our founders originally imagined. Whew, did I say all that?"

Raif pulled a worn copy of the Constitution out of his overcoat pocket. "I carry this along with my Bible. Both make our suffering and sacrifice bearable." He flipped through the pages. "Look how few the pages are. My version has twenty-nine, yet that's all the pages the Constitution needs, if we'd stop messing with it.

"Because of the 10th Amendment, our country fought one civil war already. It was really our first revolution for states' rights, as seen through the eyes of Madison. I can't remember when the Civil War's emphasis was put on freeing the slaves. Since my ancestors were slaves, I'm thankful for the freedom. So don't get me wrong when I say there was more to that war than freeing slaves. In our present civil war, we mean to free American citizens from another kind of slavery. It appears that too many, me included, were mere serfs for our former government. No matter which way you look at it, the same situation applies in this civil war, too. Most would have gladly paid the high, confiscatory taxes if doing so would have prevented all this. Unfortunately, it only served to fuel the problems. The corruption, partisan politics, economy, social security, Medicare, tax cuts, Arabs, Islam, and terrorism all conspired together as culprits causing a great nation's decline as it lost its focus."

Raif smirked, disarming Justin with his casual demeanor. "Damn it, Northcutt, how'd you get me on my soap box? I'm sorry I got carried away."

"Yeah, Raif, but don't be sorry. I'm enjoying your dissertation, Professor. I agree we don't have enough paper to list all the things gone wide of the mark that led us to this moment. In my opinion, they have been turning us into a third world nation: open borders, moral corruption, the list is staggering."

"You know what, Justin, maybe when this war's over, I'll write its history, not only of the battles, but of the cause and effect. We'll have to win first, or I'll be too dead to write it all down." Raif chuckled, his attitude relaxed.

"Raif, you'd make one heck of a good politician, a rare one, I grant you, 'cause you're too damn honest. Heck, I'd vote for you." Justin snickered, enjoying this opportunity for conversation with his commander and mentor. It was a rare treat. Raif didn't open up to many, and the extreme circumstance of pending battle made it all the more memorable.

Suddenly, with horrific impact, the ground exploded as an errant Rebel shell fell short, shaking the temporary building. Fragments of shrapnel penetrated its thin walls. Justin looked in disbelief and horror at the blood flowing freely from Raif's torn chest. Justin, in a choked, high-pitched voice called, "Medic, here quickly! The general's been hit!"

Justin quickly tore a sheet from a nearby cot. While cradling Raif's head in his lap, he tried desperately to press the ripped fabric against the wound but failed to stop the bleeding. Justin was covered in his commander's blood.

"General! Talk to me! Please hold on. I'm getting you help. You'll be OK," he whispered in a raspy and calming voice.

Raif looked at his young general, his eyes blurred. Pain filled his every fiber. "Justin," he repeated, "Justin, I'm done for. My time ..." Raif spat blood. Choking, he tried to speak. "Justin, my time is over. My number's up."

"Sir, don't talk! Rest! Please. Help's coming." Justin tried to soothe him. He knew his friend was dying. He'd seen too much death.

"Justin, it's getting so dark. Do you hear me?" Raif mumbled his words, barely able to hear his own voice.

"I hear you, Sir," Justin spoke softly.

"Tell everyone to stay the course. Do you hear me? Stay the course. Tell my wife ... I ..." His eyes turned towards Justin and fell into a blank, cold stare.

"Yes, General, I hear you. I'll tell her."

Raif did not hear Justin's acknowledgment.

"General, we will stay the course. I promise." Tears unabashedly fell from Justin's swollen eyes. Raif's personal doctor arrived in time to see Justin close Raif's staring, startled brown eyes.

"He's gone, isn't he? General Northcutt, I'm sorry I can't do anything." The doctor's expression turned pale as he babbled on, tears running down his cheeks. Justin was numb.

"We're all sorry, Doc. We all are."

"You're hit, Sir. Let me help you."

Justin, too numb with grief, didn't notice nor even feel the blood running down his back. The doctor, seeing Justin's daze, bandaged him where he sat. He had seen this scene played out too many times in his young medical career. He knew his new, temporary commanding general needed time to himself.

Justin sat for several minutes, cradling his general's head, staring blankly at his fallen comrade and mentor. *What next?* He allowed himself the luxury to grieve until Raif's body, draped in a hastily found Texas flag, was removed from the debris.

Wincing in pain, Justin stood slowly and finally felt his injury. He called to a nearby staff officer who was openly crying. "Captain, get a grip and get word to Austin that we have a situation!" Justin grabbed his weapon and called for his orderly.

Justin's driver came forward, shouting above the din, "Sir, the lieutenant's dead. I'm the only one left!" He offered his hand to help Justin. Six men had traveled here with Justin; only he and the sergeant had survived the errant bomb's wrath.

"Sergeant, thank you. Find us transportation. I'll call you when you're needed."

Justin felt more alone than he ever had during his young life. *I must put aside this terrible feeling and the hurt from this damn wound and somehow find a way to navigate through the confusion. Order must be restored.* It was all he could do for the moment.

Quietly, he made a vow to his mentor. "Raif, I promise I'll never forget you or your history lesson. And I will carry on the cause, so help me God."

When things go wrong don't go with them. Think things through then follow through.

—Eddie Rickenbacker

CHAPTER TWENTY-FOUR

December 16, 2020—Northeastern Kansas Border

General Sinsome's accidental death dealt the Rebel Army a terrible blow. Meanwhile, the war's most recent battle was fought to a precarious draw, giving little advantage to either side. The extreme casualties suffered added universal strain to the moment. The Federals, though, considered it a victory. Even though they had nothing to do with Sinsome's death, the loss of a great Rebel leader, no matter how it came about, gave reason to rejoice.

Justifiably, the Federals believed Sinsome could never be replaced. Even to his enemies, Sinsome had been considered a military genius. The Federal press, such as it was, likened the Rebel loss to Stonewall Jackson's death at the Battle of Chancellorsville in May 1863. Then, as now, a great Rebel general was felled by friendly fire.

Sinsome's death had rekindled faltering Rebel fervor in its darkest hour. Jackson's death had occurred when the Confederate cause was at its zenith. Raif's death and his last selfless words, "Stay the course," hammered home to anyone in doubt that the Rebels would not go away.

The day after Sinsome's death, Lieutenant General Tarkington, a New Yorker and the Second Army commander, was named to replace Sinsome over Justin Northcutt. Justin was not unhappy.

Once appointed, Tarkington immediately chose to continue Sinsome's strategy for the upcoming campaign. He understood the problems he'd face filling the shoes of a legend. He did the only thing he could—moved on and refused to look back. He was determined to stay Sinsome's course until they reached its destination or his death, whichever came first.

x x x x

After a brief memorial service, Tarkington personally oversaw preparations to send Sinsome's remains to his Austin home for burial. He then called an emergency meeting of his corps generals at his new field headquarters, a mile from where Sinsome had fallen. His military demeanor, like his predecessor's, was all West Point. With an air of determination, he commenced his first meeting.

The room was filled to capacity. The chill did little to change Tarkington's positive attitude. He knew the next few minutes might be the most important, both for him personally and for the rebellion. He opened the meeting with a short prayer and then got to the point.

"Gentlemen, as you were. Today, we mourn a great leader, a good friend, and teacher. You all know I've been given the difficult assignment to replace a legend. You'll agree Raif has a large pair of combat boots to fill. I pledge to do my best to live up to the trust our government has placed in me. I earnestly need your help, cooperation, and support.

"I can't easily replace General Sinsome." Tarkington talked in a slow, measured lilt. "I only wish to lead you to the victory Raif so gallantly strived toward and now shall never see. We're here today only because of his untiring ability to keep us together, even when all seemed lost. It's for his memory we must see this war to triumph. General Northcutt told me a few moments ago that Raif's last words before he died were, 'Stay the course.' My fellow generals, that is what I intend to do.

"Word came a moment ago that the Federals are pulling back. We have reason to believe their purpose is to defend their temporary capital in Madison. I'm ordering pursuit at all cost. Gentlemen, you're aware we no longer have the luxury of a lengthy campaign. I'd like nothing better than to celebrate our final victory as an early Christmas present for the cause."

Tarkington's voice raised a few notes. "So, Gentlemen, are you with me? I say, let's do it!"

His generals cheered in approval. Each unconsciously looked to the man next to him, many wondering if Tarkington's quest for Christmas was possible. Each knew unequivocally that it must be.

"Tomorrow we move forward. Plans will be readied for your collective review at 0400. Thank you. You are dismissed."

Justin left the meeting, unsure how to read his new commander. He had briefly served under him after Del Rio and hadn't been impressed. There was little doubt Tarkington had the desire to do whatever it took to win. But could he?

Today Justin was burdened with the hard pain of loss, held within until Tarkington's meeting had brought home its vivid reality. Overall, he was content at being passed over. Even if qualified, he honestly doubted he was ready for the added responsibility.

Still, Justin's inward and outward hurt continued undeterred. He grieved not just for his fallen mentor, but for all his friends and for the thousands of unknown men serving in his command that had died or were maimed following his orders.

Feeling is a luxury ill afforded in war and dangerous for survival's sake. Justin, keenly aware of his failing—one of caring too much—required precious, but unavailable time to mourn. Today, the rebellion refused him this luxury.

After he surrendered to his weakness, his deliberate strides to his post eased the hurt. Poisonous grief, once released, gave free rein to his awakened terror, while empathy's balm moved him in a new direction. Terror aside, Justin's resolve needed to refocus on the ultimate goal—victory.

Ever observant to conditions, Justin looked for problems as he walked, and he found many. There was great need for everything: food, fuel, bandages, and all other necessities. He wondered if Raif's, and now Tarkington's, hope for one last major campaign was really possible.

Justin rummaged his tired mind fruitlessly for reasons why it might work. It was difficult. Opposing air forces were either out of planes or out of fuel. It didn't matter because airpower was only a vivid memory. Transportation was moving as fast as it could—in permanently low gear, limited by wintry weather conditions. Reintroduced was the true role of the foot soldier, wearing out shoe leather. Total conventional war now riveted the land with a madness of extremes beyond even man's cruel imagination.

Justin looked to the north. A few miles in that direction lay the end to their long journey. *The year 2020*, he mused, *must be a year to make the gods of war proud.* Justin's ever-active mind raced into high gear, thinking, *Two years ago I was dreaming of the joy of the Christmas holiday, presents, and trees, not destruction and devastation.* He prayed in silence as he walked. *Dear God, please don't let all our suffering and sacrifice be for nothing.* Plagued by his final conversation with Raif, he continued his pleading. *Lord, please lead us to a just victory and a future filled with honorable leaders in high places. Please see history does not repeat its evil in this Your Promised Land. And Lord, forever make for Raif a place of honor in Your celestial home.*

December 16, 2020—Federal Army Headquarters, Des Moines, Iowa

"General Newman, I bring great news. Sir, it has been reported by good authority that General Sinsome was killed yesterday." Newman's adjutant, Major Rodney Dunmore, was beside himself with glee. "What a wonderful Christmas present for our Union," he blurted.

Newman could understand his subordinate's pleasure at hearing the news of the death of his great adversary. He, though, could not find the heart to gloat nor take joy in the report. "There, but for the grace of God, go I," he muttered.

"Sir, did you say something?" His adjutant, confused by Newman's somber attitude, wondered why Newman wasn't ecstatic.

"No, Rodney, nothing worth repeating. You probably don't know this, but Raif once was a very good friend—always a worthy opponent. It's little known, but I was best man at his wedding. If his death had happened back in Texas in 2019, when all this crap started, it would mean something. Now it's too late.

"Major, it's like this: too much time has elapsed, allowing the Rebs to grow and create a depth in their ranks which most assuredly has rendered an adequate replacement for Raif."

"Sir, at the risk of sounding like an admirer of Sinsome, he's irreplaceable to their cause, isn't he?"

"No, Rodney, that's where you're wrong. I think it was the French leader DeGaulle who said, 'Cemeteries are full of indispensable men.' Certainly, whomever they throw at us next will never be as capable or experienced. But there's very little fight left on either side. The winner will be whoever has the strongest stomach for what it'll take to end this. Strong-minded men are now needed more than ever. We're in trouble if Sinsome's replacement fits that stalwart image. Major, simply stated, the army which is most unwavering will carry the day."

"Then, Sir, I reckon we better be that determined force." Dunmore liked showing his positive side to superiors. At this moment, he was trying more to convince himself.

"Rodney, I agree, we must drive our men to the highest limits of their endurance. I feel certain the end of this war is very near. Gather my commanders for a conference at 0800. We need to formulate a strategy to take advantage of the possible Rebel disarray. It may be our best, if not our only, chance after a long string of disappointments." Newman's voice did not carry his usual dominant reassurance.

It did not go unnoticed by the major, who thought, *Why does it seem the general is only going through the motions?*

December 16, 2020—Hutchinson, Kansas

Air in the damaged bunker was stale and damp. Sweat rolled down Luke's forehead, forming rivulets like roadways over his dirt-encrusted face and torso. He'd been digging with bare hands for two days, with little to show for it. His injuries hurt like fire, and medicine was gone. Privates Burroughs and Chelsea assisted. They were the only able-bodied men available, and they, too, carried slight wounds that slowed them down. Becky did all she could to keep the few remaining wounded alive. Still, several died. Dirt shoveled from the bunker was placed over the dead to keep the smell away and slow disease. Hunger, and now thirst, took its toll. Energy required for the seemingly endless digging was in dire need of replenishment.

"Luke, I've done all I can for the wounded. Let me help some." Luke's pride was too weary to reject.

"Sure, grab that tarp. When we fill it to about here," his hand leveled at an imaginary line, "see if you can drag it to the pile over there and cover those bodies some more."

"Luke, do you think our people are still up there?"

"I hope so, though it's anyone's guess. From the continued noise we heard, there must've been a major engagement. For all we know, we may dig out only to find ourselves prisoners." Luke leaned on his shovel, wiping his brow.

"That's just dandy. Right now, I'm not sure if I'd care. All I want to do is get out of this hole and see the sun, if only for a moment, before I die." Becky's visible fatigue spoke volumes.

Luke appreciated her frustration. Just the same, her utterance bit deep into Luke's concern. He figured they'd be lucky to end up prisoners, an unlikely event of late. Luke didn't have the heart to remind her of the enemy's recent feelings about surrender. He'd cross that river when he came to it.

"Do I dig around the air shaft, Sir?"

"No, Private," Luke's shout showed his concern. "While we should thank God for that shaft, I wouldn't probe around it. We might accidentally plug our air source. It's the only good thing we've got going for us."

"You've got a lot more than that going for you, Colonel." Becky smiled in the fading light. Dust cascaded on her worn body. Luke's heart swelled at the sight of his vivacious young fiancé, looking so alive, even in the quivering light from the one remaining lantern that hadn't run out of fuel.

"I suppose you're right, Becky." He looked at her with warm intensity. Then he noticed the diggers. "Hey, Private, move that boulder carefully. Wait, we'll help." He shouted too late.

A thunderous rumble caught everyone's attention. "Lord almighty, what was that?" Private Burroughs let out with a gasp, as dirt surged inward.

Luke yelled, "Get back and out of the way. It must be a backhoe or something large playing with the earth."

Luke took a deep breath and shouted for all his worth. The others who were able joined him with their added screams. They saw a glimmer of daylight. "Stop! Please help us! Help us! Down here!"

Above the bunker, Private Gonzales heard shouting from the bowels of the earth. He excitedly screamed to the backhoe operator to shut down his equipment.

"You, down in the hole, who the heck are ya'?"

Feebly at first, then with a vigor taking all the power his faltering adrenalin could muster, Luke yelled hard enough to break away bandages on his jaw. His voice resonated from his very toes.

"Down here, we're trapped! There's several wounded! Please hurry!"

"Do you think they're ours?" Becky looked up, temporarily blinded by the welcomed sunlight.

"I don't know, Becky. We'll have to take our chances and pray for mercy if not. Either way, it doesn't matter. I doubt we'd last much longer down here."

Someone above shouted, "Identify yourself!"

Luke took a deep breath and made a sign of the cross, an almost forgotten remnant of his faith. It still gave him comfort. "Colonel Luke Rinaldi, 7th Ranger Regiment. To whom am I speaking?"

"Friends, Colonel, friends," the voice from above shouted.

The morning sun never looked so grand. Luke emerged from their temporary tomb into a cold day filled with blinding light. Shielding his eyes from the discomfort, his first glimpse of the rolling landscape of Hutchinson seemed like heaven. His shaded eyes saw the long lines of trenches. Upon better scrutiny, he looked to a familiar point where he had remembered trees once grandly standing upon the open plains. They were gone, probably blown away by the artillery fire they had heard. The crippled landscape appeared to be a war-torn refugee, with death replacing its former grandeur.

"How'd you find us, Private?"

"Sir, we weren't looking for you. But a couple of days ago, right after the big battle, a platoon from the 36th, and later another from the 121st, came prowling around looking for MIAs. I guess you're them," he smiled. "We've been digging mass graves. There's thousands of dead that need burying. Your little hole was about to be part of another burial trench. I suspect it still will be once we clear it out."

"Well, I'll be damned! Thank you, Private. Thank you. It almost was a tomb for us." He shook the private's hand aggressively, smiling like a kid at Christmas.

"Can you get the officer in charge? We've got a lot of people needing attention."

"Sir, he's on the way, along with some medics."

"Great, Private. What's your name?"

"Private Javier Gonzales, 21st Oklahoma Regiment, at your service."

"Well, Javier, do you have any food or water handy?"

"On the way, too, Sir." Gonzales gave a large toothy grin.

Luke drew Becky to him. In an unmilitary gesture, he kissed her deeply for all to witness in the December sunlight. The two were oblivious to the twenty-three-degree temperature.

"Becky, once we're taken care of, I'll need to return to my regiment, if it's still in one piece. It looks like I missed one terrible battle. I'm feeling a bit guilty for saying this, but I'm not sorry I did."

"Luke, I know you have your duty. I don't know what I'll do, though, if you don't come back to me." Tears streamed down her face. "Please be careful."

"Becky, there's nothing that can ever get in my way from returning to you, not after all we've been through! Honey, you can bank on it. Don't worry."

Luke reluctantly climbed into the waiting transport vehicle and waved a sad good-bye.

"Luke, I love you!" she shouted, running alongside his vehicle for a few wonderful moments.

He turned, a big boyish grin painted on his grimy, swollen face. He winked, drew an imaginary heart in the air, and then held his right hand to his heart.

December 17, 2020—Headquarters, 1st Army Corps, Northeast Kansas Border—Foreign War Correspondents' Press Conference

"General Northcutt, do you really think it wise to commence action in such inclement weather, especially now that the cause has lost the stellar leadership of General Sinsome?"

Justin peered over his nose with distaste at the English war correspondent. The arrogant demeanor he displayed went beyond his routine job to question events. Justin was beginning to tire from his innuendoes. Up until this phase of the press conference, he had dutifully followed orders, giving them enough to appease their voracious appetite. With his patience rapidly waning, he observed the little man standing before him.

Gerald Whitsure came from old money. Rumor had it there was also a hint of royalty in his family line. The past two decades had built up an open hatred in Europe for everything American. Whitsure couldn't hide his obvious distaste. England didn't stand alone in its low regard for its cousins across the pond. In the past two decades, Europeans were used to having open season chiding Americans. The world, with liberal Europe in the forefront, seemed to have forgotten it had been the United States that had saved their collective asses twice in the 20th century. What happened seventy years earlier no longer mattered. All they wanted to know was what the Americans could do for them today.

Justin's mind wandered while Whitsure rattled on, drumming out his redundant questions. Justin remembered silently, *So much American blood was shed on European soil, including the blood of my great-grandfather, killed at Normandy on D-Day. American taxpayers' hard-earned money helped rebuild this ungrateful bastard's war-torn country. Two million American casualties were sacrificed in the name of freedom, over two world wars, so that this sniveling, ungrateful son of a bitch can stand before me and have the balls to talk down at me and mine.*

Justin decided he'd better respond before the better side of his nature grabbed the sniveling idiot by the neck. He returned from his internal wanderings to speak, not really answering the correspondent's questions.

He rambled for several minutes, finally concluding, "When we attack, you will no doubt hear."

"I'd like to turn the tables a bit and ask you a few questions. Why is it that on the one hand, you speak so contemptuously of our cause in your news reports, and then on the other, in bold words, speak fondly of our freedom of speech, touting our cause for independence as a struggle worthy for the world to grasp? It appears y'all preach out of both sides of your mouth."

His monologue then continued, as he gave the room's correspondents a lesson in agriculture. Justin talked for several minutes, intentionally confusing all in the room.

Whitsure was uncertain how to take the brash young Rebel general. Northcutt was, by all accounts, one of the rebellion's heroes and a man to respect. The interview had suddenly taken a strange twist, with mention of trees and roots and some such.

He came forward. "General, I mean no disrespect to you personally or to your cause. I only think it impractical to believe your efforts would be well served by continuing your present campaign after the tragic and costly battles of the past two weeks. And frankly, Sir, I am confused by your talk of agriculture."

"Mr. Whitsure, people and nations started misinterpreting our resolve as far back as our first revolution. The world, no doubt, will continue to be so misguided as to misinterpret our strong, compelling desire for freedom. On that, Sir, you may rely. Print that!" Justin gathered his papers.

"I am sorry, but duty requires me to move on; therefore, I must end this interview until another opportunity presents itself." Justin turned abruptly, entering his field office, to Whitsure's and the other correspondents' surprise. Justin's staff officers, standing within hearing distance, snickered in bemused smiles, knowing their commander's mood. Justin ignored the correspondents' pleas and their tossed questions as he left the room.

"General, we have more questions," someone shouted. "What's all this to-do about trees and agriculture? What does this metaphor have to do with the war?"

Justin walked on past the correspondent. *Damned if I'll tell you—figure it out for yourselves.*

2020: A Season to Die

x x x x x

Justin quickly closed the door to his private quarters in the bedroom of the old abandoned Iowa farmhouse. He wondered, *Was this room once filled with hopefulness, love, and peace?* He somehow knew it was. He closed his eyes a scant second to clear his anger, born mostly of fatigue and frustration. He felt bad about how he had acted with the correspondents but not bad enough to go back. He gazed upon a serene picture on the wall. It reminded him of a similar place he witnessed as a boy. Wildflowers, a quiet brook, and a warm cottage nestled beside a weathered barn. It was a little like his grandparents' home.

The sun cast heavy shadows through the weathered room while late fall winds drove furiously across the ancient plains, chilling the space. Looking out a narrow window, he saw the rolling terrain. It seemed to mirror his mood. He had not been alone for hours, too busy to properly mourn. The loss came back, striking him with sudden turbulence. *So many good men; did they all need to die?* The thought of death besieged him. Its black claws would not let go. He shook his head, searching the void, trying to see if someone, anyone, was listening to his anger. *I need to find myself—rekindle my resolve.*

Justin kneeled on the cold linoleum floor. In deep prayer, his mind raced back to that terrible day when he first saw death. It was an unholy sight. Not at all like the movies, even with their realism. He thought, *Could it be only twelve years ago? I remember it happened so quickly on that hot August day.* He started to speak at a staccato-like pace, as if he were on a witness stand defending his very conscience. He needed to clear his head from all the confusion; he hoped for relief. Often, in the past, talking out loud had helped him to grasp the common root to his troubles. *Am I going mad? No, I will not go mad.*

His whisper came in bursts as he quietly began to recite the incident that once again chose to haunt him. "Taylor and I had been visiting our grandparents' ranch in Sherman. We were out by the road riding one of Grandpa's toys. I remember it was his golf cart, when the accident happened right in front of our eyes, near the ranch's entrance. The wrecker, going at a high rate of speed, hit the shoulder of the road at a bad angle. It caused his front right tire to turn. The driver overcompensated, making the heavy vehicle cross the road in sudden flight, into a steep incline. It then turned over, crashing through the neighbor's pipe-rail fence, tearing out a whole section, mangling the scattered pipe. The flip damaged the truck and tossed the driver violently out of the one-ton vehicle's door. The driver was killed instantly. My little brother, Taylor, and I could not believe it."

Justin continued his thought, outlining this tragedy, trying in this fashion to take charge of his present confusion. He continued after a pause, still on his knees. "The man lay there for what seemed hours. Seven sheriff's cars, with lights flashing and hoods up, plotted out their investigation. They asked us questions. When I asked why the hoods were up, a sheriff's deputy told me it was their procedure to designate a death scene."

Justin took a deep breath. The memory hurt, but he knew he must continue if he wanted to recapture his sanity.

"The coroner came and the body was dutifully wrapped in sterile white and carted off without ceremony, taken away like so much garbage. I was not quite a teenager, and I was deeply troubled by what I'd seen. My grandfather got word of the accident. He joined us at the scene, in silent counsel. I recall Grandpa spoke later with heartfelt grief for the unknown man."

"Justin, you OK?" Taylor had walked into the room so quietly that Justin was unaware, his feelings too deep to be distracted. Taylor heard his brother's whispering and thought it strange. *Is Justin breaking?* He feared the worst.

"Nothing, Taylor. I was thinking. It's another bad habit I indulge too much. It's been a rough time for me, and I've been having difficulty trying to get the pieces to fit. Sometimes talking it all out to myself helps, sort of like playing chess. Do you remember the time years ago when that poor man died in front of Grandpa's ranch?"

"Heck, I'll never forget that day; it haunts me sometimes. Even after the stuff we see everyday in this war. Damn, it was my first experience with death. Justin, do you remember what Grandpa said when they put the dead man into the ambulance? Because I'll never forget." Taylor unknowingly had gotten to the heart of Justin's problem.

"Yes, it's been with me for years. And it seems appropriate now. I remember Grandpa said, 'we needed to say a prayer for this man, for his friends, and for his family.' I recall you didn't pray."

Taylor, visibly uncomfortable, said, "Yeah, you're right, and I recall you wondering why we needed to pray for his family since we didn't know them."

"Taylor, I was a confused little boy, too, and also curious at the same time. I remember I was quite disturbed by what we'd seen." Justin continued, "I'll always remember that Grandpa said, 'The poor man's worldly concerns are over. Now we must pray for his soul and his journey. May his be a quick road to heaven.' Then he said, 'Justin, it's really this man's family that needs our prayers now. We know he's gone. You saw it happen. I doubt his family has heard about it yet. When they do, it'll be difficult for them. We don't know this man. He could be a father—even a grandfather. His sudden and untimely death will be difficult for some to handle. Let's pray his family can accept the fact God called him so that they may carry on with life. Death is sometimes quick and surprising. With a sudden death like this, closure is often difficult for those loved ones left behind.' I think that's about how Grandpa said it."

Justin fidgeted nervously. "Taylor, I have the same confusion today about death as I did then. You'd think after all the carnage we've seen it would be easier," he said grimly, then wiped a solitary tear from his face.

"Justin, I feel the same. I clearly remember seeing you close your eyes and pray. You said later it could have been our dad or grandfather or someone we loved lying there."

Taylor surprised Justin with his recollection, for he never thought this incident had affected Taylor. He never once talked about it before this.

"Yeah, Taylor, I remember clearly praying that day. I now find myself praying for thousands I'll never know. Some things never change."

"You know, Justin, I didn't pray then and I can't pray now. I didn't want to know that man, and I didn't want to hurt over someone I didn't know. It bothers me sometimes when I think of my selfishness. You know, I was only nine years old. It was the only way I could cope. It's the same now. Like you said, some stuff never changes."

"Taylor, no matter how hard you try to dodge the reality of sudden death, it'll never leave you alone."

"I know, Justin. I don't have the room for the amount of hurt in my heart you seem able to carry. So, while I grieve for the whole, I can't let myself mourn for the individual. It just hurts too damn much. It's also how I survive." Taylor reached out, gently placing his hand on his brother's shoulder. "Justin, I know how close you were to Raif. I'm really sorry." Justin winced in pain from his shoulder wound. Taylor didn't notice.

"Someday it'll hit you. When it does, Taylor, let it happen. I miss so many good friends. Now with Raif gone, I hurt deeply within my soul and in places I'd rather not visit. He was not just a good leader; he was a good friend, a family man. Why, damn it? Sometimes life, especially nowadays, doesn't make sense. I've put too much death aside, and it is getting freakin' old, like so much dust swept under a rug. Heaven knows we probably have to add our baby sister to this terrible mix, too."

"Justin," Taylor's voice rose with emotion, "I feel what you feel, believe me. I can't let go yet. Someday, maybe I'll face my private hell, but not until this shit's over. I need to cope with it in my own way. Thanks, though." Taylor's somber mood turned suddenly to excitement.

"Hey, your melancholy almost made me forget why I'm here. Not that it could this time. It's great news for a change, and it sure looks like you can use it." Taylor's contagious smile lightened the room, changing instantly the dour atmosphere.

"What are you waiting for? Speak. I can use good news." Justin arose from the floor, matching his brother's grin.

"Word just came in that my 7th Regiment's commander and Becky are OK. It seems they were stuck in a bunker that collapsed during the initial bombardment in Hutchinson."

Justin beamed. Taylor had finally told him about the missing couple after the Battle of Hutchinson. "Are they both in one piece?"

"Both are a bit worn from their trial, no more than what you'd expect. They were buried in a forward command bunker. It saved their lives, though the ordeal had to be terrible. Luke's bruised up and anxious to lead what's left of his regiment. He'll be here shortly. Becky's already on her way back to her unit somewhere in southern Kansas."

"This is wonderful news. I don't have anything to add to make it any better. You do know that Tarkington plans to follow Raif's lead and try to end this by Christmas." Justin's smile turned grim.

"Bro, I was there. Remember? I think he's nuts! We're at an all-time low in morale. Hunger is rampant. Jeez-Louise, our men aren't strong enough to face another battle so frigging soon."

"Taylor, I'd like the luxury to feel as you. Yet, I agree with him. We can't last much longer. The Feds are as tired and hungry, and worse, their untried aliens outnumber the Americans in their ranks. We're also hearing from Fed deserters that they resent the foreigners. It appears this may be our best, if not our only, chance. To wait would be the same as suicide. We just can't allow them to consolidate."

"I sure hope you're right on this one."

"You can be assured, I'm certain." Justin's face turned positive.

"Oh, by the way, did you hear we received several tons of Texas pecans today, cracked and all? It should help to stifle the hunger."

"Justin, that's great news. I was wondering if they took your sorry-ass advice to send the Home Guard to harvest the crop. With all the rain we had last spring it had to be a bumper crop. I suppose we confiscated as much as our commissaries could find."

"Yeah, it sure was. I did send word to go to Grandpa's ranch. With his 1,000 trees, I figured it's what he'd want us to do. But actually, Rinaldi found most of the pecans on a large pecan ranch outside of Messilla, New Mexico. Rock said that place had over 180,000 trees. Can you imagine?"

"Justin, as for Grandpa's place, that's probably wishful thinking. Locals more than likely raided it already. There's plenty of hunger to go around, you know. But 180,000 trees in the New Mexico desert—now that *is* something to talk about."

"Taylor, I say, who cares where the pecans came from. They're more than welcome. I'm issuing orders to have the men stuff themselves first and then pack to carry at least three pounds of raw nuts per man. They'll soon get sick of pecans, but there's a lot of nutrition in just a couple of ounces. By the way, I've had a few roasted. My orderly had the cook add some honey we found. Would you like some to take back?"

"Damn straight, I would. Thanks. Hey," Taylor paused, "one of your staff said you were pretty pissed off over some English correspondent. What ticked you off? I'm the one who usually loses his temper. Didn't HQ pick you to talk to them because of your ability to bullshit?"

"It wasn't any one thing, but a combination of all the crap coming from that pompous Brit. If I were a private citizen, I would have choked his skinny chicken-shit neck."

"He's probably just doing his job. Many Brits seem to come across in that 'I'm-better-than-you' air of theirs anyway." Taylor imitated a bad British accent. "They don't mean anything by it. What's so new and different about today?"

"Nothing new or anything we haven't heard. I didn't lose control with him. I only exercised my right to move on when I had about as much of his crap as I could take. Kinda like before I lost it." Justin playfully parodied his brother's bad British accent.

"You know, the Europeans in general haven't been very supportive except with their damned mercenaries helping the Feds. Heaven certainly knows they, along with the rest of the world, are at best only convenient friends. I guess I was taken aback when he said ..." at this, Justin lifted his lip, raised his nose, squinted his eyes, and said in a lilting British accent, 'You Rebels have had the good fight, but I do believe you have reached your depth and are now at the mercy of your fate.' Even though it was crystal clear to me he was talking about what he really wished, not observed, it still set me off, and perhaps he did hit a sore point."

Taylor, amused, chuckled at his brother's expressions.

Justin continued, "I reversed the interview, finding myself asking him questions. I asked if he felt we no longer could carry on the fight just because we lost Raif. The bastard said I was right on point."

"So that's it! Surely you said more."

"You know me too well, Taylor. Yes, a lot more, and then I proceeded to give him a lecture about trees and roots."

"What! Did you actually say trees and roots?"

"Yeah, trees and roots. I told the pompous ass our cause could be likened to a large forest of trees—some big, some small. I asked if he ever wondered why trees in a forest seem to grow even if they have no light or water source. He looked at me like I was loony. It didn't matter." Justin smirked as he remembered. "I continued to explain that some trees are in the center, away from direct sunlight, while others are away from a good water source but perhaps near the sun, and so on."

"Did he have a clue where you were going with that? I seem to recall Grandpa Northcutt telling us this once. Unlike you, I didn't listen too hard."

"No, with all his lordship's learned background, he didn't have a clue. He had never heard that the roots of trees in a forest actually intertwine with each other and that the strong offer nutrients to weaker trees. Nor did he know it enables them all to survive because the weaker trees, perhaps those with more sunlight than water, receive energy through common roots from those trees closer to water, and vice versa."

"So, did he catch your drift?"

"Probably not. I didn't really care if he did. I was getting crap off my chest while I struck back at him in the only civilized way that I could. I likened the forest's resolve to survive to our cause to win our independence. I said we may lose an occasional tree, but the forest is large. And seedlings will always take the place of the fallen, now and in the future. We may lose a great leader now and again, and another will come along, taking over where he left off. If the war is lost or extended, regardless, the seed of rebellion is forever cast."

"Justin, I don't know if I really care, but did he finally get the big picture?"

"I suppose he may eventually, when he has time to reflect. He had to be stupid not to. He may be an ass, but he's not stupid. Then I said we'd not move according to his or anyone's ideal schedule, unless it is right for us. I emphasized that when we do move, he could bet the farm that no force on earth would halt our resolve. I then went on to tell him to print that in his paper. That's when I beat a hasty retreat to here."

"Justin, I'm surprised at you. It's not like you to waste energy on a fool. I'll bet it felt good, though, didn't it?" Taylor chuckled.

"It was good to get it off my chest. I'm afraid he took the brunt of my fatigue and frustration, and that's far greater than anything I received from him."

"That, I can buy. It's been good talking to you. I need to go check on Colonel Rinaldi. I'll be back to eat some pecans. Why don't you put your four stars to good use and rustle up a beer or two? I'll bring some apples that my boys liberated."

"I'll try, Taylor, but don't get too cozy. It looks like hell's on a short vacation and wants to play."

Taylor was worried about his brother. It was unlike him to lose control, even under the circumstances. He decided to return as soon as he could, knowing Justin might possibly need his best friend and brother to help him through the pain.

Luke sat on his tent cot, too numb for the cold to interfere with his dismay. He had just been briefed about the condition of his regiment. It was not good news. His command took a pounding in the recent battle. Although Major Duggins was among the wounded, happily it was thought he would live. Facing reality unnerved him.

Taylor walked into his tent and grabbed him by the hand, both men very happy to see each other.

"Luke, damn it's good to see you. We've got some catching up to do."

"Taylor, tell me I didn't lose half my regiment?"

Taylor looked at his friend, seeing the hurt. "Yes, Luke, it's true. You'll soon have replacements from other units that fared even worse. We need to keep our shock regiments intact. Can't disappoint the enemy, you know," Taylor replied, trying to lighten the conversation. It wasn't working.

Luke stared blankly, with unseeing eyes, tears falling. He muttered, "I promise they'll pay. They'll pay hard for this." Luke walked out into the solace of the cold, dark night, numbed by this latest news. Taylor followed, carrying Luke's overcoat.

Let us have faith that right makes might, and in that faith let us to the end dare to do our duty as we understand it.

—Abraham Lincoln

CHAPTER TWENTY-FIVE

December 18, 2020—121st Division, First New York Volunteers Regimental Hospital Tent, Omaha, Nebraska

The sterile atmosphere of the field hospital tent went unnoticed by Rock Rinaldi, who lay dying. The ravages of a young man's war had finally caught him. He frantically tried to bring back his body's lost vitality, but cold Nebraska winds fought his futile efforts. Once taken ill, he declined quickly. Never complaining, he had worked until collapsing a day earlier.

Rock's chest heaved in convulsive pain; his breathing was irregular. The doctor diagnosed acute pneumonia. His gasps for air continued in endless frustration, while his damaged lungs worked overtime in vain. The drafty hospital tent remained chilly, despite its overworked heater. Rock, cognizant of his plight, was bravely reconciled to the inevitable.

Through dimming eyes, he saw the unmistakable image of his son. It gave him comfort, for now he could die.

"Hi, Joe. I'm glad you made it." Rock's usual robust voice was gone. "How are things?"

"Dad, rest. You need to conserve your energy." His soothing voice was cloaked in worry. He choked aside his fear.

"I'm so cold, Son, so damn cold, and I feel like someone's standing on my chest." He shivered uncontrollably despite several blankets. The orderly had forewarned Joe that things were bad. Joe felt Rock's forehead; it was feverish.

"I know, Dad. We're moving you south with the wounded convoy as soon as they can get the trucks fueled. The damned snow has started up again, so they really need to get going. Just hang in there. You'll be fine."

"Joe, have them give my spot to someone who's going to live. I know I'm done for. It's my heart. This darn cough," he gasped and then hesitated. "It's affected my ticker. All this soldiering finally caught up with me. I'm ..." he searched for air, "I'm ready to go see my Rose. I miss her. She needs me. I need her."

Joe was surprised at his father's acceptance. It wasn't like Rock to give up so easily. It unnerved him.

Joe calmly tried to give encouragement. "Dad, stop talking nonsense. There's plenty of time to see Ma, but not now. You're going to make it. Damn it, you're still young. You've got to hang on, for me." Joe pleaded, quickly wiping an errant tear, hoping Rock did not see. He was too late.

"Dad, I've got good news. Word's come in that Luke's OK." Joe saw Rock's forced but genuine smile. "You get better. I know he'll want to see his grandpa, especially now that he's planning to marry that pretty Texan girl. He'll want you there when he ties the knot."

"Joe," Rock gasped, "thank God! I promised the Lord if that boy would just make it, He could have me instead." His open smile was strained. Shaking out of control, he stammered. "A good trade ... if I say so myself."

"Stop the foolishness, Dad. You're going to live. The orderly is coming for you soon. I just came to see you off. No telling when we'll see each other again." Joe was at a loss for words; he didn't want to accept what his eyes saw. He realized sadly, *I can't let him go. Lord, please let Dad live.*

Rock had difficulty speaking. He forced out words he needed to say to give comfort. "Son ... every day God gave me ... since he let me come home ... from 'Nam has been ... a gift."

Joe just stared, unrestrained tears rolling from his eyes. "I know, Dad. Now rest," he said with a strained attempt to comfort in his voice.

Rock stared blankly, trying urgently to focus uncooperative, tired eyes. "Joey, I'm sorry. I love you, Son." A terrible rattle escaped with Rock's forced words. "You know, Mom and I will see you soon enough." Rock's voice trailed off and his eyes opened wide to a beautiful smile. "Joey, do you see her? She's beautiful."

Whatever he sees must be wonderful.

Then Rock slipped away to the ages.

Numbed, Joe sat at Rock's cot, losing track of time. His tears felt cold on his cheeks. After almost five decades, he now faced a world without parents. It was a hollow, empty feeling.

The hospital orderly entered, walking to the cot, his breath heaving with empathetic concern. "Sir, I'm sorry, but we need to bury him right away. He was a good man. I remember talking to him at his store back in Utica. He'd always talk to us kids."

"Thanks, Private." Joe could hardly contain his emotions. "I know, but he's my dad." The orderly put a gentle hand on Joe's sagging right shoulder.

"Sir, I'll help all I can if you'd like. Word is we're moving out. I knew your dad, and well, Rock ..." he hesitated, "he wouldn't want to stand in the way of what must be done."

"You're right." Tears unabashedly streamed down Joe's face. He stood and looked at the still form of his father, and then at the orderly. "Son, what's your name?"

"It's Kevin Salvari, Sir."

"Kevin, give me a couple minutes to be alone. Then I'll take you up on your offer."

"You've got it, Sir."

Closing his father's eyes, Joe said a silent prayer. He checked Rock's meager belongings and noticed the ancient Winchester under his cot. He lovingly picked up the rifle, clutched it briefly to his chest, and put its sling around his shoulder, calling for Kevin's assistance. Together they carried Rock's body to the designated area for burial. Joe had one more stressful duty to perform in a war that demanded too much. The sudden void he felt anesthetized his entire being, shaking his distressed world as he watched while the burial detail slowly lowered Colonel Rocco Rinaldi's mortal body into the impersonal, shallow trench. Joe whispered, "Go with God, Dad. I love you."

Somewhere in the near distance, a horn cried its sweet, sad, military farewell as Private Kevin Salvari held back tears and played "Taps," his heartfelt tribute to an old friend.

December 21, 2020—Main Rebel Army Column Somewhere Near Indianola, Iowa

Everything at the front was stalled. A treacherous winter storm blew its wrath on the opposing armies, not caring which it encumbered. The weather did little to deaden the wrath of numerous threats coming from the world at large.

Europe was in total chaos and also in denial, too confused to bring back order, even in its best interest. America's conflict was threatening to turn global, making a swift end to the Civil War all the more important as the balance of the world teetered on the edge.

Running battles and minor skirmishes followed the two armies like a bad dream on a disastrous path. The Rebels continually pushed, gaining ground the hard way, one costly step at a time. Commanding General Tarkington, poised for one great surge forward, hoped to catch the Federal Army by surprise.

The terrain near Indianola was hilly and heavily treed. The beautiful farmland, cultivated through centuries by farmers' loving hands, had made it a grand part of America's once abundant breadbasket for the world. Today its dense hills were the center of a 100-mile front for two opposing, very irritated, and very determined giants.

Justin, formally promoted to command First Army and now second to General Tarkington, was on a mission. He was accompanied on his recon of the area by several staff members, including Generals Taylor Northcutt and James Rinaldi. The cold rolling hills, coated with a foot of new snow, shimmered in beautiful contrast to the tired and freezing men, searching for a weakness in the enemy line.

Trudging in the snow, Justin turned to James, retaining a formal air for the benefit of his brother, who was trailing behind. "General Rinaldi, how goes your division?"

"Sir, they're in place, sheltered and resting as ordered."

"Good, and the 36th?" Justin looked to his brother, who had frost on his beard and pain showing on his face. Taylor's hatred of the cold weather was legendary.

"Same here, Justin." Taylor, true to form, ignored military formality. "My Rangers are ready, along with my 1st Corps. I've had the chance to review the ranks. We're ready, despite our reduced numbers." Taylor, promoted to command of 1st Corps, was now a reluctant lieutenant general; his shoulder carried three stars. Since Hutchinson, 1st Corps had found its numbers cut in half.

"I don't think this ten-degree weather's going to help much. We'll have to keep the men moving." Taylor wore two field jackets and a scarf made from a cut-up blanket. He, though not alone, did not look like a general officer.

"Yes," James piped in. "I fear the constant running battles we've seen since this campaign started will seem small after we face what's ahead." Shivering, James continued, "Damn, I never knew it could get so windy or so cold. This is the pits, even for a New York boy."

"This is the Great Plains, Jimmy. Just be thankful it's not snowing." Taylor tried to sound positive. It didn't work.

"Don't be so smug, Tay," James quipped. "You obviously didn't check with the weather wizards. They think we're in for a major storm by Christmas."

Taylor was not amused. "Great, gang up on me. I needed that news like I need the hemorrhoid I have. At least there are plenty of trees to burn for warmth." Taylor laughed through his makeshift scarf.

"Taylor, I don't think I needed that little detail. Perhaps if you sit in the snow it'll help." Justin cracked a smile. "And I doubt we'll stay here long enough to worry about big fires. The enemy's somewhere over there," he pointed. "Men, we no longer have the luxury to wait."

Taylor recognized the familiar gaze that always showed in Justin's eyes when things were about to happen. He came forward. "OK, Justin, when you get that look, I know we're in for some more shit, so what do we need to ready our men for? I hope there'll be some warm food and a bed somewhere in it, because staying here is an idea that doesn't seem to want to grow on me," Taylor said, though he listened in earnest for his brother's reply.

Justin, glaring, answered, "Men, gather closer to form a break from this wind. You've heard this before—you all know we need to end this soon. We can't stay holed up here. Even if we can get ourselves comfortable defensively, we're too vulnerable. If the Feds decide to move before we do, we're screwed. We were placed at the center of the enemy defenses for one reason and one reason alone, to kick some ass."

Major General Matthew Everett, a stockbroker in civilian life, came forward. "General, according to Intel, as always, we're outnumbered at least two to one, short on food, fuel, and warm clothing. Our men have stuffed every confiscated piece of cloth within a hundred miles into their uniforms. All they think about is eating and avoiding frostbite. You're not really thinking we may attack soon? In this? We're not ready. It's insane!"

"General Everett, I hear you. And we hope this is what the enemy thinks, too. We need to keep the men occupied, or the winter will kill us. In a nutshell, here we stand in the center of our extended line." Justin took a threadbare, gloved hand from his overcoat pocket and pointed. "About ten miles north is Indianola, Iowa. I'm told it's a quiet farm community with a beautiful college in the center of town called Simpson."

"I remember that name, Justin. Didn't one of our cousins attend that place?"

"You may be right, Taylor. I think, though, it was our cousin's boyfriend. Whatever, Indianola's the center of the Federal line and pivotal for us. Des Moines is a few miles further north. That's our ultimate objective. It's there we'll find the core of the Federal Army, and General Newman."

"When's our entire army expected to be in position?" asked James, brushing his arms to rub in warmth. Answering his own question, James continued, "It may be optimistic to think it'll be soon, with the weather about to implode. Word is the fuel we captured and salvaged in Hutchinson has helped. Every diesel vehicle in the Free States has been hauling personnel and ordinance. Casualties remain high, though. It seems there's a skirmish at every intersection or twist in the road. We've been fighting nonstop from Lincoln to here, even when you count those frigging river crossings."

"It's a good thing for us the Feds didn't try to hold their strong line at Lincoln. With a little resolve, they'd've licked us good." Taylor stamped his feet, keeping time with his words.

"Yeah, I agree. It doesn't make any sense." Justin replied, brushing off newly fallen snow, harbinger of James's prediction. "That line of defense they had was over 100 miles long running from York to Lincoln to Omaha. All of it flat land and terrain impossible for hiding either army. If they had stood and slugged it out with us, we'd have been caught out in the open. It could have been disastrous."

"General, why the hell do you think Newman pulled out?"

"That's a good question, Colonel. Maybe God was looking out for us. I can only guess. Maybe his new, green replacements needed more conditioning."

Taylor said, "Probably the SOB needed to lick his wounds. We did pound them pretty hard."

Justin nodded his agreement. "By the way, the unit I ordered north through South Dakota to cut off possible enemy replacements turned out to be a dud. If you think this place is cold, those boys saw twenty below. Their recon reported enemy defenses as nonexistant. Maybe the Feds have misread what we're up to and have moved to better ground, fearing they'd be outflanked. Right now, it doesn't matter. All we need to concentrate on is what's over there." Justin again pointed in the direction of Indianola. "Somewhere over those hills is a warm town waiting for liberation."

James couldn't resist. "Well, the pricks have better ground now. This place is rife with hills, trees, creeks, and rivers. All the obstacles a defensive army loves."

"Don't fool yourself, Rinaldi. You, a New Yorker, can appreciate these hills. I hear your boys made a habit of fighting in similar terrain. And anyway, all those creeks and rivers are frozen solid."

"You got me there, Sir. New York, except for the higher hills in the Catskills and the Adirondacks, has similar ground."

Justin studied the old road as it wound its way toward the sleepy town about to awaken to war's misery.

"Down this road lies freedom. We must take Indianola and turn the enemy's center. So, Gentlemen, prepare your men. We move as soon as the promised storm starts really blowin'."

"Seems like we're about to throw chance to the winds, General. Are we doing the right thing?" Taylor's face was shielded by the clouds of condensation, like a distress signal awaiting release.

"Taylor, hopefully this is the last time we'll ask the ultimate sacrifice from our people. If it doesn't work, well ..." Justin hesitated, "there may not be another time to ask. It's that critical, and it won't hurt to tell your men. They'll understand the need. They're good men."

Justin's group worked its way back to their transportation, hidden beneath the cover of many hills. A scattering of gunshots was heard in the distance. Justin wondered. *Is it a stray cow finding itself on a campfire's limited menu or a patrol in trouble?* The sounds, so common, hardly managed to turn their heads. They rushed to the minimal warmth afforded by the vehicles.

"General, may I have a word in private?" Taylor, sitting next to his brother, waited for the right opportunity to confront Justin.

"Sure, Tay, what's up?"

"I thought you'd want to know Julia's nearby."

Taylor watched as Justin's face transformed from sternness to delight. "You know the answer to that. Lead me to her."

"No need, I've taken the liberty to have her brought to HQ. She should be at your quarters about now."

"Thanks, and ..." Justin searched for a way to say what was on his mind. "Taylor, she can be so darn stubborn. I want her out of harm's way. After we meet, I want to get her on the next convoy out of here."

Taylor chuckled. "She's stubborn, sort of like you're stubborn. Anyway, I'm not sure it'll be possible to get her out. Fuel's low. We're waiting for tankers to arrive so we can send most of the stranded trucks back for resupply and safety. Otherwise, if we start advancing like you suppose, supply trucks will be caught in the thick of it, most likely moving troops."

"Shit, another thing to worry about. I thought my plate was full enough, and then I go fall in love."

"OK then, why not assign her to a hospital unit? Heck, Justin, you can issue the orders. Have her report to Becky. Sis will look after her. Damn it, man, you're about as high as anyone can get. You're commanding general of a whole freakin' army! Stop getting tongue-tied and use it to your advantage for once. It's not a sin to want Julia safe. Hell, if she was my girl, I'd do it."

Justin smiled at Taylor's insubordination, shaking his head in resignation. "OK, Taylor, tell me what you really think!"

December 21, 2020—Federal Army Headquarters, Des Moines, Iowa

General Skip Newman did not feel very successful, even though he sat in the catbird seat in a strong defensive position. It didn't matter any longer. The past weeks had seen his army purposely fall back in running battles and skirmishes too numerous to document. Indecision had entered the equation, becoming a virus eating into the central fiber of his army. The Federal cause was in trouble, and he saw no practical answer to the dilemma. He had protested to President Rex Collins that his inexperienced troops simply weren't ready and a fallback would allow a chance to prepare. He hoped the enemy would eventually overextend their lines from their supplies. Right now, luckily, the weather was on his side. He felt sure his strategy was working and hoped Collins thought so, too.

Newman sat at the cluttered desk reviewing intelligence and was not pleased. The staggering reports were disturbing. He mentally outlined what he would say to his unexpected visitor, rattling it off silently in systematic steps. Collins sat comfortably next to the office's roaring fireplace, waiting impatiently for Newman to begin. When he did, he was startled by his commanding general's clipped, unsure voice.

"Mr. President, despite our numerical superiority, we have lacked the cohesive glue necessary to carry it to advantage. Half the army consists of mercenaries of varied languages and loyalties. Their commitment appears only as strong as their advantage lasts. We need a victory to boost morale."

Collins thought, *No surprises so far.*

"Most troops sheltered in and around Des Moines are held in reserve. The bulk of the army is spread for 100 miles from Bridgewater in the west to Oskaloosa in the east, with Indianola in the center, all mostly along Iowa's old Highway 92."

Collins interrupted. "Yeah, I remember that road. My wife, God rest her soul, loved a movie a few years back that took place near there. She made me visit the location on one of our vacations," Collins reminisced. The memory of his wife still hurt him. He forgot about the war for a moment, feeling the need to explain to Newman.

"It was a real-life love story titled *The Bridges of Madison County*." Rex Collins, for a brief moment, let his austere guard down, and Newman, surprised at seeing a soft side to the hard old man, didn't miss it.

"Sir, I don't think I recall the movie. It was a bit before my time."

Collins, annoyed with himself for showing weakness born of fatigue, said simply, "General, continue."

Newman was pleased with the interruption. It allowed him to rethink his impromptu statement. "Thank you, Sir. Recent battles and numerous skirmishes have reduced the main Federal Army to around 1.2 million men. Of this, we have 200,000 in Des Moines and, as you're aware, about 200,000 with you in Madison." Newman looked at Collins, wondering, *What does this bastard really know that I do not?*

"Reports say the Rebels have almost 600,000 facing us here. Intel believes they have relief columns of unknown strength coming in from the Canadian border and the southwest, but doesn't believe they can possibly arrive in time for the coming operation. The early arrival of winter has become our biggest ally, making transport for them all but impossible.

"In the Atlantic states, we remain locked in a standoff. We have 800,000 men in a rigid line from Jamestown to Richmond. They're poised to break out, but I'm reluctant to do so now. As you know, they're surrounded by a like number of Rebels in preferential positions. It seems everything is focused on what happens right here."

Collins was beginning to show his age. Weeks of continual stress had caused the few remaining gray hairs upon his head to fall out. His visit to Des Moines to confer with his commanding general came from a keen desire to act.

"General Newman, from what you tell me, our troops in Des Moines are well situated and dug in for any uncertainty."

"That's correct, Mr. President." Newman's office in the Iowa state capitol building didn't seem suited to its new military use. Its proud walls, though surrendered to the necessity of war, did not lose their original purpose.

"Do you anticipate an attack on our lines?" Collins challenged.

Damn, another history lesson. "Mr. President." Newman picked his words carefully. "We outnumber them. We're entrenched and have better ground. We're mostly warm and settled. Add to all this a wind factor of minus ten degrees and a forecast for snow. ... I'd think even the late General Sinsome wouldn't be crazy enough to attack."

"Oh, you mean like the Hessians thought before General Washington hit them at Trenton? I seem to recall that it was around this time of year." Collins's historical parallel did not go unnoticed.

"Mr. President, I know my history. Washington, with a small army of less than 2,000 men, attacked his enemy under similar adverse, wintry conditions." Newman, pissed off, began to cite history himself, in hopes of annoying Collins. "He took advantage of his knowledge that the German tradition back then was to imbibe heavily on Christmas Day. Washington relied on their stupor as his ally. It was a major gamble, one that could have gone either way. He was lucky in my opinion."

Undeterred, Collins asked, "We won't repeat history, will we?" Collins's eyes burned a hole into Newman's inner soul as he continued. "History seems to have repeated itself a lot in this struggle. Skip, we have superior numbers. It's time for you to attack. You do understand I can order you to attack, but I am here to listen to your options and reasoning before I do. So damn it, man, convince me."

Unfazed, Newman continued. "To attack now, Mr. President, exposes us to needless casualties when we hold preferential ground. Our weakness, despite superior numbers, is the simple unavoidable fact that over half the army consists of mostly inexperienced, untrained mercenaries and draftees."

Skip noted that none of his explanation seemed to rouse Collins. Ignoring the president's lack of enthusiasm, he continued. "I understand your concern, Sir, but with half our troop strength untried, I feel we need one more victory to convince my mercenary generals they have chosen the right side. Whenever I've used our foreigners, they've inspired the Rebels to even more of the intense warfare they have become renowned for. I fear if the mercenaries ever start to think we're losing, only God knows which way they'll go. I just don't feel comfortable with them right now."

"General, you seem more concerned about your reinforcements than you do the enemy. We have veterans. Use them!"

"Pardon the confusion I seemed to have caused you, Mr. President, but there's more. It's not simply the problem of foreign soldiers. I'm not certain how the Rebels' new leader, Tarkington, will move. If Raif were still in command, I'd expect an attack. That would be his way. Hit us whenever he had a chance, and especially when we least expect it. Tarkington's an unknown. I think he's a bit more cautious than Saint Sinsome."

"General, your analysis better be correct. A lot depends upon it." Collins stood as he snapped out his words. "Intel says the Rebels are at the end of their rope. We fooled them at Vail by feeding them false info. I've had the snoops working on some new covert ploys to keep them off guard."

"Mr. President, even if I'm wrong, we have the advantage. And the time it would take to set up another ambush like Vail may take too long to make it believable. Besides, Sir, after Vail the enemy Intel has grown wiser. We need patience. Unless, somehow, they get overwhelming replacements to refill their diminishing ranks, they won't attack. I figure the next warm front will see them move on us. By then, it'll be too late, for we'll have taken the initiative from them. Seriously, before we take any action, I need to get our army together as one cohesive unit, not a hodgepodge foreign legion. As soon as I feel they're ready, I'll move in all haste. I fear to do otherwise could prove drastic."

"I need results, General. Your gamble better be right!"

"It's no gamble!" Newman shouted back. "Trust me! Sir, you shall have your victory. Our weather reports say it's going to snow big time in the next several days. They say we're about to have a regular white Christmas blizzard."

"Well, Newman, don't forget General Washington. It snowed that Christmas too."

"Don't worry yourself, Mr. President. Washington wasn't in godforsaken Iowa. Have a nice Christmas. Stay warm. I'll watch the farm here and give you your victory."

Collins turned to leave, his wool coat draped over his arm. Then he turned once more to address Newman. "You know, a lot is riding on your assumptions. I admit I was wrong earlier this month when I insisted you move. Unfortunately, we're running low on everything, and soon we'll have no room left to maneuver. That's unless you want to fight this war in Canada. Have a good day, General, and a Merry Christmas!"

Under his breath, Newman said, "Bah humbug to you, too, Sir!"

December 21, 2020—Evening, Rebel First Army Headquarters Milo, Iowa

The fireplace's warmth cast a glow upon Julia's weather-beaten face. The cold had taken its toll, chafing her lips and chilling her throughout. Justin was aghast at how tired and haggard she looked. *Do I look as exhausted?* He would not broach the subject; it didn't matter. Here Julia was, standing before him in the flesh, new sergeant's stripes sewn on her overcoat and hat. Time was at a premium. He needed to get her out of here as soon as possible. He could never live with himself if he didn't.

"Justin, I've missed you. Are you well? You look so tired." She lovingly grasped his hands, pulling him to her warmth.

"I'm as fine as I can be under the circumstances. What's more important is we're together. Julia, this is all we really have, right now. I've missed you and love you so much."

Julia's piercing eyes captivated his heart. Their separation, a necessary evil, only served as the tinder to the spark of their love.

"Justin, I love you, too."

They embraced, holding each other, afraid to part. Justin looked into her eyes. There was no mistaking what they felt for each other.

"Sergeant Julia McKnight—oh how I love the sound of your name upon my lips. I have a favor to ask."

"How can I refuse such a charming general? What is it?"

"Let's marry the moment this war ends. You know, Honey, I can't think of my life or my future without you." The Rebel Army's most daring general was all stutters and shakes, but Julia didn't notice. Her smile reflected her joy.

"General, you mean you actually still want to marry a girl from Oklahoma? I figured you had temporary insanity a few days back on that road outside Hutchinson." She teased Justin with another loving hug, watching for his reaction.

"You bet I would. What do you say?"

Standing, holding hands, and looking into each other's eyes, Julia answered, "Justin, I can't wait for the war to end. I'll marry you now, if you want. Nothing would please me more." Julia beamed; her smile melted his heart. "Of course," she continued, "I'll wait, but you may be taking a chance I might get a better offer before this here war's over."

"You better not," he teased. "I still prefer to wait. Do you mind?" He pulled her close to him, feeling the tender warmth of her body pressed to his. Their eyes met, and their kiss, long and lingering, melted his resolve. Nothing but this moment mattered.

Julia reluctantly pulled away to speak, wearing a large, happy grin. "Justin, I'll wait for you as long as it takes."

"Honey, if I have anything to say about it, you won't have long to wait. You know, we need to break the news to Taylor, but before we do, can I see your left hand?"

Taking her hand, he kneeled as he placed a small diamond ring on her third finger. It almost fit, but was slightly too small. Julia's surprise was replaced by elation. Taylor had helped him acquire the ring in one of his scavenging patrols.

"This makes our awkward moment outside Hutchinson official," he beamed. "I plan to get you a nicer one someday. Today, though, I want the world to know you're spoken for."

"Don't you dare ever get another! This will always be my special ring, a vivid reminder of this wonderful moment." She leaped into his ready arms, embracing him, tears flowing. "Do you think Taylor will be surprised?"

"Surprised about what?" Taylor asked as he entered the warmth of the small farmhouse.

"Why, we set a tentative date to get married, that's what, Bro. What do you think?" Justin moved toward the door to greet Taylor. Julia showed him the ill-fitting ring, now safely nestled on her pinky finger.

"Congratulations." Taylor hugged his future sister-in-law. "But you're right, no big surprise, Julia. My big brother did tell me you said yes a few days ago. And anyway, he's been love-struck since the moment he laid eyes on you." Taylor, his dramatic side now on full throttle, blinked his eyelashes and turned his unkempt head upwards, teasing.

Laughing, Justin tapped his brother on the shoulder and then hugged him. "Don't ever change, Taylor. Stay the way you are. You're one of a kind. And Brother, why the heck are you here, now of all times? Your timing is sure lousy."

Julia, smiling, hugged Taylor and whispered, "We need to find someone for you, General." She had heard through the grapevine that Taylor, when wounded, had been close to a hospital nurse. Her name was Samantha Gregory, and her unit was only a few miles south.

"Oh, I'll worry about all that after the war. I wish you both a long and happy life together and a few nieces and nephews for me to spoil." Taylor, unaware his nurse had been killed two days earlier, grinned foolishly. Julia didn't know if the relationship was serious, and anyway, she didn't have the heart to tell him. She felt like a coward.

"I see it's snowing by the mess you've brought in here." Justin pointed to the growing puddle on the floor.

"Actually, Justin, that's why I came. General Tarkington's called a powwow, and all us good generals are invited, from brigadier on up. As his second, I suppose that includes you, too, oh illustrious Commander General of the First Army." He teased, "I hate to crash your love nest, but duty calls. Sorry, Julia." Julia's eyes and pretty pout gave away her sadness at hearing the news.

"At least we got the chance to agree to a time, Julia. I promise I'll do everything life allows to make you happy." Justin tried to keep a bold face. "Honey, you need to stay away from harm, so no questions. I'm assigning you to duty with the 77th Hospital Unit. Here are your orders.

You need to report to Lieutenant Rebecca Northcutt; yes, she's our sister. Transportation for the wounded has been arranged to convoy at first light. Rest here for now, and enjoy the heat while you can. My adjutant will have an escort for you when it's time to leave. I love you, Julia McKnight, and don't you ever forget it."

They kissed deeply, clinging to each other, trying to hold on for one more precious moment. It hurt for Justin to break away. He couldn't miss Julia's tears. They covered her face.

"And don't worry, I'll see you soon." Justin needed to give her hope and wished what he was about to say didn't sound like bragging. "One more thing—I'm going to do everything in my power to end this war soon so we can get married the minute it ends. I sure don't want to give you a chance to change your mind." He softly caressed her face, holding her close. "I love you, Julia, and I shall always love you."

He forced a laugh as Taylor opened the door. Both brothers left the room's warmth for the unknown, rushing into the mouth of a raging storm.

Julia rushed to the window and sadly, yet proudly, watched him leave. She was happy for her brief moment with him, yet knew the tremendous weight her future husband carried.

She sobbed, "I love you, Justin. Please be careful."

December 21, 2020—2200 Hours, General Tarkington's Headquarters Liberty Center, Iowa

The dim light cast a foreboding of doom upon the shadows of the gathered generals. The need for the meeting was obvious. Many would have preferred to hide their heads in the proverbial sand, or in this case the raging snow, rather than face this moment's dread. General Tarkington started the meeting as he walked impatiently into the crowded room.

"Gentlemen, we're at our ebb. We have little time left to maneuver in our favor. The expected storm has arrived and so has our opportunity to act. We have two days to deploy our forces. Consult your maps, please. We'll converge on Indianola, the enemy's center." Justin glanced quickly at Taylor with knowing eyes. Once again, Justin had figured the army's move.

"Sir, that has to be the strongest point in their line." Taylor couldn't resist pointing this out.

"I suppose it is. It's also their Achilles' heel. Justin, First Army's 1st Corps is to attack their center with your 36th and 121st Divisions leading the way." Taylor groaned to himself. James showed no outward emotion; inside he felt sick.

"I need our best shock troops in the advance," he said as he eyeballed Taylor. Taylor wished he hadn't been so curt a moment earlier. "If the storm continues, and reports indicate it will, you'll leave tomorrow morning at dusk and progress to your objective.

1st Corps' goal is to take Indianola at all costs. The enemy has about 90,000 men in the area, so you are about even. You'll agree that's a rarity. Intel says they're dug in."

"Where does the rest of the army figure in the scheme of things, Sir?" Justin wanted the full picture. His impatience and excitement made him jump ahead for an answer. Unlike Sinsome, Tarkington, did not readily include his second in command in his planning strategy.

"Good question, Justin. Our army will attack on all fronts during the night of the 22nd and the morning of the 23rd. Most important will be our flanking movements meant to create balanced attacks both to the east and northeast. I intend to split the Federal forces' positions aligned all the way to Oskaloosa."

Justin instantly saw the merit of a plan having all elements of the Rebel line attacking at once. It was risky and daring. *Going for broke when there is little other option makes sense.* The primary objective would be to surprise and disrupt the enemy, instilling sufficient confusion and fear to force them to move east to protect the route to Madison. He agreed it was certainly a gamble.

When Tarkington summed up his intentions, it was apparent to all he had figured every angle. However, everything depended upon coordination in the worst storm the area had seen in years.

Tarkington stood still, almost as if in attention. His stiff appearance was in direct contrast to the late General Sinsome's casual manner. "Gentlemen, it's now up to us. Unless supplies reach us soon, we have only five days left before we're forced to retreat and attempt to meet up with our supply line to the south. With this storm, we're landlocked. Retreat would be a greater disaster than attacking the enemy. It gives the Federals time to organize. And Gentlemen, I repeat, time is something we can't afford to give. We can't end up like Napoleon did in Russia."

He delivered his punch line in rapid fire. "We must attack because we can't retreat. If we move forward, we might fail, but at least we'll do a lot of damage. If we retreat, we take the chance of repeating history and possibly losing our army to the weather. For you non-history buffs who may have missed my point earlier, Napoleon retreated in similar weather after his defeat in Russia. He was slaughtered. I will not let this happen to us." No one in the cold room missed his point. Tarkington's staccato continued.

"Issue as much ammo and food as can be carried. Justin, I thank God for your pecan plan. I do say, though, I'm already tiring of the wondrous nut. See if you can capture some good old Federal food. That's a huge request and not an order."

"I'll see what I can come up with, Sir." Justin smiled.

"Justin, your men will need to travel light. With the cold weather expected, it's critical to wrap 'em up as warm as possible. Have each man carry only those damn pecans and as much ammo as they can hold. Your gear will be waiting for you when we catch up. Now, go with God and get equipped. Good luck!"

Leaving the command post, Justin gathered the First Army generals around him. "Men, we've got our work cut out for us. Get as much sleep as you can. We meet at 0400 hours."

When all his officers left, Justin, with a troubled look, turned to Taylor, who was lingering behind. "I guess my marriage plans may have been a bit hasty, if not completely optimistic tonight."

"I'm afraid it's a bit too late for that, Justin! Now if you don't mind, James and I would like to help you go over plans for tomorrow, since you have planned a wedding that's dependin' upon our success. You know, I was thinking ..." Taylor hesitated.

"Oh crap, here we go again!" Justin feigned concern.

"No, I promise no bullshit and nothing bad. I was just thinking, it's too bad Mom and Dad don't know. One thing's for sure, they'd be pleased at your choice and would want to be there for you. Do you think we could find them somehow?"

"Taylor, I sure wish they could be there, but I doubt it's possible."

"Well, Bro, you've found yourself a great girl. I hope to God I'm as lucky as you someday."

"You will be. Wait and see. Do you think Mom and Dad are still in Santa Fe?"

Taylor saw his concern. He felt it too. "I hope so; it's said the war hasn't touched it much."

James interrupted the brothers' nostalgic mood. "Hey, lovebirds, let's get to our maps and get to work. I'm a bit confused, if not concerned, about coordination."

Taylor scooped up a handful of snow, made a snowball, and threw it at James, laughing.

"Are you crazy, Taylor?" Justin shouted above the wind. "If James knows anything, it's snowball fights."

The three generals, all laughing, walked quickly toward Justin's headquarters. Large snowflakes quickly covered the landscape and the footsteps of the three men; its swirling white fury had suddenly become both their hope and their hell.

A mile distant, Julia, wrapped in several blankets and clutching a warm thermos, climbed into the cold passenger seat of a truck's cab, headed for Becky's hospital unit. Her heart was all aglow, but the dour middle-aged woman next to her didn't seem to notice. All she knew was she had to drive 200 miles south into a blizzard. The driver nodded to the soldier, noticing, in time, her sergeant's stripes.

Julia reached across the cab to shake the driver's hand. "Soldier, I'm Sergeant Julia McKnight. Happy to meet you, Private."

"Sergeant, I'm PFC Liz Forbes, at your service. Glad to have the company." Liz retightened the scarf covering her face. "Sarge, it looks like we're about to face some terrible weather. I can't imagine what military genius thought this here trip up." The scarf made her voice seem muffled and distant.

Julia, not commenting, smiled. *If you only knew, Honey, if you only knew.* Laughing, Julia said, "Soldier, let's get these wheels turning. We've a long way to go and a lot of road to burn." Smiling, she lingered on the memory of her parting kiss. *Please, Lord, don't let him be harmed.*

You may have to fight a battle more than once to win it.
—Margaret Thatcher

CHAPTER TWENTY-SIX

December 22, 2020—Rebel Advance, Five Miles East of Indianola, Iowa

Taylor and James's light divisions joined ranks near the intersection of Iowa's Old Highway 92 and County Route 532, five miles east of their objective, chomping at the bit, ready to advance. The Rebel coordinated effort placed them in the army's forward position. Their ambitious objective, simply to break through the Federal center nomatter the cost, weighed heavily on everyone, from general on down. The Ranger Division's line covered two miles, running east and slightly southeast. It linked with the 121st, whose ragged line spanned a two-and-a-half-mile ridge, driving westerly for about a mile before slanting in a thirty-degree angle northwest. Thousands had stood in the cold morning flurries since 0330 hours, cold, uncomfortable, and anxious to pounce. Snow and howling winds made the frightful wait more unbearable for even the stoutest of souls.

Men huddled together for warmth, though the wind chill of eighteen degrees was actually warmer than expected. Troopers didn't see it making much difference in their comfort; they focused their minds on staying warm rather than on the anxiety of the coming battle.

Taylor, shivering, shouted into the wind toward James. "General, the 36th is ready; are your men set?" As 1st Corps' latest lieutenant general, Taylor commanded the advance. "Damn cold weather. How does anyone live here?" Taylor's body ached; the cold cut through him as he jumped in place, trying to stay warm.

James answered, a light snow covering his helmet and shoulders, "We're ready to go on your order. Any change in plan?"

"Nope, we're to hold tight and try to keep warm. This howling wind should help conceal our advance if we don't freeze to death before we start." He rewrapped his weathered scarf around his face, again muffling his voice. "James, it's important to recap the objective to your men repeatedly before the cold freezes it out of them."

Taylor jumped up and down as he spoke. A boyish grin could be seen through his beard when his scarf fell away, victim to the howling wind. He spouted out the order by rote between shivers. "At 0500 we're to advance five miles in one foot of swirling snow. We are to disrupt and force-push enemy movement to allow balance of 1st Corps to flank the enemy's present position. Then we hold tight until Tarkington completes his work and links with us. Like Command said, it's a simple maneuver in a blizzard." Taylor made a wide sweeping gesture with his hands. "You get all this, James?"

Taylor's humor was catching. His antics broke the gloom, helping lift their sagging spirits during the difficult wait.

"Taylor, it sure sounds like a tall order to me." James found it difficult to remain serious. "I know snow. This weather's getting worse. I wish we could advance now. Do you really believe we can take these people piecemeal? It seems a lot to ask our enemy to cooperate just so we can kick their freaking butts."

"What I really think, James, is I'd rather be at some warm mall, shopping for some new, clean, warm clothes, especially nice, clean longjohns. Put the emphasis on warm. Then I'd sit down to a sizzling hot cup of black coffee with six teaspoons of sugar, a couple of warm jelly donuts, and a pretty, voluptuous blonde to share it."

"Taylor, damn it, stop! You're making me want to strike a general officer. The warm donuts sure sound good to me. And that blonde, well she sure sounds wonderful, too. Me, I'd settle for any pretty chick; anything will do, except your ugly mug, that is. But your dream moment is just that. I don't believe there're any malls left, particularly here!" James shook the gathering snow from his helmet. His stomach churned for want of food.

"That's a double-roger, Rinaldi." Taylor checked the workings of his M-16, taking special care that it was not locked or frozen shut.

"I still don't understand why we haven't seen any resistance. Even though the elements suck, our scouts haven't run into enemy pickets anywhere, in any direction." James became serious again. His nature would not allow him otherwise.

"Rinaldi, let's hope they're underestimating our desire to freeze our collective asses and leave it at that. Continue to send out your scouts no less than one mile in advance of our movement. Since you New York boys are used to this shit, I'll leave scouting in your hands."

"I'll get right on it," James replied and turned slightly, ready to leave. "Taylor, I better meet with my brigade commanders for another pre-attack briefing. If you see Luke, tell him to stay low."

"You got it. Good luck, James. See you at Simpson College. I hear our room and board has been paid." Taylor's chuckle sounded distantly muffled as he rewrapped his scarf around his face.

James brushed accumulating snow from his field jacket and angled into the wind, returning to his command. The day held promise for the unusual. He had no illusions of grandeur about their mission. Once again, his men would be used as forward shock troops—expendable for the glorious cause. His primary personal objective, beyond following orders, was to keep the price in blood low.

Taylor watched James slowly trudging a difficult path through the accumulating snow. White camouflage became unnecessary with the whiteout effect. Nevertheless, several men wrapped white sheets around their uniforms to improvise camouflage-like coverings. It added little warmth but gave them an additional measure of stealth. Taylor figured at best that his advance, now in a blinding snow, would appear ghostlike to the distant enemy in the morning dark. He reckoned his daydreams of warmth would have to be put on the back burner until they succeeded. He was confident of Justin's ability to bring in the balance of his new command. *If Justin fails to show ... no, I can't allow myself the luxury to think.*

Justin had earlier ordered Taylor to lead the advance, promising he'd take temporary command of his 1st Corps' backup divisions. Justin planned to come in with the balance of First Army, but only in the event of disaster. In the middle of this storm, Taylor was haunted by the old saying, "Best laid plans of mice and men often go wanting." *Oh well*, he sighed to himself.

At 0500, the Rebels ignited into action after what had seemed an eternity. The hour's ominous arrival was for some a joy; for others it was a hindrance to their desires to stay put despite the intense cold. Somehow each man knew previous battles had been forerunners in preparation for what was about to happen.

The blinding snow fell unabated. James's scouts continued to report zero resistance. The enemy apparently did not think them foolish enough to attack in the face of a raging blizzard. It was the Battle of Trenton all over again, only in the year 2020 with a new group of American rebels.

On Taylor's command, the troops moved in unison, leaning unwaveringly into the rushing, relentless wind. They advanced silently; no artillery announced their coming. No unearthly Rebel yell would be used to strike its surreal fear. Surprise was the key order of the day.

Initially, little to no resistance was encountered. The snow coated their irregular uniforms, giving them a ghostlike appearance as advance units, with stealth and precise movement, eliminated the few enemy pickets braving the weather.

Taylor, at the rear of the advance trudging slowly through the swirling snow, could not see his men directly ahead. His mind, numbed by heartless cold, had trouble focusing, yet he thought for no apparent reason, *I wonder if James knows some New Yorkers died in the Alamo. Where the hell did that thought come from?* Pushing aside the odd rumination, he resolved to enlighten Rinaldi later. Then just as quickly he caught himself and concentrated on the work at hand.

The dawning light of a new day, blocked by the storm, filtered over the land, slowly and dimly illuminating the area. When the Rebels' advance line reached within a quarter mile from its objective, Federal guards were awakened to their presence, and sounded the alarm. The garrison came alive with a vengeance, but their reaction was too late. At ten-foot intervals, and spread over four miles, 25,000 Rebels advanced toward their narrow objective in determined fury, overwhelming the mostly sleeping defenders. At the initial point of contact, the Rebels held a ten-to-one advantage.

The ensuing engagement turned into a furious array of hand-to-hand combat and mini-battles, with street-to-street fighting. Federal reserves were sent to counter Taylor's troops as if on cue, just the way Rebel leaders hoped they would. The enemy's maneuver opened their western line in Acworth slightly, about five miles from the center of the attack.

With precision, the balance of 1st Corps, unleashed by Justin, broke through the gap circling north of Indianola. Once successful, the Rebel Army dug in to brace for Newman's counterattack, expected to come from Des Moines.

Indianola was now encircled by the Rebels. By 1700 hours, the city was entirely under Rebel control. According to plan, Command quickly ordered the entire First Army, except for Taylor's 1st Corps, to link with Tarkington's Army marching for Des Moines. The worsening weather temporarily stranded Justin in Indianola. He planned to attempt reaching the main elements of his First Army Command in the morning. For the time being, he was content to be near his brother, satisfied his predicament was out of his control.

The number of Federal soldiers defending their center was not as high as Intel thought. The Rebels now had 50,000 Federal prisoners to deal with. Justin ordered they be marched south in the storm. Blindfolded, roped together, and cold, their war was over.

Justin refused to follow orders to kill his prisoners, more than half of whom were mercenaries. Though Tarkington's orders were explicit, Justin once again chose to follow his conscience. He knew that many would die on the march, but it would still be better than carrying out the standing order to execute all prisoners. In the end, more than 5,000 enemy prisoners would die from exposure. Later, the Federal prisoners' march would be referred to as Northcutt's death march. At this moment, though, Justin didn't care how history reported his deed.

Casualties for the 36th and 121st were lower than predicted. One thousand men were listed among the killed and wounded, many with frostbite. Orders were given to dig in and await the expected enemy counterattack. Justin worried the balance of Tarkington's weather-delayed corps would not arrive as planned.

The inclement weather continued. The snow churned into a swirling, cyclone-like mess, dusting about with the endless winds, chasing away any improvised warmth. Shelter became paramount in everyone's mind. The only plus to the weather was that it was likely to have a similar effect upon the enemy.

While Taylor braved the weather to arrange 1st Corps' defenses in a complete circle about two miles outside Indianola, Justin casually surveyed his temporary HQ in the Simpson College library. The Rebel Army's emergency escape route to the south was secure but only as long as the Federals didn't learn he had only 75,000 men to stop their expected advance. Taylor's six divisions were all that lay in the midst of some fifty Federal divisions. Justin hoped the Feds were taking the bait, though probably slowed by the weather. Justin wished he could have First Army's two other corps with him at Indianola. Orders required they be elsewhere. Justin had a different opinion.

Confirming Justin's worse fears, General Tarkington's advance was behind schedule. Justin's thinking turned to his next move in the dangerous game of chess his commander had started. Was Tarkington purposely behind schedule? His deceased mentor, Sinsome, had tried this ploy before; the last time in Cancun. Were Taylor's men, those few remaining brave souls from his old brigade, to be used as bait again? The Indianola force represented ten percent of the Rebel Army's presence in the region. With jarring impact, Justin suddenly realized his expendability. Tarkington had openly boasted he'd like to see Newman commit his untried troopers into the open killing fields; that would give the outnumbered Rebel Army the advantage. Justin pondered restlessly, *How long would Tarkington wait to show?* 1st Corps' contingent would not have long to find out.

December 22, 2020—1700 hours, Federal Headquarters Des Moines, Iowa

General Newman's adjutant rushed frantically into Command HQ, interrupting his emergency general staff meeting. "Sir, the enemy has captured Indianola; our center has been compromised! Four divisions have been overrun. It's thought they were allowed to surrender. Our outer units, those not involved, have regrouped and spread out in a thinner line to form a new perimeter. They await your orders!"

Though startled, Newman's experience and training forced him to slow down and think. Saying nothing, he motioned for his adjutant to take a seat. He'd expected something like this after reading the disturbing field reports scattered on his desk. He arose from his chair, clearing his desk to place a map on it. The disrupting turn of events was not yet ominous if it could be worked to his advantage. He urgently needed the victory he'd discussed earlier with President Collins, but the enemy's abrupt move forced him to play his hand before he intended. Without hesitation, he decided to move up the timetable to counterattack no later than today. *So be it*, he thought. *My newest mercenaries will have to get their training under fire. We'll see soon enough what they're made of.*

"Once again the Rebels are calling the shots," Newman said aloud to no one. "Damn that bastard Collins. He predicted this with his gibberish about Washington, Trenton, and frigging Hessians." His staff didn't dare say a word; they knew their boss too well to chance it.

Newman called his orderly, standing at his office entrance. "It seems our new nemesis, Tarkington, is moving out of turn in our game of war, disrupting my plans for a post-Christmas attack." Newman's voice was steady. "Well, we can show that upstart a trick or two." *Well anyway, just enough to make it a fight.*

He leaned over his desk, studying his map. He shouted for the nearest staff person. "Harry, call all corps commanders that are able to meet here at 1800. We'll see about Indianola. I do believe Tarkington may have overstepped his objective. It sure didn't take him long." Newman took a deep drag on his almost forgotten cigar, smiling. The smoke's aroma pleased his senses. "We'll see how we can turn all this to our advantage," he snarled.

"Yes, Sir, I'll get right on it." Harry Zook left in hurried passion.

It momentarily seemed odd to Newman that Harry, a Pennsylvania Amish man turned soldier and patriot, was such a passionate zealot, so contrary to his upbringing. The war had changed the lives of so many. Newman usually didn't give two cents for anyone but himself. Today, for some unknown, unnerving reason, a sudden caring urge surfaced.

Newman carefully calculated the odds, considering his strategy. He had a little over one million men spread out in a 200-mile front. His HQ Command at Des Moines included 200,000 of his elite forces. Intelligence suggested the 1st Rebel Corps was the only real obstacle in his way. He desperately needed to regain the respect his army had lost. Intel had said that Tarkington's main army was not at Indianola. He reflected. *Where is he? Was this a ruse or a gigantic blunder for the Rebels' new commander? Is now the best time to switch back to an offensive?*

As expected, not all Federal commanders were able to make Newman's emergency strategy session. Several were too far away at posts now made more remote due to the "Blizzard of 2020." Sufficient numbers showed up to deal with the current dilemma, but many of his best veteran commanders were missing. Newman would reluctantly have to make do with the generals he had available.

"General Newman, Sir." Riesling's impeccable English caught Newman's attention as the mercenary general spoke in clipped cadence. His German heritage was still strong upon his tongue. "Are you not concerned the Rebels are drawing us out into the open? I hear the enemy force that compromised our center is the infamous Rebel 1st Corps. Couldn't we dispose of them at our leisure? After all, we are led to believe they are a damaged force of less than 100,000 cold and fatigued men."

"You make a good point, General Riesling. The enemy 1st Corps has been a major nemesis to our republic since the beginning, starting with its core unit, the 36th Ranger Division. But I figure if we annihilate these bastards, we not only meet our objective but put an end to their mystique and break the backbone of the Rebel Army. General, I don't pretend I know what the Rebs have up their sleeves. It really doesn't matter." Riesling shook his head as if in disagreement. Newman ignored him.

"They're occupying our center and must be eliminated. Intel still believes we outnumber their entire army by two to one. I need," his voice slowed, "no, Gentlemen, we need a victory. You all know this." Newman's voice rose as he became incensed. "If they're foolish enough to get their elite shock troops cornered in that sleepy borough, then I guess it's up to us to make it their permanent resting place. Heaven knows they put enough of our men into the ground. Intel reports they took about 50,000 prisoners and drove them south. If we move quickly to retake Indianola, we might recapture our men. Orders for no quarter remain in effect. When we win this war, no one will give a damn about a bunch of dead traitors, especially that Northcutt bunch."

Newman stood and with determined force, slammed his fist upon the table before him.

"We will attack tomorrow, December 23rd, at 0400, in force. You, General Riesling, will lead the advance."

A large wall map outlining the plan of attack and designated assignments was put up for review. Newman's strategy deployed half his immediately available force of about 500,000 men, holding close to 200,000 in reserve. The balance of Newman's army, about 300,000, was needed to protect the temporary capital in Madison.

The strength of the Federal plan was also its greatest weakness. Little leeway was given for inclement weather, and reserves were not in place at the center of the advance. There was insufficient time to accurately implement orders that were communicated mostly by couriers. Twenty Federal divisions moved out. The gap they left open had to be filled quickly by the reserve force advancing mainly on foot.

The primary flaw in the quick plan was that the Federal reserves were several miles distant, near Pella, Iowa, marching into the wind. Newman calculated that this flaw was unimportant, feeling secure the weather's hindrance would serve to his advantage. A blizzard was still hitting the entire region. Besides, it was too late to change plans; no time was left to second-guess the Rebels.

Jim Damiano

December 23, 2020—Rebel Army 1st Corps Line, Indianola, Iowa

Rebel pickets soon forgot their concern over frostbite when a screeching enemy appeared, unafraid to hide its massive movement. Word was quickly relayed to Justin's temporary HQ at the college library. All troops were ordered to man their posts. Surrounded, 1st Corps once again was in a fight for its existence.

Justin was brusquely shaken awake from a fitful slumber by his excited adjutant. "Sir, the Feds are attacking in strength. We're under fire by an overwhelming force at every position except south. It remains open for the moment. General T. Northcutt asks if we should consider retreat while we can."

Justin, rudely awakened from two hours of badly needed slumber, quickly cleared his clouded mind. He tossed off his blanket and bounded from his cot, allowing his mind to capture the moment. He rubbed sleep from his tired eyes and focused on the officer before him.

"Captain, fill me in while I eat a piece of bread and some confounded pecans." He felt instantly guilty and saw his dead grandfather's scolding smile as soon as he had uttered his casual comment. "I think the Feds could've left us a bit more food. Yet I do admire their quick action to destroy everything before they surrendered." Justin forced himself to maintain a calm veneer while he held back anger at Tarkington's stalling and the abrupt awakening.

Captain Ellington, not new to Justin's calm exterior, recognized there was more to his commander's complaint than food.

"Sir, I've taken the liberty to contact divisional commanders. General T. Northcutt sends his regards and suggests it's proper for you to take command. He's on his way later but said he'd prefer to be at the front line where he can determine what's happening."

"Good! That's my brother, always the practical one. When did this start?" Justin's head, clearing of sleep, deliberated while he ate the meager breakfast. He chewed quickly, listening intently, still concerned somewhat that he was stepping on his brother's command.

"I'd say about five minutes ago. Word of the specifics arrived seconds before I woke you. Our defense is under heavy pressure. Right now we're holding our own, but no guarantees."

"Ellington, advise Taylor—no retreat."

Minutes later Justin's orderly handed him a mug of something hot, while 1st Corps' divisional commanders swiftly entered the quiet library, passing the old fountain at its entrance. Taylor approached Justin, giving a quick salute. "General, if you concur, I'll lead my men from the trenches. You hold the fort here. Two heads are better than one, you know."

Justin, relieved, answered, "Your plan makes sense, thanks. Together we'll get through this." He turned to the assembled commanders.

"Gentlemen, as you know, the enemy advance that Command hoped for has commenced. Harold and Mark, your divisions on our southern line need to consolidate. I need you each to send half your men to here and here." Justin pointed to the wall map. "Hold them in reserve so they will be able to move at once wherever needed. There's not much to discuss that we haven't covered or expected. We must hold until Tarkington shows. There won't be much mercy shown if we fail. The order to execute captured enemy soldiers stands. Let's make them pay dearly. And remind our boys that they'll die if they surrender. Do not take prisoners until and unless I order otherwise."

Justin's weary body ached; a searing pain radiated through his chest. Strain had begun to take control and worry had become his partner. Never had he felt this fatigued. He tried to avoid looking at Taylor, knowing his brother could read his concerns.

"Men, I truly feel we're near the end. Tell your men we need another good fight out of them, though they're tired, hungry, dirty, and damn cold. I know I ask too much from them. I also know they will respond admirably." He hesitated, grimaced. "I wish I could honestly say it'll be one last fight. I can't promise." *How expendable we've become in the overall scope.*

"Good luck, and may God bless y'all. It's a privilege to lead such good men."

Each man departed, some thinking deeply, most keeping their own counsel. Taylor stopped briefly, looked into his brother's eyes, and put a comforting arm upon his shoulder. He left without saying a word, heading to his eastern post to face the enemy's main thrust.

When alone for a moment, Justin opened his backpack, pulled out the eight-by-ten portrait. It was rumpled and worn, but the family picture gave him comfort. Gently he replaced it and stood to leave.

Thunderous battle raged throughout the city, leaving little doubt to its few remaining frightened citizens that they were caught in the midst of a giant struggle. The battle, a city surrounded in the dead of winter—a desperate enemy, was reminiscent of World War II's Battle of the Bulge.

Welcomed daylight filtered through the swirling drifts of snow. From his catbird seat, Taylor clearly saw that his defenses immediately forward were holding, though slowly compressing inward. Wave after wave of Federal advances were repulsed, with heavy casualties for both armies.

Midtown Indianola became a giant open hospital. Wounded searched unsuccessfully for comfort from the unforgiving elements. Hospital units were too few to accommodate all the wounded; the college dorms and classrooms were quickly filled, along with every available, undamaged building.

Becky Northcutt, who, according to her brother, was supposed to be safe some 200 miles south, worked frantically on a chest wound. Her desperate struggle to save the dying soldier failed.

She had requested duty with 1st Corps and was given permission to join medical replacements transferred before the Rebel assault. Her arrival intentionally was not announced to her brothers; they had enough on their agenda. Besides, she needed to be near her Luke, if only in spirit.

Across the tent, Julia cared for another wounded soldier. She had volunteered along with her future sister-in-law. After all, she reasoned, Justin's orders to assist Becky must be followed. Not to be denied, and ever independent, her need to be close to her general and the Rebel cause superceded Justin's desire for her safety.

Becky was pleased to have Julia on her medical team. For the moment both women were reassured, knowing they provided badly needed comfort in an unforgiving land. Becky, in the thick of war for over a year, knew instinctively that this was not the time to hold back.

× × × × ×

A few miles distant from Becky's hospital unit, Taylor scanned his defensive line using his binoculars. Swirling snow made the survey difficult. Runners continuously kept him informed, along with makeshift communications. Civilian handheld radios remained helpful, but their use was limited since they could be monitored.

"Sir, the enemy's pressing our right flank. It's about to collapse."

"Captain, send in the last Ranger reserves. Advise General Hanford his division's reserves need to back us up, if they still can."

A young courier arrived, and upon overhearing Taylor, interrupted. "Sir, not five minutes ago, General Hanford was forced to pull back to his original position on the southern line. I was sent to let you know you're on your own. He'll do whatever he can to secure our escape route."

The courier appeared to be on his last legs. Gasping, he coughed up blood, collapsing at Taylor's feet. The courier's helmet fell off, revealing long, luxurious blonde hair.

"Take care of this wounded soldier!" Taylor shouted, looking at the fallen soldier. She could not be more than sixteen.

"Too late, Sir, she's gone!"

Taylor, in a flashing moment of involuntary grief, looked upon the courier's opened blue eyes, her face beautiful, even in death, staring at him, reminding him of Becky. Regaining his composure, he shouted instructions. Then with deliberate calm, he grabbed his carbine, checked his service revolver, and touched his Bowie knife for comfort. Taylor, never one to back away from a fight, demonstrated bravely, though unintentionally, the primary reason his men would follow him into the gates of hell.

In another sector, James viewed his haggard line, still holding firm. *I'm damn proud of these men. So many families will be affected by today's toil.* He allowed the thought to slip away and concentrated on the nasty work ahead, firing his red-hot carbine into the mob pushing his way. It was difficult.

The blustery wind, taking a sharp twist, whipped the fallen snow into swirling mini-funnels, blinding everyone in its path. Actual snowfall had stopped; the full sun and bright blue sky lit the horrible scene. Massed clusters of dead and dying Federals were spread in horrible heaps over miles of blood-reddened terrain. Their work and sacrifice were not in vain; half the Rebel defenders were casualties, too. But the killing was not over yet. Horrific cries from the wounded were heard above the gunfire. Frenzied screams from charging Federals announced they were attacking again, smelling victory.

"Where the hell is Tarkington?" James shouted in dismay, calling for his adjutant. "Captain, are there any reserves available?"

"I've already checked, Sir. The answer's 'no.' We're surrounded and on our own."

Luke's 7th Ranger Regiment, helping to defend the northern line, held fast, his men heeding Taylor's call for sacrifice. They had witnessed first-hand the enemy's brutality. There was no need to tell them to fight to the death. Outside their position's line of fire lay hundreds of dead and dying Federals. Newman's untried mercenaries were now deceased veterans.

"Here they come! Don't those foreign idiots ever get enough lead?" Captain Carey shouted. No one heard his anger, except Luke.

What the rebels didn't know was that the mercenaries had no option but to go forward. Federal officers and men were placed at the rear to make certain everyone went forward. Several who had been bold enough to refuse to attack in the face of the Rebel's murderous gunfire were shot on the spot for cowardice, along with anyone foolishly trying to desert.

After the battle, this horrendous fact would become clear to the Rebels. Right now, it didn't matter much. The amassed human waves continued their brutal, unrelenting assault. Soon the Rebels feared they could not hold.

Luke's life seemed to flash before his eyes. Through gloves containing almost frozen fingers, he aimed his M-16, taking down three targets. He didn't enjoy killing his old comrades in arms. That no longer mattered either; he had no choice as he slammed another magazine into his rifle. *This is what we've become.*

"How's ammunition?" Luke turned to his adjutant.

"More is supposed to be coming up, Sir. It's getting pretty scarce. We may have to go out and relieve the enemy dead of theirs."

"Did you check ammo pouches on our casualties? We don't need to take an unnecessary chance to break cover. We'll try to wait for nightfall, though even then it's still risky. What's our current strength?" Luke, head low, reached for a handful of pecans in his pouch.

"Sir, we took ammo from casualties already. We're down to company strength, about 250 effectives. That includes the walking wounded. We've taken over seventy-five percent casualties."

"Jesus, Mary, and Joseph," Luke choked. "Are we getting the wounded to protection?"

"So far we have. Soon we won't be able to spare the men to carry them; we need every gun we have."

"I agree." Luke understood. By his last words, he was sentencing severely wounded to their deaths. He had no option. It had been reported the attacking enemy outnumbered them by five to one. However to his immediate front, he figured it was more like ten to one.

Justin, leaving the comfort of the college's library, circled the confiscated, enemy-built command bunker's wooden-planked flooring, pacing endlessly while listening to couriers convey the ever-changing situation. The question on everyone's tongue was, "Where's Tarkington?"

An urgent report just received indicated that over half of Newman's expected force in the area was attacking Indianola, doing, it seemed, Tarkington's bidding. Justin again shouted to his adjutant, pounding his fist in frustration. "We're doing our part, damn it! Captain, does anyone know where the hell he is? Have any of our scouts found him? He should've been here by now. Goddamn it, is 1st Corps to be sacrificed for nothing?"

His questions were interrupted by a courier entering, shaking snow from his uniform. "Sir, the enemy has breached our western defense. General T. Northcutt advises he has sent two companies to fill the gap. It has forced him to weaken his position. He had no choice. I am to await your orders, Sir."

"Charge!"

"Did you say charge, Sir?" Both Justin's adjutant and the courier looked at him in confusion.

"You heard me right! Tell my brother I'm taking it right from his book. Remind him it's Cancun all over again. Where he charged right into the Cuban ranks when they least expected it. Up until now, many of these foreign pond-scum bastards have never heard the Rebel yell. It's high time they did. Let's pray its shocking effect will regain the slight edge we've lost. Order bayonets and pieces fully loaded. Have the men carry as many grenades they can find." Justin turned to a staff officer. He grabbed his arm and led him to the wall map.

"Major, my verbal order for all remaining couriers to carry is as follows: we will coordinate our counterattack to take place at 1230 hours. You got that? My watch reads 1125 hours. Mark yours and make sure everyone calculates from it. Have the men advance only, I repeat, only, until they turn them. Then get the hell back to our lines. We move out from all but the southern line. Understood? The southern route must be kept open if we need to fall back. Now get your collective asses moving."

Justin spoke to his aide with a sense of finality. "Captain Marceles, if we fail, we must go down fighting. We must not forget Vail Pass. On my order, no prisoners until I say otherwise."

"They won't need a reminder, Sir."

The runners fanned out, energized, none doubting their commander. At precisely 1230 hours on the 23rd of December, 20,000 Rebels advanced as one, surprising their cold and tired adversaries. The fierce and frantic Rebel onslaught made up for its lack in numbers. The line, now temporarily restored with Rebel blood, brought the battle to new, dizzying heights. The Federals, thinking the Rebels would only charge from the protection of their works if reinforcements had arrived, retreated to regroup. It gave the Rebel 1st Corps a temporary advantage and then unexpected victory, one they had forged from imminent defeat.

Three miles outside Indianola, Tarkington's Army finally arrived, late. Linking successfully with the First Army's remaining two corps, they attacked Des Moines, their path wide open due to Newman's attempt to retake Indianola.

Rebels broke through at Norwalk, Sandyville, and Bevington, disrupting the Federal line, encircling the tattered Federals who had previously surrounded 1st Corps. The battle raged on through Christmas Eve Day. Every available trooper in the opposing armies engaged in the widespread battle. Over 1.5 million men fiercely clashed, fighting nonstop in the desperate struggle.

With the Federal center compromised, giving sudden relief to the remnants of 1st Corps, Justin ordered Taylor to move his able remaining men to join with 2nd Corps to continue the attack northward. Both corps suffered heavy casualties in the slugfest. With primitive satisfaction, Justin calmly noted in his journal that the Federals had suffered more.

December 24, 2020—Federal Army Headquarters, Des Moines, Iowa

General Newman, not attempting to mask his anger, stared blankly at his second in command, Lieutenant General Sam Jeffords.

Jeffords said, "General, we must regroup and counter, or all is lost." Newman's face appeared sinister to his subordinate.

"Sir, I fear all is already lost."

Newman looked upon the harried face of his chief of staff, Lieutenant General Griswold, and knew with certainty that his gamble had failed. Somehow, the Rebels' northern army had managed to arrive just as he was about to finish off the pesky 1st Corps and recapture his center.

It was precious few hours to Christmas. He had always loved Christmas; he didn't feel in the holiday spirit today. In all, he had committed 900,000 combatants and now could account only for half; the rest had been killed, wounded, or captured. More than 150,000 had fallen in the Indianola fiasco alone. *If only I had generals like Northcutt.* But he didn't. He snickered to himself. *Even if it is over and we lose, I shall play out this saga to its end.*

Newman spoke. "General Griswold, if we pull back to Dubuque and cross the Mississippi, we can make a stand in Wisconsin. I've called for replacements from the Eastern Department. They're on the way. They should be here in about a week."

"Very well, Sir, I'll make immediate preparation for our retreat."

"No, General, not retreat. Regroup, if you please."

"Very good, Sir, regroup it is."

In a pig's eye, regroup. Griswald silently mocked the word "regroup." He wondered why the old man played with words when it was apparent they were in dire trouble.

Christmas Day, December 25, 2020—Rebel Army Temporary Headquarters, Des Moines, Iowa

The airport in south Des Moines served as the Rebels' temporary HQ for General Tarkington, commanding general of the Allied States Armies. He was late for his own meeting, chasing a new emergency. Several corps commanders cooled their heels while awaiting his bidding.

Justin impatiently paced the large hangar. He was doubly anxious to visit his badly wounded sister and his fiancée. Word had reached him earlier that both were injured by shrapnel, apparently coming from federal shells that had destroyed their hospital tent and most of its occupants. Taylor had said Becky owed her life to Julia. He smiled at Julia's stubborn disregard for his good intentions. Although Julia was slightly injured, she still courageously managed to save Becky and several others with her quick action. He could never get angry at her for not following orders, especially now. He loved Julia more at this moment than ever before, if that was possible. He deeply longed to see them to be certain they were fine.

Tarkington walked briskly into the unheated room; it was cold, the weather again uncooperative. "Men, good news. The enemy is in full retreat. It looks like they're heading for Wisconsin. It's a very merry Christmas and a huge victory present for our cause."

They all cheered, raising their canteens in tribute. Christmas Day in the year 2020 was barely two hours old. The anxious men awaited Tarkington's orders.

"Men, I'd like to pursue Newman's army to the gates of his demise. What we must do is contrary to good judgment, but first we need to regroup. At present we're in no condition to pursue our advantage. Get some rest and prepare your troops. We move out at 0400 on December 26th. Our destination and ultimate objective will be the temporary Federal capital. I'd like us there by New Year's Eve, where I intend to end this campaign. May God grant we all live to toast the New Year in 2021. Here's to a new beginning for our newly revived republic!" Tarkington raised his canteen in salute.

"Now," said Tarkington, "let's review how we're to accomplish our intentions."

The next hour was spent in appraisal and analysis, until all participating were comfortable with the strategy. Standing, Tarkington signaled for silence. "Men, I believe we are ready for the next move. What do you say?"

Tarkington again lifted his canteen. "Gentlemen, I give you a toast to our president." Tarkington took a long pull from his canteen, filled with something stronger than water.

"Here, here!" the men cheered wildly, temporarily forgetting problems, giving in to the moment's excitement.

Tarkington raised his hand for attention. "Men, after our joint review, I firmly believe our next strategy will end this campaign and, hopefully, this war. You will all agree it is as lofty as it is audacious. And yet it's really no different than past maneuvers where stubborn resolve worked in our favor. I'm certain this plan will fly. Are you with me?" Tarkington shouted, steam billowing from his mouth in the cold room.

All his generals cheered wildly, their enthusiasm unchecked—all except Justin. Everyone noticed.

Justin, deep in thought, felt alone though sitting in the cold, crowded room. For several minutes he had sat as in a stupor, not participating, not listening. Blankly, as if in shock, he rose from the chair slowly and prepared to leave. He bent down and buckled his overshoes and wrapped a scarf against the cold.

A voice startled him. "General Northcutt, I haven't dismissed this gathering. Please wait a minute. I need another brief word."

Justin, dazed from fatigue and preoccupied, hadn't realized the meeting was still in progress. Several fellow generals were quietly confused by Justin's unusual behavior, so unlike him.

"Gentlemen," Tarkington signaled for his corps commanders' attention. "I have one last announcement." He turned to address Justin.

"General Northcutt, there isn't a medal made which can properly signify the brilliant stand First Army's 1st Corps made at Indianola. Your men have paid the highest price for our victory, more than any unit in the history of this rebellion. Their sacrifice in blood and deed is a tribute to our cause. 1st Corps is without doubt the bright Christmas Star of our army and the main reason we celebrate today. Therefore, and I will not hear otherwise, Taylor's 1st Corps is to stand down and act in reserve capacity for the coming action." Justin stood listening, too tired to comment or care.

"Justin, I personally order you and 1st Corps to report to our reserve position in Dubuque by 0400 hour on the 27th. This group of gallant men deserves better, and I sincerely wish I could send them south for extended R&R. I hope—no Justin, I hope beyond hope, that I'll not need to call on this elite corps' courage again. It has time and time again gone above and beyond what anyone could ever expect of mere mortals. When conditions clear sufficiently, it's my intention to formally and properly recognize 1st Corps with a Presidential Unit Citation and to award you with our new nation's highest honor, the Medal of Freedom."

"Thank you, Sir." Justin, visibly surprised, was relieved for Taylor's men but not crazy about leaving his position as second in command and his responsibility as First Army's commander. "Sir, I can not leave my responsibilities. I therefore request you rescind that part of your order which requires I take R&R."

Justin, weary, listened as if in a fog as Tarkington's voice droned on. "Justin, I cannot risk losing you. Tired men soon become dead men; I don't want that for you. Again, I thank you, we all thank you, for a job above and beyond the call of duty."

Again Justin's peers burst out in cheer, which only embarrassed him more. He abhorred the limelight.

Dazed, Justin accepted the order and turned to his commanding general. "Sir, I'll advise my brother of your order immediately." Taylor, delayed, had not been able to make the gathering.

Justin hid his relief at their assignment. Worn beyond feeling, he didn't honestly think his troopers could face another immediate challenge. He continued, "For the record, 1st Corps went into Indianola with close to 75,000 men. Now my wonderfully gallant corps has only 30,000. The rest, 45,000, are casualties, including 10,000 killed." His voice trailed as he tried to hide his grief.

Justin's Christmas wish was to end the war with no more men killed under his command, but his First Army command still had two corps advancing on Wisconsin. *Merry Christmas, men,* he thought. He took his leave from the group. All who knew him understood his need for solitude.

With tears blurring his vision, Justin entered the cold, snow-packed path returning to his command.

James, wounded during the advance at Indianola, rested, his right arm wrapped in a bloody sling. He awaited, in deep pain, the removal of the Federal slug from his shoulder. The crowded field hospital had been quickly set up in an abandoned hangar next to command.

Ironically, he owed his life to a Federal officer who had saved him after he fell wounded. He smiled fondly at the memory of the familiar enemy officer who had quickly covered his body with his own to protect him from further harm. They had both played dead to avoid the combined wrath of their armies. Now both lived, one to become a prisoner again. But James quickly issued an order to release the large first baseman from Albany. He had repaid James in full for saving his life a thousand miles and seemingly endless years ago.

James sat mulling it all over and over while he waited for his turn with the overworked surgeon. He smiled, reliving that frightening, fast-paced moment when Lieutenant Washington's selfless action in covering his body saved him. Above the roar of battle he had shouted, "Hey, Syracuse, do you remember me? This here's your lucky day, and you can thank your mama for it."

James fondly thought of Washington's big white-toothed smile and peaceful brown eyes. He had never forgotten the big man he saved from certain death in Utica months earlier, so shortly after burying his brother.

James could now look forward to the war's end with positive hope for the first time, it seemed, in ages. *One day*, he thought, *I will become a real friend with that gentle giant.*

Julia stood at Becky's hospital cot, holding her limp hand, talking quietly and hoping to revive her spirits. Becky's exhausted and injured body slowly responded to treatment. So far, she had gallantly resisted the temptation to give up and die. However, were it not for Julia's persistence, she might have succumbed. She slept now; her prognosis was good.

A hospital orderly brought Julia a chair. Sitting felt good. Her wounds, though slight by comparison, were still painful. She looked past Becky's bed, wondering if her general was alive. She had seen enough death in the last several days to last several lifetimes. "God," she sighed, "please end this war."

Becky moaned, "Julia, what did you say?"

Julia leaned over from her chair and grasped her intended sister-in-law's hand. "It was nothing but an idle wish. You rest. I'll be here if you need me."

Sometimes in life a person must act, not because it feels right, but because it is the only honest and right thing to do.

—Jim Damiano

CHAPTER TWENTY-SEVEN

December 28, 2020—Federal Army Headquarters
Temporary Federal Capital, Madison, Wisconsin

An army is only as strong as its resolve. The Federal Army, still willing and able to continue, faced strong pockets of resistance within its ranks. Once a determined force, its tenacity slowly diminished with each frustrating defeat. General Skip Newman could not miss the road signs nor did he care.

The Federal army reached Dubuque after an orderly retreat across Iowa. President Collins then overrode Newman's desire to regroup mainly for the defense of Madison. He realized, that without a quick victory, there would be no need to defend Madison.

Word had just reached President Collins of Canada's unexpected peace treaty and subsequent alliance with the Rebels. His sister's diplomatic coup was about to turn the balance of power. Canada responded immediately, sending its army south to link with Tarkington in Iowa. The Rebels, only a few miles from Madison, could not wait for their delayed arrival. There was not time.

Newman, expecting defeat, had no desire to take further action. Although stubborn, he was not ready to totally capitulate either. This was not how he had planned or imagined the outcome. His unbalanced psyche could not allow it. Newman never intentionally deviated from his plans, no matter how wrong he had been. And right now he had no plan or idea of what to do.

President Rex Collins's physical appearance expressed the terrible strain and high price his leadership had cost him. His youthful image, that supporters had grown to expect, though mostly enhanced by makeup artists, no longer existed. Luckily for Collins, most loyal supporters would never know; TV no longer existed to promote his propaganda or his positive image. With each subsequent military loss, he carried the weight of the times upon his broad and now slightly bent, aging, and somewhat fragile shoulders.

He stared coldly at the supreme commanding general of the Federal Army, motioning Newman to sit at the chair opposite his desk. "General, cut to the chase. What are our options? As I see it, we still have 1.5 million men at arms and a very strong navy."

"Sir, no disrespect intended," Newman replied. Collins's face gave away his distrust of Newman's sincerity. Newman continued, "But what you see on paper doesn't mean a rat's ass. It's right here and right now where our concern lies. If Madison's lost, so are we. We put all our hopes here in one neat and tidy package. In short, Mr. President, it's true—we do have about 600,000 men to defend the Capital. Let's take a close look at this army. We are short on morale, ammo, fuel, supplies, and most important, patriotism. Last, but by no means least, our army is shy of English-speaking, goddamned American citizens."

Newman looked to see if his words had any effect; they didn't. He continued anyway. "Over half my men are foreign mercenaries, with only a few able to speak English. Sir, our strategy to bring in mercenaries soured after the first battle they participated in. To put it bluntly, we're in a world of hurt."

Livid, Collins replied. "Newman, are you telling me you can't get your troops to fight?"

"No, Sir, I didn't say that. They'll fight, or at least most will. Hell, in the last battle we killed over 2,000 cowards who refused to face the Rebels. I honestly expected more to run."

Collins shouted, out of control, rage coloring his tone. "Newman, out with it! No lame excuses. I want results. You, General, are beginning to try my patience."

Newman wondered, *What patience?* He answered as respectfully as his barely-contained anger allowed. "Sir, I would not want to try your patience."

He emphasized the word "patience," hammering it out staccato-like at the president, like sharp nails driven into the lid of a pauper's cheap, wooden coffin.

"Please bear with me for a moment. This frigging war has cost our side countless lives and, worse, the benefit of future achievements from those poor souls lost. The tide has turned against us. Sorry, my conscience and common sense forces me to speak the obvious. We might have to accept the fact we're licked and negotiate for desirable terms while we still can. Give the Rebels their damned freedom and save our half of the country. Perhaps with diplomacy, we'll mend our differences in time and reunite."

"The hell I will! You, General, are a traitor with such talk. You hear this, Newman! You hear it good! I will not be remembered as the president who lost the Union." Collins's temper went into overdrive. He threw his empty coffee cup onto the floor. It shattered completely, seeming like an omen.

Collins's venomous words echoed off his office walls. "I will never, repeat, never, give in to those damn Rebels!"

"Mr. President, your concern is noted. As I see it, though, you have little choice. Our enemy, in its quest for 'freedom'—ironically, something that the bastards already had before this mess started—wants this conflict to end as much as we. I have received what I believe to be a genuine feeler suggesting it's time to stop the killing and parley about the possibility for a temporary truce or, at worst, a surrender."

"Newman, you damn fool, they'll hang both of us if we surrender; it's common knowledge I worked with the Mexican and Canadian governments, and others, to invade my own country. Canada's siding with the Rebels is proof enough. Can't you see, or are you blinded by your own stupidity?"

"Mr. President, I agree that was a blunder. But, Sir, you were doing what you sincerely believed necessary to save the Union."

"That's enough, General!" Collins's open anger changed to bestial hostility. Standing, he leaned over his desk, pointing a shaking and accusatory finger at Newman. "I'm placing you under arrest. I figured you for a traitor. So, just in case, I arranged a few things." Collins pressed a button under his desk. Several armed military police rushed into his office.

"Lieutenant, General Newman's under arrest. Shackle him and take him to the building's basement cells. This incident is to be kept quiet. I do not want to rouse his loyal followers. He's to be guarded around the clock. And Lieutenant, send someone to fetch General Jeffords. Have him report to me at once."

"At your command, Mr. President!"

The MPs started to lead Newman out the office door. Newman wrestled free and looked directly at Collins with hatred in his eyes. The hostility in his look was second only to what Satan's stare might convey. Newman, no longer needing to deliberate in silence, shouted in rage, spittle foaming at his mouth, "You'll regret this Collins," he sneered. "If I must follow you to hell, I'll get revenge. You should have listened to whatever it was your sister learned. She's the real diplomat in your family!" Newman, gleeful, knew he had struck a sore point.

General Jeffords entered the president's office as Newman, now subdued, was being led away. Jeffords showed no surprise. Nonetheless, he tried unsuccessfully to avoid direct and embarrassing eye contact with his former boss.

Upon seeing his second in command, Newman's rage was renewed. "You sniveling turncoat son of a bitch!" Newman shouted, seeing instantly where Jeffords stood. His voice boomed off the walls of the old state building. "I promise you'll both pay for this!" The MPs abruptly shoved him away.

Jeffords stood in front of Collins's desk. Collins firmly grasped his hand in welcome, feeling relief. Jeffords spoke, breaking the tension. "I see the general didn't take too well to your revised opinion of him, Mr. President."

"No, I suppose he didn't." Collins didn't choose to belabor his decision. He continued abruptly. "Jeffords, let's get straight to the point. The enemy's at our proverbial gate, and you, Sir, are my best hope. Let's talk about how we're going to defend Madison—more importantly, let's talk about an offensive." Collins sat, motioning his accomplice to do likewise.

Jeffords had been Collins's secret confidant for years. In truth, though, Collins believed Jeffords could never match Newman's knowledge, strategy, or leadership. Jeffords, of course, felt differently.

The Rebel tornado would have to be tamed, and Jeffords sincerely believed he was the one to tame it. Like all men who are full of themselves, he was confident he could make a difference, inabilities aside. Jeffords always chose the easy course. Today was no different. So he tread carefully with Collins; the best move for the proverbial "yes man."

"Mr. President, four replacement divisions from Illinois have arrived. We now have about 600,000 effectives." His numbers confirmed Newman's earlier report. "To be brutally honest, the Canadians' entry into the war limits our options to one, and we must exercise it before they link with Tarkington."

"And that is?"

"We must attack, Mr. President. We've stayed with General Newman's planned defensive through the debacle in Indianola. We must press the attack and take back the momentum. General Newman's ploy to pull back and wear out the Rebels' persistence has not worked. Instead, it appears to have strengthened their ire."

"General, if we attack, what are chances for success?" Collins had a sharp edge in his voice, the strain of the moment showing despite his inner urge to repulse it.

"Mr. President, I'd predict our chances are even, at best." Jeffords fidgeted, worried his honesty might spark Collins's monumental temper.

"Then do what you must. And do it quickly before the dwindling determination of our fighting men is totally lost."

"I'll begin planning immediately, but Sir, do you think we can break through any more reinforcements? I'd prefer to see more well-trained veteran soldiers from the eastern front. I'm not that happy with the mercenaries. If you ask me, so far they've been an abject failure."

"You weren't asked!" Collins snapped, quickly putting down Jeffords's attempt at original thought. "I'll see what I can do. You know, I never disagreed with your late commander that we needed to bring more of our citizens into the army. Truth is, and you know it as well, we can't train them fast enough. We'll get more men. For now you must slow the

Rebel bastards down a bit and give our army the time to regroup. I'd say you need to get things going before New Year's Day. In your opinion, is this possible?"

"Yes, Mr. President, I agree. If we wait any longer, the Rebs will have time to gather enough men to outnumber us. We must move now, or we'll lose the minor edge we currently enjoy. I'll get you the time we need."

Collins nodded his agreement. "Get on it then, General. Report to me as soon as you're ready. You know, being outnumbered never seemed to bother the Rebs much. I certainly don't want it to be our turn at being outnumbered. Oh, and General, for the record, every mercenary that died was one less American that had to be sacrificed."

Collins watched his new commanding general exit. He had little faith in him. Yet he was the only man he presently trusted to follow his lead. All his best men were dead, captured, or in irons. *The good thing about Jeffords is that he is a man I can count on to follow orders. Best of all, he can be led by the nose when necessary.* Collins contained his sickening, demonic laugh until Jeffords was out of hearing.

December 28, 2020—First Army Headquarters, Montfort, Iowa

Justin took a long, lingering drag on the cigar he held in his muddied right hand. Its aroma was enticing, and the clouds of smoke it created looked like Indian smoke signals. Justin had been given the cigars by a Ranger lieutenant. Where the young officer commandeered the Cuban cigars remained a mystery, but Justin was not about to ask. He had always tried to avoid the nasty smoking habit, but today, the cigar fit his somber mood. Its mild tobacco offered him the restful moment of calming reassurance needed before sorting the difficult work ahead.

He smiled, remembering bugging Grandfather to quit his three-a-day cigar habit, which he finally did, to Justin's relief. Today, with the only guarantee being this moment, future worries over mouth cancer, or even longevity, seemed foolish.

The weather had turned crisp and cold. The forecast finally showed a clearing trend; the light winds and sun made the day bearable. Large fires, surrounded by ragged men seeking warmth, dotted the countryside for miles. Smoke billowed in every direction, giving away the Rebel reserve's position. It didn't matter; General Tarkington was actively looking for a fight a good twenty-five miles east of 1st Corps' position.

Justin's battered men were on R&R with several other similarly exhausted units. The scattered and broken units totaled more than 100,000 soldiers, the nucleus of which was the remnants of the 1st Corps. All were under his temporary command. His two active corps were assigned to Tarkington on the drive to Madison. He still felt guilt over being left behind. Even though ordered to take this rest, an uneasy premonition rumbled in his gut.

Taylor, watching the placement of a combined battery of artillery from three broken units, shouted orders to its commander, not noticing Justin standing nearby.

Justin called to get his attention. "I see you're keeping yourself occupied."

"Well, Commander, I see it as my obligation to stay prepared and out of trouble," Taylor laughed. He was enjoying himself, doing the work of an artillery officer, keeping busy, filling time.

Justin moved next to Taylor, smiling, his palms up. "Don't get too settled, Taylor," Justin whispered. "It looks like we're to move forward in a couple of hours. It's a precautionary move."

"What gives? We're supposed to have this long overdue rest. Shit, what now?" Taylor grasped one of his brother's hands, while taking a fistful of the offered cigars from the other. "Where'd you get these?"

"Long story. I'll tell you later. Word reached me moments ago—the enemy's moving in force out of Madison—headin' right at our center."

"That's nuts! Are you sure?"

"Yep. I doubt they'll break through Tarkington. If they do, you know who they'll call to fill the gaps."

"No, let me guess!" Taylor smirked.

"You got it, Bro. Keep your troops alert and ready. By the way, for the record, I didn't feel right about taking over your command."

"For gosh sakes, Justin, you're second only to Tarkington. Give me a break. You're the head muckedymuck hereabouts, regardless of where or who I am." Taylor laughed, and Justin returned a loud guffaw. "Any news on Becky or Julia?"

"Like you—last I heard, Becky's doing fine. I'm told her wounds will take several weeks to heal, but she'll walk again. Thank God Julia was there to pull her out of the rubble. I'm happy to hear her wounds are doing nicely too." Justin sighed, relief resonating in his voice. "Becky was lucky, very lucky. I heard several wounded were killed, along with most of the medical staff. Those sniveling Federal bastards! If I had known about it at the time, I wouldn't have taken prisoners."

"Yes, I heard over 120 needless deaths were added to the war's tally because of that one enemy shell. It's a miracle Sis and Julia were spared. I sure hope you're wrong about the pullout. If not, I'll see you on the road." Taylor saluted, smiling. "And by the way, for the record, you wouldn't have killed those prisoners. So don't make yourself crazy talking that way. Don't ever forget that I've known you for the empathetic person you always try to hide, long before you were my general."

There was no mistaking Justin's smile of acceptance on hearing Taylor's opinion.

0500 Hours, December 29, 2020 —
Rebel Army Headquarters, Mount Vernon, Wisconsin

Commanding General Tarkington's offensive line was spread over 150 miles in a giant semicircle around Madison, with Mount Vernon its center. Word came announcing a huge Federal advance, originating from the Federal defensive position in Madison. The Federals were moving with direct intent, straight for the Rebel center. Tarkington had not expected a Federal attack and was reluctant to move immediately, fearing an enemy diversion.

By the time the Rebels realized what happened, it was too late. Like the thunderous force of jackhammers hitting cement, Jeffords's offensive hit the Rebel center, driving the stunned defenders into temporary retreat and collapsing but not totally breaking its jagged line. With the Rebel line partially broken, it bent to meet the sudden reversal of fortunes.

Tarkington, unaware of Newman's dismissal, had no way of knowing this was the desperate move of the newly appointed Federal commander testing his wings. General Jeffords, hoping to alter the course of history, moved with revived determination, knowing this might be their only chance at success. He unleashed veteran storm troopers followed closely by his bloodied mercenaries. They charged in waves, throwing caution to the wind. Any Federal soldiers reluctant to advance had little choice. It was go forward or die.

Tarkington was in trouble. He had let the Federal offensive, so unlike Newman's past actions, catch him unprepared. His men paid the ultimate price for his miscalculation.

Tarkington, on a rampage, shouted for a staff member. "Major Kim, get word to Northcutt at Montforth. He is to advance all, I repeat, all his reserves at once. Have them go to our center." Kim, a fourth generation Chinese-American, looked gravely at his commander; his grim face reflected the urgency of the moment.

"Yes, Sir, I'm on it." Kim left, passing Colonel Masters, who was entering the command center. A covering of what appeared initially to be mud encased him from head to foot. Masters, a stickler for neatness, something rare in the Rebel Army, helped break the ice when he was within wind of Tarkington. The smell said it all. The Rebel commander held his nose, but not his laughter.

"Sorry, Sir, the enemy scored a direct hit on the officers' latrine. I was close enough to, well, uh," Masters stuttered, "become involved. I need to report our line is bent severely but not broken. We've filled the center with men from our flanks. Sir, I estimate we can hold out for a while, though not for very long."

"Damn, you smell bad, Colonel. I suspect it's worth a Purple Heart for anyone coming in contact with you." Poor Masters felt the sting of embarrassment; Tarkington's sharp wit at his expense unsettled the soiled perfectionist.

Tarkington continued. "Tell your boys we expect them to hold for at least five to six hours. It'll take that long for Northcutt's troops to arrive."

"Yes, Sir." Colonel Masters saluted and started to leave.

"And Colonel, go roll in the snow or get into a borrowed uniform. See my orderly for one of mine. I know the Feds think we're full of shit, but we don't ever want them to think they're right."

Masters broke out in laughter, hoping privately this would be the worst thing to happen to him. Later on, when things cooled down, the incident would be the talk of the army and the centerpiece of the Battle of Madison—to the continued, humiliating chagrin of poor Colonel Masters.

From that moment forward, though, Tarkington's primary concern was the clear and present danger at hand. He was distressed by his oversight but not perplexed. With cool, calm reason, he quickly planned his move for a counteroffensive. Once again, his now sadly diminished elite shock troops would figure in his calculation. With luck, he could turn the aggressive moves of the enemy to his advantage.

"Sorry, Northcutt, I need your brave men. I know they've sacrificed too much for so long. But you're my best and I need you," he muttered to himself. Only his adjutant heard him, and now so would posterity.

1115 Hours, December 29, 2020—Rebel Reserve Relief Column, Command Vehicle

"General Northcutt, we're close to the front. I'm told it's about an hour's distance. Communication is set up for your use as requested. Sir, you know this is highly unusual and, worse, dangerous. Do you still want to address the troops?" Colonel Stanley, Justin's communications officer, still couldn't believe he was serious.

"Yes, Colonel. I appreciate your concern and it's noted. But while we're still several miles from the front, I want the men to understand why I'm about to ask them to risk their lives again just when they thought they had some overdue R&R."

"Sir, with all due respect, our men know their duty." Justin's pensive mood unraveled the colonel.

"Thank you, Colonel Stanley; I realize that because of my rank, I owe you no explanation. But here it is anyway. I've made up my mind to do this. I owe it to 'em. You of all people are aware—I've led some of these men from the beginning, including you. They need to know why I'm asking them to return to harm's way when I told them a couple of days ago they'd have rest. Now, is the setup ready for me?"

"Yes, Sir!" Stanley pointed to the control panel. "I'm sorry, Sir. I was out of line. Just hit this button when you're ready. The men are gathered as requested."

"No apology necessary, Peter. We go back too far, and you're only saying what you think is best. I realize this is chancy. Hand me the mike, and thanks, Colonel," Justin said, warmly grasping the colonel's hand.

Justin grasped the microphone with unfaltering determination. The engineers had performed a miracle with makeshift gear, covering an area where his spearhead force of more than 100,000 reserve troopers would hear his voice. The men, knowing they were headed to battle, wondered what the fuss was about.

Justin, covering the mike, cleared his throat. His stomach felt familiar jitters as he began to speak. Though this was not his first speech by a long shot, he still felt queasy. It felt like a time in high school, when he first confronted an audience at a debate competition. He returned to the moment when his rumbling gut caught up with his duty.

Justin gave the signal to his staff that he was about to start. Sergeants throughout the columns called the rag-tag troopers to order. As one, the battered legions snapped to attention in perfect unity. The Rebel Army had become a complete army, second to none.

Justin began to speak, then hesitated. It personally hurt him, for what he had to say did not come easily. He knew he had only a minute or two to speak. Any more time could prove dangerous. Justin was sweating and it was fifteen degrees.

"Men, I have fought and served with some of you from the beginning. Today, I want to talk to you briefly, not just as your commander, but as a fellow soldier. Shortly, you will once again be asked to fight for freedom and our new independence. The Federals have broken through our hard-won line at the army's center near Madison. Our people need us to help retake the position and straighten things out." Justin fidgeted with the mike, getting more comfortable.

"Y'all have a right to feel you've done more than your fair share. I want to tell you how damn proud I am of your service to our country. It is, and has always been, my exalted privilege and honor to lead you, to fight alongside you—to know you. Before we go into battle, I urge you to look to your left and then to your right, and remember the face of your comrade in arms. Think of lost friends and loved ones. Most of all, remember them. And when you engage the enemy, fight—not only knowing that you are in the right, but fight so their memory will not ever be forgotten. What we're about to do is for all our futures and that of our loved ones we hold dear. Most important, though, we battle for those not yet born, that they will never taste the tyranny we have faced. May God bless you with His grace and grant you the courage to face the next few hours and days. I thank you for the privilege of allowing me to lead such a gallant corps. I salute you all." Then he shouted in his excitement, "We will not fail! Long live free men everywhere!"

James felt a chill upon hearing Justin's stirring words. He watched as several of his men stopped to look at the troopers next to them. No one said a word; each soldier understood.

Listening with his men, Taylor felt the sting of tears of pride for his big brother. He shouted to those men nearby, "Three cheers for General Northcutt and victory!"

The Ranger Division, in unison, cheered for five minutes until their sergeants quieted them. In the spur of the moment, Luke, standing a few feet from Taylor, started to sing the Ranger marching song in his beautiful baritone. Slowly, ten more took up the refrain, then hundreds, and then, as if on cue, all the men from Justin's old 36th Division broke out in song, about-faced, and marched toward their next encounter in the Devil's den. Without hesitation, every unit started to sing, 100,000 voices in all. They sang the third verse of "America the Beautiful." It had begun as the marching song of the 36th, now adopted by the entire Rebel Army. Their voices spread over several miles of cold countryside; three long, projected columns headed west to uncertain destiny, singing:

> O beautiful for patriot dream, that sees beyond the years,
> Thine alabaster cities gleam, undimmed by human tears,
> America! America! God mend Thine every flaw,
> Confirm thy soul in self control, thy liberty in law!

Justin listened as the beautiful sound resonated for miles, with each unit adding their voices. These few, simple words gave meaning to why they fought, putting all in proper perspective. Justin, with tears temporarily clouding his vision, looked at his proud columns marching before him, many cheering as they passed. He knew that many would never live to see tomorrow. Quickly, with deliberation, he gave the order to move forward at double time. His exhausted legions did not hesitate to follow his command.

Upon reaching the shattered Rebel lines, Justin received orders from Tarkington. They were simple and direct. "After a fifteen-minute rest, your mixed corps is to attack the Federal center and retake lost ground."

Justin gave orders to check weapons and ammo and prepare for the immediate advance. The mixed corps would attack in coordination with a combined frontal assault of Justin's entire First Army, which had judiciously caught up with its commander. It was time to hit the enemy's jugular.

Orders were given along all lines to lock and load as 500,000 Rebels, including Justin's relief force of 100,000, advanced in unison.

Exhausted after a meager breakfast of pecans and hot water, followed by five hours of forced marching in below-freezing temperatures, Justin's mixed corps led the advance elements. The ragged and enraged 36th and 121st Divisions moved toward the enemy's center. Their controlled wrath epitomized the mood of the entire Rebel force.

Justin's men had no way of knowing this would be their final advance and the last chilling Rebel yell of the war. The terrible impact of their coordinated advance brutalized the already dispirited Federal Army. Mercenaries ran from the fighting, dropping their weapons, no longer interested in promises of riches and Rebel plunder. Federal soldiers surrendered by the thousands. Some simply slipped away, dropping their weapons, having seen all they cared to see; having done their best, they knew their war was over.

Something happened that day that would always amaze Justin. His men's fury did not follow the course it had taken in previous encounters. They just let the enemy go, universally choosing to disobey orders to shoot prisoners. As one, the Rebel Army sensed a sudden end to the bloody conflict. There was no needless slaughter, not even for the mercenaries. Sympathy for the fate of fellow men at arms was given, along with emotional mercy. Fellow Americans, men and women, all hugged, whether Rebel or Federal; even some mercenaries joined in the celebration. Everyone except the politicians believed it was over. All that remained was the mopping up and for the reality of everyday common sense to come forth.

The Canadians never reached Rebel lines in time to be a factor. When they finally arrived, their abrupt, reassuring presence lifted the spirits of all, giving rise to the certainty the end had finally arrived.

0030 December 30, 2020—Temporary White House, Madison, Wisconsin

At fifty-five, General Newman was still a powerful man. The ex-Green Beret overwhelmed his lone guard, killing him instantly. He unlocked his shackles and relieved the dead guard of his weapons. He did not need stealth; confusion reigned, and everything was in disarray. He walked the corridors unnoticed going directly to the president's sleeping quarters. Collins was not there.

Newman walked as he always did, erect and with purpose. No one paid attention to him. His five stars gave little cause for anyone to question him, and his arrest had been kept quiet for fear it would rouse his loyal men. Returning the salute of an officer, he overheard startling news—the Rebs had overrun the army outside the city and General Jeffords had been killed. *Good,* he thought, *it saves me the trouble of killing the bastard myself.* Preparations were underway for an orderly retreat. The Federal Army was apparently not ready to give up.

"Captain, where's the president?"

"He's about to leave, Sir. Don't you know we're evacuating?"

At first, the captain hadn't noticed the cluster of five stars on Newman's collar strap. Now that he saw them he wondered, but not too deeply, why a five star seemed unaware.

Newman scowled. "Thank you, Captain. I'm very aware," he lied.

Newman entered the president's outer office. Everything was in turmoil. Papers were being burned or shredded in preparation for the rapid departure. Newman directed everyone to leave. They didn't question him. He turned the knob on the door and entered Collins's office, locking it behind him.

"Mr. President, how nice it is to see you so soon." Newman's measured tone dripped with sarcasm. "I see you're in a hurry to leave," Newman said, pointing his pistol menacingly at Collins. He picked up a blank piece of paper from the desk and wrote for several seconds, never lowering the pistol. The pen's scratching sound irritated the frightened Collins, who wondered what he was writing. He had never seen Newman act so sinister. But it was no real surprise to him, either.

Collins couldn't resist his need to retake control of the situation. His anxious voice filled the office. "How did you escape, Newman? You can't get away with this! I'll see you put back in chains and shot, in that order. Guards!" Collins shouted, foreboding resonating in his voice.

"Sorry, Mr. President," Newman sneered, his voice hushed. "I've sent the guards on a mission." His words were stern and measured, as if he were spitting out an unwanted, bitter pill. "Your days have come to an end." Newman waved the pistol in a taunting, menacing manner. "It's all over. It appears that our army's been defeated. Give it up!"

"I was wrong in not listening to you," pleaded Collins trying to turn the conversation to reason. Newman would have none of it. Still Collins protested, "We still have our army in place in the east, and over twenty states still fly our flag. We'll regroup and fight on. Skip, we make a good team; it would be a shame to end it now."

"Nope, Mr. ex-President of the once Free World," he said smiling cynically. "It's over! I always knew the Rebels would win. I started to believe in their cause when you began to plan an Empire instead of a way to restructure a real peace. That's why I slowed things down until the Rebs caught up. I wanted us to re-unite, not implode, you blithering asshole!" Newman shouted. "You never saw it because you were so engrossed with yourself." Newman's words stung Collins to the core, hurting him even more than Newman expected.

He continued to aim the pistol at Collins's head, speaking deliberately. "Theirs is a worthwhile cause as long as tyrants like you exist! By the way, fool, your sister knows about my treachery. I've been her deep throat all along. It was the best way for us to control your once superior army."

Newman snarled, "You, Mr. President, are hereby unelected."

Newman calmly and deliberately aimed the pistol at Collins's balding head. Its distinct click was the last thing Collins heard. The bullet hit the president's forehead at such close range that it blew a jagged piece off the back of his head.

Newman, blood all over his once pristine uniform, tenderly took his scribbled, now blood-spattered note from the president's desk and placed it on Collins's chest, using a paper clip to attach it to his shirt pocket. He then put the pistol into his own mouth, taking one last parting glance at the assassinated president's eyes, wide-open in death, staring forever in fear and surprise. They seemed focused on the bloodied American flag still standing proudly beside his desk.

"I'll see you in hell, Mr. President. Unlike you, I can't live with myself as a traitor, regardless of how right I believe the Rebel cause or my actions." Newman, without hesitation, put his left hand reverently on Old Glory and pulled the trigger; his body slumped, clasping the Stars and Stripes, as he slipped forever into the blackness only eternity understands.

On Collins's chest, Newman's note, still legible though spattered with both a tyrant's and a traitor's blood, said simply:

Here lies a tyrant for the ages, a man who would be king, now only known to history as a man who would dismantle a nation by his greed and arrogance, killed by a man who once foolishly followed him because duty demanded it.

Long live King Rex Collins, the First and the Last.
May God forgive me, and may God always bless America.

Skip Newman,

Forever and always an American, a general, and I pray history will remember, a true patriot.

December 31, 2020—Madison, Wisconsin

The Rebel Army occupied Madison on New Year's Eve Day. It was the job of the politicians and the patriots to formally end the conflict and reunite the nation. Ironically, it was the Russians who helped in negotiations for peace. Their faltering democracy knew full well that a strong American economy was needed to return Europe and the world to order.

Troops were jubilant. The last land battle had not amounted to much when measured against the scale of past battles.

With the hostilities ceased, casualties on both sides needed attention. An additional 30,000 had been wounded in the last clash. Thousands were cared for as battlefields throughout the nation quieted and the recovery began. The War for New Independence, as it came to be called, would account for over 30 million casualties, with more than 17 million deaths. It was a terrible price to reestablish the freedom that had always been deeply rooted in a nation gone haywire.

The Rebel First Army marched into Madison unopposed. Taylor and Justin rode together triumphantly. Their battle-worn Humvee led the victorious column.

"Justin, what's with that ugly, egg-shaped building still standing? It seems like we should've bombed that one just to put it out of its dreadful misery."

"It looks like it might have been some kind of insurance company or something. No matter; it sort of represents the need for change and the rebuilding that's ahead of us." The long column entered the center of town, where the undamaged, beautiful state capitol buildings stood proudly. "Hey, Bro, the Wisconsin Capitol looks like the one in Washington." Said Taylor.

"Yeah, I once heard it's the exact duplicate of Washington's Capitol building. Someone told me that during World War II, they planned to use it as the country's temporary capital if the enemy ever forced us to move inland."

x x x x x

The two brothers stepped into Justin's spacious new headquarters situated in the Wisconsin capital. Justin's regimental officers and division generals were starting to arrive.

"Justin, was all this worth it? So many dead, so many maimed," Taylor continued somberly as they entered.

"I don't really know. We may never know in our lifetime the real cost of this war in human suffering." Justin looked at his brother's unkempt uniform and his unkempt blond beard, speckled with mud and pecan pieces. He fixed his eyes on Taylor's faded shoulder patch. The glorious Ranger patch that had been in the forefront of so many bloody encounters was faded but never beaten. Justin touched his T-patch for reassurance. He had never changed the shoulder patch on his jacket either, even when promoted to First Army commander. He then felt for the Texas Ranger Star fastened on his shirt pocket and smiled. His brother and the 36th made him proud to be a Texan.

"Taylor, I hope the 36th will forever be a memory of our fight for freedom and that it'll be retired forever."

"I'll drink to that." Taylor lifted a mug of hot coffee that had been handed to him by an alert orderly. Several of Justin's officers were already gathered in his office.

Luke walked over to the Northcutt brothers. By his wobble it looked like he had been drinking something stronger than coffee. "I still can't believe Newman killed President Collins and then himself." Luke was seemingly unaware that his bandaged forehead still showed a bloody, crimson trail. His wound was in need of attention, but Luke didn't seem to care. His priority after the required festivities was to visit Becky.

"Luke, we'll never know why he didn't surrender. I suppose he didn't want to face the music," James, who had been listening, replied, his voice wavering as he limped to the table to refill his cup of coffee. He was trying to slow the effect of the liquor Luke had given him. His leg wounds would hinder him for the rest of his life.

With equal reverence, Justin eyed James's tattered shoulder patch—the glorious orange cross of the New York 121st Division, now forever entwined in brotherhood with the Texas 36th.

"He probably saved our nation further grief. Whatever Newman's reasons, the killing is almost over because of it. I for one am ready to go on with my life, but as a civilian." Smiling, Justin pulled an unopened bottle of commandeered sour mash from the sack he'd been carrying. He passed it to Taylor.

Everyone in the small room cheered when Taylor passed the bottle. Each poured an ounce or two of the rare treat into his canteen cup. Justin raised his cup in salute, proposing another toast, purposely raising it in salute to a higher being. He hoped God and his mother wouldn't mind, just this one time.

"May God bless and guide us to a new peace and freedom, and may He bless the New United States of America forever."

They cheered and raised their cups as one, downing the slightly chilled liquid, cheering happily. The sour mash slid down gently, warming both their stomachs and their attitudes. It somehow felt right that in their midst were several Federal officers, unshackled prisoners who joined them in the common toast; all were happy to see an end to the conflict. Federal Lieutenant Isaiah Washington was amongst them, his huge arm draped on James's shoulder, both brothers, now and forever fashioned in the brotherhood of war.

Everyone's eyes suddenly turned as a beautiful brunette sergeant entered the closely packed room. Justin ran towards her, excitement in his step. He engulfed her possessively as she melted into his long arms. Though she winced from wounds that were still healing, she would not allow pain to interfere with the moment's excitement. It was the first time they had seen each other since their last encounter at the old Iowa farmhouse a few days earlier.

"General, I was told I'd find you here. I didn't count on all the company though." She smiled at the men milling around her, but her wistful smile was meant specifically for Justin. It sent waves of love's gentle warmth, like Cupid's arrow, through the center of Justin's heart, cutting deeply to his very soul. The warm, loving feeling mingled nicely with the preamble of the slithering warmth from the whisky. Julia removed her garrison cap, adjusting her long, flowing hair. She seductively whispered, "I came as soon as I could."

Justin spoke softly, almost in a hush. "Honey, it's good to see you, and now," he emphasized, "I can honestly say it's time we got on with our lives." His smile said it all. He held her securely in his arms; yet still she trembled as he kissed her in an embrace that signaled a new beginning. The symbolic moment elicited another robust cheer from Justin's men. The couple would remember that joyful sound for the rest of their lives.

Taylor, his arms around Luke on his left and James on his right, hugged the Rinaldi brothers, now forever members of his family. Tears glistened from every eye as all the combat veterans cried happy tears of joy. When the clock in the old Capitol room struck twelve times, announcing the year of our Lord, 2021, they welcomed the nation's new beginning together.

Justin and Julia, wrapped in an inseparable embrace, kissed again. "Hey, General, I seem to recall you wanted to get married when this war's over. Rumor has it that it's about that time," Julia laughed.

Justin hugged her, holding on to her for dear life, still not really believing their terrible ordeal was over. "Julia, am I dreaming, or are you really here?" he whispered.

"Oh, I'm here, and don't you ever forget it."

Their next kiss sent up a roaring cheer that resonated throughout the old building, but they did not hear the loud crescendo. They heard only the pounding of their own beating hearts.

It isn't for the moment you are struck that you need courage, but for the long uphill climb back to sanity and faith and security.

–Anne Morrow Lindbergh

CHAPTER TWENTY-EIGHT

February 1, 2021—Austin, Texas
Temporary Capital of the New United States

President Barbara "Babs" Collins-Smythe was as distressed as she appeared. Her strained disposition was a byproduct of the wearisome work of hammering out a lasting peace treaty to end the war. It was finally time to repair the torn nation, but the rigorous process had zapped her once-vivacious energy and caused a decline in her fragile health.

Today, she dressed simply, wearing a navy blue skirt, white silk blouse, and navy blue pumps. Knowing a comforting tone was required for the message she would soon give to the nation, she practiced her speech. Yet no matter how hard she tried, she still felt like a foolish schoolgirl facing an audience for the first time.

With hostilities over, Babs anxiously looked forward to peace, and time to spend on simple luxuries. Her idea of simplicity was not what one might imagine of a woman who should be spoiling grandchildren. Her uncomplicated desire was only to have proper time to mourn.

"Madam President, we're ready." John Appleton, her press secretary, entered the media room, excited about the momentous occasion about to unfold. "Is anything wrong?"

"John, I'm guilty of thinking too much. It seems to me that no matter how hard our generation will try to forget, the bloody price paid for our freedom will never allow total peace. How can I tell our people that we must allow our nation to heal itself?"

"Babs, it's only right that the nation remembers the sacrifices. It'll hurt, like you say, probably for the rest of our lives. But if you're having regrets, don't. When we're long dead, our great-grandchildren will enjoy the freedom bought by our sweat, tears, and blood. A debt, you once said was stamped and paid for in full."

"Yes, I know all this. Yet, I've had the eye-opening luxury of a precious moment to reflect. So many things plague me still, like the death of my brother. I still carry many fond memories of Rex, and mourn his death. Despite his treachery, he was still my brother. I've prayed constantly for his troubled soul. John, we've all lost so many friends and relatives. Look at you. Both your boys killed serving the cause. So many good folks lost; how can I give a speech, any speech, that does justice to what they've sacrificed?"

"Babs, I've known you for almost half a century. Heck, we go as far back as when we were college kids at the University of Texas. Just talk from your heart and forget the canned words. Keep it simple but memorable, and you'll do fine. So what if it is not remembered as your best speech? What is important is simply that it is a new beginning. That's all—nothing more, nothing less."

"John, my dear friend, right now my sole purpose in life is to heal our crippled nation. The thought that I might fail scares the wind out of me."

"Babs, the country needs to hear your words of assurance. Tell them everything is OK. If you truly believe this, it's really all you can do. Whatever you tell them, give it to them straight. Just be yourself. The Battle of Madison ended this war. Yes, a few skirmishes have followed, even up to yesterday, tarnishing the peace with needless death. Your speech must be about a new start, the beginning of the end.

"Now, Madam President," he continued, "show the nation and the world the wonderful lady I admire, the woman who is standing before me. Give us the brilliant woman who has held the pain of a nation in her heart and has the empathy of a saint. Show us that wonderful faith you never lost, even when most of the less stalwart did." He hugged her, turned, and guided her to the podium.

"Thank you, John, and God bless you for your friendship." She took a sip of water and a deep breath, stepping up to the microphone. Babs had aged beyond her years since the terrible conflict had begun. Worry lines stood prominent on her face, underscoring a sadness that showed in her loving eyes. Yet she radiated a glow of hope as she began to talk reverently about her newly reunited homeland.

Only those few countrymen within range of her voice actually heard her speech. Television, radio, and all other media still remained in disrepair. Though her words were recorded and filmed for posterity, most citizens would ultimately read the text of her missive. Her short message was one of joy and excitement for the new peace. It spoke volumes about her vision for the future New United States and rang out for the rebuilding of a great nation once lost but now found. As John suggested, she spoke from her heart. Her primary theme was reconciliation.

As she concluded, she borrowed words from Abraham Lincoln. She spoke with great emphasis, a noticeable tremble in her matronly voice. "President Lincoln never lived to carry out his great vision to rebuild our nation after his civil war. His life was cut short by an assassin's bullet only forty-one days after he had spoken this famous and insightful last paragraph from his Second Inaugural Address to a similarly tarnished nation on March 14th, 1865. His death prevented the realization of his honorable vision to gently unite a terribly divided nation. Instead, his murder gave rise to animosity and a general outcry that would cause a pall over our nation for the next 136 years." Babs took a deep breath before continuing.

"My fellow Americans, we must not let this happen to us. History need not repeat itself. The choice is ours, and it is surely in our power to make. We must also follow Lincoln's path to the beautiful future he once envisioned. You, the citizen, must ultimately decide if Lincoln was correct. I, as your president and your lowly and faithful servant, sincerely believe it so."

President Lincoln closed his address with these immortal words, which I truly believe apply to us today. I quote in reverence:

> With malice toward none; with charity for all; with firmness in the right, as God gives us to see the right, let us strive on to finish the work we are in; to bind up the nation's wounds; to care for him who shall have borne the battle, and for his widow, and his orphan—to do all

> *which may achieve and cherish a just, and lasting peace, among ourselves, and with all nations.*

"End of quote. Now, my fellow Americans, I ask you this one favor as the torch of reconciliation is passed to us, the victors. If we are to become a great nation once again, we must lay aside our malice and our politics. We must hope, NO, more important, we must DEMAND, that the spirit of patriotism prevails in every heart and every soul and every mind. We must never overlook the mistakes of our past." Babs hammered home each point with a fervor that instantly inspired all who heard her. All her generals were in the audience, including the Northcutt and Rinaldi brothers. They listened intently, gratified to be able to witness this symbolic end to the conflict they had fought so hard to win.

"We must dare to learn from our errors, and more important, we must not allow them to plague us. Our misfortunes must not ever be repeated. Politicians will always exist; they are a necessary ingredient for a free republic." Bab's face looked tired and she became faint, but she didn't allow her illness to tarnish her joy. She continued, ignoring the sudden burst of pain coming from her chest. "We must never forget why we had to fight this war. To do so would tarnish the memory of those who died for this opportunity.

"My wish for our homeland is that it may always be blessed with honest, caring political servants who value integrity over greed. My fellow citizens, we must always remember that as true patriots, we are the keepers of the keys of our democracy. Therefore, we must take the time to remind future generations of politicians that they are only servants of a just and honorable nation that is first and foremost, of the people, by the people, and for the people.

"Now, my fellow Americans, it is time to stop talking and to go to work to rebuild what we had to tear down in order to renew the great ideas fostered so long ago by our forefathers in Philadelphia in 1776.

"Let us never forget the immortal words penned by Madison in 1787, in the Preamble to the Constitution. Those words launched a war that has seen 17 million souls perish. I take this opportunity to repeat these famous words that announced our nation's true beginning, long ago.

These words must also foster our rebirth as we go forward into a bright future. Hear again what Mr. Madison penned:

> *We the People of the United States, in Order to form a more perfect Union, establish Justice, insure domestic Tranquility, provide for the common defense, promote the general Welfare, and secure the Blessings of Liberty to ourselves and our Posterity, do ordain and establish the Constitution for the United States of America.*

"I truly believe a wondrous future awaits us all. And so, my fellow Americans, may God Bless the New United States of America!"

x x x x x

Babs' speech was not her best. Like John Appleton said, it didn't matter. What mattered was that the people understood. And when Americans understand what has to be done, miracles happen and mountains are moved. The nation began to rebuild and heal and with the help and spirit of the revival, God returned to His promised land—once more, a nation under God, indivisible, with justice for all.

Jim Damiano

The present is the ever-moving shadow that divides yesterday from tomorrow. In that lies hope.

—Frank Lloyd Wright

EPILOGUE

Babs Collins-Smythe remained president for two years. After taking ill, and secure in the knowledge that the nation was on the right track, she voluntarily stepped down so that national elections for the first elected president of the New United States could take place. Her message to heal and rebuild the nation became her legacy to a grateful country.

She died suddenly, six months after stepping down from the nation's highest office. Her death was as much a casualty of the war for freedom as that of any combatant. The country mourned her passing and declared her greatness equal to that of Washington and Lincoln.

When the last battle ended in Madison on December 31st, 2020, the long road to rebuild a nation began. Following President Collins-Smythe's example, citizen soldiers returned to their homes, or whatever was left of them, with renewed faith. They participated with vigor in the American adventure. Unlike the aftermath of the nation's earlier civil war, bitterness did not linger for years, never to be settled. But the road was not easy. Patriots, though sorely tested, remained fervent. Citizens stepped forward voluntarily to help lead, guide, and heal the nation and restore it to its rightful place in the world.

The New United States evolved to encompass most of the North American continent with the exception of a reunited Canada, which remained a staunch ally. The original Constitution of September 17th, 1787, continued as the nation's centerpiece and foundation for government. The New United States Congress would not break apart a work that was reparable. With renewed energy, the country strived to fix only what had gone awry. The original concepts, as adopted by the Founding Fathers in 1787, remained the basis of the nation's strength, insuring its longevity.

In the nation's first civil war, known to history as the American Revolution, its battle cry was "Taxation without Representation." It was ironic that even the wealthiest American at that time paid less than five percent of their income in taxes to the British king.

The second civil war's paramount issues were states' rights and slavery. Slavery thankfully ended, yet ironically, all Americans slowly became enslaved by a tax system that promoted serfdom to the government, a government that eventually went overboard in spending and bureaucracy. By the beginning of the third civil war, the average American worked almost seven to eight months of each year just to pay various federal, state, and local taxes. These Americans were the silent slaves and proverbial serfs who were freed by the third civil war.

In the two decades immediately following that war, the people corrected what was wrong and saved forever all that was good for the nation. The war for a new independence resulted in the creation of a simplified federal government, streamlined and in tune with the original powers granted it by the Constitution. The powers reserved to the individual states were returned to those states, and the national government was no longer part of the everyday life of its citizens. Bureaucrats, lobbyists, and corruption were eliminated, or saw their power greatly reduced.

The red, white, and blue stars and stripes remained the symbols on the nation's banner. The Pledge of Allegiance to a nation under God also remained. Northern Mexico initially entered the Union, with the rest of Mexico soon to follow after meeting the new requirements established for statehood.

Mexico's energetic people, though initially citizens of a conquered nation, retained their identity. Their new liberties and rights made them truly a free people, giving them energy and wealth they had never known. Each Mexican state eventually joined the United States and received equal status. The nation's flag boasted several new stars, including Cuba and Puerto Rico, in addition to the stars representing the new Mexican states.

All foreign languages were encouraged by the renewed nation, but not at the expense of English, its chosen language. By a change in the Constitution, English was made the country's official tongue. Spanish and French became required languages taught in all schools because people who understand each other's background and heritage have a better opportunity to live in harmony.

Washington, D.C., was moved near Kansas City, Kansas, on a forty-square-mile piece of land cut out of the Midwest. The location was purposely chosen to be as close as possible to the center of the country's original forty-eight states and as far away from the old capital's faults and bad memories as necessary. Unlike residents in the old capital in Washington, citizens of the new capital were given representation in the federal government. It was another long overdue adjustment.

Arab oil was no longer required or consumed in large quantities as alternate fuels replaced the commodity once known as black gold. Use of oil was reduced to the construction of roads and the production of clothing, plastics, and other everyday items. No longer would oil's byproducts pollute the air and water, nor would the nation be held hostage to an enemy because of its dependence on petroleum. Arab countries dependent upon oil sales to western nations had to seek other means of revenue. With the decline of their wealth the Middle-Eastern terrorist movement failed.

The war's end gave greater meaning to the Thanksgiving holiday. Pecans became a staple in most everyone's menu. No one would have been happier than Justin Northcutt's grandfather, Dick York, had he survived the war. Dick had always praised this illustrious fruit of the hickory tree family.

April 19, 2040—Prosper, Texas

It was a warm, sunny spring day in Texas. Justin looked fondly at his youngest child who was playing with the yellow Lab puppy he just received for his seventh birthday. Julia's radiant beauty still stood out as she smiled at her son running in carefree circles with his as yet unnamed companion. A slight breeze caressed Julia's brunette hair, which now showed a hint of gray. The noonday sun sparkled in her vivid green eyes. This moment's peace felt so right to her.

"Governor, do you often think back to those terrible times?" She had decided to change her pet name for her husband from General to Governor, and used it for the first time today. After all, they were moving to Austin the next day to serve the Lone Star State.

Still infatuated, the governor-elect of Texas gazed fondly upon the woman who was the love of his life. His love for Julia grew stronger every day. The past 20 years had flown by with such speed, but he had never missed a chance to thank God, for he knew without question that each treasured moment was a joy and gift to be cherished.

"No, Honey, I try to look to the future. You know how I am about the past. Memories can be both dear and deadly. By the way, where are the twins?" Their oldest children were fifteen, sophomores at Prosper High School.

"You remember. They're at a going-away party."

"A party?" Justin seemed troubled; his casual smile gave away his unease.

"Yes, don't you recall? Justin and Brooklyn were given this party by their friends. It's at the Downings'."

"Oh boy, sometimes I think I'd lose my mind if my head wasn't screwed on. Yes, I recall. I'm sure they'll have a great time. It was sure nice of them to throw a party for the kids."

Justin turned, facing Julia with concern in his eyes. "Honey, I'm a bit embarrassed to say this, but this governor's job is somewhat more frightening to me than commanding First Army. I'm not sure I'm cut out to be a politician. Are you really ready to be a politician's wife?"

"Oh, don't fret so much. You always do well, and Texas has total faith in your ability, General," Julia responded lovingly, rolling her first pet nickname for him sweetly from her lips to ease his tension.

"Thanks, Doll. The day I saw you on Preston Road, only a few short miles from here, will always be the luckiest day of my life. I love you so much." His warm, honest smile never ceased to melt her heart. They hugged, clinging comfortably to each other. It was a familiarity only true lovers ever enjoy or understand.

"You better love me more and more each and every day, you big, beautiful lug." Julia gave him a long, lingering kiss.

The puppy barked in the background, while little Taylor, named for his famous uncle, laughed at seeing his parents kiss.

"Mom, Dad, I know what I'll call the puppy."

"What name did you choose?" Julia smiled warmly at her son.

"I'm going to call him Ranger."

Justin smiled, a tear forming. "It's a good name, Son." Justin picked Taylor up and hugged him, not wanting to let go. This, after all, was what he had fought so valiantly for.

"Daddy, why are you crying? Don't you like the name?"

"Taylor," Justin smiled, holding his son in his arms, "Ranger is a wonderful name. I love you so much."

"I love you, too, Daddy."

April 19, 2040—Syracuse, New York

Across the vast nation, in upstate New York, Taylor and his bride of two years were visiting Luke and Becky Rinaldi. Luke, a history professor at Syracuse University, had embraced his father's dream to expound upon the American experience. He and Becky had two beautiful children—Rocco, fourteen, and Savannah, ten. Becky had returned to college after the kids reached school age and now practiced contract law. She had recently become a full partner in her firm. Life was good for the Syracuse Rinaldis.

"So, Taylor, when do you return to the Capital?"

"Next week. We need to find a home for the six years I plan to serve. Thank God for term limits. I don't think I want to be away from Texas any longer than that."

"So, my senator sibling, do you plan to change the country during your term?" Becky liked to tease her older brother. Her infectious smile always lightened Taylor's load, no matter what problem he might carry. "And will my new niece really ever live in Texas?"

"Sis, my only wish is that I'll make a difference and do the best I can. As for our baby, I prefer that she be raised from her birth in Texas, but she'll get her chance in six years."

Jill, seven months pregnant, looked in admiration at Taylor; the love glowed in her eyes. She was never concerned about whether he'd be successful. "Taylor, you'll make a great senator from Texas, don't you worry. Our baby will know Texas soon enough. Isn't her daddy the legendary general of the famous 36th Texas Division? How can she miss?"

"Hey, don't forget I also commanded the 1st Corps."

"Sorry, Dear, I'll try to remember next time."

"Heck, Taylor, I thought you'd be president by now," Luke chuckled. "Jill, you better plan on giving your daughter lessons in Texan. I think your man will be at the capital longer than he's willing to admit."

"No, I may look crazy, but it's all an act. And who would want a president who walks with a limp anyway?" Taylor dragged his leg in exaggeration, making faces.

"Well, just advise us when you change your mind so that we can start making campaign posters." Becky poked Taylor playfully.

"Guys, give me a break. I'll leave that move to Justin; he's the real politician in the family."

Becky broke in, "Only the governor-elect doesn't know it yet."

Justin's popularity never seemed to faze him. It was a common gag of his siblings at how Justin unsuccessfully denied his fame.

Becky asked, "Have you two chosen a name for the baby yet?"

"Actually, we'd like to name her Cheryl. Taylor says it means 'dear one' in French. We thought it fit," Jill answered.

"Well, Cheryl Northcutt," Taylor patted his wife's extended tummy, a big grin on his face, "did you hear all that? Let's go to dinner. Any suggestions, Luke?"

"Anything but pecans will be OK with me."

They all laughed as they entered Taylor's new Cadillac, a sleek, solar-electric car.

"Wow, Uncle Taylor, this car is something!"

"Thanks, Rocky. In a year or so, you'll have to get your parents to buy you one just like it."

Luke glared at Taylor, who couldn't resist a smirk as the two old friends entered the car.

April 19, 2040—Utica, New York

James was readying for their trip to visit his brother Luke, in Syracuse. His wife and two children watched as he carefully packed the car. He looked forward to seeing Taylor and his wife, Jill, too. The last time he had seen the senator-elect was as best man at his wedding two years earlier. He and Taylor had remained close friends since the war's end, corresponding almost weekly. Their bond, molded in the war's intensity, was as great and lasting as that of birth brothers.

"Sara, Dad should be here shortly. Are you about ready?"

Sara Bennigan-Rinaldi was all that James could ever ask for in a marriage partner. He had met her fifteen years earlier and his passion for her had never cooled. After his release from the army, James had searched for his Jennie Allen for five long and frustrating years. He never found her, but he never looked back; to do so was too sad and bitter. She was another missing person from an unforgiving time, mourned and never forgotten. Meeting Sara had helped him to find love once again and move on.

Sara playfully poked James, interrupting his thoughts. "I've got an idea. Since Taylor's parents invited us to Santa Fe, let's take the kids there sometime soon. I hear it's beautiful, and I'd really love to go. What do you say?"

"Sara, I don't see why not; let's look at our calendar when we return from Syracuse. The summer's coming up, and since I won't be teaching this semester, we'll have plenty of time to enjoy a vacation."

"Do you think Utica College can do without your history lessons a whole summer, Professor?" Sara teased, enjoying every opportunity to rustle his forever straight-laced feathers.

"Here's Papa!" The children shouted in unison. Joe Rinaldi opened his car door and kneeled as his two grandchildren, Billy and Betty, raced to greet him, almost knocking his frail body over trying to be first to hug him. At sixty-six, he looked much older; he carried too much hurt and loss. The memory of the war continued to plague him. His recovery, though never complete, was given a new lease every time he saw his grandchildren. Today he would see all four. It had been weeks since he had hugged Luke's brood. It would also be good to see little Savannah and Rocky again. He grasped Betty's little hands warmly and picked her up, hugging her closely. He lovingly reached for Billy's firm ten-year-old grip and smiled, walking with them to the car.

"Let's go!" James closed his door and started the car. Its hydrogen-electric engine hummed to life as James aimed it toward Syracuse and a beautiful setting sun.

Two red-tailed hawks, perched in a nearby towering maple tree, watched the car leave as they majestically stood vigil over their nest filled with eggs about to hatch. It was the close of another peaceful day in the New United States of America, in the historic Valley of the Mohawk.

THE END

2020: A Season to Die

Jim Damiano

Organizational Structure of the Federal and Rebel Armies

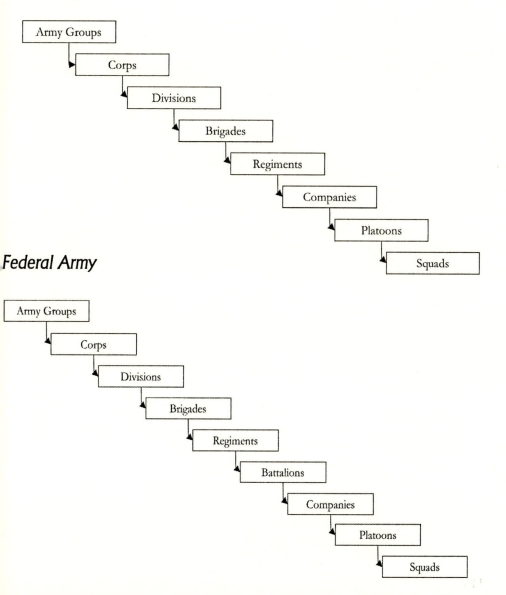

CHRONOLOGY OF MILITARY PROMOTIONS FOR KEY CHARACTERS

Justin Northcutt

January 2020 – Colonel, 2nd Regiment, 1st Brigade, 36th Ranger Division, Army of the Republic of Texas

April 2020 – Brigadier General, Commanding – 1st Brigade, 36th Ranger Division, Army of the Republic of Texas

July 2020 – Brigadier General, Commanding – Besieged Ranger Forces of 1st and 4th Ranger Brigades, Home Guard Units of Del Rio, Texas, and Elements of New York 121st Division

August 2020 – Major General, Commanding – 36th Ranger Division, Army of the Republic of Texas

October 2020 – Brevet Lieutenant General, Commanding – Allied States Expeditionary Army, Mexican Invasion

November 15, 2020 – Lieutenant General, Commanding – 1st Corps, First Army of the Allied States Army

December 20, 2020 – Commanding General, First Army of the Allied States Army

Taylor Northcutt

January 2020 – First Lieutenant, 2nd Platoon, Company C, 2nd Regiment, 1st Brigade, 36th Ranger Division, Army of the Republic of Texas

April 2020 – First Lieutenant, Adjutant to Brigadier General Justin Northcutt, 1st Ranger Brigade, 36th Ranger Division, Army of the Republic of Texas

May 2020 – Captain, Adjutant to Brigadier General Justin Northcutt, 1st Ranger Brigade, 36th Ranger Division, Army of the Republic of Texas

July 2020 – Field Promotion to Major, Commanding – 2nd Regiment, 1st Brigade, 36th Ranger Division, Army of the Republic of Texas

July 2020 – Colonel, 2nd Ranger Regiment, 1st Ranger Brigade, 36th Ranger Division, Army of the Republic of Texas

September 2020 – Brigadier General, 10th Brigade, 36th Ranger Division, Allied States Expeditionary Army, Mexican Invasion

November 2020 – Major General, 36th Division, 1st Corps, Allied States Army

December 2020 – Lieutenant General, Commanding – 1st Corps, First Army of the Allied States Army

Luke Rinaldi

January 2020 – First Sergeant, 3rd Platoon, Company G, 140th Regiment, 3rd Brigade, 10th Mountain Division, Second Army Corps, Army of the United States of America (Federals)

April – June 2020 – Prisoner of War

July 2020 – Sergeant, 3rd Platoon, Company B, 2nd Ranger Regiment, 1st Brigade, 36th Ranger Division, Army of the Republic of Texas

October 2020 – First Lieutenant, Adjutant to Brigadier General Taylor Northcutt, 10th Brigade, 36th Ranger Division, Army of the Republic of Texas

October 25, 2020 – Field Promotion, Captain, Commanding – Mixed Services Defensive Unit, Cancun 10th Brigade, 36th Ranger Division, Army of the Republic of Texas

November 2020 – Colonel, 7th Ranger Regiment, 4th Brigade, 36th Ranger Division, 1st Corps, First Army of the Allied States Army-Midwest Division

James Rinaldi

April 2020 – Sergeant, 2nd Platoon, Company C, 7th Regiment, 4th Brigade, 121st Division, First New York Volunteer Corps

June 2020 – First Lieutenant, Commanding Company C, 7th Regiment, 4th Brigade, 121st Division, First New York Volunteer Corps

July 2020 – Captain, 7th Regiment, 4th Brigade, 121st Division, First New York Volunteer Corps

August 2020 – Brigadier General, 4th Brigade, 121st Division, First New York Volunteer Corps

November 15, 2020 – Major General, 121st Division, 1st Corps, First Army of the Allied States Army

Rebecca Northcutt

April 2020 – Nurse, 77th Field Hospital Unit, Army of the Republic of Texas

September 2020 – First Lieutenant, Nurse, 77th Field Hospital Unit, Allied States Army

Julia McKnight

June 2020 – Private, Women's Auxiliary Corps, Motor Pool, Army of the Republic of Texas

August 2020 – Corporal, Women's Auxiliary Corps, Motor Pool, Army of the Republic of Texas

November 2020 – Sergeant, Women's Auxiliary Corps, Motor Pool, Army of the Republic of Texas

December 2020 – Sergeant, 77th Field Hospital Unit, Allied States Army

Rocco Rinaldi

June 2020 – Major, Supply Unit, Headquarters Staff, 121st Division, First New York Volunteer Corps

August 2020 – Colonel, Supply and Procurement, 121st and 20th Infantry Divisions, First New York Volunteer Corps

Victor Rinaldi

May 2020 – Private, 2nd Platoon, Company C, 7th Regiment, 4th Brigade, 121st Division, First New York Volunteer Corps

June 2020 – Corporal, 2nd Platoon, Company C, 7th Regiment, 4th Brigade, 121st Division, First New York Volunteer Corps

Joseph Rinaldi

May 2020 – Major, Intelligence, 20th Division, First New York Volunteer Corps, and then of the Allied States Army

ABOUT THE AUTHOR

V. R. (Jim) Damiano, Jr.

Jim is semi-retired. When he isn't writing, he spends time consulting for insurance and bond clients.

After obtaining a degree in Retail Business Management from Mohawk Valley Community College in 1965, Jim started his insurance career in Syracuse as a bond underwriter trainee for United States Fidelity and Guarantee. At age 21, he became the youngest Bond Manager in this company's history. He worked for various insurance companies over the next eighteen years, serving in management. In 1975 he was transferred to Atlanta Georgia, where he had a chance to develop his love for American History and the Civil War.

In 1980, Jim transferred to Dallas, Texas where he was introduced to Texas history. Over the next sixteen years this move served to introduce his three wonderful children, Cheryl, James, and Becky, to three marvelous Texans, Shane, Candace, and Chris, all high school sweethearts.

In 1983 Jim started his own Insurance Agency. It grew successfully to a state-wide organization under his guidance. In 1998, a New York Stock Exchange Insurance Company looking for acquisitions made him an offer he could not refuse. After working for the new owners, for one year as a Surety Vice President, Jim was forced to resign, due to ill health.

His first passion is writing poetry. Several of his works have been published, including some found in this, his first novel, *2020: A Season to Die*.

Since resigning from full-time insurance and surety work, he has dabbled in real estate, insurance sales and consulting, farming, poetry, his loves for all things historical, and, most important, writing his first novel.

He currently lives on his pecan farm outside McKinney, Texas with Betty, his wife and best friend for the past forty years, their Siamese kitten, Blue, and their dog, Ranger.

Betty and Jim enjoy spoiling their grandchildren, Justin, Taylor, Savannah and Brooklyn.

Jim maybe contacted through his web site: **www.jimdamiano.com**

Jim Damiano

Printed in the United States
33396LVS00003B/34-306